THE DRAGON QUEEN

ALSO BY WILLIAM ANDREWS

Daughters of the Dragon: A Comfort Woman's Story

The Essential Truth

The Dirty Truth

THE DRAGON QUEEN

WILLIAM ANDREWS

This is a work of fiction. Names, characters, organizations, places, events, and incidents are either products of the author's imagination or are used fictitiously.

Published by Lake Union Publishing, Seattle

www.apub.com

ISBN-13: 9781503900349
ISBN-10: 1503900347

Cover design by PEPE *nymi*

Printed in the United States of America

To My Master, Kang Heu-in

Colors fade with age. Rich tones grow dull
When touched by rain or smoke of fires.
It may be that, at last, your fame will live
In poems which are pictures turned to song.
Age cannot dim the fire of jeweled words
Nor steal the scent of breezes that will blow
Down through the ages from your soul.

Sung Kan (1427–1456 AD)

ONE

Korea. Damn. I'm exhausted and we're not even there yet. Fifteen hours in the air and not a minute of sleep. God, I wish I didn't have to do this now. Timing couldn't be worse for Jin-ee and me.

I'm sensitive to every move the airplane makes, so I feel when we begin our descent into Seoul. Derek, my flight attendant, takes my trash and asks if I need anything more before we land. Yeah, I do. A few more of those twelve-year-old whiskeys they have here in first class. But I say no and raise my seat back for landing. My skin is clammy from the airplane's close quarters, and a nasty headache is coming on.

I go over my mission to take my mind off the situation at home. "Help us prevent World War Three," the secretary of state said when she sent me off. Actually said, "World War Three." She does that. Exaggerates. They all do in DC. It's a seven-days-per-week soap opera on the world's biggest stage. The Middle East is where war was supposed to blow up, but that's last year's show. The people are bored. The show needs a new act. With what's going on here, maybe they aren't exaggerating this time.

Never thought they'd tap me for something this big. Nate Simon, special assistant to the secretary of state, on a mission to prevent World War III. Right. It's that I'm an American who speaks Korean. Three years of it in high school and four at Michigan. My Korean must have looked good on my résumé. After Cal Law, an offer from my senator to work in his DC office, where I met Jin-ee. That helped, marrying a Korean woman. A few years later another call, this time from State. Two years in Korea, then back to DC. A few promotions, and now this.

Damn, what a rebel Jin-ee was when I first met her. Two braids of long black hair and fire in her eyes. Out to change the world. I had it, too. Passion. The sex was the best I ever had. Intense, purposeful, exhilarating. Each time like it was both the first and last time we'd do it. Then marriage, two kids. What happened to me after that, I can't say. Got caught up in the race, I guess. Status, money. Things that, after Jin-ee's bombshell, suddenly don't seem so important.

There's a ding from the speaker system announcing that we're preparing to land. The cabin lights blink on. Derek gets on the intercom and recites the landing instructions. Everyone around me is waking up, putting away their stuff, getting ready for Korea. Me, I gotta focus on this mission. I gather my papers and shove them back in my case with the gold State Department insignia. Inside I see the stainless-steel box containing the comb. Oh, yeah, the comb. Big mystery this comb. Top secret. I have to find out why someone from North Korea sent it to the president of the United States. Some high-ups in Intelligence think it's important. I take it out of my briefcase and turn the box so the other passengers can't see what's inside. I open it and there's the comb. It's stunning. The expert from the Smithsonian said it's made from the finest tortoiseshell. The rim is solid gold, and the inlay of a two-headed dragon is in pure-white ivory. He said it's definitely Korean. Said it was made during the nineteenth century. Woman's comb, he said. Wasn't so sure about the two-headed dragon, though. I study the dragon. The impossibly tiny ivory inlays make the dragon look almost real. The expert said the comb belongs in a museum, and looking at it now, I believe him. Then there's the message that came with it. Two words:

"One Korea." So do the North Koreans want reunification through diplomacy or war? Guess that's what I'm supposed to find out.

I close the box and stuff it inside my briefcase. I turn the monitor to the channel showing the airplane's nose camera. After fifteen hours at thirty-eight thousand feet, it helps to see the ground again. It's still so far away.

The jet leans to the side and the airplane drops. I look out the window and try not to think of Jin-ee. The sunrise has chased us since we crossed over Japan. Looks like we'll beat it to Seoul. I look down at the city in the soft morning light. Millions of people in all those apartment towers, dragging themselves from their low Korean beds, brewing their god-awful bori cha tea. Hard to get to know them. Most Confucian country on earth. I wonder if they're worried about World War III.

I look for where Jin-ee and I lived. Don't see it. The city is even bigger now, like my job. Back then it was all so clear, simple. Save the world from destroying itself. Funny, that's my mission now, but it's not simple this time. Different rules. Jin-ee never lost sight. Still has the passion. Can't say that I do.

Head's beginning to pound. I grab Derek as he walks by and ask for a couple of aspirin and water. Finally the monitor shows the lights and the airport's open space far off. It looks so small. After a thousand landings at a thousand airports, I still hate this point in a flight. It scares me how quickly the ground comes up when you land. One minute it's miles away, the next the runway is right underneath you, moving at 140 knots.

I look over the city. Korea, the new stage in the show. Seventy-five million people in this act. Maybe if I hadn't taken all that Korean, I could be back in Virginia talking it through with Jin-ee, trying to find the truth again.

The engine whine falls several notes, and I hear the landing gear drop. The jet shakes in some turbulence, and I'm feeling nauseous. As the plane weaves into position for landing, I taste stomach acid in my mouth.

Prevent World War III. That's why they've locked me in this aluminum tube for fifteen hours straight with no way to talk to Jin-ee. World War III. I'm sweating like a pig, and I can't find my breath. World . . . War . . . Three. On the monitor, I see the runway coming up fast. I squeeze my eyes closed and see Jin-ee's young face, her long black braids and fiery eyes.

Damn it, Jin-ee. Why did you have to do this now?

An embassy guy in a dark-blue suit and trendy black-frame glasses meets me when I finally get off the plane. Tells me his name is John. Behind him stands a goon wearing a sport coat a size too small for all of his muscles. He has an earpiece and that professional focus on everything, everyone.

I'm relieved to have my feet on the ground again. As John and the goon hustle me through the airport, I take off my suit coat to let my sweat evaporate. The aspirin Derek gave me starts to work, but I still feel like crap. The lack of sleep and worry about my marriage have drained me. I have to force myself to push on.

It's early, so there aren't many people in the concourse. A few businessmen with briefcases run to catch their flights. A woman helps someone who's probably her mother make her way to a flight. A group of high school kids waits at a gate. The boys wear white shirts and ties; the girls are in knee-length skirts. They look happy, excited. If they only knew . . .

The terminal has hundreds of typical airport stores and restaurants. There are high-end boutiques—Chanel, Dolce & Gabbana, and Ascot Chang. There's a McDonald's next to a sushi bar, and a Pizza Hut across from a noodle shop. There's something different here, though. It's the signs. They're in Hangul, English, Japanese, and Chinese. You don't see that in Tokyo, Beijing, or Singapore. Only here.

As we head for the exit, I nod toward the goon. "Why the muscle?" I ask John.

"Orders," he replies. "There are people who want to push the situation here over the edge."

"Meaning?"

"An American official, like you, is a target."

Me? A target? Suddenly I'm not so tired. I think of Jin-ee and our kids eleven thousand miles away. Like the goon, I notice everyone and everything.

When we get outside, there's a stretch town car and driver waiting for us. Idling in front of it is an Escalade with blacked-out windows. When he sees us, the limo driver opens the car door and John and I climb in. The goon sits next to the driver, and we follow the Escalade into the city.

John sits across from me as we drive the airport expressway over the Yeongjong Bridge into the Incheon lowlands. I look for coffee inside the limo's black leather interior. Don't see any. Just a bottle of water that I grab and gulp down. John's all business as he launches into my itinerary, rapid-fire like bullets from a machine gun. "Your first meeting's at nine with Ambassador Morris," he shoots. "We'll get to the embassy about eight forty-five. That should give you time to freshen up." Freshen up . . . I wonder if I look as bad as I feel.

"And by the way," John says, "the ambassador invited General Dunning."

Great. General George Washington Dunning, commander, US Forces Korea. "I thought we were meeting with just the ambassador and her staff," I say.

"You know how it is," John says with a look.

Yeah, I do. When armies and tanks and missiles with nuclear warheads start moving, and when superpowers take sides and make threats, everyone gets a little scared. Stock markets crash, people start building bomb shelters and buying canned goods. The voters demand tough action. That's when generals like Dunning think they should be in charge.

John continues firing away. "This afternoon, we'll meet with the Koreans—Defense Minister Han, Foreign Affairs Minister Kim, and the Minister of Reunification, Mr. Park. Tomorrow morning, it's meetings with experts on what's going on in the North."

In other words, spies. "Anything new there?" I ask.

"No. And nothing new from the Chinese or Russians, either. It's a Mexican standoff, as they say."

John levels his eyes on me and says, "Your afternoon tomorrow is blocked off, but we weren't told what for." He raises an eyebrow.

The meeting is with some "people" at the CIA about the comb and the note that came with it. They haven't cleared anyone at State to know about it other than the secretary and me, so I simply say, "Classified."

John doesn't say anything more as we drive to the embassy. The trip usually takes an hour, but it's rush hour so it'll take two. As we drive, I turn on my phone and check messages. There's one from Jin-ee who wishes me luck and promises that we'll talk more when I get back. There's a message from our daughter, Jenny, who just last week got her first cell phone. I love getting messages from her, although we told her she had to limit her texts to me to one or two per day. Our son, Will, isn't old enough to have his own phone, and he really doesn't care. Thinks phones are for girls, not for a future NBA star like him. I answer the texts. Eleven thousand miles away, I realize Jin-ee's right, I haven't been there for my kids. We should travel more. Take a year off. Or two. Show them the world so they can see past our upper-middle-class sliver of northern Virginia. Teach them that they can change the world.

We've entered into Seoul's Bucheon district. I look out the window. It's good to be back. Reminds me of the happy times when I lived here with Jin-ee. Tiny cars and truck vans with Hangul letters on the side fill the expressway. All over the city, tall apartment buildings, like an army of soldiers, stand at attention. We drive along the Han River for a while, then cross over the Seongsan Bridge into the heart of Seoul. The city is dense with modern buildings. Glass and steel and concrete and aluminum. Seems like they're building new ones on every block. Everywhere there are cars, buses, trucks, and people on motorbikes. Car horns honk, trucks roar, commuter trains glide along tracks. On the narrow streets intersecting the boulevards, merchants are opening their doors for business. Pedestrians jam the sidewalks. The city smells like a combination of exhaust and kimchi. It throbs with energy. I marvel at these industrious, intelligent people. What they call their "Miracle on the Han River" is on full display—the rise from a dirt-poor nation to one of the world's most modern in a short fifty years.

I just hope I can save it all from being destroyed in World War III.

TWO

The limo approaches the US embassy building where I worked when I lived here. A few blocks away is Gyeongbok Palace, the last home of the Chosŏn Dynasty. Through the big-city haze, the open air of the palace grounds is visible just to the north. Beyond it is Bukhansan Mountain standing over Seoul like a giant Buddha smiling down at his subjects. We drive to the embassy's huge iron gate with big red stop signs. The embassy reminds me of something from the Cold War Soviet Union, an eight-story block of concrete. Every time I see it, I think we should tear it down and replace it with something more modern. You know, image and all. Seoul police are on guard outside the gate. Makes sense. Anything outside of the embassy is their turf. However, just inside there are a dozen US Marines holding M16s. You know, image and all.

Once inside the embassy compound, I climb out of the limo and John escorts me into the building. The interior is just like it was twelve years earlier—what some architect fifty years ago thought was progressive is now only depressing. The once-modern lobby furniture is shabby and the lighting is harsh. At the security checkpoint, they scan our IDs. When the guard asks to search my briefcase, John tells him it's okay and he waves us through. We take an elevator to the eighth floor. I go to the bathroom and look in the mirror. There are bags under my eyes, and my skin is pasty like someone who hasn't slept in two days. I smooth my hair with my fingers and splash water on my face. It helps some, but I still look awful. I leave the bathroom, and John leads me to the windowless conference room. It has the same navy-blue carpet as when I worked here, but now it's even more threadbare and the mahogany paneled walls need fresh varnish. There's the old conference table that can sit twenty-five people with enough room for everyone to spread papers around. At the head of the table is the American flag on a brass stand. Next to it on another brass stand is a South Korean flag with its red and blue yin and yang and trigrams in each corner. I go to the credenza and pour myself a cup of coffee. I gulp it down and immediately the caffeine starts to pick me up. I take a seat near the head of the table. I take my papers from my briefcase but leave the box with the comb inside. Jin-ee is in my head and so are Jenny and Will. I want to be with them instead of here. Work things out. I push them aside. I'm here now and I gotta stay focused.

The conference room's double doors open, and Betty Morris, the US ambassador to Korea, comes walking in. Good-looking middle-aged woman. She's wearing a tailored navy-blue suit and a white blouse. Her jewelry is pure Fifth Avenue. Everything about her screams East Coast money, which is, in fact, how she got to be ambassador. There are rewards for the rich who support a presidential bid. However, her medium-length blonde hair, which I've never seen less than perfectly coiffed, is unkempt like she hasn't been in front of a mirror for a while. Yeah, I bet.

With Betty are two aides. One is Craig Matthews, her chief of staff. He's wearing what would be a State Department–issued suit if the State Department actually issued suits. Craig is Harvard and as smart as they come. But he's one of those lifers who never has an opinion and only takes sides when he knows which one will win. I wonder if I've become like him. Betty's other aide is someone I've never seen before. A young Korean woman, petite and attractive.

Marching in behind Betty is General George Washington Dunning in his army dress blues. Betty introduces me to Dunning and I shake his hand. He's smaller than I expected. Not even five nine and probably shy of one seventy. He's wearing wire-rimmed glasses and has close-cropped hair. He'd look like a nerd except there are three stars on each shoulder and rows of combat medals on his chest. With my sweat-stained shirt, I'm way outmatched.

The general has with him a one-star brigadier general and a full-bird colonel. They too are in dress blues and are cut from the same military-first mold as Dunning. They each carry a thick briefcase.

The army guys take a seat on the other side of the table from me.

Of course, Dunning speaks first. His voice is surprisingly big for someone his size. "This is General Jeffries, my chief of staff," he says. "And this is Colonel Nielson, military intelligence. They're here to answer your questions." Yeah, he brought the guns with their stars, eagles, and medals, straight-as-a-board military posture, and hard-as-nails stares. Don't get me wrong. I respect these guys and I sleep better with them on our side. But they're not here to answer my questions. They think diplomats like me don't even know the right questions to ask in a situation like this. They just might be right.

I nod a greeting to Jeffries and Nielson. They nod back without expression as if I'm a private in a reviewing line. I say, "Ambassador, I know Craig, but I haven't met your other aide."

"Oh, sorry," Betty says from the head of the table. "This is Anna Carlson. She's an international law attorney and one of our new aides."

Sitting behind the ambassador and Craig, Anna Carlson wears a smart gray suit jacket and matching skirt. She has her long black hair neatly pulled back. She looks about thirty, young to be a player in a meeting with ambassadors and generals. But when she acknowledges me, I see something—something that Craig and Betty don't have. It's the look that Jin-ee had—still has. Intelligence. Depth. *Conviction.* As if she knows something no one else does.

The meeting begins. Betty sits in her chair fingering what's probably a six-carat Harry Winston. Seeing her up close, she looks exhausted, like she hasn't slept in a week. She lets Craig do the talking. He launches into his briefing. Thank God the coffee does its job and I'm able to concentrate. There are a dozen angles to this mess, and, according to Craig, it's more serious than what they're reporting in DC. The sanctions against North Korea are threatening to break the country apart. To stay in power, the "Dear Leader" is threatening war. He's moved a half a million troops to the border. Craig says that the Chinese have moved troops to their border with North Korea on the Yalu River, prepared to give what they call "humanitarian relief." Right. The US has warned the Chinese to stay out, and for the time being, they're complying. Naturally, the Russians want to be part of the show, and they're rushing troops and tanks to Khasan on their border with North Korea. Both direct and back-channel diplomacy between all parties has degraded into nothing more than threats and saber rattling.

And now, the Japanese—our dear friends, the Japanese—are taking advantage of China's distraction in Korea to beef up their military presence in the disputed Senkaku Islands. Craig says the Land of the Rising Sun has their eyes on a few other islands, too. How nice.

After forty-five minutes, Craig finishes his report. I ask him about the mood in South Korea. He says the people are scared. The South Korean president has adopted a stiff upper lip and a business-as-usual policy. But the Korean stock market has tanked and businesses are laying off workers. There are anti-communist protests nearly every day. Anti-American ones, too. Some want war to end the tensions once and for all. Most, however, just want peace.

Next General Jeffries gives a briefing about our military response. The general opens a folder and reports that they've moved twenty-thousand troops into South Korea, upping our total to fifty thousand. Another fifty thousand are ready to deploy on a moment's notice. We've relocated one carrier group to the Sea of Japan and another just outside the Yellow Sea.

The brass has canceled R&R for troops in South Korea, and all bases are on high alert. After twenty minutes, Jeffries concludes that the US military is ready for any "exigency," as he says, and closes his folder.

General Dunning leans forward. "There's one more thing," he says in his big voice. "The nuclear threat. Intel says the North has the ability to deliver nuclear ordinance to Seoul, Tokyo, and possibly the US West Coast. We have a deterrence plan, but frankly, Mr. Simon, we aren't sure what we're up against." He gives me five seconds of his cold glare and then leans back.

I let out a sigh. Sure feels like World War III. Armies are marching, missiles are pointing, and people in charge are making threats. The superpowers are engaged in a stare-down across a divided nation about the same size as my home state of Michigan. And they have nuclear weapons. What a mess.

I look around the room. Betty has stopped fingering her diamond ring and looks like she needs to get back to her penthouse on Park Avenue for a long vacation. Craig is expressionless as usual. The army guys are stone-faced, and Anna Carlson hasn't said a single word. When I look at her now, I get the sense she's studying me as if she's trying to decide if I'm up to handling this assignment. After listening to the briefing, I'm beginning to wonder that myself.

General Dunning hasn't stopped staring at me. "Mr. Simon," he finally says, "you've been sent here to assess the situation and help the president formulate a strategy. Which way is the president leaning—a military solution or a diplomatic one?"

I shake my head. "General, it's not my duty to guess how the president will respond. It's only my duty to report what I learn here."

The general's eyes narrow, telling me he isn't at all happy that I didn't answer his question as he ordered me to. "And what do you see, Mr. Simon? A situation that requires military action or more diplomacy?"

"Well, General," I say finally, "there are seventy-five million Koreans depending on us to get this right. There are potentially millions more if this situation escalates beyond the peninsula. There are tens of thousands of US troops—"

"Don't think you need to tell me about our troops!" Dunning booms. "They are *my* responsibility, and I know full well what's at stake."

Dunning pushes away from the table and stands. Somehow, he looks a lot taller than five nine. "Yes, Mr. Simon," he says, "it is our job to get this right. But the fact is, at some point military action saves more lives than diplomacy. Just be sure that the secretary of state and the president know when that point is. Am I clear?"

Here, I could stand like the general and use my six foot three inches to tower over him. I could remind him that I'm in Korea at the behest of his commander in chief, and that I'm confident his superiors in Washington will get it right. But my head spins with everything Craig and General Jeffries have said. The coffee has worn off and I'm tired again. So I stay seated, and nod.

Dunning sits and crosses his arms over his medals. Betty nervously looks from the general to Matthews to me. Matthews looks straight ahead at nothing.

After a long pause, Colonel Nielson says, "Mr. Simon, we heard that you have a meeting with the CIA tomorrow about something that was sent to the White House. Can you fill us in?"

Everyone turns their eyes on me. "It's classified," I answer. "All I can tell you is that the White House received a message from someone we believe is a credible source in the North. We want to check it out."

"A message?" Dunning snarls. "What does this message say?"

"I'm sorry, General," I answer. "As I said, it's classified."

The general unfolds his arms and leans across the table. "You're telling me that the president and the secretary of state do not feel they need to share with the head of US Forces Korea a message from our enemy?" He pushes his chair away and puts his hands flat on the table as if he's going to leap over it. "Did you hear anything Mr. Matthews and General Jeffries said about our situation here? Maybe in DC they don't feel the danger. But our enemy has five hundred thousand troops fifty klicks from this building's front gate. If the White House expects me to protect Ambassador Morris here, fifty million South Koreans, and fifty thousand American troops, perhaps they better tell me what's going on."

I draw a breath. "I'm sorry, General," I say trying to find the right tone between firmness and respect. "I can't."

The general looks like he wants to grab me by the throat. Jeffries reaches out and touches Dunning's arm, but the general doesn't seem to notice. Betty Morris looks like she doesn't have the energy to mediate our little quarrel, and Matthews clearly doesn't have a clue what to do.

Then Anna Carlson speaks for the first time. "Gentlemen," she says in a surprisingly calm voice, as if the tension in the room is nothing more than a friendly disagreement about who will win the World Series, "perhaps we should take a break. Mr. Simon has had a long flight, and we've given him a lot to think about. Let's give him some time. How about if we reconvene at eleven? That's thirty-five minutes."

"Good idea," Betty says quickly.

After a few moments, General Dunning lifts his hands from the table and stands straight. He nods once. "Okay," he says. "Eleven o'clock." Then he marches out of the room with General Jeffries and Colonel Nielson in single file behind him.

Ambassador Morris does a weary shake of her head and leaves. Matthews sweeps up his briefing papers and follows her, leaving Anna and me alone.

Anna looks at me matter-of-factly. "You should take a walk, Mr. Simon," she says. "It's a beautiful morning in Seoul, and the persimmon trees are in bloom in Gyeongbok Palace. It's lovely there now. The palace has stories to tell. It will clear your head and help you relax."

"Yeah," I say. "Maybe I will. Will I be safe there?"

"We'll send someone with you," she says as she opens the door for me.

THREE

After I leave the conference room, all I want to do is call Jin-ee and the kids to make sure they're still there, then curl up on a couch to get some sleep. But it's midmorning and I have only two days to find out what's going on here before I have to fly back to DC. And Anna is right—I need to clear my head. I used to love to take walks in Gyeongbok Palace when I worked here, so I decide to follow her advice.

I go down the elevators to the lobby where the goon who escorted me through the airport greets me. He's still wearing an earpiece, and I notice a bulge under the arm of his jacket. "I'm Mike," he monotones. "I'm your security. Pay no attention to me. I'll just follow behind you."

Right. Pay no attention to big Mike with a pistol under his jacket. I consider staying at the embassy, but I really need some fresh air. I shrug and go outside to the street. Mike follows. I turn toward Gyeongbok Palace. The morning haze has lifted, and as Anna said, it's a beautiful day. The May breeze sweeps away the airplane fumes that still cling to me. The sun is warm on my back, and soon I stop worrying about needing to have Mike escort me. I walk across the street to the wide plaza that leads to the palace's Gwanghwamun Gate. The gate's twin pagoda roofs spread their eaves over the three arched entrances. Within the eaves are intricate green, blue, and orange painted buttresses and brackets. I walk through the entrance into the palace grounds. Before me are several buildings whose green tiled roofs curve gracefully upward, like the wings of giant birds rising into the sky. At the other end of the courtyard is a pavilion with a long porch. Hundreds of tourists stroll across the stone-paved walkways. They take selfies or gaze in awe at the buildings.

I stroll toward the pavilion and suck in the heavy spring air. There's the earthy smell of freshly mowed grass and the soft scent of persimmon blossoms. My legs stretch, and blood flows through my body. The kinks and cramps from the long flight are working their way out. The information overload from the meeting is beginning to ease.

I take a good look around. Gyeongbok Palace, Korea's most sacred place. For over five hundred years, it was the center of the Chosŏn Dynasty. There are new buildings since I was here last. I remember that the Koreans vowed to rebuild hundreds of palace buildings torn down by the Japanese during their thirty-five-year occupation before World War II. Looks like they're making progress. Good for them.

I look beyond the palace, north at Bukhansan Mountain, tall and proud in the cobalt-blue sky. I look south toward the heart of Seoul, the glistening, modern city among the hills overlooking the Han River. I let the sun wash over me and the spirit of Korea fill me. I can almost feel what it's like to be one of them.

I've made it to the pavilion. Mike's a few yards behind. In his navy sports coat and gray slacks, he's doing a poor job of pretending to be just another tourist. I check my watch. Fifteen minutes until I have to be back at the embassy for more meetings. What have I learned so far? What do I think we should do? Come on, Nate, try to get an idea. The secretary and president want a report, and I can color it any way I want. Wish I could take an hour here at the palace. Or all day. It might help me find an answer or two and maybe even find the passion I had when I lived here. But people are waiting. They want to tell me what's going on and what they think we should do. And I need to learn about the comb with the two-headed dragon and the message that came with it.

"One Korea," I hear a woman say behind me. I quickly turn around and there above me on the pavilion porch is Anna Carlson. She looks down at me with the same look of confidence—or whatever it is—that I noticed when I first saw her.

"What'd you say?" I ask.

She comes off the porch and stands in front of me. The top of her head doesn't even reach my nose. She looks out over the courtyard. "Aren't the persimmon blossoms lovely?" she asks.

"No, no," I say. "What did you say before, just now, when you were on the steps?"

She gives me a knowing smile and points me to walk with her along the pavilion. She says, "Did you know that in 1394, King Taejo—he was Chosŏn Dynasty's first king, of course—planted persimmon trees here because he believed they would keep tigers away? Tigers are nearly extinct now in Korea, so apparently it worked." She lets out a soft chuckle.

She is indeed a beautiful woman, and there is a deep intelligence in her face. There's a serenity about her that's out of place here, now, with everything that's going on. I want to ask her again about what she said when she was on the pavilion porch, but I decide I must not have heard her right. I let it pass.

"Yeah, well," I say. "I think Siberian tigers are endangered everywhere, not just where they planted persimmon trees."

She points to an open space in the courtyard. "There, right there. That's where the queen's quarters were before the Japanese tore it down. Do you remember what happened?"

"Ah, no," I answer.

"Queen Min?"

"She lived here?"

"And died here, on October 8, 1895. She faced many tigers during her reign, if you recall your Korean history."

I remember only a few things about Korea's last queen. "Yeah, she did," I say, hoping the conversation about Korean history doesn't go much deeper.

We continue to stroll. "The queen was a remarkable woman," Anna says. "Hers is a story you can learn here. She had strength and courage and love for her people during a very difficult time in Korea. Of course, now, just like then, many tigers threaten this country. They come in all forms, speak different languages. They make promises and threats. I don't think persimmon trees will keep these tigers away, do you?"

I'm not comfortable with where this conversation is heading. Anna is a junior aide and there's a pecking order, a protocol to follow when discussing policy. People can take words out of context, say things they shouldn't. Someone in my position needs to be careful. I stop walking and turn to her. "Look, Anna. I just met you and, uh, well . . . I don't know you. You work for the ambassador. It isn't appropriate for us to discuss US foreign policy without her. And we have to get back."

She shakes her head. "It's not just about US foreign policy, Mr. Simon. It's not just about communists and capitalists and yet another conflict between the superpowers. It's far deeper than that. It goes back hundreds of years. It's primal to what this country is."

I cock my head. "What are you talking about?"

She levels her eyes on me. Then she says, "One Korea." She holds her eyes for a few seconds more, and turns and walks toward Gwanghwamun Gate.

One Korea. I heard her right the first time. She knows the two-word message someone from the North sent to the president along with the comb with the two-headed dragon. How could a junior aide to the ambassador possibly have anything to do with it? How could she know?

I check my watch again. I have less than ten minutes to get back to the embassy. I'm going to be late. I turn for Gwanghwamun Gate. As

I hurry through the gate's center arch, I see Anna getting into the back of a car. The car speeds off, and I'm puzzled why she isn't walking back to the embassy. I mean, it's only a block away. Then I notice a crowd surrounds me. They are all ages, men and women, even children. They look like tourists, dressed in street clothes. There are dozens of them, maybe fifty in all. They're all looking at me, grinning. I try to push through them, but they don't give way. I look for big Mike. I can't see him anywhere.

The crowd moves and forces me to move with it. We go to the street where a car idles. I remember what John had said about me being a target. I start to panic. "Hey!" I say as the crowd pushes me forward. "Mike, *help*!" I shout. The car's back door opens and hands shove me inside. I fall onto the seat. The car door slams, and someone puts a sack over my head. I try to fight, but someone has a firm grip on me. I shout again for help, but inside the car, my calls go nowhere. I feel the car accelerate and turn a corner. I struggle, but whoever has a grip on me knows what they're doing. Inside the sack, I'm breathing hard. My mind races. I start to panic.

"Who are you?" I demand. "What are you doing to me? I'm with the US Embassy. I have diplomatic status." There's no response, the car speeds on, turns a few more corners. I think of Jin-ee and the kids. I promise God that I'll be a better husband and father if He lets me live.

After a few minutes, the car stops and they pull me out with the sack still on my head. Hands on my arm and back lead me down a set of stairs and into what feels like a long tunnel. The air is cool and it smells like we're underground. In my mind, I picture a cell and a torture chamber. I yell and try to twist free, but the hands hold tight and drag me forward. Finally we stop. They let go of me and take the sack off. Slowly, my eyes adjust to a dimly lit room. I want to run, but I'm disoriented so I just stand in place. The air is slightly musty. There are shadows of people moving around. Some are lighting candles, others are starting a fire in a fireplace. Eventually the light comes up. When I see where I am, I think I'm in some bizarre nightmare.

The room is large for being underground. It's two stories tall and twice as wide as it is deep. Wooden columns and painted beams support the roof. In the center, four columns hold up a wooden dais topped with a canopy. On the dais is a throne painted red. Hanging behind the throne is a ten-foot-high faded-blue tapestry that looks very old. Woven into the tapestry with what looks like gold thread is a two-headed dragon—the exact same dragon as on the comb sent to the president of the United States. Its tongues curl up and its claws reach out. Its eyes seem to be staring at me.

I'm still terrified, but clearly this isn't a torture chamber. I don't see a cell, either. My panic eases some, but I'm terribly confused.

Off to one side of the throne are several women dressed in dark loose-fitting blouses and slacks who are attending to a woman with her back to me. The attendants remove the woman's clothes. Naked, her cream-colored skin glows in the candlelight. Her figure is lean and athletic. She stands straight as the women slip on a layered hanbok petticoat. They support her as she steps into a blood-red *chima* with a gold design above the hem. When they tie it to her chest, the long skirt reaches all the way to the floor. The woman steps into brown *namaksin* clogs that make her several inches taller. She holds out her arms, and the attendants put on a gold *jeogori* jacket with a white collar. They close it across her chest with a maroon bow. As they apply makeup to the woman's face, someone brings in stools and more attendants stand on them and go to work on her hair. They brush it with long deliberate strokes. They fold it onto her head and pin it with a gold *binyeo*. They place something on top of her head and secure it with more ornamental hairpins. The entire ritual feels like a holy thing that I should not interrupt. Finally the attendants are done and they bow as they back away, out of sight into the room's darkness. With her back still facing me, the woman bows her head. I think she's praying.

I look around. There are people lighting candles, preparing tea, stoking the fire. They all wear the same dark loose-fitting clothes. I notice there are two men standing behind me.

I'm still confused, but for some reason, I'm not so afraid any more. It's peaceful here, almost like a church. The fire in the fireplace has burned away the mustiness. The great room is now pleasantly warm. I get a strange feeling that I'm about to go on an extraordinary journey.

"Come forward," says the woman, speaking Korean. She's still on the dais facing away from me, but she no longer has her head lowered. Her voice is strong and firm and echoes off the walls. I'm not sure she's talking to me, so I don't move. The men behind me take my arms and lead me forward until I'm standing just below the dais. I look up.

She turns to face me. She's magnificent, like a beautiful, terrifying queen. Her face shimmers gold and orange from the fireplace's flames, almost as if she herself is on fire. The hanbok gracefully drapes her figure. The makeup on her face makes her look both delicate and strong. They've arranged her hair in strips and folds and have put on a headpiece that snakes around her hair. It adorns her face like a picture frame. Her dark eyes are intense, but touched with compassion. In her hand is a folded fan.

"Anna?" I mutter. "What's this abou—"

"Take off your shoes," she says in Korean.

"Uh, what?" I say.

Her eyes flash. She points her fan at my feet. "Your shoes," she says. "It isn't proper to wear street shoes inside a place like this. Take them off."

The men behind me put their hands on my back so I slip my shoes off. Someone places a pair of zori on the floor in front of me. I don't put the sandals on.

"Christ, Anna. What are you doing?"

"Speak Korean," she says, still speaking Korean herself. "I hear you know it." She goes to the throne and sits with her back perfectly straight.

"Yeah, but . . ."

"Use it. You are in Korea. Speak the language." She holds her chin high and looks down at me.

Finally my mind starts to work. "Who are you working for, Anna?" I ask. "The North? The Russians?"

"Working for?" she says in Korean with a smirk. "Do you think this is about money? You *have* turned corporate, haven't you, Mr. Simon? You weren't always that way. I've read your dossier."

"You have?" I wave. "Look, just tell me what this is about."

"One Korea," she says.

I lean forward and cock my head. "One Korea?" I say. "How could you know—"

"Speak Korean!" she thunders.

The power in her voice and the fire in her eyes startle me, so I switch to Korean. "What's going on here, Anna? Who are these people? Where are we? You're in a lot of trouble."

"As I suspected, your Korean is pathetic," she says, looking away. "To honor the people whose language you use, you must learn it. Without an accent. With proper grammar."

"Well, I'm not a native speaker like you," I say.

"I'm not, either," she sniffs. "I was raised in America since I was a baby. I didn't start learning Korean until a few years ago."

I can't believe it. Her Korean is flawless, as if she's spoken it all her life. There's no accent, and her vocabulary is much better than mine. So much for seven years of Korean. "Anna, Jesus. What's going on here?" I say, carefully choosing the right Korean words and struggling to minimize my accent. "The two-headed dragon. The message sent to the president. What do you know about it?"

"It's not what *I* know that's important. What is important is what *you* learn about it. Perhaps your experience here will bring back that fire you once had." She lifts her chin at the people behind me. They bring a high-backed wooden chair. A hand on my shoulder gently pushes me to sit.

"Please," I say, "I don't know what you want with me, but . . ."

"Why are you here?" she asks. She opens her fan and fans herself with quick flicks of her wrist. "Why did you come to Korea? What is your mission?"

"To get a ground-level view of what's going on. To help formulate a strategy for the secretary of state and the president."

"To achieve what goal?" she asks.

"What?"

She stops fanning herself and glares at me as if I'm stupid. "Strategies support goals. You said you're helping formulate a strategy. What goal will your strategy support? It's a simple question."

"To support US policy here in Korea. To protect our interests in East Asia."

"Ah, yes. Our interests," she says, fanning herself again. "American imperialism is not the recipe for world peace, Mr. Simon."

"It's not imperialism," I counter, switching to English. I shake my head and stand. "Look, I don't have to sit here and debate US policy with you, whoever you are. Okay?" I look for my shoes, but a hand pushes me back into the chair. It's not so gentle this time.

Anna snaps her fan closed and nods. "You are correct," she says. "We are not here to discuss policy. Instead, you need to hear a story," she says. "It's one not many people know."

"I don't care about your story," I say. "If you really work for State and want to ruin your career with this charade, then by all means. Just do it without me."

"My career?" she replies with a raised eyebrow. "So I can be like you and Craig Matthews—harmless, but dead? That is not why I'm here."

"I'm not dead," I protest half-heartedly.

"Stop worrying so much about your career, Mr. Simon," Anna says. "I assure you this is far more important to your mission than anything the ambassador or a general or the CIA can tell you. This is the story of the dream of One Korea and the two-headed dragon."

I look at the tapestry again. The two-headed dragon stares back at me. The words "One Korea" ring in my head. "Well, Anna," I say, "looks like I don't have a choice."

"Call me Ja-young," she says. "That is my Korean name. When I'm in Korea, it is the name I prefer."

I'm pissed about having been abducted and being forced to be the audience for Anna's show. But with her guards behind me, there's nothing I can do about it. And I sense there's something important to learn here. "Okay, tell me your story," I say. "I hope, for your sake, it doesn't take too long."

"It will take as long as it takes, Mr. Simon. You must listen carefully. Listen and learn."

And then the pleasantly warm room and Anna's queen-like demeanor start to pull me into a spell. It feels like the Korean folk plays Jin-ee and I loved to see when we lived here. I cross my legs and lean back. I hold my gaze on the remarkable figure sitting on the throne above me. Damn, she looks a lot like Jin-ee.

She sits straight with her hands folded in her lap. She starts in a voice clear and strong. "It was the first warm day of spring when the palace messenger came galloping up the road to the House of Gamgodang where I lived."

FOUR

March 1866. Seoul, Korea

It was the first warm morning of spring when the palace messenger came galloping up the road to the House of Gamgodang where I lived. Only a few days earlier a warm rain had made the leaves burst into a sweep of green, and the flower buds on the fruit trees were ripe to open. The new bamboo shoots had pushed through the garden like ivory needles through black silk. The air was heavy with new life.

I first saw the messenger while I sat on the Chinese bench in the bamboo grove reading poems by Chŏng Ch'ŏl. The messenger drove the horse along the wall surrounding the compound and pulled to a stop at the gate. He wore a red tunic jacket and a black *joenrip* hat with a thick red tassel and a long beaded strap. His horse was a splendid Chinese Datong, tall, muscled, and draped with a polished leather saddle. As the horse snorted and stomped, the messenger called out from the gate, "*Anyohaseyo!* I have an important message from His Excellency's court. Come out at once!"

"His Excellency" was Korea's powerful regent, the Taewŏn-gun, "Prince of the Great Court," father of the boy king Gojong. The Taewŏn-gun often summoned my uncle to the palace only a short distance away. So naturally I assumed the messenger had come for him. But I remembered my uncle had left earlier that day for Yongsan-gu on official business for the crown. Surely, the palace would know he wasn't here. I didn't think anything of it and was returning to my poems when my uncle's valet, Mr. Yang, and my aunt came out and exchanged a few words with the messenger. I turned my ear to hear what they were saying, but they were too far away. My aunt exchanged a few words with the messenger and then looked across the bamboo garden and pointed at me. The messenger examined me from atop his mount and nodded. He pulled on the reins and kicked the horse with the heels of his oxskin boots. The horse reared and galloped down the road back toward the palace. My aunt gave me a quick look, lifted her purple chima, and hurried into the house followed closely by Mr. Yang.

A few seconds later, the back door swung open and Mr. Yang ran to the stables. He roused the stableman and pointed to my uncle's fastest horse. When the stableman had saddled the horse, Mr. Yang mounted it and went for the gate. As he drove the horse down the road in the opposite direction from where the messenger had come, he shot a disapproving glance at me from behind his wire-rimmed glasses. This, from someone who I thought didn't even know I existed, sent a shiver through me.

I couldn't believe all this commotion was about me. Who was I to have the attention of the palace? I was an orphan girl, dependent on the charity of my father's brother and the Min clan of the House of Gamgodang. To them, I was like a beggar that appeared at their doorstep four years earlier. And just as people try to avoid beggars, they did their best to avoid me. I didn't care. In fact, it was the way I wanted it to be. If they could not love me, I wanted them to leave me alone. So I talked only when I was spoken to and was careful to stay out of their way.

But I had once been loved. I'd been my parent's only child, and they had nurtured me as only loving parents could. My father had been a scholar and a spiritual man. He insisted I read the teachings of Confucius and Buddha and encouraged me to take up the same studies as boys my age. He told me I was an excellent student and that I learned quickly—faster than the boys. He was tall, strong, handsome, and, though he was a scholar, he liked to do hard work—work usually assigned to servants or put out to cheap labor. He had me help when he fixed roof tiles on our house or when he built a coop for our chickens and ducks. As we worked, he talked about the teachings of Confucius and the poems of the great Korean poets. I loved listening to him, and my heart soared when he put his hand on my shoulder and smiled at me after we had finished our work.

My mother had been more earthly. She was beautiful and petite like me. She had more spirit than anyone. She delighted in growing orchids and loved the wildlife along the Han River a short distance from our house. Her favorites were the red-crowned cranes. She told me the cranes lived for a thousand years and were a sign of good luck and longevity. She would take me to the river's high banks and we would watch the snowy-white birds with the long black necks and little red caps as they stalked their prey. When one speared a fish or a salamander, she would cheer and grab my hand and I would cover my mouth and laugh. We talked about spirits and the meaning of things that I could not talk about with my father or anyone else. Through her, I knew the cranes, the fish, the trees and flowers, the mountains and sky.

Together, my parents were heaven and earth, the truth and life, and all the year's seasons at once. They loved each other like no two people ever did, and I blossomed inside their circle of love.

But one day, my mother started to change. What was once warm and light turned icy and dark. She stopped talking to my father, as if he was a stranger to her. He desperately tried to bring her back, and his heart broke more every day as she drifted away. Although she was never cruel, my mother didn't talk to me, either, except to order me away from my books to come help in the kitchen or the garden. I often wondered if she was angry with me. She never went to the river anymore to watch the red-crowned cranes. She would spend hours in her garden talking to her orchids. In the last days, she never asked me to help in the garden when she was there and scolded me to stay away whenever I came close.

One night, I awoke to voices in the garden. I crawled off my sleeping mat and went to the window. Outside, my mother was angrily talking aloud to no one. "What is it?" she cried. "What do you want from me?" I thought she was talking to her orchids again. Then she said, "Go! Leave me alone!" This time, I thought she was talking to me, so I quickly went back to my mat and covered my ears. I never looked out again when I heard her in the garden at night.

My father died when I had just turned eleven. One day he was there, looking at me from over the top of his books as I studied Confucius and the classic Chinese teachings. The next day, he was gone like the cranes that vanish on the first cold day of fall. The medicine woman that came from Mapo said that the blood in my father's head had turned to wood in the middle of the night. After the eight days of mourning, my mother no longer talked to her orchids or tended to the household chores. She stayed in bed, longer and longer each day, until she never got up. I tried to feed her, but she refused to eat. Her orchids died. I often heard her sobbing at night.

One day she called me to her bedside. Though the nurse had opened the sliding wall to the outside, the room was warm and clammy. My mother was thin and frail, and her eyes were lifeless like those of a dead fish. Lying on her mat, she motioned me to come close. I kneeled beside her.

"Ja-young," she said, "soon I will go to the land of our ancestors where I will finally be at peace."

"Please stay, *Ummah*," I cried. I was afraid of being alone, and I wanted my life to be as it was when my father was alive and she was happy.

My mother shook her head weakly. "No, I cannot. The spirits scare me, and I cannot convince them to leave me alone."

I looked at my hands so she could not see my tears. Outside, the birds chirped gaily, mocking my despair. "What will become of me?" I asked.

She sighed deeply. "Oh, my daughter, I have not been a good mother. I should not have left you. But you are stronger than I am. You are smart and beautiful. Like me, you see things others do not. I was not able to find peace with these things, but you must or they will lead you into the dark as they have done to me. And when you find your peace, you must use your gifts."

I shook my head. "But what will I use them for, Ummah?"

My mother closed her eyes. Then she said in a faraway voice, "The spirits tell me they fear for Korea. I think, my daughter, you who sees so much must try to understand what they are saying. Speak for them. It is your duty to me and your father, and the spirits of our ancestors. It is your duty, your children's, and your children's children's. Find your way. Be strong and do not fail. Promise you will."

"Yes, Ummah," I said. "I promise." She nodded weakly, and turned away.

Early the next morning she got out of bed for the first time in weeks and threw herself into the Han River.

Now, as I sat in my uncle's bamboo grove, I remembered what my mother had said about my duty. I had been fortunate to have my uncle take me in to the House of Gamgodang after my mother died. It was a lovely place and I did not want for anything. But living here, I wondered if I would ever find my way as my mother said I must. Since I had arrived, I'd spent my time in comfortable idleness. I wasn't unhappy, yet I was not happy, either. I didn't hear the spirits my mother spoke of. My life was like the days in late winter when everything is quiet and still and you think spring will never come.

So I passed time reading my uncle's books. I loved his books. I was very careful not to soil them or wrinkle a single page. I was always mindful to put them back where I found them on the bookshelf in my uncle's study. I was thankful that he never said anything to me about sneaking into the male area of the house to borrow his books. Though I didn't understand everything in them—after all, they were meant for scholarly men much older than me—they gave my life some perspective. Through the pages of those books, I tried to hear the spirits of my ancestors, the kings and queens of Korea. I tried to understand the meaning of things as I had done with my mother sitting on the bank of the Han River. But I heard no spirits and I didn't find any understanding.

After the palace messenger left and Mr. Yang gave me that look, I tried to read another poem, but I could no longer focus on the words. I shut the book and wondered why they had regarded me the way they did. I looked at the House of Gamgodang. It was the house of a wealthy man—a *yangban*—much larger than my parents' house near the Han River. It was a compound with many buildings. The main house where my uncle and aunt lived was built on a timber-frame platform two feet off the ground with steps leading up to it on all sides. It had white stucco walls and a dark-blue tiled roof that turned up gracefully at the corners. Off to one side were rooms for the staff and other members of the Min clan. Outside was a courtyard, gardens, a small orchard, stables, and storehouses. A four-foot wall topped with the same blue tile as the house surrounded the entire compound. Beyond the wall were the streets of Seoul. As befitting a man of importance, the house was on the main boulevard a mile south of the king's residence, Gyeongbok Palace, where the messenger had come from.

Suddenly a kitchen maid came out of the back door carrying a bamboo-leaf basket and ran to the storehouse. Another ran to the fowl coop and disappeared inside. I could hear the chickens squawk and flap their wings. The house's heavy wooden front door opened, and my aunt and her lady's maid came out. My aunt could be described as being statuesque and having a pleasantly round face. She held her chima above her ankles as she walked through the bamboo grove toward me. Her maid was as short and plump as my aunt was tall and lean. Her face was always red. She walked three steps behind her mistress with the half bow she employed when my aunt was upset.

My uncle's wife, her name was Su-mi Kim, came to me and held out her hand. "Someday, child, you will fall into a book and have to live the rest of your life among the pages. Come, the king's mother is coming to see you."

I was stunned. "Lady Min?" I said. "Coming to see me?" I couldn't believe the king's mother even knew I existed. "Why?"

"I do not know," my aunt said. "Now come, quickly. We do not have time to waste."

I handed the book to my aunt and followed her to the house. Her lady's maid walked behind still in a half bow. We went inside. The house had a large main room with dark-wood ceiling beams and wood floors covered with dried rush mats. Along one wall was a zelkova-root wooden chest with polished brass fittings. Against another was a Chinese tray table with thick bamboo-formed legs. A blue-green celadon pot sat in one corner, and an oil pendulum lamp on an iron stand was in another. There was a kitchen off to one side, and the servant's quarters were beyond that. Separated from the main room by sliding walls were a series of rooms—sleeping rooms, a bath area, and my uncle's study. Altogether, the house was simple and clean, as a proper Confucian house should be.

Inside, the entire staff was busy at work. A housemaid dressed in a commoner's cotton *durumagi* hurriedly dusted the lattice on the windows. Another moved the floor mats and swept underneath. In the kitchen, maids fussed at the sink and the cast-iron stove. The footman hurried in from the back with a bucket of coal and placed it on the kitchen floor. The scullery maid dragged in two pails of water from the well. Now that she was inside the house, my aunt's lady's maid—her name was Eun-ji—stood from her half bow and began clapping her hands and barking orders at the staff. "Get the large celadon pots from the storeroom and place them along the wall, there," she said, pointing. "Make sure they are well cleaned. You," she said to the housemaid sweeping the floor, "be sure to shake out the mats. Do a good job of it or else!" She raised a finger. "Plum blossoms! We should have plum blossoms." She lifted her chima and marched into the kitchen, her face redder than usual. "Have the gardener cut stems. Prepare some warm water and sugar to force them to open. Quickly! The king's mother is coming!"

My aunt, Eun-ji, and Mr. Yang had trained the staff well. Everyone moved with purpose and haste, taking quick steps across the wooden floor and keeping their heads low. They did not dare make a mistake or overlook the slightest detail for fear of being demoted or kicked to the street.

As the staff attended to their duties, my aunt gave me a long look. "You should have a bath. Eun-ji, come," she ordered.

Eun-ji scurried into the main room and gave my aunt a small bow. "Yes, ma'am?" she said.

"We need to bathe and dress Ja-young for Lady Min," my aunt said. "She looks like a peasant girl."

"I do not," I protested as I looked down at my smudged and wrinkled clothes.

"Yes, you do," Eun-ji said, inspecting me with the same pose as my aunt. "She does not have a proper hanbok," she said to my aunt. "And yours will not fit her skinny bones."

"We'll have to make do with the hanbok she has," my aunt said. "Bathe her now, and prepare her hair. Do your best with her hanbok."

"I do not want to meet Lady Min," I said. "Why does she want to see me?"

"This is not a time to argue, child," my aunt said. "Now go with Eun-ji."

Eun-ji grabbed me by the arm. "Myeong-ki!" Eun-ji called out to the senior housemaid as she led me to the bath. "Make hot water for the bath and fetch Ja-young's hanbok. She must be well turned-out for the Grand Lady Min."

A few minutes later, I sat in the big iron tub as Eun-ji and Myeong-ki scrubbed me with a coarse wool cloth and honey locust-seed soap until I was afraid my skin would come off. Normally, I would have protested such a harsh treatment, but they were preparing me to meet the Grand Lady Min and I knew that protesting would do no good. They dried me and put me in clean undergarments—*gojaengi* pants and a *jeoksam* blouse. Then they went to work on my hair. As two maids dried my hair with bamboo-leaf fans, Myeong-ki combed out my tangles. She was none too gentle. She tugged so hard I thought my hair would tear right out of my scalp. But I refused to cry out or even complain. I knew that if I did, she would have only pulled harder. When my hair was straight, they twisted it into three tight braids and tied them together with a red *daenggi* ribbon.

My aunt came in with my hanbok, which they had just pressed in the kitchen. It had a pink chima and yellow jeogori with a black bow. It was a plain hanbok, not like the silk embroidered one with gold trim my aunt wore to formal events. But I liked mine just the same. Eun-ji and Myeong-ki slipped the skirt over my legs and wrapped the jacket around my waist. They had me step into a pair of my aunt's brocade silk slippers that were too large for me.

My aunt took a long step back and examined me. "She is thin like a willow stick," she said.

Eun-ji stepped back, too, and posed alongside my aunt. "We can put another layer underneath," she said.

My aunt shook her head. "No. Lady Min is too shrewd for that. She will know what we are trying to do. Ja-young will have to meet her being skinny."

Outside, there were horses galloping toward the house. They stopped at the gate. My aunt and Eun-ji ran to the main room. I stayed back, just behind the sliding wall. My uncle came through the front door followed closely by Mr. Yang. My uncle's name was Chul-jo Min, and he was a leader of the Min clan. Like my father, he was tall, lean, and had soft, onyx eyes. He wore his goatee and mustache closely trimmed like a diplomat rather than long and loose like a scholar. As he took off his topcoat, he addressed my aunt. "Mr. Yang tells me Lady Min will attend my house today. Do we know why?"

My aunt said, "The messenger only said she wants to see Ja-young."

"Why does Her Excellency want to see my niece?"

Eun-ji stepped forward. "Master," she said bending at the waist, "there is gossip on the street that the Taewŏn-gun has not found anyone in the Yi clan that his son wishes to marry. They are searching the countryside to find someone who will please the boy king. Ja-young is the right age."

"But wouldn't Lady Min have us bring the girl to the palace?" my aunt asked. "Why is she coming to this house to see Ja-young?"

My uncle nodded knowingly and folded himself down onto a floor cushion. My aunt did the same as Eun-ji and Mr. Yang stayed standing. "Because," my uncle said, "the king's mother is a Min and the palace is the House of Yi. Perhaps Lady Min wishes our clan to have a seat on the throne, and she doesn't want the Taewŏn-gun to know about Ja-young until we have had time to prepare her."

"Yes," my aunt said, "that is a good explanation."

My uncle scanned the room. "Where is Ja-young? I want to see her."

Eun-ji clapped her hands. "Ja-young!" she shouted. "Come!"

I stepped from behind the door into the main room.

"We readied her for Lady Min as best as we could," my aunt said.

"Come closer," my uncle ordered. He inspected me with his dark eyes for a few seconds. I thought he would say something about how skinny I was or that a silly girl who spent all day reading books wasn't fit to be the king's wife. But he said, "Listen to me carefully, Ja-young. When Lady Min arrives, you will not make eye contact with her and you will say nothing unless she asks you a question. You will address her as 'Your Excellency' and answer her questions directly. You will say nothing more. Do you understand?"

"I do not want to marry the king," I said.

My uncle nodded. "Well, for now all you need to do is meet Lady Min. And this, you must do," he said firmly.

"Yes, sir," I answered.

"Good," he said. "Now wait in my study. My wife and I will see to it that the house is ready to receive Lady Min."

FIVE

I did as I was told and waited for Lady Min in my uncle's study. It felt strange to be allowed in the male quarters of the house. The room had the smell of burnt sandalwood from the incense my uncle liked to burn when he worked there. The study had a low desk with an inkwell, several quill pens, and calligraphy brushes in a small pot. Along one wall was his bookshelf filled with books. I went to it and ran my hand over the books' spines. I had read nearly every one, and I loved their stories and poems. I wished that instead of meeting Lady Min, I could do as my aunt had said earlier and fall into a book and live forever among the pages.

I left the bookshelf and went to a wall that looked out over the garden and the street beyond. My uncle's house had windows with real glass panes from China. The glass was wavy and had bubbles in it, but I found a corner where the view of the street was clear. I positioned myself to watch for Lady Min.

I had seen Grand Lady Min once before. I was with my mother on the way home from the market when royal guards on horses came trotting down the street. They shoved and kicked people away and said, "Move aside! Her Excellency is coming on this street." My mother pulled me next to a wall and told me to lower my head. As the entourage passed by, I was so curious I couldn't resist sneaking a look. I lifted my eyes and in front of me was an extraordinary red and gold palanquin carried by eight barefoot porters dressed in black robes. The palanquin had a high roof topped with a bulbous finial. On each corner was a carved head of a dragon with its long tongue curled up. The palanquin's box was three wooden panels painted red and decorated with painted cranes and landscapes. In the front was a yellow curtain made from what looked like Chinese silk. The palanquin's long poles rested on the shoulders of the porters, who stepped in perfect unison so that the palanquin traveled smoothly along the street.

Then I looked through the palanquin's curtains and caught a glimpse of the grand lady riding inside. For just an instant, our eyes met. I quickly lowered my head and prayed she would not send a guard to whip me for looking at her. No guard came and after the entourage had gone, my mother and I went home. As I waited for her now, I worried that she would recognize me—the disrespectful girl who dared to make eye contact with her five years earlier. I was taller now and I was no longer a girl. But it was said that Lady Min was very quick. I prayed she wouldn't remember that day at the market when our eyes met.

As I watched the road, I thought about what Eun-ji had said about why Lady Min was coming to see me. I slept in a room next to the servant's quarters and had heard the maids talk about how the Taewŏn-gun was looking for a wife for his son, King Gojong. They practiced in the kitchen passageway, bowing to a pretend king. One of the older girls joked about what she would do on her wedding night if she was the one who they selected. The other girls giggled at the joke, covering their mouths as they did.

But I knew better. Unlike the maids who were *nobi*—slaves and indentured servants—my father and mother had been yangban, though in the last few years they had fallen on hard times. My father was a fine Confucian scholar. The palace sometimes employed him, and he told me about their eccentric ways. I knew they would never choose a nobi to marry the king. I also doubted very much that they would choose an orphan like me. No, certainly they would choose a noble yangban girl, someone worthy of sitting on the throne.

I had never thought about marriage when I lived in my house by the Han River. Perhaps I was too young. Or maybe I was too content. Now, waiting for Lady Min in my uncle's study, I tried to picture myself marrying the king, but I could not. I had never been inside the palace, and I couldn't imagine being part of that world. The royal family was a mystery to someone like me. The housemaids gossiped about extravagant affairs at the palace with strange people from faraway lands. They said the palace had rare animals and foods and inventions most people had never heard of. Surely, none of it could be true. Then again, I really did not know. As for King Gojong, though he lived only a mile away, I didn't even know what he looked like, or if he was kind and gentle, or coarse and mean. As far as I was concerned, he might as well have lived on the moon.

I heard horses coming down the street. Two palace guards dressed in long red robes and broad-brimmed black hats rode high in the saddles of their horses. Following them were two more guards on foot, each carrying a long lance with a wide shiny blade. Behind them was Lady Min's palanquin that I had seen years earlier, flanked by guards and carried by eight barefoot porters dressed in black robes. Behind them was a smaller, less ornate palanquin carried by only four men. These porters did not step in unison, and their palanquin swayed and bounced as they moved. The procession came to a stop at the gate. Then, as if they were performing a slow dance together, the first palanquin's porters lifted it from their shoulders and carefully lowered it to the ground. The other palanquin's porters lowered their load less carefully and the palanquin wobbled and came to a thud on the street.

A guard on horseback called out. "Anyohaseyo! Her Excellency, Lady Min, calls on this house. Come and receive her."

There was movement in the main room, and I heard the clink of the latch on the front door. Outside, a guard stepped to the palanquin and lifted the curtain. He took a woman's hand and bowed low as Lady Min stepped out. She was younger than I'd expected. She looked to be not much older than my mother had been when she died. Her figure was full and adorned with an elaborate gold and blue hanbok. She wore a headpiece of a noble married woman made from two wide braids of fine cloth that covered her hair and the back of her neck. She stepped from the palanquin to the front of the house and out of my sight. Out of the other palanquin stepped a short man with a long mustache. He wore a top hat, woolen slacks, and a European-style waist jacket. He followed Lady Min.

I went to the wall between the study and main room and listened. I heard my uncle welcome Lady Min into his house. He called for Mr. Yang and Eun-ji. I heard the kitchen staff bring out tea and food. After a few minutes, my uncle and Lady Min began to talk. I listened as best as I could, but I could only hear a few words: "our clan" and "opportunity" and "the king" and "the girl." My heart skipped a beat at those last words. I still couldn't believe they were talking about me. I hoped they were discussing the merits of some other girl and Lady Min was only asking my uncle for advice about her. But then I remembered that the messenger had said she was coming to see me.

My uncle called to me from the large room. "Ja-young, come at once," he ordered.

I was stricken with panic. I thought about running out the back door, past the stables and over the compound wall, disappearing into Seoul where they wouldn't make me their queen. But I didn't know where I would go or who would take me in. I would be alone on the streets with no food or place to live. To survive, I would have to become a slave, a nobi, like the housemaids and the thousands of slaves throughout Seoul, bought and sold as chattel among the yangban and merchant class. Or I could step out into the great room and present myself as someone who would be queen. If they chose me, I would live among strange people in their strange world, the wife of a man I did not know. My choice was simple. I could run and be a slave or present myself as someone who could be queen. Both choices terrified me.

"Ja-young!" my uncle repeated. I took a deep breath and walked into the main room with my head low. I felt everyone's eyes on me, watching for any mistakes I might make. Though I had my head bowed, I saw that my uncle and Lady Min were sitting at the Chinese table. I went to them. Lady Min held out a hand and someone helped her to her feet. My uncle stood with her.

"Come closer," Lady Min said. Her voice was low and full of authority. I took a step forward and bowed low. She reached out and lifted my chin. I kept my eyes down, not daring to look at her face as I did when I was young. She turned my head from side to side and muttered, "Hmmm." She brought her hand to my breast and squeezed it, first one, and then the other. "Uh-huh," she said, taking her hand away.

She said, "She is pretty like a bird but thin like one, too. A little more eating will help with that." She sat at the Chinese table again and my uncle sat with her. She took out a fan and fanned herself. As I stayed bowed before them, I could feel Lady Min inspecting me from her cushion. "What is her sign?" she asked.

My aunt spoke up. "She was born in the year of the pig, Your Excellency."

"Ah," Lady Min said. "Is she ambitious like a pig?"

"She does not seem to be, Your Excellency," my aunt replied. "In fact, she doesn't seem to be . . . much of anything."

"Hmmm," Lady Min said. "Well." There was a long silence as Lady Min continued to study me. I hoped she would say I was too skinny to be the queen or that someone born in the year of the boar would be a bad match for the king. Instead she said, "I think this one might please my son. I will propose to my husband that she be a candidate. The Taewŏn-gun is the leader of the Yi clan and is not inclined to let a

Min on the throne. But this Min is an orphan with no father. I believe my husband will look favorably upon her. And perhaps my son will approve of her, too."

"That is good, Your Excellency," my uncle said. "It is good for our clan."

"Yes," Lady Min replied, "but we must be careful. My husband is clever. If he thinks we are putting this one forward to someday challenge the House of Yi, he will reject her."

"Yes, Your Excellency," my uncle said.

"She must be prepared," Lady Min continued. "I have brought a tutor who will train her. His name is Mister Euno." The short man from the second palanquin bowed behind Lady Min. "Mister Euno has trained geishas in Japan, and he will be able to train this girl so she will please the king. Be sure she gets plenty to eat—goat's milk to make her bones strong and duck fat to fill her out. I will arrange the meeting with my husband and son. She must be ready in fifteen days. Mister Euno will know what to do."

"Yes, Your Excellency," my uncle said.

Lady Min closed her fan and presented her hand again. She and my uncle rose from their cushions. She stood in front of me. "Listen to me, Ja-young," she said, tapping my head with her fan. "I am giving you a chance to be my son's wife, the new queen of Korea. My son has rejected everyone he has seen, but he might like you. Mister Euno will teach you how to impress him. You will do everything he asks of you."

"Yes, Your Excellency," I said.

"And if my son chooses you, you must always remember that you are a Min and that we are the ones who made you the queen. Do you understand?"

"Yes, Your Excellency," I said.

She nodded. "Good. Your training will begin immediately."

She turned for the door and someone opened it. My aunt and uncle bowed as she walked outside to her palanquin. A guard helped her in, and the porters lifted the palanquin in perfect unison. They turned as one and marched back to Gyeongbok Palace.

My uncle clapped his hands and his eyes sparkled. "This is an extraordinary thing! It has been a hundred years since a Min sat on the throne. And now we only need Ja-young to impress the king and we will have it again!" He took me by the shoulders. "Ja-young, you must learn the lessons Mister Euno has for you. Learn them well and you can be the queen." He smiled at me and nodded.

I shook my head. "Please, Uncle, do not make me do this," I begged.

My uncle's smile dropped and he gave me a harsh look. "Listen, Ja-young. I brought you into my house when you had nowhere to go. I have given you a place to sleep and food from my storehouse. For four years, we have never asked anything from you. You've been treated kindly here and now you must do this. It is your duty to our clan and to your father and your mother."

I lowered my head. He was right. They had treated me well—or, at least, they had not mistreated me. Without them, I would have been an eleven-year-old girl alone on the streets, and there's no telling what would have become of me. It was also true that I had a duty to honor my father and mother. My father had often told me that I should be proud of my clan and that I must always honor my ancestors as the writings of Confucius taught. And I had made the promise to my mother that I would speak for the spirit of Korea, although I did not know how.

"I am sorry, sir," I said. "I will do what you say."

My uncle nodded and put a hand on my shoulder. "Good," he said. "And now, you must prepare yourself to impress the king."

SIX

Mister Euno stepped forward. He held his top hat along his leg. He was short like most Japanese, but not thin. He looked to be about the same age as my uncle. His hair was pulled into a short *chonmage* topknot. "We must begin at once," he said with a slight Japanese accent. "First, we will work on her posture. I assume you have a courtyard we can use?"

"Yes," my uncle said, "through those doors." He pointed to the back of the main room.

"Excellent. Put her in plain clothes and bring her there."

My aunt and Eun-ji took me to the kitchen where I stepped out of my hanbok and into my day clothes. My aunt took my arm and led me to the courtyard.

Mister Euno stood in the courtyard waiting for me. His hat was on the wooden step that ran the entire length of the courtyard. He held a bamboo switch. "Stand here, girl," he said pointing his switch to a spot just in front of him. My aunt let go of my arm, and I went to the place Mister Euno pointed to.

The courtyard was surrounded on three sides by the sleeping quarters, the main room, and my uncle's study. The house's roof with its blue-green tiles hung far out over the steps, making the space underneath like a long porch. Here and there along the courtyard's edges were large pots planted with herbs and small trees. Stone tiles covered the ground. The courtyard's open side faced an orchard where the plum blossoms were ready to open.

"Bring several pots of all sizes," Mister Euno said to my aunt. "And then leave us be. We are not to be interrupted. The first lesson will last the rest of the day."

My aunt left, and I stood in front of Mister Euno as two housemaids brought pots from the kitchen and storerooms. They placed them on the step and then left me alone with Mister Euno.

"You have poor posture," Mister Euno said, eyeing me. His long mustache jumped like a cricket with every word he spoke. "We must make you straight. Cross your hands at your waist, left over right, and pull your shoulders back and down."

I did as he said, and he shook his head making his topknot dance. "No," he said. With his bamboo switch, he pushed my shoulders down, one and then the other. But as they went down, they moved forward. He poked his switch into each shoulder to push them back. And when they went back, they went up again. He struck the top of my shoulder with his switch. The blow shot spikes of pain into my chest. I winced and stepped away.

"Why do you hit me?" I cried.

"It is for your own good. You heard Lady Min. You must do as I say without complaining. Now your shoulders. Both down and back at the same time." He pointed his switch to the spot in front of him. "Stand here. Do it again."

This time, I pressed my shoulders back and down. It strained my back, but I held the pose anyway.

"Not so far back," Mister Euno said, "and a little more down." I adjusted my shoulders as he said, "That is correct. Now raise your chin level with the ground. Keep your buttocks pulled forward and your hands crossed at your waist." I did, and he said, "Good. Now stand like that until I say you can stop."

The position was uncomfortable and hard to hold. It was as if someone had a knee in my back and was pulling on my shoulders. But I didn't want Mister Euno to hit me again with his switch, so I stood perfectly still while he sat next to his top hat on the step with his legs tucked underneath him. From his waistcoat pocket, he took out a pipe, tobacco, and a sulfur match. With his thumb, he packed the tobacco into the pipe and lit it. As he puffed, the blue smoke rose high into the air and over the roof. It smelled sweet, like burnt plums.

I stood in that position for ten minutes, and then for twenty. The muscles in my shoulders and back grew more and more fatigued until they screamed in pain. It was hard to breathe. In spite of the morning's pleasantness, I was sweating. I desperately wanted to release my muscles to make the pain go away, but I continued to hold it. All the while, Mister Euno watched and said nothing. He finished smoking his pipe, tapped it against the step to remove the ash, and put it back into his pocket.

After forty minutes, the pain was unbearable. I slumped forward. Mister Euno jumped from the step and came to me. He hit my shoulders with his switch. I cried out and fell on my knees. He stood over me.

"Do it again," he said.

"I can't," I said. "It hurts too much. I won't."

He raised his switch and brought it down hard on my back. The blow hit me like a strip of fire and made my stomach clench so hard I thought I would vomit.

"It hurts because you are weak," he said, pointing his switch at me. "If you are to impress the king, you must learn to be strong. Now stand and do it again."

I slowly rose to my feet. I did not want Mister Euno to hit me again, so I clasped my hands at my waist and pulled my shoulders, chin, and buttocks into position. Mister Euno adjusted my shoulders with his switch until they were exactly to his liking. He went back to the step and sat.

This time, after a half hour, the pain grew to a dull ache. As I held the pose, the day grew warm. Mister Euno removed his jacket, exposing a white shirt with buttons in front. He smoked three bowls of tobacco, and the sweet aroma filled the courtyard. He fanned himself with his hat. After forty-five minutes, I could no longer feel anything and I was afraid I might faint, but I gritted my teeth and forced myself to hold his pose. Finally, after an hour, he said, "Good. Now you may sit." I almost collapsed to the ground. He went to the water barrel and brought me a cup of water. I drank it in big gulps.

He said, "Rest for five minutes, and then you will do it again. Only this time, you will do it with a pot on your head. For each pot that falls, you will get a beating."

That day I broke three pots.

For the next several days, I worked on my posture standing in the courtyard with a pot on my head while Mister Euno smoked his pipe and watched for my slightest mistake. On the third day, he added a pot to each shoulder. He made me walk that way and lower myself into a chair all while keeping my shoulders properly positioned and a pot balanced on my head. Each time a pot fell, he beat me with his switch. By the fourth day, there was a pile of broken pots in the courtyard and I was so stiff and sore I could barely move. By then the plum blossoms had opened, filling the air with their scent. The new bamboo had turned from white to green, and the housemaids had made the season's first harvest. The bamboo plants they let grow to send off new shoots for the next harvest were over two feet tall. Normally, I would have enjoyed watching them grow—so fast that on warm days you could almost hear them stretch toward the sun. But I could not. Every day Mister Euno rose when it was still dark, came to my room, and poked me with his switch to wake me. We worked from sunrise to sunset on my posture, on how to sit like a proper queen, and on how to walk so that my body glided as if being propelled by some unseen force.

Those days, no one from the house said a word to me. The servants avoided me—I could tell my aunt had told them not to talk to me—and so did Mr. Yang and Eun-ji. They put out food for me at day's end—cups of goat milk and plates of fatty meats like Lady Min told them to. I was always very hungry and ate everything they gave me, but I never had enough to make my hunger go away. After I ate, I would go to my room, aching from the day's work and Mister Euno's beatings, and try to sleep. He would go to sleep in my uncle's study.

At the end of the sixth day, my uncle came into the courtyard. "How is she doing?" he asked.

"She is hopeless," Mister Euno said, shaking his head. "I do not think she will be ready for the king."

"Perhaps if you let her rest, she will do better," my uncle said.

"She will get no rest," Mister Euno replied with a shake of his head. "She has too much to learn."

My uncle looked at me for a moment, and I could see in his soft eyes that he was concerned about me. I wanted to speak out, tell him I couldn't take any more of Mister Euno's lessons. But I didn't say anything and my uncle went back inside the house.

That night after a particularly difficult lesson, I didn't sleep at all. Lying on my mat, I tried to find a position to ease the aches in my body. I couldn't lie on my back because it was sore from Mister Euno's beatings. When I tried my side, my ribs felt like they were poking right through my chest. When I rolled onto my stomach, I couldn't breathe. So I sat instead of lying and I didn't sleep, though I was terribly tired.

As I sat on my mat, I thought about what they were forcing me to do. I had endured Mister Euno's cruelty for six days, and there were eight more to go. I couldn't see how I could possibly make it another eight days. I believed I would die first. I wanted it to end. I wanted to go back home where I could read with my father and go to the river with my mother. But my mother and father were gone and I was alone. And so I cried. I cried into my hands so no one would hear. I had never known pain like this. I'd never had to suffer. I had never been beaten, insulted, or made to feel worthless. And I had never been afraid of what would become of me. I cried and I cried until I could not cry anymore, but my sorrow did not ease.

I wiped my tears away with the back of my sleeve. It was dark outside. I sat quietly and listened. The wind promised rain. I winced as I pushed myself up and slipped on my zori. I put on my robe. I went to the door and slowly slid it open. I stepped out into the servant's hallway, then to the garden along the house. The night air was heavy and cool. The wind came in gusts. I crept along the house to the front and then to the gate. I carefully lifted the latch and stepped out into the street.

And then I ran. My body was sore and stiff, but I pushed myself to run away from Mister Euno and his cruel lessons, away from ever being the queen. As I ran through the dark streets of Seoul, past houses, stables, and gardens, I started to hear voices in my head. There were only a few and they spoke in a whisper. I kept running to where the streets angled down to the Han River. My lungs burned and my legs protested. The voices were louder now, but I couldn't make out what they were saying. I shook my head to make them stop, but the farther I ran, the louder they grew. I stopped running and put my hands over my ears. I looked up and there was the black open expanse of the Han River a half mile across. I smelled its dampness and the coolness rising from it. It started to rain, first in big drops here and there, then in loud splashes. Soon, it was raining hard. The rain's splatters clashed with the voices in my head. I was scared and confused. I scrambled to a place away from the street and crawled under bushes. I pulled my knees in tight and put my hands over my ears. Eventually the voices faded away and the rain turned into a gentle patter. The cool rain soothed my skin. I didn't feel the soreness in my body. I crossed my arms over my chest and closed my eyes. Soon I was asleep.

Someone was dripping water on my face. A drop on my cheek, another on my nose. I twitched my nose to flick the water away, but then another drop hit me. I forced open my eyes and thought I was dreaming. It was daylight and the rain had stopped. Gray clouds were giving way to a light-blue sky. I looked up and saw hundreds of sparkling droplets like glass beads on the bush I was under. I was wet and shivering from the cold. I couldn't feel my legs. With effort, I stretched them out, and the pain of six days of torture shot back into me. I groaned and shut my eyes, wishing that the peace of sleep would come again.

The voices in my head were gone, but now I heard movement on the street and boots splashing in mud. The splashes grew louder, and soon the boots were next to me. I opened my eyes and there, looking down at me, was a man. In my fog of weariness and pain, I thought it was my father coming to take me home. But as my eyes adjusted and my mind cleared, I saw that it was my uncle.

I was afraid he was going to scold me for running away. Instead, he reached out a hand and helped me stand up. "Come," he said. "I know a place nearby where we can get you dry." He took off his overcoat and put it around my shoulders. He took my arm and helped me walk up the street. We turned into a house. A short, elderly man with a long white beard greeted us. He bowed low to my uncle.

"Bori cha and rice cakes," my uncle ordered. "And stoke the fire." The man bowed again and went inside the house.

We followed him. The house was that of a merchant, a *chungin* man. It was small, modest and filled from floor to ceiling with books. I had never seen so many books. It was like all the books in the world were there in this one man's house. My uncle helped me onto a cushion. He opened the latticed windows to a view of the city down to the Han River. Sunlight poured in. I recognized the places on the river where I used to watch the cranes with my mother. I could feel heat rising from the home's *ondol* under-floor heating system. Still wrapped in my uncle's coat, I no longer shivered.

My uncle took off his wide-brimmed hat and sat on a cushion next to me. He was my father's older brother and had the same long chin and soft, wide-set eyes. I had never noticed before how much he looked like my father.

The old man brought in bori cha and sweet rice cakes and set them in front of us. He left, bowing again. "I do business with this man," my uncle said. "His name is Chuk-so Pak. He is a book merchant and I am one of his best customers. He can get any book anyone might want. Drink some tea. It will warm you and ease your pain."

He poured my tea, which surprised me. As my elder and as a man, he should not have poured tea for me. But for some reason, it was right that he did. I took the cup from him and drank. Immediately, the strong tea began to soothe my aches and clear the fog in my head.

"Have some *dduk*, too," my uncle said.

I took a rice cake and bit into it. I hadn't had anything sweet since I'd begun my training with Mister Euno, and it was delicious. I took another bite, and then two more and I had eaten the entire cake.

My uncle chuckled. "You are hungry. I can understand why." He looked out the window with his eyes like polished black onyx. "Ja-young, you should know that this morning, I talked with Mister Euno. I told him you ran away because his training is too harsh. No one, not even someone strong like you, can do what he demands. He threatened to quit and report to Lady Min. But I assured him that I, too, had Her Excellency's ear and that she would not approve of his methods for someone who might someday be queen. And so he agreed to my demands. Then I came to find you."

He took a long look around the room at the stacks of books and said, "I brought you here because you like to read. I've seen you in the bamboo grove reading my most challenging books. Even I struggle with some of them. Yet you seem to enjoy them."

"Yes, Uncle, I do. Thank you for letting me read them."

"Those books are meant for men and scholars, and I should not let you read them. I do because I see something in you. You are beautiful like your mother. And though you do not say much, I can tell you have my brother's intelligence. I must say, he was smarter than me, although I never admitted that to him." My uncle grinned.

"And your mother," he continued, "she understood the spirits of the animals and mountains and of the Han River and of the dead. She would say the most peculiar things about the world. I would think about what she said for days, and sometimes I would understand. She could see what others did not—until she started to see what wasn't there at all."

"I miss them," I said.

My uncle nodded. "Yes, I do, too. But when I look at you, I see them both again. That's why I was so pleased when Lady Min said she would recommend you. You have the heart of a queen, Ja-young. I believe you are worthy of the throne."

"I do not want to be the queen," I said. "I believe it would be terrible. I would rather stay with you and read books."

My uncle nodded. "You are wise to see that side of it. Most do not. The crown is glorious to those who see it, but a burden to the one who wears it. If you become queen, your subjects will bow to you and call you 'Your Majesty,' all the while behind your back they will plot against you. Some will love you, some will hate you, and you won't know which ones they are. They will tell you that you can do no wrong, yet in private, they will criticize your every move."

He took a sip of tea and let his words sink in. Then he turned to me. "Ja-young, Korea is entering a challenging time. We must become an independent nation, but we face threats from many directions. It will be very hard to be the queen during this time. So if you don't want to do this, I will talk to Lady Min. But hear me. I believe it is the right path for you. I believe with what you have—your beauty and intelligence, how you are able to see things—it is your duty to be Korea's queen."

My duty. My mother's last words were about using my gifts to fulfill my duty. I had promised her that I would. Now my uncle was saying it, too. Maybe it was true. Maybe it was my duty to be queen. It seemed incredible—me, an orphan girl, the queen of Korea. But if I were to be queen, I had to learn to be strong, as Mister Euno said.

Then, as the warmth from the floor soothed my bones and the strong tea cleared my mind, I realized that I hadn't known my uncle well. I had always been aloof, absorbed in my own world, and he was a busy man. We hadn't spent much time together since I had come to the House of Gamgodang. But now I saw that he truly cared for me. For the first time, I felt a kinship with him. I saw that he was a lot like my father, true and honest, and I did not want to disappoint him.

I looked out toward the river. A lazy fog drifted over the water. Through the fog, I saw the ghost of my mother sitting on the bank and watching a red-crowned crane stalking prey. She looked up and smiled at me, not with the mad face of those last days, but with the smile I remembered from when I was a child. I looked at the stacks of books in the room, and there was the ghost of my father there reading a book. He, too, looked up at me and nodded the way he did when we had finished a chore. Their spirits were like hands pushing me up, giving me strength, urging me to go back to Mister Euno and learn his lessons. They were encouraging me to do my best in an audience with the Taewŏn-gun and King Gojong.

I set my teacup down and turned to my uncle. "Thank you, Uncle, for coming to find me and bringing me here and making me warm." I lifted my chin. "I will go back with you and do my best in my lessons."

He nodded and smiled at me.

"We should go right away," I said. "Today Mister Euno wants to teach me the proper way to bow."

SEVEN

"Five hundred eighty-one." Thump. "Five hundred eighty-two." Thump. Mister Euno counted as I sat on a cushion in the courtyard with my back straight repeating the correct way to lift a teacup to my lips. His top hat sat on the bench next to him, and with every count, he tapped his switch on the top of it like a drum.

"Five hundred eighty-six." Thump. "Five hundred eighty-seven." Thump.

After I'd run away, Mister Euno's training was only slightly less harsh. I still had to hold his poses for hours and repeat his lessons until I was so tired I was practically senseless. And he still hit me with his switch when I did something wrong. But each day, the lessons grew a little easier, and I believed I was learning how to perform as he wanted me to.

Even so, I still wasn't sure I wanted to go through with it. The spirits I had felt in the bookseller's house were only a memory now, and doubt filled my heart. At night when I went to bed sore and exhausted, I cursed the gifts my mother and uncle said I had. I thought about scratching my face or cutting off my hair so that I wouldn't be pretty anymore. But I had promised my uncle that I would do my best, and I didn't want to disappoint him. So each morning I crawled out of bed when I heard Mister Euno get up. I followed him out to the courtyard and tried to learn his lessons.

"Five hundred ninety-two," Mister Euno counted as he thumped his hat. "Five hundred ninety-three."

A horse galloped along the street. When it stopped at our gate and a messenger called out, Mister Euno stopped counting. He told me I could rest. I followed him into the main room. Mr. Yang went out the front door to talk to the messenger. After a few minutes, the messenger galloped back toward the palace, and Mr. Yang came into the house with a rice-paper envelope closed with a red wax seal.

My uncle came out of his study, and my aunt came from in from her garden. Eun-ji came in from the kitchen. "What is it?" my uncle asked.

Mr. Yang pushed his wire-rimmed glasses up his nose. He held out the envelope. "It is a message from His Excellency, the Taewŏn-gun."

My uncle took the envelope and examined it. "Yes. It has His Excellency's seal." He broke the seal and read the message. He looked up and said, "His Excellency orders Ja-young to stand before the king tomorrow morning." My aunt and Eun-ji brought their hands to their mouths. Mr. Yang gave me a look.

"But she isn't ready!" Mister Euno protested, the small man's mustache twitching more than usual. "She still has two more days of training."

"It would not be wise to disobey the Taewŏn-gun's orders," my uncle said. "I will take Ja-young to the palace tomorrow."

"Then we must work all night," Mister Euno declared. "She has much to learn." He grabbed my arm and turned me toward the courtyard.

"No," my uncle said. The word filled the main room like a cannon. Mister Euno stopped and turned back. My uncle flashed his eyes at him. "Your job is done here, Mister Euno. Let her rest now."

"But she is not ready!" Mister Euno said again. "She is not perfect."

"You have said that," my uncle replied, "and I say her training is done."

I took a step forward. "Uncle," I said, "I am willing to work with Mister Euno all night. I want to present myself well."

My uncle nodded. "Yes, I believe you would do that. But no, you are done." I nodded and stepped back.

My uncle turned back to Mister Euno. "Thank you for your service, Mister Euno. Now you may go."

Mister Euno huffed and did not bow as he should have to a higher-ranking man. He went out to the courtyard to gather his waistcoat and hat. Marching through the great room, he pushed his hat over his topknot and went out the door without a word.

My uncle turned to me. He said, "If you are tired, you will not perform well. Mister Euno has given you all you need, though I must say, I do not approve of his methods. You will do well in your audience with the Taewŏn-gun and the king. All you need now is rest."

"Yes, sir." I nodded. Truthfully, though I was willing to, I was thankful I didn't have to work anymore that day. My uncle was right. I was exhausted from nearly two weeks of Mister Euno's cruel lessons. I needed to rest.

"May I borrow one of your books, Uncle?" I asked. "I'm most relaxed when I'm reading."

My uncle grinned and nodded. "Of course. I recommend *Songs of Dragons Flying to Heaven*. It was the first book written in Hangul. You will find it on the upper shelf in my study."

"Thank you, Uncle. I will read that one."

Ten minutes later, I sat on the Chinese bench in the bamboo grove with *Songs of Dragons Flying to Heaven* in my lap. The book was thick and bound with sheepskin. On the cover was stamped the title in Hangul and a small picture of a dragon. It was so peaceful in the garden. The sky was high and blue, and the spring air was comfortably warm. The bamboo they had left to produce new shoots was five feet tall. Days earlier, the plum blossoms had fallen, and petals covered the ground like patches of pink snow. Now the apple blossoms were in bloom, and the air was rich with their perfume. Behind the house, the stable-mate groomed the horses and the gardener pulled weeds around the young cabbage plants. The maids and servants expertly went about their chores. I expected to see my aunt in her rose garden, watering and trimming the new canes. She delighted in growing roses and was proud of the lush blossoms she grew. Sometimes I helped her, and she would show me how to prune the bushes so they would yield the most blossoms. But I didn't see her there this morning.

The warm sun soothed my sore bones and relaxed my aching muscles. Yet relaxed as I was, I sat straight with my shoulders back and down. I held my knees together. It was natural to sit that way now. Perhaps Mister Euno's lessons had changed me after all.

Even so, I wasn't sure if I was ready to meet the Taewŏn-gun, the all-powerful regent, and his son, the king of Korea. I was terrified that I would perform poorly or say something silly. Maybe the young king would think my nose was too small or that I was too skinny to be his wife. Maybe the Taewŏn-gun would think I was dim. Maybe all the work I had done over the past twelve days was for nothing.

I opened *Songs of Dragons Flying to Heaven*. I was surprised that my uncle had recommended a book in Hangul. Scholarly men and yangban like him shunned the written language of Korea, opting instead for books written in Chinese. They said Hangul was for *chungin* and *sangmin*—merchants and commoners. But my father, though he was a scholar like my uncle, encouraged me to learn to read both languages. I knew a few words in Japanese, too. My father had said I was smart with languages.

I turned to a page my uncle had marked by a silk ribbon. I read the poem there.

A tree with deep roots,
Because the wind sways it not,
Blossoms abundantly
And bears fruit.
Water from a deep spring,
Because a drought dries it not,
Becomes a stream
And flows to the sea.

I thought about what the words meant. I turned the pages to the introduction and read that the book was written four hundred years earlier by order of Sejong the Great, Chosoˇn's greatest king. I remembered from history books that King Sejong invented the Hangul written language and tried to move Korea away from Chinese culture toward independence. I remembered my uncle's words from a week earlier about how Korea needed to become an independent nation, and I knew why my uncle recommended this book. *A tree with deep roots . . . Water from a deep spring . . .*

My eyelids grew heavy. I put the ribbon back at the page and closed the book. I put it aside. I lay on the bench and closed my eyes. I tried to picture myself dressed in a queen's robe sitting on a throne. Before the image formed, I was asleep.

Eun-ji woke me in the middle of a nightmare about a tree's roots holding me under a stream. It took a minute for me to realize where I was. The sun had moved to the other side of the bamboo grove, and the late afternoon coolness had set in.

"Yes?" I said, trying to focus on the plump woman before me.

"Your aunt wants you in the house," Eun-ji said, trying to disguise a grin.

I followed Eun-ji into the house, and there, in the main room, my aunt held up a new hanbok. It had a yellow chima with a floral pattern on the hem and a light-blue jeogori closed with a dark-green bow.

My aunt sparkled. "I thought you should have a new hanbok for your audience with the king. We've been making it all the while you were working with Mister Euno. Here, try it on."

I couldn't take my eyes off it. "It's beautiful."

"Come, come!" my aunt said. "We had to rush to get it done when you were called early. Let's see if it fits you. We'll need to make the last adjustments before tomorrow."

I stepped out of my regular clothes, and my aunt held my arm as Eun-ji pulled the chima over my legs and closed it across my chest. My aunt helped me into the jeogori. She and Eun-ji struck a matching pose with their hands on their chins as they examined the fit. "It's close," Eun-ji said. "A tuck here and there and it will be perfect."

Eun-ji got some pins and as my aunt looked on, she pinned the hanbok where it needed adjustments. When they were done, I put on my regular clothes and said, "Thank you, ma'am."

My aunt smiled. "The kitchen staff has prepared a meal for you. Go. Tomorrow is a very important day for the Mins."

I smiled back at her and headed to the kitchen.

The next morning I awoke when the maids got up to prepare the house and the morning meal. I went to the kitchen for tea. The housemaids bowed to me. When I came near, they backed away with their eyes low.

After the morning meal, Eun-ji and my aunt helped me into my new hanbok and prepared my hair. They put it into the three-band braid customary for an unmarried woman and tied it off with the same red daenggi I wore for Lady Min.

My uncle waited for me at the door. My aunt, Eun-ji, and Mr. Yang watched as I walked across the main room to go to the palace with my uncle. When I got to the front door, I turned to them. Eun-ji and Mr. Yang bowed to me, which they had never done before. My aunt smiled and said, "You are beautiful."

I drew a nervous breath, then walked with my uncle through the streets of Seoul for my audience with the Taewŏn-gun and King Gojong.

I had only ever seen Gyeongbok Palace from the pine trees outside palace walls. When we approached the Gwanghwamun Gate, my stomach started to jump. I had always been in awe of the massive gate with its colorful, complicated wooden brackets in the eaves. I never dreamed that someday I would go inside. We went to the entrance where my uncle showed the guard the Taewŏn-gun's letter. The guard let us through into the palace grounds, and when I saw the palace from inside the walls, I thought I might be sick. It was as if I had stepped into a different world. All around were buildings with green-tiled turned-up roofs. The one in the center was the tallest building I had ever seen, with three pagoda roofs. There was a long pavilion with an extravagant two-roof pagoda. Guards holding long lances and wearing red tunics and tall black hats stood at each gate and each doorway. Groundskeepers swept the stone walkways. The persimmon trees were clouds of yellow blossoms, and the cherry trees were clouds of white. I tried to take it all in but it was impossible. Surely I wasn't worthy to rule over such a wondrous place. I felt small and foolish for agreeing to meet the king and the Taewŏn-gun.

I had to push myself to keep walking. My uncle led me through a pavilion gate into the biggest courtyard I'd ever seen. Knee-high rank stones lined the pathway. Towering above the courtyard was the tall building. I had to tilt my head back to see it all. We climbed two sets of stone steps to where Lady Min met us. My uncle and I bowed to her.

She pointed her fan at me. "Why does she wear that hanbok?" she huffed. "It looks pretentious."

My uncle bowed again. "We wanted her to look her best for the king," he said.

Lady Min shook her head. "Pray that the Taewŏn-gun doesn't think she's too fancy. Come with me." We followed her to the building.

When we got inside, it was all I could do to not run back home. The room was almost impossible to take in. It was so big you could have fit my uncle's entire house inside with plenty of room to spare. Holding up the ceiling were a dozen pillars so big two men couldn't reach their arms around them. In the ceiling were thousands of brightly painted support beams and brackets similar to Gwanghwamun Gate. In the center of the room was a red dais, ten steps above the floor. On the dais was a high throne with a gilded top. Behind the throne was the most beautiful tapestry I had ever seen. In great detail, it depicted a lovely scene of trees and mountains, and in the sky, both the sun and moon.

My mouth was open as Lady Min led us toward the center of the room. As we approached the dais, Lady Min struck my arm with her fan. "Close your mouth," she said. "You look like a monkey." I snapped my mouth closed and focused my eyes straight ahead so the majestic room wouldn't overwhelm me. I pushed my shoulders down and back and my buttocks in so that I glided as I walked. I brought my chin level with the ground. Out of the corner of my eye, I saw someone sitting on the throne and someone else in a low chair next to it. I didn't dare look at them.

When we got to the dais, my uncle bowed low. As he bowed, I overlapped my hands at my waist, the left over the right as Mister Euno had taught me. I bowed my head and bent at the waist as I had practiced thousands of times. I bent my knees so they didn't catch inside my chima and knelt just so on the stone floor so that my chima spread out around me. I brought my hands, still with the left over the right, out in front of me and placed them out on the floor. I closed my eyes, bent all the way down, and put my forehead on top of my hands. And there I stayed, waiting for someone to tell me I could stand.

Lady Min spoke first. "This is the girl I told you about. Her name is Min, Ja-young."

"You may wait outside, Chul-jo," a man said to my uncle. His voice was high but strong. "Leave us alone with the girl."

"As you wish, Your Excellency," my uncle said. I stayed on the stone floor as my uncle's footsteps faded away behind me as he left.

"You say she is an orphan?" the Taewŏn-gun said with his high-pitched voice.

"Yes, husband," Lady Min answered. "Chul-jo is her uncle. She has no paternal lineage. She lives in the House of Gamgodang."

"Yes. A Min house," the Taewŏn-gun said. "Have her stand so we can see her."

Lady Min took my arm and helped me stand. I assumed Mister Euno's proper standing posture but kept my eyes low.

The Taewŏn-gun came down from the dais and stood in front of me. All I could see was the hem of his robe, which was white with gold embroidery. My knees started to shake and I was afraid he would notice. I tried to breathe as Mister Euno had taught me, but my breaths came in shallow gulps.

"She is small," he said. "But she has a pleasant face. Why do you recommend her, my wife?"

"Because she is no one," Lady Min said. "She will not challenge your authority."

"But like you, she is a Min."

"That is true. But without a father, she is a Min in name only."

"A Min is never a Min in name only," the man said. He turned to the throne. "Your Majesty. Come see this girl. Tell me what you think."

"I can see her from here," a young man said from atop the dais. "I do not like her."

"Come here, son, as I said," the Taewŏn-gun demanded.

King Gojong came from the dais. He stood next to his father. The trembling in my knees spread to my entire body. My breathing was so difficult I thought I would faint. "She looks better up close," the young king said. "But she is too small."

"Yes," the Taewŏn-gun said. "She is small."

"May I go back now, Father?" the king said. The Taewŏn-gun waved his hand, and King Gojong returned to the dais. The Taewŏn-gun stayed in front of me. "What would you do if we made you queen, girl?" he asked.

Mister Euno had anticipated this question. He had made me memorize the answer and rehearse it hundreds of times. I kept my eyes low as Mister Euno had told me to. I steadied my nerves and said, "Your Excellency, I am nothing more than a humble orphan girl. If His Majesty honors me by making me his queen, my greatest honor would be to serve him and make a son for him."

I could see Lady Min nod. The Taewŏn-gun nodded, too. "We have seen enough," he said and went back up the dais.

Lady Min took my arm and led me out of the room into the sunlight where my uncle waited. She said, "The king has seen Ja-young, and we will let you know what his decision is." She turned and went back into the throne room.

As my uncle and I walked out of Gyeongbok Palace, he asked, "What did the king say?"

"He thought I was too small," I answered.

"Well," my uncle said, "we will have to wait and see."

EIGHT

After my meeting with the Taewŏn-gun and King Gojong, I was convinced the king didn't like me and that his search for a queen would go on. And after seeing the inside of Gyeongbok Palace with its grand buildings, and after how rude King Gojong was, I didn't care. I put the entire affair out of my mind. The twelve days of Mister Euno's lessons had been unnecessary, though I didn't feel it was a waste of time. I had learned how to act in front of royalty and the proper behavior for a yangban woman. And I'd learned something about myself, too. I had survived Mister Euno's abuse and had performed in front of the king precisely as he told me I should.

When I got back to my uncle's house, I settled into my regular routine—reading in the bamboo grove and helping my aunt in her rose garden. At first the household staff continued to treat me with deference, but after a few days, they went back to the way it was before and regarded me as just another household member. But the experience left me unsettled. If I wasn't going to be the queen, then what would become of me? My mother had said I must use my gifts to speak for the spirits of our family, clan, and country. My uncle had said it, too. But I didn't hear the spirits now, and I certainly could not speak for them if I didn't hear them.

Then one morning I awoke and felt something was going to happen. It was like a day in late winter when the snow melts away and you feel spring is coming. It had rained the night before, and the morning was glorious. The sun had chased away the morning mist, birds sang their after-rain songs, the horses lazily chewed their oats, and the chickens strutted and pecked at the ground as chickens do. The household staff moved around the compound as if they were performers in a well-rehearsed play. The spirit of the day spoke to me. It said, "Remember me."

I tried to push the spirit aside and go about my regular routine. I took one of my uncle's books to the bamboo grove where new shoots were almost ready for harvesting again. And then directly above was a chattering screech. I looked into the sky, and there was a flock of red-crowned cranes heading to their breeding grounds in the north. I ran to an open area where the trees didn't block my view. There must have been twenty of the white and black birds with red caps on their heads. They flew straight and strong, and my spirit soared with them. After they flew out of sight, I sat on the Chinese bench and the feeling I had about the day returned and was heavy on me.

A short while later, my uncle came through the front door and walked with purpose down the path to the bamboo grove. He had never before come to me there. He'd always had Mr. Yang or Eun-ji call me to the house if he wanted me. Now, my uncle came to me and sat on the bench. He folded his hands in his lap. He told me the palace had summoned him the day before to meet with the Taewŏn-gun. The regent had said that King Gojong had chosen me to be his wife—the new queen of Korea. There was only one condition—that with me as queen, the Mins would never challenge the House of Yi.

"I agreed to His Excellency's terms," my uncle said. "And you must agree to them, too. If you do, you will be queen and the wedding will be in twenty-one days."

"I didn't think the king liked me," I said.

"The Taewŏn-gun was impressed with how you carried yourself. And he told me King Gojong was especially struck with your beauty. Apparently Mister Euno knew what he was doing after all."

"So I am to be the queen?" I asked.

"You only need to promise to let the Taewŏn-gun run the country."

"I would not challenge His Excellency," I said, shaking my head. "I couldn't possibly."

"Yes, that is what you say now," my uncle said. He turned to me. "Listen carefully, Ja-young. The Taewŏn-gun has many allies and is a ruthless man. Do not take this oath lightly. You will be queen, yes, but the Taewŏn-gun is the regent and he will rule. If you ever choose to challenge him, you must be very careful. He is powerful and cunning."

We sat in silence for some time. I had only been inside the palace walls that one time and it had made me feel small. Now I would be its queen. I tried to picture myself dressed in a queen's robe sitting on the gilded throne in the throne room. I tried to imagine what it would feel like to have everyone bow to me and call me "Majesty." It seemed so strange, as if it were a fairy tale in a book happening to someone else. But it was happening to me. I was about as ready for it as I was to be a fish.

After some time, I asked, "How does one be a queen?"

My uncle turned his onyx eyes to the grove and studied it as if he could read the answer to my question among the bamboo shoots. "Ja-young," he said finally, "you are an intelligent woman and you are strong. I am sure you will quickly learn how to be a queen. And when you do, you will have a choice. You can wear the crown on your head and sit silently on the throne like the stones in the palace walls. Or you can wear the crown on your heart and be like a dragon who rules the forest. If you choose to be a stone, you must make yourself dead. If you choose to be a dragon, you must be alert and quick because many will want to slay you."

My uncle continued. "This afternoon you must make your promise to the Taewŏn-gun. But in time, that promise will be of little consequence. As I've told you before, Korea faces far greater challenges than age-old fights between the clans. The Taewŏn-gun thinks that ignoring them will make them go away. But they will not go away, and I fear for our country and our people. If you choose to be the dragon queen, you must find the truth for Korea and fight for it as a dragon would. It will be the more difficult choice."

"I hope I choose what is right," I said.

He turned to me and looked at me as my father used to do. "Well," he said, "in the end, a queen is first a person. Do as all people must do. Do your best." He gave me a smile and went back to the house.

After my uncle disappeared inside the house, everything looked different. The bamboo shoots seemed sharper and whiter, like an angry dog's fangs. The earthy smell from the stable was as strong as if I were there with the horses. The chicken's clucks sounded like a fox was just outside the coop. The sounds, the smells, the colors overwhelmed me. I turned my back to the house. Then, I didn't know why, but I cried.

That afternoon I bowed low to the Taewŏn-gun and made my promise, and he issued a proclamation that I was to be Korea's new queen.

After the Taewŏn-gun issued his proclamation, it seemed like the entire country went to work. That day, the palace sent dozens of messengers on fast horses to the entire peninsula to announce that I would be the new queen. They dispatched a ship straightaway to Shanghai to fetch silk, spices, and flowers for the ceremony. They sent oxcarts to Taegu for garlic and the vegetables that grew in the temperate climate there. They sent more carts to the Port of Pusan for herring, anchovies, squid, and tuna from the East Sea. Farmers from the countryside brought in cattle and pigs so the palace chefs could select the fattest ones for slaughter. They employed artists and calligraphers to commemorate the affair. They commissioned dancers and musicians to prepare a pageant. Writers wrote poems and plays, and actors rehearsed them. It seemed like a hundred tailors came into the palace to make the robes for the ceremony. They had me stand on a stool for hours as they measured every inch of me and carefully recorded each measurement in a book.

As for me, I spent my days in the queen's quarters, though I was not yet the queen. It was a building not far from the throne room, much less elaborate than that great room, but far more so than any place I had ever lived in. It had two rooms. There was a bedchamber with a bed off the floor the likes of which I had never slept on before. It was big enough for four people and was covered with layers of fine silk sheets and blankets. Separated from the sleeping room by rice-paper walls was a study of sorts. It was grander than the sleeping quarters, and it was there I received my visitors. Sliding latticed walls lined the room. Opposite the entrance was a raised floor two steps above the rest of the room and polished with soybean oil. There was a low mahogany table where I could sit on an embroidered silk cushion with gold tassels when visitors came in. All around were celadon pots, brass statues, and beautiful inked paintings of nature scenes.

It was there where I met the tailors and sat for artists as they painted my portrait. Maids and servants far more skilled than my uncle's attended to my every wish. Most of the time, I was in my study under the direction of Lady Min and Mister Euno, learning the royal court's ways. Mister Euno was not harsh now, but his lessons were not any easier and I had much to learn. He instructed me on the proper way to greet foreign dignitaries, how to preside over the royal court, how to address the king, and how a queen should receive her subjects. I learned about foods that I'd never heard of before, and the proper ways to eat them. I learned how to preside over a tea ceremony. There were lessons on what to say in specific situations, how to answer questions, and what questions I myself should ask. And just like in the courtyard of my uncle's house, I rehearsed each lesson hundreds of times until I could do them just so.

One day, Lady Min came into my quarters with two of her maids and the royal perruquier. The wigmaker was a tall, thin man with a pointed nose and a closely trimmed goatee. He bowed to me—as everyone did now—with only a half bow, since they hadn't yet crowned me queen. I sat in a chair as he measured my head and examined my hair. When he was done, he said, "She is small. Perhaps we should make a lesser headpiece than is customary for a royal wedding."

"No," Lady Min replied, fanning herself. "Make it grander, instead."

"But, Your Excellency, she will not be able to bear it."

"She will," Lady Min said simply.

"As you wish, my lady," the perruquier said, and bowed out of the room with his assistants.

After the wigmaker left, Lady Min dismissed her maids. Being alone with her made me uneasy, and I had to remind myself that I did not have to bow to her or even lower my eyes. She wore a red day-hanbok and the same *jokduri* headpiece of a married court lady as she wore when I saw her at my uncle's house. She sat on a cushion and I sat alongside her.

She lifted her chin but kept her eyes on the room, instead of on me. She fanned herself. "Soon you will be queen," she said. "You will be the first Min to sit on the throne in one hundred years. It is a great opportunity for our clan."

"Opportunity, Your Excellency?" I asked.

"Yes, of course! The House of Yi has ruled since King Taejo, and they have always treated our clan poorly. The Yis take the highest positions in government and impose stiff taxes on us. They are arrogant and pretentious, and their corruption keeps our country poor. But now you will sit on the throne with them."

She stopped fanning herself and looked at me. "Mister Euno tells me you are strong. And your uncle says you are intelligent and that you read scholarly books. My son does not take his studies seriously," she said, fanning herself again. "He prefers to spend his time in the company of his friends playing games. And he is weak. When you become queen, you will have the power to make things right. I will help you."

"But my lady, I promised your husband that I will not challenge his authority."

Lady Min's jaw stiffened and she fanned herself faster. "Yes, my husband," she replied. "You made a promise, but you are young. You have no way of understanding the promise you made. And some promises are not worth keeping."

She stood from her cushion and I stood with her. She closed her fan and tapped my head with it. "Keep this conversation to yourself. Do well in the ceremony. Be a good wife to my son. Make a prince for him. For the time being, do what my husband tells you to do. And though you are the queen, hold your tongue with him. Our time will come soon enough."

Lady Min called her maids. As the maids came in, she pointed her fan at me, "Remember, your father was a Min and it was I who put you on the throne. Your duty is to your father and me, and to your clan." Lady Min lifted her hanbok and left the room as her maids followed close behind.

The next day, three tailors and their assistants fitted my wedding robe on me. It was spectacular. There were five layers of petticoats under the chima and two layers of *sok* jeogori under the jacket. The robe was dark blue. With fine silk thread, they had embroidered one hundred fifty-six pairs of pheasants in nine rows. The robe's red borders along the neckline, front opening, cuffs, and hemline had thirty dragons imprinted in gold leaf. Underneath the robe was a red silk chima with a long train that flowed out, imprinted with a phoenix and clouds. Attached to the chest, back, and shoulders were the queen's medallions with more five-toed dragons. For my feet, there were indigo-blue silk shoes decorated with clouds and the same dragon motif as on the robe. Altogether, the petticoats, jeogori, chima, and robe were so heavy, I could barely stand when they put it on me. I worried that I would not be able to walk or bow or do anything I had to do during the wedding ceremony.

As the tailors made their adjustments, the Taewŏn-gun came in. The tailors and their assistants backed away and bowed low. "Leave me with Ja-young," the Taewŏn-gun said. The others quickly left and I stood in the middle of the room dressed in my regalia.

The Taewŏn-gun was not tall and was slightly round in his face and body. He had a medium-length mustache and goatee. Over his sharp, keen eyes, his eyebrows rode high as if he was always searching for something.

He sat in a chair, and in my heavy clothes, I struggled to sit on a cushion in front of him. Though I would be queen soon, I kept my eyes low to the great man who until a few weeks earlier, I hadn't dreamed I would ever meet.

He cleared his throat. Then he said in his high-pitched voice, "Ja-young, in a few days, you will be queen. You will rule alongside my son. But you are young, only a girl. And you are uneducated. You do not know what our people need or how a government works. You don't know about foreigners with strange ideas who threaten who we are. We must stay away from them. It is all very complicated and something you need not worry about. I have served in the government for a long time. I know what's right for our country and I have plans. I agreed to let you be queen because of your beauty and poise. You and my son will be good figureheads for our country as long as you let me run it."

"Of course, Your Excellency," I said.

"Good. Now, on your wedding day, I will introduce you to two Japanese dignitaries, Minister Yamamoto and Mr. Takata. Smile at them and be deferential. It is important that they think we are weak."

"Yes, Excellency."

"I will also introduce you to two Chinese dignitaries, Mr. Ha and Mr. Zhong. Hold their eyes and do not smile at them. I want to end their authority over us, so it is important they think we are strong."

"Yes, Excellency."

He let some time pass. Then he said, "I suspect that my wife has talked to you." He shook his head. "Like you, Lady Min knows very little about government, and she is blind to what threatens us. She thinks only of the Mins, but I must do what is right for everyone. It would be dangerous to listen to her."

"Yes, Excellency," I said.

He pushed himself out of the chair and looked at me as a schoolteacher looks at a student. He said, "Remember, it is I who let you be the queen. Your duty is to me. You must keep your promise and do as I say."

"Yes, Your Excellency," I said. He nodded and left me alone in the room.

As Lady Min had ordered, my wedding wig was a grand and extravagant thing. The perruquier had made it out of ebony. It swooped and looped over and around my head, intersecting my hair here and there so it would stay put. The wigmaker's assistants pinned it to my hair with two huge binyeos made from gold and silver and encrusted with gems. Among the wig's swirls rested a jeweled crown lined with pearls and topped with blue, green, and red ceramic baubles. The wig and crown were extraordinarily heavy, and I was certain I wouldn't be able to bear it throughout the ceremony's long day. I said so to the wigmaker as his assistants fit it on my head in my study the day before my wedding. "It is what Lady Min ordered," he replied inspecting it with a sniff. "We will have to have slaves hold it for you."

Then King Gojong came in. Everyone except me bowed low. Of course, I should have bowed, too, but if I did, the heavy wig would have made me fall on my face. I held the wig to my head with both hands and stood, facing the king. He looked at my wig and said, "Well, it certainly is big." He waved his hand. "Wigmaker, take it off for now. Then all of you leave me with my future wife." The wigmaker quickly did what the king told him to, and he and his entourage bowed out of the room. It was the first time I was alone with the king. He looked much like his father, only twenty years younger. He had a round face and high eyebrows, and the hair in his goatee and mustache was wispy, like a man who only a year earlier was still a boy. His eyes were not as keen as his father's, and he held his mouth slightly open as if he was vaguely puzzled by everything going on around him. He wore a white robe and a small black hat.

He came toward me, and I thought I should bow low to him as one was supposed to bow to a king. But I hadn't bowed when he came in, and I would be his wife soon and certainly could not be expected to bow all the time. So I didn't bow, but I kept my eyes low.

He sat on a chair and said, "Tomorrow you will be my wife. What do you think of that?"

"I am honored, Your Majesty."

"Huh, yes," he said, twisting his mouth a little. "You thought I didn't like you when I first saw you. Am I right?"

"Majesty, I'm glad you did."

He looked at his fingernails. "I thought you looked like a queen. In the face, anyway. I will need someone who looks the part when I run the country."

"When will that be, Majesty?" I asked.

"Soon. My father says I am too young, but I think he just wants to run the country himself. He says that I'm feebleminded and I will always need him. But he is wrong about me. And when the time comes, I will have him step aside."

"Yes, Your Majesty. When the time comes."

He scoffed at me. "Do you think I couldn't do it now? Do you think I am afraid of my father? I'm not afraid. I am being smart. I am going to wait for just the right time."

"Of course, Majesty," I said. "Waiting for just the right time is smart."

"In the meantime, you will serve me by giving me a son. I will be in a stronger position to take over from my father if I have an heir to the throne. I expect you to bear one for me."

"Yes, Your Majesty."

"Good," he said. He stood to leave. He paused a moment and then ran the back of his hand over my cheek. He said, "Remember, Ja-young, I will be your husband and your king. Your duty is to me. And when the time comes, I will rule Korea with you at my side."

"Of course, Majesty," I said. "It will be my utmost honor to be at your side."

He looked at me a while longer with his mouth still half-opened. Then his mouth turned into a crooked grin, and he left.

The wedding, coronation, and celebration went precisely as planned. Two palace slaves held my wig, and I struggled to bear the ceremonial clothes as King Gojong and I did our part and we were married. In a short coronation service, the Taewŏn-gun pronounced me queen and I received the queen's seal. Then the king and I were paraded in an open palanquin carried by eight eunuchs through the streets of Seoul past thousands of our subjects, who bowed and looked genuinely happy to have a new queen. I was delighted that the people seemed to like me.

But they didn't know me and I was terrified that once they discovered who I really was, they would be disappointed and wouldn't want me to be their queen anymore.

That afternoon when I met the Japanese dignitaries at the reception, I bowed just low enough and diverted my eyes so they would think I was weak. When I met the Chinese, instead of bowing I simply nodded and held their eyes so they would think I was strong.

When my uncle and aunt greeted me, they bowed low and said, "Your Majesty."

I was so excited to see them that I replied, "Uncle, Aunt, how are you? How is everyone at the House of Gamgodang?" They stayed bowed and did not answer. Standing next to me, Lady Min motioned for them to go on and gave me a stern look. After that, I did not say anything more to the people I greeted.

By the end of the day, the dancers had danced, the musicians had sung and played their instruments, the poets had read their poems, and the actors had performed their plays. And I was the new queen of Korea.

NINE

Present day. Seoul, Korea

"What do you think of my story so far, Mr. Simon?" Anna Carlson asks from the throne. As she tells her story, I'm struck by the similarities between her and how I picture Ja-young Min. Like Korea's last queen, Anna is petite and has a beautiful face. And dressed as she is in her red and gold hanbok, sitting high above me, it's as if she herself is a queen.

"It's interesting," I answer, "but I don't see how it has anything to do with my mission. Frankly, you'd better let me go so I can get back to it. There's probably a ruckus with me missing."

"Do you know what Ja-young's uncle was talking about when he said Korea faced challenges?"

"Threats from the Japanese and Chinese?"

"Those and others, too," Anna declares.

I let out a sigh. "Yeah, I get it. The world has always fought over Korea. It's always been caught in the middle, just like now."

"Yes, caught in the middle, just like now," she says. "There's something more you should know about the queen's coronation. There were other dignitaries there—from Russia, England, Spain, and from France. The Americans even sent a diplomat in spite of the fact the Civil War had ended only one year earlier. They were all there for the same reason. They regarded the peninsula as strategic high ground for their own imperialistic plans. And here we are again one hundred fifty years later, still fighting over this country."

I shake my head. "The United States doesn't have imperialistic designs on Korea," I protest.

"Really now, Mr. Simon?" she says. "Why then do we have fifty-five thousand troops stationed in this country even though most Koreans don't want us here? Why do we spend as much on our military as the rest of the world does combined? What do we want?"

I'm offended that this junior aide talks to me as if I'm some sort of rookie. And I want to get back, make a call home to tell them I'm all right. I stand up angrily and immediately there's a hand on my shoulder. The hand makes me hesitate a moment, but I launch in anyway. "Look, Anna, this is nuts. I can read all about your Queen Min when I get back to DC. Or if it's important, I can read about her on the airplane, okay? Right now, I have to get back to the embassy before your little kidnapping becomes an international crisis that makes this entire thing blow up. Did you ever think of that?"

She snaps open her fan and fans herself with quick flicks of her wrist. "Of course I thought of it," she says. "And I can tell you, Mr. Simon, that the right people know exactly what's going on with you. Your disappearance will not cause the situation to 'blow up,' as you say."

"The right people know?" I repeat. "What the hell, Anna?"

"Sit down, Mr. Simon," she orders, pointing her fan at me. "There is much more to my story." The hand on my shoulder pushes me to sit, and I'm so flabbergasted that I don't resist. Anna continues, "It's important to remember what was happening in the world when Ja-young became the new queen. We were talking about it before. Imperialism."

I nod. "Yeah, I know my history. The Age of Imperialism."

"Correct. It started one hundred fifty years before Ja-young was crowned queen," Anna says, "and it didn't end until . . . well . . .

historians say it ended after World War Two. But let's be honest, it hasn't really ended, has it? How many wars have been fought for it, Mr. Simon? How many innocent people have died? *When will it end?*"

"It's different today," I say.

"True, it is a different form. Today the goal is to control markets. It's directed by corporations and driven by greed. But it is still imperialism with a different name."

Anna continues, "Our young queen came to the throne when the old Age of Imperialism was at its apex. The more powerful nations were dividing the entire world. Back then they called Korea the 'Hermit Kingdom.' It was poor and undeveloped. In the mid-nineteenth century, it was a target, exactly as it is today."

"Okay," I say, crossing my arms. "I admit there are parallels. Fine."

"And that's why you must hear Queen Min's story."

I shoot a glance over my shoulder. "Doesn't look like I have much of a choice."

"True." She smiles. "But you are missing a larger point. You think I'm just lecturing you about imperialism. What's more important is that you understand the spirit that the queen searched for. What it means to be Korean. It's the spirit of the two-headed dragon."

Anna stands from the throne. She goes to the faded blue tapestry with the two-headed dragon and runs her hand over the edge of it. "This tapestry is remarkable, isn't it? It's plain compared to most Korean tapestries because it's very old. We believe King Taejo himself had it made. He, of course, was the Chosŏn Dynasty's first king. That would make this . . . let's see . . . well over six hundred years old." She stands back and admires the tapestry. "Did you notice that the two-headed dragon is the same as the one on the comb sent to the president?"

"What do you know about the comb?" I ask.

She laughs softly. With her back to me, she lifts her left hand to show me that she's holding the comb with the two-headed dragon. She must have taken it from my briefcase in the embassy conference room when I wasn't looking.

"You took it!" I say.

"It belongs to me," she replies, still admiring the tapestry. "I'm the one who sent it to the president."

"Ah . . . that's not possible," I say, shaking my head, pleased with myself that I caught her in a lie. "It was sent by someone in North Korea. We know because of the channels it went through to get to the White House."

"Yes, I did send it from the North. I did so to get the president's attention."

"Yeah, right," I say.

She turns to me and puts a finger against her chin. "Let me see if I can remember. On March third, a CIA operative—that is, a spy—stationed in Pyongyang slipped across the border at Sinuiju, North Korea, with this comb in a stainless-steel box. Jae-hee Huh was her name. She was met by another of our operatives in Dandong, at the Great Wall's farthest eastern point. His name was Xiong Wu. On March sixth, Mr. Wu delivered the comb to the US Embassy in Beijing. The instructions were that it was to be given to the US president and that it was important to the crisis here in Korea. The two-word message with it—rather well done by me in my finest calligraphy, I might add—was, 'One Korea.' Correct?"

My God. She has it dead right, all the details. I can't believe it. This junior embassy aide knows what the CIA had said fewer than five people in the entire world know. Suddenly I feel like I'm in some sort of bizarre game of espionage where nothing is real and you can't trust anyone. I wonder if the CIA or Defense or maybe even my own people at State are setting me up. I thought they'd chosen me for this assignment because I speak Korean and I'm somewhat of an expert on the country. Now I think they chose me to be a pawn in some grand deception.

My mouth is agape and all I can do is stare at Anna. I snap my mouth closed and try to regain my composure. "Jesus, Anna," I say. "Who the hell are you?"

She slides the comb inside her robe and returns to the throne. "Just a junior aide at the US Embassy in Seoul," she says.

"Ah . . . I don't think so."

She shrugs. "I suppose, if you really want to know. I was born in Seoul thirty years ago. My birth mother died giving birth to me. Her mother—my birth grandmother—was very poor so she put me up for adoption. I was adopted by a couple in Minnesota who were loving parents. I came back to Korea ten years ago and met my birth grandmother. She helped me discover who I was, especially my Korean heritage. After that, I vowed to learn more about the country where I was born. I learned to speak Korean. I got an international law degree. I landed a job with the State Department. Three years later, I was sent here."

"Yeah," I say. "But that's only part of the story, right?"

She smiles. "I suppose everyone is more than what they appear to be on the surface."

"Maybe you better tell me what's going on."

"That's what I'm doing, Mr. Simon," she says. "Only I'm giving you the big picture. Sit back. Relax. Now where were we in our story?"

I lean back and force myself to calm down. "Ja-young had just become queen," I say.

"Ah yes. Can you imagine? She was queen at just fifteen years old. She became queen as Korea entered its most crucial era. Traditionalists fought progressives. The poor were beginning to rebel against the caste system. There were the century-old fights for power between the clans. And the imperialists from Europe and America were at Korea's doorstep. All that and only fifteen years old. At that age, I was hoping to make the cheerleading squad. You were probably trying to make varsity basketball." She chuckles and waves her hand. "Let's not get ahead of ourselves. Before she could take on those challenges, Ja-young had to become the dragon queen."

TEN

Summer 1866. Seoul, Korea

The day I had agreed to become queen, my uncle told me that a queen was first a woman. That was true. And what was also true was a queen was a wife. And while they had spent the weeks before my coronation teaching me how to act like a queen, no one ever taught me how to make love to a man. I supposed it was something that a mother would do. But before we could have talked about it, my mother had thrown herself into the Han River to silence the spirits that haunted her. And I had never talked with my aunt about it. It would have been awkward, and anyway, before they chose me to be their queen, I'd never thought it was necessary. While I was at the palace during the days and weeks before the wedding, I'd wanted to ask someone about it. But whom could I ask? I certainly could not have expected Lady Min to tell me about how I should make love to her son. And my servants, ladies-in-waiting, and slaves were there to serve me and wouldn't dare give me advice about such a thing even if I had asked them.

Of course, I had thought about it many times. I'd had my monthly bleed for several years now, and I looked at men differently than I had only a few years before. I'd become aware that I was attractive to men, and I was thrilled when I saw how my beauty affected them. I often wondered what it would be like to be in a man's embrace, to kiss him, hold him close, to make love to him. When I lived at the House of Gamgodang, I'd heard Mr. Yang and Eun-ji grunting and making all sorts of muted sounds in the middle of the night in her room next to mine. I'd listen to my uncle's servant girls talk about the men they liked and about their secret trysts in the stables. But for me, it was all a fantasy, something still far off. So on my wedding night, I didn't have any idea what to do.

The same was not true of my new husband, however. He had several courtesans at his beckoning, and he used them regularly. It was rumored that he was quite fond of sex and that sometimes he would stay up all night with his mistresses. So when I went to the king's bedchamber on our wedding night, I had to depend on him to tell me what to do. When I got there, he'd already taken off his ceremonial robe and hanbok and he lay in his undergarments on an enormous bed with a carved ebony headboard. Red, blue, and yellow silk sheets and pillows covered the bed. Oil lamps on iron stands cast soft light throughout the room. Though he was about my age, Gojong was half again as big as I was. His arms and legs were fleshy like a boy's and his stomach was round. When I came in, he grinned at me.

Still dressed in my robe but without my heavy wig, I stood in the middle of the room confused and flustered. I could tell he expected me to do something, and I wanted to please him to start our marriage the right way. But all I could think to do was to keep my head lowered and wait for something to happen.

"Take off your robe and hanbok," he finally ordered. My heart beat hard as I unfastened my robe and slipped out of my jeogori and chima and let them fall to the floor. Though I still wore layers of sok petticoats, I felt small.

My husband laughed at me, making me feel even smaller. "I see with all those layers they tried to make you look bigger than you are," he said. "Take them off and let me see what you look like underneath."

Slowly, I removed the layers of chima and my inner jacket so that all I wore was a chest band and inner pants. As I undressed, Gojong watched me with his silly grin. His boy's mustache and goatee twitched. I began to tremble and my undergarments' light fabric shook with me. Gojong said, "Take off your undergarments. They shake like an aspen leaf in the wind. Remove your chest band, too."

I did as he said and stood in front of him, naked as a newborn baby. I had never been naked in front of a man before, but I didn't try to cover myself. The man before me was my husband, and I wanted to please him.

My trembling was now a full-body shiver. The king threw back his head and laughed at me again. He shook his head. "Your breasts are small like plums before they are ripe. And you are skinny like a twig. I'm afraid I will break you! Come here on the bed with me."

The shaking in my legs made it hard to walk, but I forced myself to go to him. As I sat on the edge of the bed, he reached around me and cupped my breast with his hand, which caused me to jump a little. "Yes," he said, "small like an unripe plum. Ah, well." He pulled to make me lie back.

What we did then wasn't making love, not as I had imagined it would be. It was a clumsy, sloppy, painful affair that hurt and made me bleed. Many times, he tried to penetrate me, but it was too painful, and each time I begged him to stop and pushed him off. After several attempts, he rolled over on his back and said he was disappointed in me. "I'll have to call for a concubine," he said. "Go now."

I choked back tears as I put on my clothes and ran back to my quarters. When I got there, I threw myself on my bed and burst into tears. There in my bedchamber surrounded by luxury, I felt like a complete fraud. I was sure that my husband would never want to have me in his bed again, and that I would be an awful queen. I wanted to run away and never come back to the palace. But I knew it was impossible. I was the queen now and a wife, too. And as my uncle had said, I had to do my best. I prayed that I would soon get another chance to be a proper wife to my husband.

In the weeks and months afterward, the king never mentioned that night, but he didn't call me to his bedchamber, either. I was determined that the next time I was with him I would not push him away or ask him to stop. I wanted to give him a son as he had asked me to. I wanted to be a proper wife and queen. So I waited patiently for him to call for me.

I had to learn how to be a queen to my subjects as well as a wife to my husband. Unlike being a wife, being a queen was not very hard. I was smart and observant and I started to believe that being queen was something I could do. And I had help. As it was before the wedding, I received instruction from Lady Min and Mister Euno about my role as queen and how to act toward dignitaries, the yangban, and my subjects in the lower classes. Mister Euno was deferential now. He addressed me as "Your Majesty," and the short man always bowed low. When I made a mistake, he would say, "Majesty, no one can be expected to get it right every time." I smiled to myself as I remembered how only months earlier, he would beat me with his bamboo switch when I made a mistake. I must admit it pleased me that he worried that someday I would seek revenge for having treated me like that.

As for Lady Min, she addressed me as "Your Majesty," too, but only when others were with us. And she never bowed low. Instead, she simply nodded her head. When we were alone, she treated me like the daughter-in-law that I was. She called me "Ja-young" instead of "Your Majesty" and she never bowed, not even with just her head. She often scolded me for progressing so slowly in my lessons with Mister Euno, even though he said I was learning fast.

After my morning instructions, I was free to roam the palace grounds, which I did nearly every day with several servants a few steps behind and my lady's maid—a prim, middle-aged woman named Han-sook who walked with small steps like a Japanese woman. I loved exploring the palace's many halls, pavilions, courtyards, and gardens. A few months earlier, the Taewŏn-gun had commissioned new buildings and a large pond with an island and a cupola. As I strolled through the palace, laborers in straw hats dug foundations for the new buildings. Workers caked in mud dug the new pond with shovels and buckets. Two-man carts—they allowed no beasts inside the palace walls—hauled the dirt away. All around, gardeners dug holes for trees and plants. The palace was alive with activity, and I couldn't believe this was my new home.

Now that I was the queen, the servants, guards, and workers all paused from their work and bowed when I came near. Everyone addressed me as "Your Majesty," even the Taewŏn-gun. At first, I must say, it was very strange. After all, only a few months earlier, I'd just been a girl who no one paid much attention to, reading books in my uncle's bamboo grove. But now everyone noticed every little thing I did. Eventually I grew to accept it, although I often wished I could be that girl back in the bamboo grove.

Most afternoons, the king and I would go to Sajeongjeon Hall, "Where the king thinks deeply before deciding what is right or wrong," across a courtyard from the king's quarters. There, we would attend meetings on the country's affairs with the Taewŏn-gun and palace ministers. Sajeongjeon was smaller than other buildings and was less ornate. It housed the palace's administrative offices and had several rooms separated by sliding latticed walls. In the main meeting room, the king sat at the head of a long, low table on a throne-like chair with gilded edges. I sat on a low chair well behind the king, facing away from the group because affairs of the state were for men only. The Taewŏn-gun sat on a cushion along one side of the table, and eight or ten ministers sat on the other side. We would all listen as messengers and scholars and dignitaries read letters and made presentations at the table's far side. Then the Taewŏn-gun would discuss what to do about each case with his ministers. King Gojong rarely said anything and looked positively bored at the proceedings. Once he fell asleep, which embarrassed the presenter so much that the poor man begged for mercy for putting the king to sleep and ran out of the room. I never said anything during these meetings, but I listened carefully and studied how my father-in-law worked with his ministers, handled the proceedings, and made his decisions.

For months after our wedding, we received wedding gifts that the royal secretary presented to us at the end of the meetings. People and countries from all over the world sent gifts. When it was time to receive wedding gifts, I would face the group since receiving gifts was not an official affair of the state. The servants brought them in, and the royal secretary read aloud the letters that came with them. There were hundreds of gifts from yangban and government officeholders eager to secure our favor. The Chinese sent a large jade sculpture of monks among mountains, waterfalls, ponds, and trees. They had inscribed the sculpture with a blessing for King Gojong and me. The Japanese sent a six-panel screen with a painted scene of fishing boats on the sea in front of a conical, snowcapped mountain and a red, setting sun. Queen Victoria of England sent an ornate sterling silver tea set, and Napoleon III of France sent a pair of etched leaded-crystal vases that everyone thought looked strange. We had heard about America's struggle to recover from its bloody civil war, so we were surprised when the White House of Andrew Johnson sent a large wooden tobacco box filled with superb American tobacco. The top had tiny inlays depicting a frontiersman dressed in deerskin hunting an American bison. The scene was like nothing anyone had ever seen before.

King Gojong was summarily unimpressed with the gifts except for the tobacco box with the bison scene. On the other hand, the Taewŏn-gun took particular interest in each gift as it was presented. He asked the scholars about the value of each one and what the gift's hidden meanings were. He asked more than a few questions about the jade from China and even more about the screen from Japan. When the Taewŏn-gun finished asking his questions, guards hauled the gifts away to a storage house in the back of the palace grounds.

One day someone delivered a gift of a tapestry. The servants brought it in and unrolled it at the table's far end. Compared to the other wedding gifts the king and I had received, it was nothing special. It was obviously old. The blue background fabric was slightly faded, and the years had frayed its edges. In the center was a two-headed dragon embroidered with what looked like gold thread. The dragon's tongues curled up and its claws reached out.

"What is this thing?" the Taewŏn-gun asked in his high-pitched voice. "Who is it from?"

The royal secretary nodded. "Your Excellency, it was delivered early this morning at the gate. The courier only said that it is a wedding gift for the king and queen. He did not say who it was from, and the letter that came with it does not say, either."

The Taewŏn-gun studied the tapestry as the servants continued to hold it up at the head of the table. "I see," the Taewŏn-gun said. "What does the letter say?"

"That is a puzzle, too, Excellency," the secretary said. "It simply says, 'One Korea.'"

These words caused something to stir inside me. It was as if a spark went off. "One Korea." I stared at the dragon, and I had a strange feeling it was staring back at me.

Suddenly King Gojong came to life. "What kind of gift is this?" he asked. "It's a rag! Send it back."

"That will be difficult, Majesty," the Taewŏn-gun said, still inspecting the tapestry, "since we do not know who sent it."

"Then burn it," the king said, folding his arms and slouching in his chair again.

As I looked at the tapestry, it seemed that the two-headed dragon was begging me to save it. I wanted to argue for keeping the tapestry, but I didn't dare go against the king.

Then the minister in charge of culture, Minister Kim, leaned forward. He was a thin elderly man with a long gray beard and pure-white eyebrows. He always spoke slowly, as if each of his words held great meaning. "Begging your pardons, Your Majesty . . . Your Excellency . . . ," he said, nodding to each. "Would you allow me to take . . . a closer look?"

"You may," the Taewŏn-gun said.

Minister Kim gathered his robe around him and slowly stepped to the tapestry. "Uh-huh," he said as he stroked his beard with long, gnarled fingers. He produced a monocle from inside his robe and used it first to examine the blue fabric, then the gold dragon. "Hmmm," he said. He tucked his monocle back inside his robe and returned to his cushion.

"Excellency," Minister Kim said, "I notice two things about this tapestry that give us a clue."

"Go ahead," the Taewŏn-gun said.

"First . . . there is the fabric. It is Korean silk. I would say with quite some certainty. It is not from China. Nor is it from Japan. No. It is clearly . . . Korean."

"And the other thing?" the Taewŏn-gun asked.

"It is the dragon's toes, Excellency," the minister said. "You will see . . . there are five toes on each foot."

The Taewŏn-gun leaned forward and examined the dragon's feet. "You are correct. That is interesting."

"What does it mean?" King Gojong asked. "Why is that important?"

The minister nodded a slight bow. "Your Majesty, a five-toed dragon is only used for something belonging to . . . the king or queen."

The room went quiet for several seconds while everyone stared at the tapestry. Then King Gojong said, "I do not care. Five toes, three toes, or eight. It's an insult. It is dirty and musty and worn. It is no more than a peasant's rag. Whoever sent it should be beheaded. Don't you agree, Father?"

Minister Kim looked sideways at the Taewŏn-gun, who returned his look. "Minister," the regent said, "have you ever seen anything like this before? A dragon with two heads?"

The thin minister with the white eyebrows shook his head. "No, Excellency," he replied.

"Well," the Taewŏn-gun said, "it is indeed old and worn and not much of a gift."

I didn't know why I did what I did next. I had not said a single word in months of these meetings. No one had ever asked for my opinion, and I truly could not have expressed one if someone did. Anyway, I didn't have to. The Taewŏn-gun had everything under control, and I had promised that I wouldn't challenge him. Until then, it had been prudent to keep quiet. But the spark that I felt when I heard the words "One Korea" smoldered inside me. The dragon still stared at me and its claws reached out.

"Excellency," I said. All the heads snapped around to look at me. Even King Gojong raised his head and stared. I sucked in a breath. "If Your Excellency and Your Majesty do not mind, the tapestry pleases me. I would like to have it."

"But it's old!" Gojong said. "It's not fit to hang inside the palace walls."

I nodded my head. "I see your point, Your Majesty. And of course, you are right as always. But because I have no living ancestors, old things like this tapestry remind me of where I have come from. So if you please, Majesty, I would like to have it. It speaks to me. Think of it as a wedding gift for just me."

The king looked confused for a second and then blew out a laugh. He waved his hand. "Such a foolish thing. All right. If that's what you want. Father?"

The Taewŏn-gun hadn't taken his eyes off me since I'd started talking. "It speaks to you," he said as he stared, "this tapestry with a five-toed dragon?" Finally he nodded. "If you wish, Your Majesty," he said.

"Thank you, Excellency," I replied.

That night servants took the tapestry to my quarters, and I had them hang it on a wall in my study. I sat on a silk cushion and looked at it. It was indeed old and worn, and the king was right, it wasn't fit for a palace. But as I stared at it, the two-headed dragon's spirit seemed to talk to me. I sensed that the words "One Korea" meant something important, though I didn't know what it was. But somewhere deep inside where I could not put my feelings into words, I believed that someday, I would be thankful I had saved the tapestry with the two-headed dragon.

There was a knock on my door. "Enter," I said.

Han-sook, dressed in the yellow and blue hanbok that identified her as the queen's lady's maid, stepped in and bowed low. "Majesty," my lady's maid said, "the king wishes to have you in his bedchamber tonight." Han-sook bowed again and backed out.

As I looked at the two-headed dragon, I smiled. The king had not ordered me to his bed since our wedding night. Now months later I would go there again, and I would be his wife for the first time.

ELEVEN

One of my most important functions as queen was presiding over palace banquets and ceremonies. In my morning instructions, Mister Euno drilled me on the proper ways to act during these occasions. He taught me how to flatter those the Taewŏn-gun wanted on our side and how to snub those he did not. Mister Euno was especially clever about how to deliver the flattery and snubs for the desired effect. A lift of the chin here, a look away there. He had me practice them until I could do them just so. When I got it wrong, the Japanese man used his own precise expressions and words to convey his displeasure with me—diplomatically, of course, since I was the queen. And when I got it right, he complimented me and bowed to show his pleasure. When he did, my chest would fill with pride and he made me feel that I was playing a most important role in the success of my country.

One day many months after my coronation, the Taewŏn-gun asked to meet with the king and me regarding an upcoming visit by some Japanese dignitaries. We met in the king's study, a room Gojong rarely used. At one end was a low rosewood desk perched on a platform so that the king, sitting on embroidered silk cushions, was higher than the people he met with there. Several excellent silk screens depicting nature scenes lined the walls. A rosewood chest held stiff, unopened books that betrayed the king's disregard for his studies.

The king sat at his desk and I sat behind him when the head servant showed the Taewŏn-gun in. The regent lowered himself on a cushion in front of us. He gave us a bow with a nod of his head, but below his high eyebrows, his eyes—a stern father's eyes—were set to remind us both that he was in charge. From the corner of my eye, I could see that the king was uneasy in the presence of his father. He looked down at his desk and turned quiet.

The Taewŏn-gun began. "Your Majesties," he said, "in three days, we will have a meeting here in Gyeongbok with ministers from Japan. They will demand that we open our borders to them for trade. They will make promises and they will make threats. As you know, I want us to align with the Japanese to loosen the grip that China has over us. However, we must stay away from these treaties, and I do not want to give the Japanese too much. It is a delicate situation. We must handle it carefully."

The Taewŏn-gun studied us with needle-sharp eyes. "They have asked that you both attend the meeting so that the proceedings will have a royal endorsement," he said. "But they are clever. What they really want is to see how the new king and queen of Korea will do in such situations, how you will act, what you will say. They are looking for a weakness that they can exploit. You must not give them one."

Gojong continued to look at his desk and didn't respond, so I spoke up. "We understand, Excellency. Tell us what you want us to do."

The Taewŏn-gun said, "When you meet them, you must not show any emotions. Do not look pleased or displeased. In the meeting, you are to say nothing. If they ask you a question, do not respond. I will answer for you. Keep your eyes forward and do not look at them or anyone else. When the meeting is over, do the same as when you met them."

My father-in-law turned his head to the side and fixed his eyes on a scroll hanging on the wall. "There will be a reception afterward," he said. "The Japanese are very cunning. They will try to talk to you, flatter you. Perhaps they will say something provocative to see how you respond. Do not take their bait. Short, simple statements are best. I will not be far away."

He turned back to the king and me. "It is very important that you both do well. Mister Euno will instruct you, Majesty," he said to me. The Taewŏn-gun gave a dark look to his son. "And I will instruct the king."

"Yes, Excellency," I said. Gojong continued to look at his desk.

After the Taewŏn-gun left, the king said, "He treats me like a child, yet I am the king."

"Yes, you are the king, my husband," I said. "But I think for now, we should do what your father says."

"My father," Gojong said. He gave me a look that was both fearful and sad. "Leave me now."

I bowed my head to him and went back to my quarters.

The meeting with the Japanese took place in Sajeongjeon Hall, in the same room where we had our afternoon meetings. Han-sook and my maids had spent all morning dressing me in the hanbok I wore for diplomatic engagements. It was not as elaborate as the one I wore for grand palace ceremonies, but it was impressive nevertheless. The jeogori was deep red with long, full sleeves. There was a brocade chima embroidered with green and blue cranes. Underneath it all, I wore several layers of undergarments to fill me out. On my head, I wore an intricate gold crown. These many layers were dreadfully hot in the late summer, but I was determined not to let my discomfort show.

The king's outfit was more modest than mine. He wore his official robe that he used for state affairs. It was royal red with a long front apron hemmed in gold thread.

Together we must have made a striking pair, although I must say, Gojong looked utterly miserable at having to put on such a show. He twitched and pulled at his robe and fanned himself nervously. He stared at the ground.

When they came in, the Japanese dignitaries were wearing Western-style suits with starched upturned collars, silk ties, and coats with tails and broad lapels. They all had top hats like the one Mister Euno wore. When the secretary introduced the lead Japanese delegate—an older man with a thick gray mustache and long chin—he studied King Gojong for several seconds. Then he set his gaze on me. I held his eyes and looked neither pleased nor displeased. I did the same with others in the Japanese delegation.

As far as I could tell, the meeting went well. The Japanese were not at all subtle. They didn't present their goods for trade and did not talk about how trade would benefit us. Instead, they made demands and threats that the Taewŏn-gun and his ministers respectfully listened to. All the while, I sat behind the king with my back straight, chin high, and my hands in my lap. I sat sideways to the group so I did not make eye contact with anyone. The king, however, slouched in his chair as if he wanted to be somewhere else.

When the head Japanese diplomat asked what Gojong thought of their proposal, the king said, "I'm the king and you don't scare me. I think—"

The Taewŏn-gun cut his son off. "Our distinguished guests come here in peace, Majesty," he said with a glance at the king. "Their proposal intends to strengthen the bond between us." He turned to the Japanese delegation. "We will have to discuss your ideas among ourselves," he said with a diplomatic smile. "While we certainly see the advantages of your proposal, we must be certain we are doing what is best for our country. I am sure you would not mind if we answer you in due time."

Gojong slumped into his chair again. The head Japanese dignitary eyed the king, and the corners of his mouth turned up. He nodded at the Taewŏn-gun and agreed that they would await our answer. And with that, the meeting was over.

Later, we held a reception in a small pavilion next to Sajeongjeon Hall. The Taewŏn-gun chafed at having such a modest place to host foreign dignitaries. He often complained that it made our country—and him—look backward and weak. During the reception, I performed exactly as the Taewŏn-gun and Mister Euno had instructed me to. I answered the Japanese dignitary's questions with short, diplomatic answers. I kept perfect posture throughout—my shoulders down and back, and my chin level. I was the very picture of royalty and grace. The king, however, showed no interest in the festivities. He kicked at the ground and eyed his father when the regent wasn't looking.

In the end, the Japanese dignitaries went back to Japan, and as far as I could tell, the Taewŏn-gun never gave them an answer.

I worked very hard at learning what I must do as queen, and in a less than a year, I had become quite skilled at it. When I performed as the Taewŏn-gun wanted me to—which I always did—he gave me a small smile and a nod to show he was pleased with me. I began to appreciate how important Mister Euno's lessons were, though I felt they were becoming repetitive.

Even so, I wondered if I was fulfilling my destiny as my mother and uncle told me I must. Of course, my performance as queen with foreign dignitaries and clan leaders was valuable to the government, but I certainly was not speaking for Korea or using my gifts to see what others did not. I wasn't terribly concerned about this, however. I enjoyed what I was doing, and I was delighted that everyone approved of me.

Everyone, that is, except for Lady Min. She treated me as if I were an awful queen. When we were alone, she hit me with her fan for little things she thought I'd done wrong, even though I had done exactly as the Taewŏn-gun and Mister Euno had told me to do. She criticized my looks and said I was too small to be queen. She looked down her nose at me and said it was a good thing that she was the Grand Lady Min, the regent's wife and still the most powerful woman in Korea. I never fought back or objected to her insults. I simply did my duty as best as I could.

And much to my surprise, I enjoyed being queen, especially attending the afternoon meetings. In my place behind the king, I took great interest in the proceedings, the debates among the ministers, and how the Taewŏn-gun made his decisions. Though there were times I wanted to speak up or give an opinion, I didn't feel I should because I knew little about the topics they discussed. So as King Gojong slouched and sometimes dozed at the head of the table, I watched and learned how the government worked.

I was amazed at how much there was to do. There were requests from the public—mostly yangban—for changes in how the country was run. The Taewŏn-gun had levied a new household tax on the upper classes—what he called "voluntary offerings"—to pay for projects like a new grand pavilion for Gyeongbok Palace. The yangban protested and recommended scaling back on the projects or suggested other ways of raising revenue. I listened carefully to the presentations and debates among the ministers and tried to understand why the Taewŏn-gun rejected the proposals.

There were presentations from emissaries of countries other than Japan as well. These were usually requests to open trade with them. They brought strange and wonderful goods—ornate porcelain and gold clocks from France, bolts of plaid wool fabric from England, pungent spices from Spain, intricate wood carvings from America. The emissaries promised great prosperity for us if we would sign their treaties and open our borders to them. After each country's presentation, the palace secretary would show the dignitaries out of the hall, the ministers would debate, and the Taewŏn-gun would make his decisions. No matter how persuasive the presentation was, no matter how forcefully the ministers argued, the Taewŏn-gun always decided against the treaties. His ministers—especially Minister Kim—warned that there was a budding fascination among Koreans with the strange Western nations of Europe and America, and that the pressure from these countries would only grow. But the Taewŏn-gun argued that the West's eccentric customs and ideas were dangerous for Korea, and he always held firm.

At night, if he called me, I would go to King Gojong's bedchamber. I had become much more comfortable with sex, although there was no passion in it. Our relationship was based on only one thing—that I was the vessel that would bear him a son. We never talked about life in the palace, or gossiped about the royal court or the palace visitors. We certainly didn't discuss politics or the decisions his father made in the afternoon meetings. The king was always aware of my monthly cycle, and when it was my time of month, he would ask if I was with child. When I told him I was having my monthly bleed, he would scold me for not giving him a son. He told me I was a worthless wife and a horrible queen. He threatened to take on a second wife and have me banished from the palace. He sent me away and didn't call for me for weeks.

TWELVE

One particularly warm evening a year after I had become queen, I sat alone in my study. I had prepared myself to be with the king, but he had not called for me. I worried that he was with one of his concubines, or was drinking with his friends. I could tell Han-sook felt sorry for me. My prim, middle-aged lady's maid offered to have my attendants pour a bath with rose petals and lilac perfume, but I declined. I thought about going for a walk through the palace, but I had grown tired of the same scene every day. Earlier, I had asked Lady Min if I could walk outside the palace walls. She said the Taewŏn-gun wouldn't allow it and that I could only leave the palace grounds when I went with King Gojong for a Yi clan picnic on the Han River, or a hike in the pine forests behind the palace near Mount Bukhansan, which we rarely did. So I sat on a silk cushion in my quarters and sulked.

Then Han-sook was at my door. "Minister Kim is outside, Majesty," she said. "He wishes to speak with you. He said it is important."

I was surprised that the minister was calling. I'd never had anyone from the government visit me in my quarters. They had only talked to me at Sajeongjeon Hall, and only then about an upcoming ceremony or feast I was to preside over. I couldn't imagine why Minister Kim had come to talk to me. "Let him in," I said.

Han-sook stepped aside and the thin elderly man with the long gray beard and snow-white eyebrows came through the door. He was dressed in the simple white robe of a scholar. He bowed low and said, "Your Majesty."

"Minister Kim," I said, "what is on your mind that you want to see me at this time of day?"

"Majesty, it is . . . the tapestry," he said in his halting style. "I asked the Taewŏn-gun if I could study it further. If it would not be too much trouble . . . I would like to see it now."

"You may," I said. "It is there, behind my desk."

Han-sook stood back from us as a lady's maid should. Without moving toward the tapestry, Minister Kim looked sideways at her and then lowered his eyes. "Perhaps, Majesty, you could show it to me . . . alone?"

I immediately understood. I turned to Han-sook, who gave me a worried look. "Leave us," I said to her.

"But Majesty," she began, "I—"

"Leave us now," I said. My lady's maid hesitated a moment, then bowed out of the door with her small, Japanese-style steps.

I was now alone with Minister Kim. "Do you really want to look at the tapestry?" I asked.

"Yes, Majesty," he said. "I do."

"But you also have something to say to me. That is why you had me dismiss my lady's maid."

Minister Kim lowered his head. "Yes, Majesty. Please forgive the nature of my visit to your quarters . . . at this hour. I told the Taewŏn-gun that I only wanted to see the tapestry. But there are things you must know . . . and this is the only way I could think of to tell you about them."

"I see," I said. "Come, look at the tapestry. Then tell me what you have to say." I pointed at the tapestry hanging on the wall. Minister Kim took his monocle from inside his robe and a candle from the wall. He went to the tapestry and studied it closely. He ran his long, gnarled fingers over the gold, two-headed dragon with its claws and curled tongues. He examined the border. He stepped back, took off his monocle, and looked at the entire tapestry. He stroked his beard. "Yes," he said. "It is as I thought."

"What do you see?" I asked.

"Well, Majesty," he said, "when I first saw it . . . I suspected it was an important artifact. I was relieved when you said you wanted to keep it . . . and that they did not burn it. I took it upon myself to find out who made it. I also took it upon myself to learn what the message 'One Korea' meant. I read books and made inquiries . . . all secretly. I did not want the Taewŏn-gun to become . . . suspicious."

"And what did you learn, Minister?"

"Majesty, notice how the dragon's heads face in opposite directions but come together in one body. And because the dragon has five toes . . . well, I believe King Taejo himself commissioned it. The tapestry and the words, 'One Korea' are a message from him. It is a message that we must strive to be one nation. And I believe that those who wish Korea to be independent and free have passed along this tapestry and message . . . for hundreds of years."

A message from King Taejo, Chosŏn's first king. Was it possible? I looked at the tapestry. It certainly looked five hundred years old. And the dragon had always stared at me as if it were trying to say something.

I turned to Minister Kim. "Minister," I said, "why haven't you told this to the Taewŏn-gun? Why don't you want him to know? And why are you telling me?"

Minister Kim said, "Because, Majesty, Korea needs a new leader. There are many who fight over us. The Chinese wish to keep us their protectorate. The Japanese wish to take us for themselves. The yangban fight to retain their position in society. The clans battle each other for power. You are the one who will bring us together as one nation. You are the hope . . . for One Korea."

"Me?" I said. "How do you know, Minister?"

"Majesty," the old man said, "I am a man of science and reason. While I believe in the spirit in all things . . . I am not inclined to believe in magic. But according to the books, each time the tapestry appears . . . a great leader rises. It is not a coincidence that the tapestry found its way to them. And Majesty . . . it is not a coincidence that the tapestry has found its way to you."

The old man looked directly at me for the first time. There was earnestness in his face as he opened his mouth to say more. I held my breath. Suddenly there was a commotion in the reception room. Minister Kim stiffened and whispered, "Do not reveal this to anyone. There are agents from all sides within the palace. Trust no one. The walls . . . have ears."

Then Lady Min rushed into the study followed closely by Han-sook. "Majesty," Lady Min said without even a nod, "your lady's maid tells me you have a visitor. I thought I could be of assistance." She turned to the minister. "Minister," she said, "you have come to look at the tapestry?"

Minister Kim lowered his head. "Yes, Excellency. I wanted to see if it was genuine. I'm sorry to say that, upon closer inspection . . . it is a fake. I'll make my report to the Taewŏn-gun tomorrow."

"I see," Lady Min said. She produced her fan from inside her yellow robe and fanned herself. "Well now that you have seen the tapestry and made your assessment, you may go."

As Minister Kim went to the door, I forced myself to take a step forward. I had been the queen for over a year, and it was still difficult for me to give orders. But Minister Kim's claim that I was the one chosen to be a leader stirred something inside me. "Wait, Minister," I said. "Tell the Taewŏn-gun that though the tapestry is fake, I wish to keep it."

"Yes, Majesty," he said.

"And now, Minister," I said, "you may go."

After Minister Kim left the study, I turned to Lady Min, who stood in the middle of my study fanning herself. I was angry with her for interrupting Minister Kim before he could tell me more about the tapestry and why it had come to me. I thought of how she controlled where I went, what I did, and whom I talked to. I thought of how poorly she treated me when we were alone. I lifted my chin and said, "Lady Min, I would thank you not to interrupt me when I am meeting with someone in my quarters. Also, let *me* dismiss my visitors."

Han-sook cowered behind Lady Min, who stopped fanning herself and looked at me with her mouth half-opened. It was the first time I had ever talked to her that way. I thought she might slap me or report me to the Taewŏn-gun.

But before Lady Min could say anything, I said, "And now, Your Excellency, I would like to be alone."

Lady Min's mouth dropped farther. She closed her fan and cocked her arm to hit me with it. Before she could, I wrapped my hand around her fan and stared at her. She glared back, but after a few seconds, she took her fan away and slipped it inside her robe. Then, without addressing me as she should have, she lifted her hanbok and left the room with Han-sook scurrying close behind.

That night as I sat in my bedchamber, I thought about what Minister Kim had told me. "You are the hope for One Korea," he said. I didn't understand what he meant. After all, I was already the queen, so what more could I be? He also said Korea was in danger from invaders. It didn't seem to me we were in danger of anything. Sure, the Japanese wanted to open trade with us and made threats, as the Japanese do. Other nations wanted trade with us, too. But China was the true power in Asia, and they would certainly come to our aid if Japan or anyone else followed through on their threats.

I remembered that my uncle had told me that someday, I would have to choose between being a stone queen or a dragon queen. I went to my study and stared at the tapestry and the two-headed dragon. I remembered the promise I made to my mother that I would speak for the spirits. It seemed that the two-headed dragon spirit was trying to talk to me. Its eyes looked straight at me, and I thought I saw its long tongues move. I turned my ear to the dragon, but I didn't hear anything. I wondered if it was true what my mother and uncle had said, that I saw things that others did not.

I went to bed, but Minister Kim's words haunted me and I could not sleep. If Korea needed saving and I was the one who had to do it, I needed to do more than preside over ceremonies and feasts. Perhaps I should start asking questions and give my opinions in the afternoon meetings. But I didn't know enough about government or the outside world to give a learned opinion. I was afraid I would say something that would show my ignorance or that I would ask a foolish question. Though I had enjoyed reading since the time I was with my parents, I was still uneducated. I decided I had to take charge of my education instead of letting Lady Min and Mister Euno drill me in the rituals of my office. I had to learn about the world beyond the palace.

Books. I remembered my father's and uncle's books. The teachings of Confucius and Buddha, the reflections of great scholars on the lessons of life, the poems, the parables. Of course, there was a palace library and since I was the queen, I could go there at any time. But scholars were men, not women. And as queen, I was expected to be a living example of Korean traditions. Hence, I never once visited the library.

Lying in bed with these thoughts spinning in my mind, I realized how much I missed reading. I tried to remember the poem my uncle recommended from *Songs of Dragons Flying to Heaven*, but I could not. I tried to remember my uncle's other books. Then I remembered *The Analects of Confucius* and the saying, *"They must often change, who would be constant in wisdom."*

I had read this passage many times. They were only words before, but now I understood them as clearly as if I had written them in my own diary. I was now sixteen years old and coming into my own. I had to change or I would spend the rest of my life as a stone queen and I would never be able to speak for the spirits of Korea. Whatever my challenge would be, I would need the wisdom of the great scholars and prophets. Though the Taewŏn-gun and my husband would disapprove, I had to teach myself what I needed to know. And then I would decide if I wanted to become a dragon queen.

The next morning Lady Min and Mister Euno came to my quarters at their usual time. I could tell by the way she held her mouth that Lady Min was angry about my behavior from the previous night. We went into my study, and Lady Min took a seat in a Chinese chair and crossed her arms. Dressed in his Western-style suit as he always was, Mister Euno announced that we were going to work on the finer points of hosting a tea ceremony. It was something we'd rehearsed dozens of times already, and I was convinced there was nothing more I needed to know. Mister Euno ordered Han-sook to have my attendants fetch a tea set and brew some tea. As my lady's maid headed for the door, Confucius's words, "They must often change . . . ," ran through my head. I gathered strength and raised my chin. Before Han-sook reached the door, I said, "Wait, maid."

Han-sook stopped and looked at Lady Min. "Look at *me*, maid, not Lady Min," I ordered. My maid faced me and lowered her eyes. "Do not fetch tea. Instead, have the palace manager bring a writing table for my study and a *bat* chest for books. Be sure they are fit for a queen. And bring pens and paper, candles, and a reading glass, too." Han-sook raised her eyes slightly as if she didn't know what to do. "Go now," I commanded. "I want everything this morning."

At my tone, Han-sook did not hesitate, and said, "Yes, Your Majesty," and quickly stepped out of the room.

I turned to Mister Euno. "Mister Euno, your services are not needed here today. When I want you, I will send for you. Leave me now with Lady Min."

The short man's expression did not change as he bowed respectfully and said, "As you wish, Majesty." He put his hat over his topknot and walked out of the room.

"What are you doing?" Lady Min insisted after Mister Euno had left. She sat in the Chinese chair with her arms crossed. Now that we were alone, she talked to me like a mother-in-law again. "You need these lessons." She pointed her fan at me. "Do not challenge me."

Her Excellency—Grand Lady Min, wife of the Taewŏn-gun, mother of the king—was my mother-in-law and an important leader of the Min clan. Since they had crowned her son king three years earlier, she had ruled over the palace as if she herself were the queen. She was the most powerful woman in Korea—at least until they put the crown on my head and had bowed to me at my coronation. Even Lady Min had bowed. And if I were to be queen, I would have to be her queen as well.

"Your Excellency," I said. "Of course, you are right. And I would not challenge you. But before I was crowned queen, you told me I could change the government and make things right for the Mins. That is something I want to do. You said our opportunity would come someday. I need to be ready when that time comes. I do not believe I can do that by just learning how to host a tea ceremony."

Lady Min stared down her nose at me. "Hmmm," she said. She rose from the chair and slowly paced across the room, fanning herself as she did. "Do you think you are ready for more?"

"Yes, Excellency." I went to her side as if we were partners in a grand conspiracy. "Naturally, you know what is best," I said, "but I was thinking . . . the Taewŏn-gun and the Yis have an advantage. They have knowledge that you and I do not have. We need books and lessons so we have their knowledge when our opportunity comes."

"I see what you mean," Lady Min said with a slight nod.

"But only if you think it is the right thing to do, Excellency," I said humbly. "If so, then I am willing to do the work."

Lady Min stopped fanning herself and brought a finger to her chin. "It couldn't hurt. We will have to be careful, however. The Taewŏn-gun will not look favorably on a woman taking up scholarly matters, especially you. But if we put it to him in a way he thinks will help him, he might agree. I will see what I can do."

"Thank you, Excellency," I said with a respectful nod. "And regarding last night, please forgive my rudeness. I was only thinking that if we are to be successful, you and I, I must act like a queen. For our clan, Excellency. For the Mins."

"Yes," she huffed. Then she tucked her fan inside her robe and her face slid into a sly grin. "Very well," she said. "For the Mins."

After Lady Min left, I sat at my desk and stared at the tapestry with the two-headed dragon. I thought about what I was doing. I had taken a step toward being a dragon queen. I tried to see my future, sitting on the red throne commanding armies and making important decisions.

I asked the dragon, "Am I doing the right thing?" He stared back at me and did not answer.

THIRTEEN

Two years later

By the time I'd settled into my role as queen, Korea was undergoing great change. The Taewŏn-gun had sacked hundreds of corrupt government officials and replaced them with mostly Yi clan members who were only slightly more honest. With Lady Min applying her influence, some new officials were from the Min clan—more than the Taewŏn-gun had wanted. Though there was bickering between the Yi and Min officials, the government ran more smoothly than it had before.

The regent had also raised taxes again. There were land taxes, fallow-field taxes, cloth taxes, taxes on having a baby, and even a death tax. The rival clans—the Kim, the Pak, Ch'oe, and the Min—constantly complained that the taxes were ruining them. The Taewŏn-gun was unmoved. He used the new funds to restore civilian authority over the military and to expand it, adding hundreds of new troops, acquiring new weapons, and building two new warships. He formed an alliance with the Japanese to counter China's authority. He convinced the scholars and yangban that his isolationist policy was right for Korea. In short, through guile and intelligence, and by the force of his personality, the

Taewŏn-gun had consolidated control over the country for himself and the House of Yi.

But none of his projects was as grand and conspicuous—or as costly—as the rebuilding of Gyeongbok Palace. There had been a flurry of construction since I'd arrived. The Taewŏn-gun wanted the palace to be a grand symbol of sovereign Korean power for the entire world to see—especially the empire of China. And so it was. Thousands of workers built dozens of new halls and pavilions with broad upturned roofs. There were lovely new courtyards, gardens, and lakes. They built vast new quarters for King Gojong and named it Gangnyeongjeon, meaning "Health to the king." It had several buildings, pavilions, courtyards, and even a private library—which, for the king, seemed to be a waste. Gargoyles and statues surrounded the quarters to keep evil spirits away. There were expansive new quarters for the Taewŏn-gun and Lady Min. They'd finished digging the pond in the back of the palace grounds, filled it with water, and put in hundreds of red and white koi fish imported from Japan. They built an island with a lovely hexagonal pavilion that they named Hyangwonjeong. And the Taewŏn-gun finally had his grand banquet hall—a two-story structure named Gyeonghoeru Hall. It was surrounded by a square lake on three sides.

They built a new queen's residence for me, too, and named it Gyotaejeon. Like the king's residence, it wasn't just one building but a group of buildings for me and my servants and staff. There was a large main building that housed my bedchamber with a high bed, and a sitting room with a Chinese couch and watercolor scrolls on the walls. There were servants' quarters and a private courtyard planted with mature persimmon trees. They built a study for me, and I had them move in the writing table and bat chest I had requested the day I dismissed Mister Euno. It was a proper queen's table made from cherrywood and ornate brass hardware. The matching bat chest had ten drawers where I kept paper, brushes, inks, and wax for my seal. I had my servants hang the tapestry with the two-headed dragon on the wall behind my writing table.

It was in my study that I took on my education under the unblinking eyes of the two-headed dragon. Lady Min had convinced the Taewŏn-gun that I should learn the classics to most effectively serve him and the king. He had agreed to let me study rudimentary books, which I quickly learned. I pressed Lady Min to bring me more—the advanced books that only scholars read, the ones the Taewŏn-gun didn't want me to read. When she was able to get them to me, I devoured them. Though they were thick, dense books that few were supposed to understand, they were easy for me. I read each one from cover to cover three or four times. I carefully thought through the concepts and theories on Confucianism, Buddhism, Western philosophy, and logic. I wanted to discuss them with others, but I didn't dare. I wanted to ask for more, but I had to be careful not to raise questions.

One day, the palace assigned me a new guard, who replaced the one who had been with me since I had arrived at the palace. I was surprised at this because the guards I had seemed to me to be perfectly fine. The new guard's name was Kyung-jik Kim. He was tall and handsome and had a strong square jaw. I asked my sergeant of the guard why they had assigned Kyung-jik to my staff. He replied that the palace did it as a favor to Minister Kim. "You see, Majesty," the sergeant said, "Kyung-jik is the minister's nephew."

I remembered when Minister Kim had visited me in my quarters two years earlier and warned me not to trust anyone. *The walls have ears,* he had said. Perhaps the guard that Kyung-jik replaced was one of the ears in the walls. Perhaps Minister Kim had assigned Kyung-jik to me because he was someone I could trust.

That is, if I could trust the minister. I had tried to forget about his late-night visit to examine the tapestry with the two-headed dragon. I had not heard from him since that day and had decided to dismiss his musings about the tapestry—and me—as those of an old man's overactive imagination. But I had no one else to trust. And more than once when I was exhausted from my studies and my eyes grew heavy, I thought I heard the two-headed dragon trying to speak to me. I would open my eyes and look at the tapestry. I sensed that something important was at hand and that somehow, I would play a critical role. And if I did, I would need help. I decided that I should trust Minister Kim and his nephew, the handsome, square-jawed guard Kyung-jik.

Eventually I tired of reading the classics, and one day on a pleasant walk in the pine forest near Mount Bukhansan, I told Lady Min I wanted to learn about Japan. She was surprised and asked why. As we strolled and took in the fresh pine air under the gray granite mountain, I replied, "The Taewŏn-gun and the Yis are using the Japanese to move away from China. We, the Mins, need to know about the Land of the Rising Sun for when our opportunity comes."

Lady Min glanced at our guards to make sure they were out of earshot. Then she whispered, "Yes. That is the right thing to do. We will have to be careful. My husband will not look favorably on you knowing too much about Japan. He has questioned me on how I am helping you, but I have revealed nothing. I will talk with Mister Euno in private and have him visit you straight away." We continued to stroll through the pines and said nothing more about it.

A short while after we got back to the palace, Mister Euno came to my quarters alone. When he arrived at the door of my new study, he took off his hat and bowed, exposing his topknot. I let him stay bowed for a while. By now I had become comfortable with everyone bowing to me and was learning how to use my position to my advantage. Finally I said, "You may sit here, by my table." He sat on a cushion in front of me.

I had only seen Mister Euno occasionally since that day I had sent him away. When necessary, I willingly submitted to his training to handle a delicate diplomatic situation. Though I depended on him, I never trusted him. I remembered how he looked and dressed like the Japanese diplomats who pressed us to open trade with them. I remembered how he beat me with his switch before I was queen. And there was a mysterious side to Mister Euno, too. He was secretive and clever. He always listened to everyone and everything, yet he never gave his own opinion or said anything unless someone asked him. Then he would choose his words carefully, never revealing too much. Sometimes on an early morning stroll, I would see him in a courtyard, dressed in a white *keikogi* robe with a long black belt, practicing the movements and techniques of the Japanese samurai. I was surprised at the small man's grace and speed. I wondered why a diplomat like him felt it necessary to practice the military arts.

Sitting in front of me now, Mister Euno asked how he could be of service. To be higher than him, I sat at my writing table on several cushions with gold tassels. I said, "As you know, I have been studying the classics so that I can be most helpful to the government as queen. I must say, the books are difficult and I don't understand them."

"You are too modest, Majesty," Mister Euno said. "But do not be concerned. They are teachings only a few truly understand."

I scoffed to myself at this. I did not see what was so difficult about the concepts that "only a few" could understand. They were easy for me. But I didn't want Mister Euno to know, so I said, "Yes. We should leave the understanding to scholars instead of a silly young woman like me. But it is my duty, so I do my best with them as I should."

"It is good that you do, Majesty."

"Mister Euno, I was thinking," I said. "These books are all in Chinese. It seems that everything is from China. But surely, your people, the Japanese, have scholarly books as well. Shouldn't I study them, too?"

Though he was always careful not to express an emotion, I saw a sparkle in his eyes and his long mustache lift a little. "Majesty," he said, "you are very wise. It is true; there is much you can learn from Japan. I, myself, am a Kokugaku scholar."

"Kokugaku scholar?" I exclaimed. "That sounds impressive. Tell me, what is a Kokugaku scholar?"

"We believe in the Japanese way, Majesty," he said, lifting his chin. "We seek to—how shall I say?—distance ourselves from China. We study the Japanese classics instead."

"The Japanese way," I repeated. "That is interesting. Why have I not heard of this before?"

"It is new, Majesty, and perhaps a little controversial." There was a slight hardening in Mister Euno's jaw. "But I believe it is the true way for Japan."

I stood and pretended to study one of the fancy watercolor scrolls that they had hung in my new quarters. "Your Kokugaku teachings sound like they are too difficult for me, but I want to try to learn them anyway. I assume I will need to learn more Japanese, too. You will help me. In the mornings, as we used to do."

"Yes, Majesty," Mister Euno said from his cushion.

I turned to him. "Japan and Korea are neighbors. We should be closer allies. I believe this is a good course of action for me. Do you agree?"

"I do, Majesty," Mister Euno replied.

I sat at my desk again. "Good. We will begin tomorrow morning. That is all."

Mister Euno bowed, put his top hat over his topknot and left my study.

The next morning, I awoke earlier than usual. It was cold outside, and a strong wind blew from the north. My servants had closed the walls tight against the wind and had stoked the flame in the firebox outside to warm my quarters through the ondol heating ducts under the floor. I sat at my desk waiting for Mister Euno. I was excited to learn something new instead of reading the same books I had studied for the past few years. I was especially keen on learning about Japan, our neighbor less than one hundred miles across the Korea Strait. The Japanese had always fascinated me, but like most Koreans, I distrusted them. They had invaded our country many times during our history, burned our homes, and looted our land. Although the Taewŏn-gun had improved relations with Japan, they were becoming more aggressive to their neighbors in Asia. It was rumored the young Emperor Meiji was modernizing the military.

Mister Euno did not come at his usual time, which concerned me. In the time I knew him, he had never once been late. After I had waited for a while, Han-sook came in. She bowed and said, "There is a messenger here from the Taewŏn-gun."

"Let him in," I said.

The messenger came in. "Majesty," he said from a bow, "the Taewŏn-gun wishes to see you in his quarters."

"Now?" I asked.

"His Excellency says as soon as it is convenient for you. I have been ordered to escort you."

"What does His Excellency want?" I asked.

"I was not told, Majesty."

I waved a hand at him. "No matter. I cannot possibly see him this morning. I have an appointment."

"Majesty," the messenger said, "if it is Mister Euno you expect, I was told to tell you he will not come."

"He isn't coming?" I said. "Hmmm. Well, I suppose then I shall see the Taewŏn-gun."

Han-sook helped me put on an outer robe, and I followed the messenger across the main courtyard to the Taewŏn-gun's quarters. The regent's residence was smaller than mine and simpler, too, which somehow made it more impressive. The messenger took me to the

Taewŏn-gun's personal study and a guard showed me in. My father-in-law sat on the floor doing calligraphy. Spread before him on a low table were ink bottles and pots with brushes sticking out. A large sheet of paper rested on the desk in front of him. My father-in-law had a reputation as an expert calligrapher. He spent hours on it each day, and his finest pieces were on display throughout the palace.

He didn't look up from his work when I came in. He said in his high voice, "Majesty, thank you for coming to see me."

I was surprised that he didn't stand when I came in. I wasn't sure what the protocol was in this situation—how we should address each other or who should bow and show deference. I decided I should keep our encounter balanced, and so I stayed standing where I was. "*Ahbonim*, father-in-law, your messenger said you wanted to talk to me about something important?"

The Taewŏn-gun dipped the tip of his brush into an ink bottle and held it steadily over the paper. "Yes," he said. "It is about your course of study." He carefully touched the tip of the brush on the paper and made a slow, deliberate stroke. He cocked his head and examined the line he had just made. He said, "I hear you want to learn about Japan. Why?" He continued to hold his brush above the paper and inspect his work as he waited for my answer.

"Ahbonim, Japan is our neighbor. I think it is important for me to know them, don't you?"

The Taewŏn-gun dipped his brush into the ink bottle again. "No, I do not." He held his brush over the paper again and kept his eyes on it. "I have also learned that Lady Min provides you with books that I have not approved. I think she is using you to advance her own agenda."

"I only wish to be helpful to you and the king. I thought that—"

"You are already doing a fine job of being helpful. You have learned to be a gracious hostess. Foreign dignitaries and clan leaders compliment me on your skills. That is valuable to the king and me. You need not do more." He made another line on the paper with his brush.

"But, Ahbonim, I want to."

The Taewŏn-gun set his brush down and looked at me with sharp eyes framed by his high eyebrows. "You haven't forgotten your promise, have you?"

I took a step farther into the room and shook my head. "No, Ahbonim. I just—"

"Good," he said. "Since you intend to keep your promise, you do not need the lessons you requested from Mister Euno. Furthermore, I will take charge of your education from now on, not Lady Min. And I will provide you with books more . . . suitable for a young queen. In the meantime, you should perfect your skills as a hostess."

"Someday I will have to help the king run the country. Then, I will need to be much more than a hostess."

"That day is a long time away," my father-in-law replied. "You do not need to take up studying Japan or anything more until then. I am in charge now." He gave me a polite smile. I met his eyes and held them. It was the first time I dared to look at him that way. His smile slowly dropped. After some time, I looked away. I wanted to argue with him, make a case for my education. But he was the Taewŏn-gun, Korea's mighty regent, and I was afraid to confront him.

"That is all I wanted to tell you," he said, finally. "Thank you for coming to see me, Majesty." He picked up his brush and turned back to his work as if I weren't there.

I walked through the cold back to my quarters. When I got there, Han-sook took my outer robe and I went into my study. I looked around. I had everything a person could want—a beautiful place to live in, servants to attend to my every need. Everyone bowed and called me "Your Majesty." It was more than I could have ever imagined only a few years earlier. And yet, the Taewŏn-gun had controlled my life, and now he would control what I could learn.

I went to the lattice wall that looked out over the main palace courtyard. I slid the wall open and let the cold breeze blow over me. I looked beyond the palace, north toward Bukhansan Mountain on guard over Seoul like a steadfast soldier. I looked the other way out over the city of Seoul and thought of my thousands of subjects who lived there. Queen Min, they called me. But what kind of queen was I? If I were to speak for the spirit of Korea, I would have to be a dragon queen. But the Taewŏn-gun was only ever going to let me be a stone queen. To him, I was like his new palace—something to behold and impress, but silent like the courtyard stones.

I slid the wall closed against the cold and went back into my study. I opened a drawer in my bat chest and retrieved paper, a pen, and ink. I dipped the pen into the ink bottle and wrote a short note. I closed it with hot wax and my seal.

I clapped my hands for Han-sook. She came in and said, "Yes, Majesty?"

"I want to visit my uncle at the House of Gamgodang," I stated. "Arrange it. And send him this note at once announcing my visit."

"Yes, Majesty," Han-sook replied. "What should I tell the palace the visit is for?"

I glared at Han-sook. I wasn't sure she was someone I could trust. Maybe the Taewŏn-gun himself appointed her my lady's maid to spy on me. Perhaps she had told him about my lessons. So I said, "He is my uncle and I have not seen him in a long time. Now do as I say and do not ask questions."

Han-sook bowed low and left with my note for my uncle.

FOURTEEN

I thought the Taewŏn-gun would not allow me to visit my uncle, though it was only a short distance from the palace. As was the way with all women in Korea, men controlled where I could go and who I could see. I did not complain about it. I was still young, and to my disgrace, I had not yet given the king a child. Hence, I didn't feel I could ask for more freedom, and indeed, I was not given much. So I was surprised when Han-sook reported that the visit was set for midday and that I could take my own entourage.

Since I had become queen, they rarely let me leave the palace. Many times I had wanted to see my uncle and aunt, but the palace didn't allow it. When I did leave, I was with the king, Lady Min, and a large following of guards, porters, servants, and slaves, who provided everything we needed while we were away. Sometimes the Taewŏn-gun would go, too, although he usually stayed at the palace to work or was away on government business. On hot summer days, we would go to the countryside for a picnic or an afternoon stroll to escape the heat. Twice we took a ferry across the Han River to Seolleung, to visit the tomb of King Taejo, the founder of the House of Yi. Once, we made a two-week journey to Pusan in the south so the people there could pay their respects to the king and me. There, I saw the sea for the first time and it thrilled me. As I gazed across the water that looked like it was falling off the earth's edge, I wondered what else there was for me to see in the world and I desperately wanted to see it. But most of the time I stayed inside the palace. So I was excited to be going to the House of Gamgodang on my own.

When it came time to go to my uncle's house, eight porters carried my palanquin. The barefoot eunuchs dressed in long red robes were trained to keep the palanquin level and my ride smooth. Behind the palanquin were servants and maids on foot led by Han-sook, stepping along with her small steps. Four guards—the new guard, Kyung-jik, another on foot, and two on horseback—led the procession through the streets of Seoul, pushing people aside and making sure they bowed as I came by. As we moved toward my uncle's house, I lifted the curtains of my palanquin and looked out at my subjects. They were mostly poor, dressed in drab robes and frocks against the winter wind. None dared raise their eyes to me, and I realized that though I was their queen, I didn't know them.

When we arrived at my uncle's house, the eunuchs lowered the palanquin to the ground. Bowing at the waist, a eunuch lifted the palanquin's curtain and offered me his hand. When I stepped out, my uncle's valet, Mr. Yang, was waiting at the gate. When he saw me, he pushed up his wire-rimmed glasses and bowed low. I went to the gate and Mr. Yang said, "Majesty, welcome to the House of Gamgodang."

I smiled to myself at Mr. Yang's servility. Years earlier when I lived with him under the same roof, he never once acknowledged me. To him, I had been useless, nothing more than a beggar in the household he managed. Now, I was his queen, someone to whom he had to bow.

Since Mr. Yang was a mere servant and I was the queen, the protocol was that I shouldn't greet him and I didn't. After a few seconds of bowing without a response from me, he scurried into the house. Soon, my uncle and aunt were at the door, bowing and inviting me in. I walked the path to the house and went inside to the main room. My uncle, aunt, and Han-sook followed. My uncle said, "Majesty, it is a great honor to have you grace our house. Welcome."

Mr. Yang and Eun-ji were stationed in the back of the room in front of the entire household staff. All were dressed in their finest robes and bowing low. They had set out a tray of tea and rice cakes on the low table. As everyone stayed bowed, I looked around at the dark-wood ceiling beams and polished parquet floors. They had brought out the best celadon pots and placed them against the latticed wall leading to the courtyard where I had trained with Mister Euno that awful spring years earlier.

"Uncle," I said, "I wish to talk to you alone." My uncle clapped his hands, and immediately, the entire staff and even my aunt left the room. Han-sook stayed. "You, too, maid," I said. "Leave us." Han-sook bowed and went out through the front door, and I was alone with my uncle.

I went to the tea table and sat on a cushion. My uncle stayed standing with his eyes low. I hadn't seen him since my wedding day, and I was thrilled to see him now. He was dressed in his finest hanbok and looked much the same as before—tall and handsome. There were new streaks of gray at his temples, which made him look distinguished. "Sit," I said. "Have some tea with me."

My uncle hesitated a moment, then sat on a cushion across from me. He still didn't raise his eyes. He poured a cup of tea for me, and one for himself. As I took a sip, I said, "It is strange to visit this house now, as queen."

My uncle smiled. "I am sure it is, Majesty."

I leaned into my uncle who hadn't touched his tea. "I believe I am doing well," I said. "His Excellency, the Taewŏn-gun, compliments me on how I conduct myself with the yangban and dignitaries. Mister Euno still instructs me, but with a delicate hand. I have learned much."

"That is good, Majesty."

I sighed. "Still, it is not so easy to be happy in the palace. You told me it wouldn't be, and you were right. You told me something else, too. You said I would have a choice, that I could be a stone queen or a dragon queen. Do you remember?"

"Yes, Majesty, I do."

"Well, Uncle, I have decided."

"And what is your decision, Majesty?"

I set my teacup down. As I looked around the house where I had lived for four years, I was weary of having everyone treat me as if I would behead them for making a mistake in my presence. Here, in the House of Gamgodang, I had been Ja-young, a simple orphan who no one paid much attention to. I read books on the Chinese bench in the bamboo grove and helped my aunt in her rose garden. My only concern had been Mr. Yang's disapproving looks, which I had always dismissed. As I sat now with my uncle, I realized I had been happy here.

"Uncle," I said, "look at me."

My uncle slowly lifted his head and his onyx eyes met mine. I said, "I am the queen, but part of me is still Ja-young. I know I can never fully be Ja-young again, but perhaps I can be her now . . . to you?"

My uncle smiled softly and his posture relaxed. "Yes, Ja-young," he nodded. "But only when we are alone."

I smiled back at him, and for the first time since I had become queen, I was myself again.

We sat together for a while without talking, my uncle finally taking his tea. After a time, he said, "I think you want to tell me you have decided to be a dragon queen."

I nodded. "Yes, Uncle. I have decided that very thing."

"And you have come to me for help?"

"That is correct."

"So tell me, Majes . . . Ja-young, how can I help you?"

I took my teacup into my hands and told him how Lady Min had been helping me get an education until the Taewŏn-gun dismissed her from that role. I told him about my wish to learn about Japan and how the Taewŏn-gun had rebuffed my request and ended my education. And

I told him how I couldn't trust anyone in the palace and that I was like a prisoner there. I set my teacup down and said, "How will I ever become a dragon queen if I cannot learn what I need to know?"

"I see," my uncle nodded. "You are wise to seek an education. But you underestimate what you need to know." He poured more tea for himself and me. He took his teacup and began. "It is not just the classics you need to know. As I told you before you accepted the crown, the whole world is now at our doorstep. If you are to be the dragon queen, you need to learn about the world. Economics, government, politics, history, science, the ways of the West—Europe and America. You need to learn Japanese, French, Russian, and English. But most of all, you need to learn diplomacy. It will be your greatest challenge."

My head began to spin at what my uncle was saying. "Economics, science, history. English, Russian . . . ," I said.

"Most importantly, diplomacy," my uncle repeated.

"How can I possibly learn all of this?" I asked, shaking my head.

My uncle took a sip of tea. "It will take many years, Ja-young," he said. "But I must say, if anyone can do it, it is you."

"Yes, I am willing, and I want to. But the Taewŏn-gun will never allow it."

"Perhaps the king can help. He is the king, after all."

I said, "Yes, perhaps he can. I will ask him." I turned to my uncle. "I want you to be my adviser. I will arrange it through the palace."

My uncle nodded. "I would be honored, although we must be discreet about this assignment."

"There is something else," I said. "I think Minister Kim is an ally. I need you to connect with him. Do it quietly."

"I will."

As I studied my uncle closely, I realized that I had taken him and my aunt for granted when I had lived here. Before I had come to the House of Gamgodang, they had lost two children—one to consumption and the other to a riding accident. They had brought me in as if I was their own and had given me a home. I had accepted their generosity and had not thought much about it. But now I realized that my uncle was much like my father and my aunt was like my mother. For the first time, I felt close to them. I wanted to stay here at their home, take in their love so it could be as it was with my own father and mother a lifetime earlier. But I was the queen now and I would never have that again.

I stood up from the table and my uncle stood with me. "Thank you, Uncle," I said. "I must return to the palace."

He smiled at me. "Ja-young, I am pleased that you have decided to be a dragon queen, and I am honored to be your aide. But we must be careful." And then he bowed and said, "Your Majesty."

King Gojong and I rarely had sex, and since we'd been married, we had never truly made love. Our marriage was purely functional, a working relationship with the goal of producing a son. I had tried—and I believe he did, too—to make our relationship into something more. I had seen how my parents loved each other, how they had touched when they thought no one was looking, how my mother blushed when my father smiled at her. My uncle and aunt had a similar relationship, perhaps with less passion than my parents, but a loving marriage nevertheless. There was even affection between the Taewŏn-gun and Lady Min, though they often didn't see eye-to-eye on matters outside their marriage.

It was not the same with the king and me. We were too different. While I was studious and reflective, he was just the opposite. He didn't care about his studies and lived without regard or regret for his actions. He drank *soju* wine with his friends deep into the night and often slept past midday. He indulged in all-night orgies with his concubines. And some said he liked to smoke opium.

While his behavior enabled the Taewŏn-gun to stay in power, it worried Lady Min terribly. She often asked me about him and our relationship. I always told her that I thought he would be a good king and that he treated me well, though his regard for me was no different than it was for his chopsticks. I was simply a tool he used to give himself a son.

Unfortunately, I was not a very useful tool. Since the king and I had become husband and wife, I had never missed my monthly bleed. At first Gojong had expressed his disappointment in me. But after years of telling him that once again I wasn't pregnant, he simply shrugged and sent me away. I worried that he would take a second wife, one who would bear a son for him, but he never did. Instead, our relationship languished as he fell into a habit of drunkenness and debauchery.

In spite of the drudgery, we kept trying. It was our prime duty to provide a prince for our country so that the royal lineage wouldn't be broken. So a few days after I had visited my uncle, the king summoned me to his bedchamber. It was another cold, starless night as I walked across the main courtyard to the king's residence. When I arrived at the door of his bedchamber, a guard bent at the waist, opened the door for me, and I stepped inside. The king's new chambers were more spacious than mine. In the room was a bed large enough to sleep five people. It was covered with fine silk spreads. The room had superb Chinese scrolls and the finest chests, tables, chairs, and embroidered cushions. When I came in, there were only a few candles lit and the room was deep in shadows. I smelled incense and a faint odor I didn't recognize. It was a sweet, smoldering smell, as if someone had spilled perfume on a candle. I removed my slippers and made my way through the shadows to the bed. The king, covered with silk sheets, laid on his back, a shadowy lump.

He raised a hand. "Come, wife. Be with me tonight." His speech was slow and he slurred his words.

I took off my clothes and slipped under the sheets with him. The smell of burnt perfume hung strong on his breath. I put my fingers on his chest. His skin was cold and clammy. He did not respond to my touch. I tried to arouse him with my hand, but again, he didn't respond. He sighed, and then chuckled lazily. "Well," he said, "perhaps not tonight."

I took my hand from him, but I didn't leave his side. "Let me stay," I whispered, "just for a while."

"If you want," he said.

He closed his eyes and rolled his head from side to side. He groaned. "I'm thirsty," he said to the ceiling. "I want some wine."

He picked up a small bell from a side table and rang it. Immediately, a servant in a white robe was at the door. "Yes, Your Majesty?" the servant said.

"A jug of soju," the king said.

"Yes, Majesty," the servant replied and disappeared out the door.

Gojong rolled to face me. "How come you never drink with me? You never have, not even once."

It was true; I never drank with him. I had only tried the rice wine once, and I didn't like its sharp taste. I always refused when it was offered, taking tea instead. But now I said, "I would like to drink soju with you my husband."

The king grinned. His eyes were dilated and unfocused. His grin was loose and as thin as his mustache.

He pushed himself off the bed and put on a robe. He stumbled to a table and lit more candles, making the room brighter. I stood from the bed and put on my robe, too. I sat on cushions next to him. The servant came in with a celadon carafe and blue porcelain mugs on a tray. He placed them on the table and expertly poured the clear white wine into the mugs. He stood with his head bowed and his hands in front of him at the waist. "Is there anything else you wish, Majesty?" he asked.

The king waved his servant away with the back of his hand. "Not now," Gojong replied. When the servant was gone, Gojong lifted his mug to me. "Drink," he said. I lifted my mug and took a sip of the strong wine. As Gojong watched me drink, his face slid into another sloppy grin. He took a big drink from his mug. He wiped his mouth with the back of his hand. "It is good, huh?" he said.

The strong drink bit my tongue and burned my throat. I didn't like it any more than the first time I had tried it. Even so, I said, "Yes, it is good."

"Drink more!" the king said. I took another drink, and the liquid started to warm me.

Gojong took a long drink from his mug and filled it again. "Ha, ha!" he said. "I like wine. It makes me feel strong."

"Strong? Why do you need to be strong?"

"It is not easy being king!" he huffed. "I know they talk about me behind my back. They think I am stupid and lazy, but I'm not. I only let my father run the country so they can't criticize me. If he made a poor decision, I would step in. I am not afraid of him."

"Of course," I said. "You would have to." I took another sip of wine.

Gojong took another drink and turned serious. "I will have to take over soon. Things are not going well. Everyone complains about everything. When I take over, you will help me."

"I will," I said. "We will make a good team."

"A team. Ha!" the king exclaimed. "You are not a very good teammate. You haven't given me a son."

I lowered my head. "I am sorry that I have not given you a son, my husband. I will try harder. I believe the day will come soon."

"It better," Gojong said.

We both took another drink. The wine made my head spin. I had to force myself to concentrate. "I can do something in the meantime," I said. "To help when you must take over."

"What is it, wife?"

"I would like to use your library. Perhaps I can learn something that will be useful to us."

The king gave me a sly look. "You are ambitious, aren't you? My father says you are. He tells me you study the classics. My mother thinks

I should study them, too, but they bore me. Poems about the ghosts in mountains, devils who talk to people through stones, teachings from men who died centuries ago. It is all very conceited, and I do not have a use for it."

I nodded. "Yes, it is silly, isn't it? But they think it is important. They think a king who will run the country should know these things. They will not listen to you unless you do." I took another sip of wine.

"I will not do it," Gojong said.

"Then let me," I said. I set my mug down and moved close to him. "Let me use your library. You are the king. They won't go against you."

Gojong eyed me and chuckled. "You *are* ambitious." His eyes were now very red and he looked tired.

I touched his arm. "I live only to serve you, my king. Let me serve you now. Let me do this for you."

My husband sighed deeply. He closed his eyes and curled up on the floor. "As you wish," he said. "But make me a son, too."

In a few seconds, my husband was asleep on the floor. The making of a son wasn't going to happen that night. I dressed and pulled on my outer robe for the walk back to my quarters. When I got to the door, I looked back at Gojong who now snored softly on the floor of his bedchamber. I could still smell the odor of burnt perfume. Although I'd never smelled it before, I knew what it was.

The king was using opium.

FIFTEEN

As it turned out, the king didn't need to talk to the Taewŏn-gun about letting me use his library. Over time, the laws and policies the Taewŏn-gun had passed started to cause trouble for him. That summer, the Americans sent the US General Sherman, a heavily armed merchant schooner, up the Taedong River loaded with cotton, tin, and glass, hoping to force trade with what they called the "Hermit Kingdom." The ship made it all the way to Pyongyang, but the Taewŏn-gun stuck to his "no trade" policy and threatened to sink the ship if they didn't leave immediately. In response, the Americans captured two officials from the Yi clan and held them hostage. When an angry crowd at Pyongyang harbor demanded their release, the General Sherman fired its cannons into the crowd, killing several civilians. Eventually our navy rammed the American ship with a boat filled with explosives, setting the schooner ablaze. When the American crew swam ashore, the civilians killed them all. This infuriated the Americans, and there were reports that they were sending warships to the peninsula. The Taewŏn-gun spent long hours with his ministers trying to prevent war.

Then there was the argument about relations with China and Japan. The Taewŏn-gun argued that closer relations with Japan was a way to break China's hundreds-of-years-old domination over Korea.

"As a child must leave his mother," the Taewŏn-gun said in an afternoon meeting one day, "so should Korea wean itself from the protection of China."

A traditionalist minister leaned forward. "A man must respect his mother and never turn his back on her," he countered.

The ongoing dispute split the nation between isolationists and progressives, so no clear policy emerged.

There were issues inside Korea as well. The yangban and chungin began to protest the Taewŏn-gun's high taxes and were refusing to pay them. When the palace sent soldiers along with the tax collectors to force payment, the rebellion stiffened. The soldiers killed several rebels, including prominent members of clans that were rivals of the Yis. There were rumors that the people were planning to storm the palace and end the reign of King Gojong and the House of Yi.

And there was age-old fighting between the clans, too. The Kims were angry with the Paks about land they believed the Paks had stolen from them. The Chungs were fighting with the Ch'oes about a large unpaid loan. And all clans hated the Yis, blaming them for the high taxes and government corruption.

Threats from foreigners, arguments about ideology, anger with taxes, quarreling between clans. The debates inside the palace and out grew loud and emotional and sometimes broke into fights. In all, the country was in turmoil, and the Taewŏn-gun had his hands full.

During this time, I kept quiet. I did not challenge my father-in-law or express an opinion or even ask questions in our meetings. My silence and the country's turmoil turned the Taewŏn-gun's attention away from me so that I could further my education without him knowing. In a matter of a few months, I was spending most of the day in the king's new library. It was an extraordinary place. There were rows of shelves stacked with books in Chinese, Hangul, and a few in Japanese, all there for me to read. I spent months with them. Eventually I worked my way through the entire library. But the library only had the classics, and most of them were in Chinese. I wanted more. I wanted to read the modern books on topics my uncle had told me I needed to learn. But I knew that if I requested them directly, the king's staff would alert the Taewŏn-gun.

So I turned to my uncle. When I had visited him at the House of Gamgodang and told him about my situation, he had agreed to help. When I told the palace I wanted him to be my adviser, they did not object. I supposed the Taewŏn-gun thought it was natural for me to have a member of my family on my staff. The palace even paid my uncle a handsome stipend. So he visited me every week, sometimes twice a week, and when he did, he brought books. They were on a wide variety of topics—economics and history and science and even novels that my uncle got from the bookseller who lived near the Han River. The books were from all over the world—Japan, America, and Europe—translated into Chinese or Hangul. My favorite was Shakespeare. I devoured his stories, especially the ones about kings and queens. I kept these books in my sleeping quarters, hidden from my staff, and read them deep into the night. When I was done with them, I demanded more. I was obsessed with learning.

I also had my uncle get tutors for me. He brought tutors for each subject I studied, and I spent hours listening carefully to their lessons and asking questions. Their lessons were easy for me and I learned quickly. "Majesty," they would say with genuine surprise, "you are indeed a gifted student."

I supposed what they said was true. I was smart like my mother and uncle said I was—certainly much smarter than anyone at the palace knew. What they didn't see was how hard I worked at my lessons. When I was alone in my study or on a stroll around the palace grounds, I would practice my lessons until I could do them with ease. And when I mastered one lesson, I would demand more. But it was strange for me, being an intelligent woman in a world dominated by men. I often wondered why it had to be that way.

One day I told my uncle I wanted to learn Japanese. The next week, he brought a Japanese teacher, and I started to learn the language. I memorized words and phrases as I lay in bed at night. I listened closely to how the teacher pronounced the words and copied him so I wouldn't have an accent. After I learned Japanese, I moved on to Russian. And though that language was strange and the words came together in an odd way, I learned rudimentary Russian. I wanted to learn English and French, too, but my uncle could not find instructors in those languages so easily. Still, I learned some words of both languages when I heard or read them, and eventually I had a small working vocabulary. Learning a new language was like a game to me. I was good at it. Still, I had to be very careful that I didn't show how much I knew.

Neither the Taewŏn-gun nor the palace ever questioned why my uncle visited me so often and brought tutors with him. And Lady Min no longer watched over me. I only saw her to plan palace events, or when we went on one of our picnics. I sensed that the Taewŏn-gun had quashed Lady Min's ambitions for the Mins.

My husband never questioned what I was doing, either. Since the king rarely read or used his own tutors, he didn't know how much there was to learn about the world outside the palace. Of course, when I was with him, I made light of my obsession with books, pretending it was a silly thing like taking up painting or growing orchids. But he wouldn't have cared if he did know. While I spent months and years learning, he sank deeper and deeper into his hedonism until he couldn't see anything beyond it. And I must confess, as I went about my business, I did nothing to help him.

But there was a problem with my education. The more I learned, the more restless I became. When I was alone, I would close my eyes and imagine myself traveling to the places I had read about—Europe, America, Africa, and India. I daydreamed about debating the world's great thinkers and impressing them with my knowledge. I tried to imagine how it felt to ride the new invention called a bicycle or to fly high into the sky in a hot-air balloon.

And I wanted to use my education to show everyone that I was not a stone queen. But like the sex I had with my husband, my hard work yielded no fruit. I tried to take comfort in the fact that I was still young, not yet twenty years old, that there would come a day when I could use what I had learned. But I felt like a caged bird yearning to be free.

One day after the Taewŏn-gun had made a decision in the afternoon meeting, I said from my position facing away, "Excellency, the king is fortunate to have you run the government on his behalf. But if you please, explain to the king why you feel this is the correct decision." It was the first time I had asked such a question, and I could hear the ministers murmuring to each other. My father-in-law proceeded to explain his position, and I asked nothing more.

As the weeks and months went on, I asked more questions but never challenged my father-in-law. That is, until one day after the regent made a decision, I said, "Excellency, you are wise and make excellent decisions for our king and country. But what would happen if we took another approach?"

This time, the ministers went quiet. My father-in-law cleared his throat and gave a good answer to my question, and I said nothing more.

And then one day many months later, the regent made a decision that I thought was wrong. I turned to face the group and said, "Excellency, the king and I are most thankful for your governance of our country. However, on this matter, I do not agree with this decision." This time, the ministers stared at their hands and the king raised his head and looked at me. The Taewŏn-gun glared at me from under his high eyebrows, and I knew I had gone too far. So after the regent explained his decision in detail, I did not disagree with him and his decision stood.

After I started to challenge the regent's decisions, I noticed that he did not include the king and me in some important discussions.

When a particularly prickly situation came up, the regent would set the discussion aside "to talk about later," as he said. Then, afterward, the issue would be resolved without ever having been brought up again in the afternoon meetings. I wanted to challenge my father-in-law about it, but I decided to keep quiet. Still, with all that I was learning, it was increasingly difficult to hold my tongue.

It did not help my standing with the palace that I had still not gotten pregnant. The king needed a son to assure the Yi dynastic line. I had tried everything—the herbs the medicine woman had prescribed and the exercises my maids had suggested I perform after I had visited Gojong in his bedchamber. I consulted fortune-tellers. One read my palm and said my time for childbearing was near. Another examined the bones in my face and predicted I would "have a son by the time the snow flies." Both were wrong. I began to believe someone had put a curse on me. When the king planted his seed in me, it landed on infertile soil. Every month my bleeding announced that I had once again failed in my most important responsibility to my king and country. Every month the menstrual cramps in my stomach were like my people punching me for not giving them a prince. I knew everyone was staring at me, watching, wondering what was wrong with me, as if I was broken somehow. I wanted to hide in my quarters away from their stares. I was afraid that they were right and that I was broken somehow. I was relieved when the king didn't call me to his bedchamber.

I couldn't use my education and I couldn't bear a child. I was as useless as wings on a cow. I had come to regret agreeing to be queen.

During this time, I kept an eye on Minister Kim's nephew, Kyungjik. I asked the sergeant about the handsome guard, and he said that he was a capable and earnest man. He was skilled at empty-handed fighting methods, and he was learning sword fighting. "He will be a great swordsman someday," the sergeant said. I told the sergeant to promote Kyung-jik to the head of my night guard, which, of course, he did.

And I set out to see if I could trust Han-sook. I needed someone close to me who I could depend on, and now that the Taewŏn-gun was keeping Lady Min and me apart, my lady's maid was the logical choice. When I first became queen, I thought the demure, middle-aged woman was a spy for Lady Min or perhaps even the Taewŏn-gun. But as I thought back, it was possible that I had misinterpreted her actions then and she was just trying to help me. She had always been proper, humble, and willing to do anything for me. So I started to ask her advice on important matters, and she seemed genuinely pleased that I did. And when she gave her opinion, I discovered that she was smarter than I had thought. She was honest and wise, and had a sharp sense for diplomacy. Gradually, but cautiously, I brought her into my confidence.

My uncle met with me every week. He walked the mile from the House of Gamgodang to the palace through pouring rain, summer heat, and on the cruelest days of winter. He never missed a meeting. Until one summer day, he did. I didn't think much about it at the time. I thought perhaps he had forgotten to tell me he would be away, searching for a rare book for me, or hunting for an English tutor, although it was not at all like him to forget. But then he missed another week, and then another and another.

Sitting in my study, I clapped my hands and Han-sook came in. Her hair was pinned back, framing her pleasant, round face. She bowed to me from the door and said, "Yes, Majesty?"

"Come closer," I said. "Here by my desk." Han-sook kept her eyes low as she padded to my desk with her small steps. "Han-sook," I said, "you have been an able lady's maid for me. But now I need you to be something more. I need someone who I can trust. Can I depend on you?"

Han-sook swallowed hard. "Majesty," she whispered, "I will give my life for you."

"Good," I said with a nod. "I fear that something has happened to my uncle. He has not come for several weeks now. I want you to find out why."

"Yes, Majesty."

"Han-sook, listen to me," I said. "You must do this quietly, without raising suspicion. You see, my uncle helps me learn about the world against the Taewŏn-gun's wishes."

Han-sook nodded. "Yes, Majesty, I know."

I cocked my head. "You know?"

Han-sook wrung her hands. "Please forgive me, Majesty, but I have known for some time. The palace has asked me why your uncle visits you so often and why he brings tutors with him. I see that you hide your books, so I tell them he is only helping you learn the classics and how to be a proper queen, although I know your lessons go far beyond what the Taewŏn-gun has approved."

I paused for a moment. I realized that over the past few years it would have been impossible to hide my activities from my lady's maid. She was always with me, or only a few steps away. I recalled the times she warned me that someone was coming so that I could hide my books or have a tutor sneak away through the courtyard. I remembered the times I found my books hidden in my bat chest after I had left them out in the open. And then I knew that Han-sook was someone I could trust. My heart went out to her and I wanted to hug her. But I was the queen and she was a servant, so I kept my emotions to myself.

"Very well," I said giving her a look of approval. "Can you find out what happened to my uncle?"

"I will try, Majesty. I have friends who work for the Taewŏn-gun. I will ask them in a way that will not raise suspicions."

"Good," I said. "Let me know as soon as you hear."

"Yes, Majesty," my lady's maid said and she bowed.

A few days later, Han-sook reported that no one knew where my uncle had gone. At first I was puzzled. If my uncle would be away for this long, he certainly would have told me beforehand. I thought about contacting Minister Kim to see if he knew what happened to my uncle, but I hadn't talked to the minister directly in years. I thought about sending a message to the House of Gamgodang, but there was no guarantee that a message would get through. I said to my lady's maid, "Rouse Kyung-jik. I am going to my uncle's house at once."

"Yes, Majesty," Han-sook replied. "Shall I inform the palace?"

"No. I am the queen; I do not need the palace's permission to visit my uncle and aunt. You and Kyung-jik will escort me. I want no one else along. Go now. Quickly."

A few minutes later, Kyung-jik, Han-sook, and I marched across the main courtyard to the Gwanghwamun Gate. There, two guards saw us coming and held their positions. "Open the gate," I commanded.

"Majesty," one guard said, "we weren't informed that you would be—"

"Open the gate now or I will have your head," I stated. The guards bowed and quickly opened the gate's heavy door.

The House of Gamgodang was on one of Seoul's broad streets. The three of us walked, with me in the lead, Kyung-jik in his guard's uniform slightly to my side, and Han-sook wringing her hands three steps behind. It was a hot summer day with no breeze. As my tiny entourage walked by, people on the streets stared at us with their mouths agape, then quickly backed away and bowed. I noticed that the merchants and yangban were stern-faced when they saw me and did not bow as low as they should have. I also noticed many were ragged and dirty. No one had swept the streets of horse and oxen waste. The city smelled of sewage and sweat.

It had been several years since I had gone to the House of Gamgodang to talk to my uncle about helping me, and when we arrived there, I barely recognized it. Tall weeds choked the rose garden, and they had not harvested the bamboo. There was no livestock in the pens, and the outbuildings were unkempt. There were no servants working in the compound, and the stablemate was not at his station.

I went to the gate. "Anyohaseyo," I called out. "Is anyone here at this house?" There was no answer. Kyung-jik called out, but still there was no reply.

"Go to the door," I ordered.

Kyung-jik went to the door. He pounded on it and called out again. "Anyohaseyo!" he said. "Her Majesty, the queen, calls on this house. Come out at once!"

After a few seconds, the door cracked opened and Mr. Yang stuck his head out. "Please," he pleaded from behind his glasses. "We are not prepared to receive the queen."

I pushed through the gate and went to the door. As I approached, Mr. Yang stepped out and bowed. "Mr. Yang," I said, "I have come to see my uncle. I do not care if you are prepared or not. Let me inside."

"Majesty," Mr. Yang said, "I regret to tell you that your uncle is not here."

"Where is he?" I asked.

He pushed his glasses up his nose. "Forgive me, Majesty. I do not know."

I stood outside the house looking at Mr. Yang who kept his head low. He was a skilled valet, and it was his job to always know where his master was. Yet he was telling me he didn't know.

I pushed past Mr. Yang and went inside the house. Except for a few cushions on the floor, the room was empty. The zelkova-root wood chests and Chinese table were gone. There were no celadon pots anywhere. The kitchen was dark, and the maids and servants were not there. The house was ghostly quiet and it smelled musty.

Mr. Yang followed me inside. "Please forgive the condition of the house, Majesty. Perhaps if we had known you were coming . . ."

As I stood at the door staring at the empty house, the wall from the courtyard slid open and my aunt stepped into the room. Eun-ji followed close behind her. My aunt looked at the floor. She was dressed in her everyday robe. But unlike when I knew her before, her robe was smudged and wrinkled. Her shoulders drooped. She appeared to have lost weight. "Majesty," my aunt said, "I wish you would not have come. I am ashamed that you have to see us like this."

"Where is my uncle?" I asked.

My aunt began to cry. Eun-ji put an arm around her. Mr. Yang said, "We think the palace arrested him. There is no other explanation."

"Why would the palace arrest my uncle?" I demanded.

"I am sorry, Your Majesty," Mr. Yang said. "I think it was because he worked for you."

My heart went out to them. My once-proud aunt looked defeated and sad. Eun-ji, who had run the household staff with a firm hand, had no one to manage anymore. Mr. Yang had lost his master and his purpose in life. I went to a cushion and sat. "Come," I said, "all three of you. Sit. Tell me what has happened here."

At first, they hesitated, then all three sat on the floor in front of me. They started slowly, but eventually they told me what had happened. They said that my uncle had disappeared three weeks earlier. They told me he was supposed to have been with me at the palace that day but he never came home. When Mr. Yang went to the palace to find him, they told him they didn't know where he was. Mr. Yang investigated and concluded that the palace had secretly arrested my uncle. They had tried to get a message to me at the palace, but they never heard from me.

I asked them where the servants had gone. "We had to let them go a year ago," my aunt answered. "We could no longer afford them. We cannot afford Mr. Yang and Eun-ji, either, but they refused to leave. We have been doing what we can."

"I don't understand," I said. "The palace paid my uncle for his services to me."

Mr. Yang nodded. "That only lasted for a short while. A few years ago, they stopped paying him, but he insisted that he continue to work for you without pay. And since then the palace has given him no other work."

I thought about the months and years my uncle had worked for me. He had never told me the palace had stopped paying him. He must have been paying for my books and tutors out of his own pocket. During the past several months, I had noticed his robe was soiled and that his shoes were threadbare. I hadn't thought anything of it, assuming he must have been working too hard to attend to his grooming. I never even considered that he had run out of money.

"Do you think he is still alive?" I asked.

My aunt put her head in her hands to stifle a sob. Eun-ji put a hand on her arm. Mr. Yang leaned forward. "Please forgive me, Majesty, but before he disappeared your uncle was concerned that his work for you was upsetting the palace. He told me to be on the lookout for threats against this house. I thought he was exaggerating or just being cautious. But now this has happened."

My aunt looked at me. Tears ran down her face. "Help us, Majesty," she sobbed. "Help me find my husband."

The Taewŏn-gun. For the past several years, I thought my father-in-law didn't know or care what my uncle did for me. But apparently the regent had found out, and he did not approve. My father-in-law was intent on keeping me under his control, uninformed and uneducated so that I could not challenge him. As I looked at my aunt, sobbing for her lost husband, and as I looked around this once-proud house that had fallen into disrepair, I felt the color rise in my face.

I stood and the three of them stood with me. I turned to my aunt. "I promise I will find your husband," I said firmly. "I do not believe they have killed him. I will find a way for us to get messages to each other. In the meantime, do nothing until you hear from me."

"Yes, Majesty," my aunt replied.

I left the House of Gamgodang, and as I headed back to the palace, I prayed that I was right that the Taewŏn-gun had not killed my uncle.

SIXTEEN

When I got back to the palace, I sat at my writing desk and my blood boiled. It was one thing for the Taewŏn-gun to try to make me be a stone queen. But it was unforgivable that he would do something to my family. It was time for me to become the dragon queen.

I pushed myself from my cushion and headed out the door. I marched across the main courtyard to the Taewŏn-gun's quarters. A guard stood at the entrance. "Majesty!" he exclaimed, clearly not knowing what to do.

"Step aside," I commanded with a voice I didn't know I had. The guard quickly backed away, and I went inside where the Taewŏn-gun sat at a low table with his advisers all around him. There, too, was Mister Euno. They all fell silent when I came in. I sensed they were discussing something important without the king and me.

"Your Majesty," the Taewŏn-gun said, trying to disguise his surprise. "You were not announced."

"What have you done with my uncle?" I asked without properly addressing him.

The Taewŏn-gun looked around at his advisers, each of whom had their eyes fixed on the table in front of them. "Leave us," the Taewŏn-gun ordered in his high-pitched voice. "I wish to talk to the queen alone."

The advisers and Mister Euno left the room in one big bustle. When they were gone, I stood at the front of the room and said, "You have Japan on your inner counsel?"

"Mister Euno is a wise man," my father-in-law said. "He has connections in Japan and knows how to work with them."

"They are treacherous, and I suspect, so is he." My father-in-law did not respond. "Where is my uncle?" I asked.

My father-in-law shrugged. "Why do you ask? Is he missing?"

I hesitated a moment to gather myself. I had come here in a rage, and the Taewŏn-gun was a clever man, skilled at turning an argument to his advantage. Instead of answering his question, I asked again, "Where is he?"

He rose from his cushion and faced me. Though he was not old, he looked much older than when I had first met him, as if the demands of running the country were draining the life from him. The lines in his face were deeper, and his long beard was turning gray. Still, he was the Taewŏn-gun, and though he was a small man, his character filled the room. "If he is missing, I can understand why you are concerned, Majesty," he said. "I know he is your closest adviser. I often wonder why you need so much advice. Perhaps Minister Kim knows what happened to him. I hear he has become an adviser to you, too."

I was stunned and didn't know what to say. How was it possible the Taewŏn-gun knew about my conversation with Minister Kim? "I . . . I don't know what you mean," I stammered. "Minister Kim has only come to my quarters to inspect my tapestry. He is your adviser, not mine."

The Taewŏn-gun went to a wall and examined a calligraphy he had done that was hanging there. It was a single Chinese character, beautifully drawn with graceful yet bold strokes. The character was for *gōnglǘ*, the Chinese word for "power."

"Yes," the regent said, "your tapestry. Well, Minister Kim is a fine adviser. He is studious and has good judgment. He and I do not always agree, but I value his counsel." Then, without looking away from his calligraphy, he said, "I do not know what happened to your uncle."

He was lying and I knew it. I lifted my chin and leveled my eyes on the regent. I said, "I don't believe you, Ahbonim. You know what happened to my uncle, and I command you as your queen, tell me."

The Taewŏn-gun still faced the calligraphy. Then, in one quick move, he ripped it off the wall and crumpled it into a tight ball. He let it roll off his hand onto the floor. Shocked, I took a step back. I had never seen such emotion from my father-in-law, and it frightened me. He glared at the crumpled paper for several seconds. "Forgive me," he said finally. "I saw a mistake in it. I do that sometimes—make a mistake that I do not see until later."

He slowly turned toward me and then returned to his cushion. "Ja-young, hear me. We—both of us—serve the king. I do what is best for him and our country. It is your duty to do the same. And the best thing you can do for the country and king is to let me run the government. Do not challenge me. Remember your promise to me and your duty to your king."

I gathered my courage and took a step toward him. "If I believed you only serve country and king, I would not challenge you. But it seems you only want to stay in power. You befriend the Japanese to distance us from China. But Japan will protect you only as long as you do what they want. You persecute the Mins and the other clans to keep the Yis in power. And now you have taken my uncle."

My father-in-law glared at me. "Be careful what you say. Your words are dangerous to the king."

"Yes, the king," I said. "There are many dangers here in the palace. But I believe he will be fine. *'There's such divinity doth hedge a king that treason can but peep to what it would.'*" The Taewŏn-gun cocked his head at me quizzically.

"Shakespeare, Ahbonim," I said.

"Shakespeare . . . ?" he replied, his eyebrows higher than usual.

"*Hamlet,*" I replied. "And you are right. I will have to be more careful from now on." I turned and stormed out of the room.

I marched to the king's quarters and threw open the door to his bedchamber. "It's time," I said as I stood in the doorway. The king was in his bed with a woman who was naked. When she saw me, the courtesan got out of Gojong's bed and casually picked up her clothes from the floor. She had a much fuller figure than I did and was taller, too. She had a pretty face and long black hair. She didn't cover herself as she walked past me out of the room without bowing.

Gojong crawled out of bed and slipped on his robe. "You should not come in here like that," he scolded.

"Who is she?" I asked. "I've seen her with you before."

"Her name is Gwi-in," he said as he tied his robe closed with a sash. "She is a Yi and she will give me a son. When she does, I will make her my second wife."

The king's slight hurt me, but I bit my tongue. He hadn't called me to his bedchamber for months, and I began to think he would never call me again. And if Gwi-in made the king a son, they would push me aside and make her the reigning queen. They would send me somewhere far away and forget about me. Or maybe they would simply kill me. I immediately disliked the king's concubine with the full figure and pretty face. But I pushed aside these thoughts. At this moment, I had to convince the king to take control of the government so I could find my uncle.

"You said it is time," the king said. "Time for what?"

"It is time for us to take over from your father," I answered, still standing at the doorway. "You said you would when the time is right. That time has come."

"Ha, ha," Gojong laughed. "And you want to help me, don't you? You, the ambitious one." He grinned and went to a low table and sat on a cushion. He picked up a bell from the table and rang it.

A servant appeared and said, "Yes, Majesty?"

Gojong didn't reply right away. He looked from the servant to me, and then back at the servant again. "My pipe," he said finally.

"Yes, Majesty," the servant said and left the room.

Gojong looked back at me. "Tell me, wife, why is *now* the time?"

I went to the table and sat across from him. "Your father pushes our country toward Japan, and I fear it could be disastrous. And his taxes are making the people poor. I have seen it on the street. They will not stand for it much longer. There is anger in their faces."

The king waved his hand. "All this worry about taxes and Japan and China and war and rebellion. It tires me. I approve of what my father does."

I leaned toward him. "Do you? Your father makes decisions without us. Just now, I walked in on him in his quarters where he was meeting with the court advisers and Mister Euno, too. They were meeting in his quarters without us! The decisions he makes are on *your* behalf. They are supposed to have your approval. If the people rebel, they will come after you, not him. If Japan seizes Korea for itself, they will take away your throne. You must take charge before it's too late."

Gojong's brow furrowed and his goatee twitched. He cocked his head. "He's making decisions without me?" We stayed silent for some time, the king staring at the table, rubbing a hand over his head as if he was trying to understand what I had told him.

There was a knock on the door, and the servant came in carrying a silver tray. On the tray was a carved wooden pipe with a long, leather-wrapped stem. Next to the pipe were brown powder and sulfur matches. Before the servant could cross the room with the tray, Gojong pointed to a chest and said, "Set it there." The servant set the tray on top of the chest, bowed and left the room.

Finally I spoke again. "I can help, my king. I have learned about the ways of the world, about politics and economics. I can speak Japanese now. Let me help you."

Gojong shook his head. "I can't do anything."

I huffed at him. "You are the king!" I exclaimed. "You can take charge. You can save your throne if you act now."

"No," he said, shaking his head. "I don't want to." He looked over at the tray on the chest and then at me. "Maybe I could if I had a son," he said simply.

I looked at him. His hair was greasy and his skin was pale. He had lost weight, and there were dark circles around his eyes. He looked sad, like a man who had nothing to live for. He was the king, the most powerful man in the country, but his laziness and hedonism had turned him into a puppet and his father held the strings.

I was disgusted with him, but I pitied him, too. Like me, he hadn't chosen his position. He was only thirteen years old when they crowned him king. But now he was the age when he should take over from his father. But he couldn't do it.

As I sat across the table from my husband, I felt a kinship with him. We had a common foe—the Taewŏn-gun and the way he controlled us. But if we didn't muster the courage to confront him now, perhaps we never would.

I said, "Did you finish with her?"

"Who?" the king asked.

I pointed to the door. "The tall pretty one."

"No," the king replied. "You interrupted us before I could."

I stood and started to undress in front of him. Gojong stared at me as I let my robe fall to the floor. "What are you doing?" he asked.

"Finish with me," I said, slipping out of my *jeoksam* and *gojaengi* undergarments. "Finish with me and I will make you a son. And then we can talk about how we will take over the government from your father."

I was naked now and I went to him. I took off his robe and pressed myself into him. At first he didn't respond. Then he pulled me in close.

The sex was like nothing we'd ever had before. There was still no love in it, no real affection for the other. It was a physical, greedy, lusty act meant to satisfy only ourselves. For me it was an expression of my anger with the Taewŏn-gun for arresting my uncle and for controlling my every movement as if I was a common woman. It was frustration with not being able to bear a prince for my king and country. It seemed that the sex was much the same for Gojong.

And when it was over, when we lay on the silk covers, exhausted but consummated, we said nothing. After a while, I got out of bed and dressed. Gojong went to the chest, took the tray of opium to his desk, and started to smoke it as if I wasn't there. As the sweet, smoky smell filled the room, I left the king's bedchamber and went back to my quarters.

Now I knew for certain what I had suspected before—the Taewŏn-gun held important meetings without the king and me. I assumed he did so because I had started to ask questions and give my opinion in the afternoon meetings. As queen, I could veto the Taewŏn-gun's decisions, as long as the king didn't side with his father. Since Gojong didn't care about much of anything outside his small world and could have just as easily sided with me, it was safer for the regent to hold meetings without us.

I had to put an end to this. I was the second most powerful person in Korea—officially, anyway—and the Taewŏn-gun was making policies and decisions on my behalf as well as the king's. I had seen firsthand that the country was in turmoil, and the Taewŏn-gun's policies were making things worse. He'd had my uncle arrested for helping me, and I was powerless to rescue him. Someone needed to do something, and if Gojong wasn't going to take charge, I would do it for him. I had to hope that my husband would support me.

A few weeks after I had visited the House of Gamgodang, an important issue came up in the afternoon meeting. The Taewŏn-gun was at his usual place, on a cushion in the middle of the table's long side, flanked by his advisers. At the end of the table, the king was in his chair positioned above all the others. As he always did, Gojong slouched, barely paying attention. I sat in my chair behind him, facing the group as I always did now. The court secretary read a letter from the court of Empress Cixi, the powerful dowager empress of China. The letter said that the Chinese were feuding with the Japanese over islands in the East China Sea and they demanded that we support them in the matter. It was a particularly sensitive issue that should have been decided with the king and me present. But the Taewŏn-gun waved off the discussion, saying the council would discuss it later.

I pushed myself closer to the group to a place just behind the king. "Begging your pardon, Excellency," I said, "but this is a decision the king should be involved in. We should resolve it here, now."

The Taewŏn-gun gave me an almost imperceptible nod and turned to Gojong. "Majesty," he said, "this is not something we should bother you with now. We will look into it and discuss it at another meeting."

Gojong raised his head from his slouch. First, he looked at his father, then he looked at me. Since the time we'd had our passionate sex in his bedchamber, the king and I had been together several times more. Each was as passionate as that first time. In this, we had developed a loose kinship of sorts. So Gojong said, "Do as the queen says." He sat up and started to take more interest in the discussion.

The Taewŏn-gun stared at the king for several seconds. Then he nodded. "As you wish, Majesty," he said.

The discussion went forward with the ministers expressing their opinions and debating the merits and pitfalls of different courses of action. Minister Kim led the group in favor of supporting the Chinese, and he made a sound case for it. The Taewŏn-gun waved off the minister's argument and said that we should support the Japanese instead. "We have had to show deference to China for hundreds of years," he declared. "It is time we break free. We will align with the Japanese. They can help us with the Chinese."

The advisers didn't dare to challenge the regent, and so the debate was over. The Taewŏn-gun was about to issue his decision in favor of Japan, but I did not agree with it. If I was going to help my husband take over, if I was going find my uncle, if I was going to be a dragon queen, I had to speak up now. "You are correct, Excellency," I said. "Japan can be an ally. But perhaps they are becoming too strong. Throughout history, nations that are closest to their friends do the most harm when they turn. The wiser course would be to maintain a balance, one ally against the other."

There was a long silence. The ministers stared at the table, not daring to raise their eyes to either the Taewŏn-gun or me. Gojong looked from me to his father. "Well, Father, she makes a good point. That is what we will do."

It was the first time the king had ever expressed an opinion, much less issued a directive. The Taewŏn-gun went slack-jawed and said, "Begging your pardon, Majesty, but we should wait before we reply to the Chinese. To see what happens."

"No," I said. "By doing nothing, we support Japan. Instead, send a reply to Empress Cixi that we support China in this matter. Then send a carefully written apology to Emperor Meiji stating that we consider the Japanese to be a great friend, but we believe the Chinese are justified in their position regarding the islands."

The Taewŏn-gun pushed himself forward, "But Majesty," he said, "I—"

"You have made your case, Excellency," I said in a firm tone that I had never used before in the afternoon meetings. "You need not promote it any further. Issue the letter."

The Taewŏn-gun gave me a look, and this time it wasn't at all subtle. He turned to Gojong. "Majesty. This is not a wise course of action. I recommend that we wait on this matter."

Gojong shook his head. "Yes, you've said that. Do as the queen says. Now, I am growing tired of this. Let's move on."

And so the issue was resolved, and the secretary noted in the record book that the palace would write a letter of support to the Chinese and another to the Japanese carefully explaining our position. Gojong went back into his slouch, and the meeting ended a short while later.

SEVENTEEN

1871

Gojong and I continued having sex . . . until I realized that I was pregnant. I was weeks late in my bleeding time when I noticed my breasts were sore. One morning a wave of nausea came over me. I called out for Han-sook, who came running into my bedchamber.

"Yes, Majesty?" she said, out of breath.

"I am sick in my stomach," I said. "But now it's gone."

Han-sook smiled a little. "Forgive me, Majesty, but I have noticed that your breasts are swelled and you are thick in your legs. And now this morning you are sick in your stomach."

"Hmmm," I said. "Does that mean . . . ?"

Han-sook broke into a full smile. "I think you are pregnant, Majesty."

I sat on my bed. The room began to spin, and I was sick again. "A bowl!" I said. "Quickly!"

Han-sook ran from the room, but before she could return, I fell to the floor and vomited. Seconds later Han-sook burst into the room with a servant carrying a large porcelain bowl. "It's too late," I said.

"Don't worry, Majesty," Han-sook said. "Lie back until the sickness passes."

As the servant cleaned the mess on the floor, Han-sook attended to me like a mother attends to her baby. She rested my head on pillows and covered me with silk linens. But I was fine after I had vomited, and I said so to Han-sook. "If you please, Majesty," she replied, "you must rest until the doctor sees you. I have sent a guard to fetch him."

Han-sook stayed by my side until, minutes later, the royal doctor came rushing in. He was a large older man with long gray hair and a shaved face. He wore the long black robe and red sash of a man of medicine. His thick glasses made his eyes look as big as fish eyes. He carried a leather bag. He bowed and came to my side. While Han-sook looked on, the doctor pressed my stomach and examined my breasts. He produced a wooden stethoscope from his bag and listened to my heart. With his glasses perched on the end of his nose, he looked inside my mouth. He asked how long it had been since I'd had my last bleed. When I said it was nearly two months, he nodded, put his stethoscope in his bag, and declared that I was pregnant. He said that I was perfectly healthy and that I shouldn't worry. And then he said with an air of authority, that all indications were that the baby would be a boy.

After the doctor's visit, word about my condition spread like wildfire throughout the palace. The happy anticipation in Gyeongbok was the same as when I was to be crowned queen. It was almost festive. An heir to the throne was on its way, and it would be a boy! A prince for the king and for all of Korea! Han-sook could barely contain her joy. She stood guard over me like a dog protects her pups. I wasn't able to do a thing before she would grab the task from me and gleefully do it herself. Three times every day, she fed me chicken broth with ginseng root. "For the baby," she said. Everyone was even more flattering than they had been before. The guards bowed lower and the servants moved faster. There were always two or three maids standing by. To them, I was more than a queen now. I was practically a god.

It wasn't until days after the doctor said I was pregnant that the king visited me in my quarters. Typically, a husband wouldn't concern himself with his wife's pregnancy. Making a child was a woman's duty. The husband only became interested after the child was born—especially if the child was a son. I was in my study when the guard announced him. I wasn't surprised that he had come. He beamed at me. Then he scowled. "You should be in bed, wife," he said.

I smiled. "I am fine. I get more rest than I need these days."

He came and sat on a cushion next to me. He was still gaunt and pale, but now, there was a light in his eyes. I hoped that giving him a son would turn him from his irresponsible ways.

He sat by my side and regarded me as if I was a delicate thing that would break if he touched me. "The doctor says he thinks it will be a boy."

"He cannot know," I said. "But I hope it is."

"It *will* be a boy," the king said, lifting his chin. "I know."

It made me happy that my husband was pleased that I was pregnant. But I hadn't forgotten about the Taewŏn-gun's secret meetings, or that my uncle was missing. I had promised my aunt that I would find her husband, but with the Taewŏn-gun in control, I couldn't. I turned to Gojong. "Husband, now that I am pregnant, we can take over the government. Your father would not dare oppose us."

The king suddenly got up from his cushion and stood with his back to me. "I don't care about that," he said. "You shouldn't, either. If you worry about these things, you will not make a healthy son."

"But it is your time to take over."

He turned to me and scowled. "It is all a silly game, you and my father. I don't want to play it anymore. We should let him do as he sees fit."

"I've already started to challenge him. We cannot stop now."

Gojong glared at me. "Be silent, wife. You will upset the baby."

"If we do nothing, what will become of our son? What kind of prince will he be? If you want our son to be a strong prince, if you want him to be king someday, you must take charge now. You must lead the way for him or he will never be king."

"Our son will be king," he declared.

"Yes, he will," I said. "But first *you* must be king. And that means you must take over from your father."

The king thought about what I said for a moment. Then his shoulders sagged, and he looked both scared and tired at the same time. He would have to give up his wine and opium, study his books, and most importantly, he would have to challenge his father.

I took his hand. "I will help you," I said. "Together, we can do it."

"I don't know," he said.

"I do," I replied. "We must, for our son."

The king sighed heavily. He turned away and said, "Be sure our son is healthy." Then he walked out of my bedchamber.

Now that I was pregnant, everyone expected me to stay in my quarters and not concern myself with the state's affairs. But I now had an advantage over the Taewŏn-gun. I had the king's favor, and no one, not even the regent, would dare upset me for fear of harming the future prince.

So I started to take charge. I sent money and servants to help my aunt, Mr. Yang, and Eun-ji. I gave the general of the army the task of finding my uncle. He always reported that he had found nothing. Eventually I came to believe that he was following the Taewŏn-gun's orders and doing nothing to find my uncle. In the afternoon meetings, I challenged the Taewŏn-gun whenever I thought he was wrong. When he fought for new taxes, I remembered how his high taxes had destroyed the House of Gamgodang and I fought to have them lowered. When he wanted to replace an official with someone from the Yi clan, I put forward a different, honest man for the position. When he argued for close relations with the Japanese, I reminded him that the Japanese were modernizing and growing more powerful under the new government of Emperor Meiji.

During these confrontations, the king sat in his chair at the head of the table and tried to pay attention. His mind was unclear and his attention was short. All the same, he was trying. And since I carried his son in my womb, he sided with me most of the time. But sometimes when the Taewŏn-gun was particularly adamant about his position, he would glare at his son and Gojong would wither like an abused dog. Then the king would side with his father.

My pregnancy proceeded as the doctor had said it would. Eventually my morning sickness subsided, and I was energized by my condition. Just like the king, I was thrilled to be fulfilling the hopes of a nation for an heir to the throne. When my stomach grew heavy, the doctor—and therefore Han-sook—only let me leave my quarters for the afternoon meetings. Once when Han-sook thought I was attending to something away from my quarters, I snuck away to the Hyangwonjeong island pavilion to watch the koi fish as they swam among the lily pads. After a short while, Han-sook came running across the walkway followed by a servant and guard. My lady's maid was in tears when she came to me. "Majesty!" she cried. "We have been searching for you. Please, you must go back to your bedchamber and rest!"

I smiled at Han-sook. Though she fussed over me too much, I was glad she was by my side. She had become my confidant and friend—at least as much of a friend as a queen could have.

And now she stood in front of me at the pavilion wringing her hands, trying her best to take care of me. "Yes, Han-sook," I said. "I am a little tired." I let Han-sook lead me across the walkway over the pond and back to my quarters. The servant and guard followed close behind us. When we got to my bedchamber, Han-sook put me in my bed and called for the doctor. The doctor came and examined me as he had done nearly every week before. He admonished me for leaving my quarters. "The cold air is not good for the baby, Majesty," he declared. After he left, I fell asleep with Han-sook at the side of my bed watching over me.

Later in my pregnancy, I had trouble sleeping at night. It was the combination of having a sore back and heartburn, and the country's problems running through my head. Some nights, I would only get a few hours of sleep. I had always been able to get by with little sleep, so it didn't bother me. In fact, other than the heartburn that was sometimes so bad it sent spikes of pain from my stomach to my chin, I enjoyed being in the quiet of my quarters, alone. I would often crawl out of bed and go to my study to read. On warm nights, I would go out to my courtyard and gaze at the moon, wondering if it was really as far away as the astronomers said it was. Sometimes, I took short strolls across the palace grounds, though it worried Han-sook terribly when I did.

Late one night I sat in my courtyard watching a half-moon do a dance with the night clouds when a shadow moved at the end of the courtyard. Since I had lived in the palace, I'd always had guards close by, so I always felt safe. But lately I had been creating a stir by challenging the Taewŏn-gun, and I wondered just how safe I was.

"Who's there?" I whispered so as not to wake Han-sook or my servants. The shadow moved again, stepping toward me this time. I quickly stood and put a hand on my pregnant belly. "I command you as queen," I said, louder this time, "who is in my courtyard?"

The clouds slid away from the moon, casting soft light on the figure in front of me. The figure was tall and dressed in a guard's uniform. He had his head lowered. "Majesty," a man said, "please forgive this intrusion."

"Kyung-jik?" I said, softly again.

The man bowed low. "Yes, Majesty. It is your most loyal guard, Kyung-jik."

"What do you want at this hour?" I demanded. "Are you spying on me?"

"No!" he answered. "I would never do that, Majesty."

"Stand straight," I said. "Tell me why you are here."

Kyung-jik straightened, but didn't raise his eyes. "I was asked to get a message to you in secret and this is the only way. The message is from my uncle, Minister Kim."

I looked around the courtyard. No one stirred in the maids' quarters, and there were no other shadows. "Come closer," I whispered. "Tell me what important thing Minister Kim has to say that he sends you at this hour."

The guard stepped closer. "He says that you are in danger, Majesty," Kyung-jik said softly. "His Excellency, the Taewŏn-gun, means to remove you from the throne. It is only your pregnancy that has prevented him from doing so already. Minister Kim tells me to keep a close watch." The guard raised his eyes some. "I assure you, I always will protect you, my queen."

I studied the man I had made the sergeant of my guard. He was handsome, tall, and strong. Over his strong jaw, he had a carefully trimmed goatee and under his guard's hat, he had pulled his dark hair back into a short tail. Though he didn't lift his eyes to me, by the moonlight I could see sincerity in them.

"What else does your uncle have to say to me?" I asked.

"It is about you challenging the Taewŏn-gun on treaties with the Japanese. My uncle agrees that the Taewŏn-gun is too close to the Japanese. But he bids that you do not challenge the Taewŏn-gun on affairs with the Japanese. He says it would be very dangerous to do so." The guard shuffled his feet. "And," he said, "my uncle says pray that you have a son, a prince for the country."

A son. A prince. A cloud slid over the moon, making everything dark. My back was sore and heartburn was coming on. I was tired and needed to go to bed and sleep a few hours before the morning came. I sighed. "Guard, tell your uncle that you have delivered your message. And give him this message from me: I am near the end of my pregnancy, and for the time I will not challenge my father-in-law. But we must be firm with the Japanese. I plan to push my agenda again once the baby is born, and I expect his help."

My guard bowed low again. "Yes, Majesty. I will deliver your message."

"Good. Go now, Kyung-jik," I said.

He didn't leave at once. In the darkness of my courtyard, his eyes nearly met mine and he said, "Majesty, Han-sook or I might come for you at any time, and when we do, I beg you, do not question us or hesitate in the slightest."

I immediately understood what he was saying and why. I looked at his handsome face. "Well," I said, "we will see if the time comes."

It was the middle of winter, and I was in my study when the labor pains first came. It was earlier than the doctor had predicted, and I was concerned that the baby hadn't fully grown inside me. I tried to ignore the pains, but they grew worse, and then something inside me gave way and a slime ran down my legs and onto the floor. I called out for Han-sook, who came running. I told her the baby was coming, and her eyes grew wide. "I'll call for the doctor at once!" she said.

Five minutes later, Han-sook had moved me into my bedchamber. She and the servants laid a mat on the floor and covered it with several silk sheets. Han-sook kneeled off to one side, barking orders at the servants to fetch water and cool cloths for my forehead. The doctor rushed in dressed in his black robe. He rolled me onto my back and placed cushions under my shoulders. He stripped away my clothes from the waist down. He had me spread my legs wide. He ordered a servant to get hot water and to make a brew of tea and herbs to ease my pain.

The doctor sat on the mat cross-legged between my legs, and behind his thick glasses, he watched for the baby to come.

Soon the pains were more frequent and more intense. Each time they came, I grabbed at the silk cover and arched my back. Han-sook wrung her hands and stared at me with a most worried expression, as if she thought I would die at any moment. The doctor stared between my legs and declared, "It is going as it should."

After some time, the pains were almost constant and each was harder than the previous one. The sweat-soaked sheets clung to my back, and I grew tired. My back ached terribly. Han-sook cooled my forehead with a wet towel and barked at a servant to get clean ones. Finally the doctor said, "The baby comes! I see the head. Push, Majesty. Push hard!"

I raised my back and pushed as hard as I could. The doctor announced that the head was out. He reached inside me and turned the baby, "for the shoulders," he said. "Push again, Majesty." I did and in one great, pain-filled thrust, a gush slid out of me. The doctor caught it in a blanket and quickly wrapped it up. The baby was quiet for a while, and I was afraid it was not alive. I was about to ask the doctor if it was okay, but then it let out a tiny squeak and whine. The doctor lifted a corner of the blanket and looked inside. "As I predicted, Majesty," he said, raising his chin, "it is a boy."

Han-sook looked like she would faint with joy. "A boy!" she exclaimed with a hand on her chest. "It is a prince!"

I lay back and closed my eyes. A wave of relief spread over me. I had made a prince for the king and for my country. I had finally done my duty. Now, the king would not take a second wife, and we would take over the country and rule as king and queen.

And I had a son! A baby to take care of, to be proud of, to love. Until now, I hadn't thought how I would feel about being a mother. But as the baby squirmed under the blanket, and as he squeaked and moaned, he touched my heart. I instantly loved him. My son! My baby! My child!

"Give him to me," I said to the doctor. "I want to see him." The doctor gave me the bundle. I lifted a corner and looked at my son's face. He was red, wrinkly, and wet. I half laughed, half cried at the funny creature in my arms. He craned his neck as if he was working out the kinks from being trapped for all those months in my womb. He wriggled, opened his mouth, and let out a squeaky cry. I brought him close and rested his head on my breast. He stopped crying and wriggling. Soon, he was asleep, warm against my chest.

I cannot say how I felt at that moment. Though I had read hundreds of books over the years and knew several languages, I didn't have the words. It was as if my baby and I were one thing; the yin and yang, earth and sky, fire and ice, mother and child. It was perfect, more than the poems in *Songs of Dragons Flying to Heaven*, more than a spring day in my uncle's bamboo garden. The soul of the tiny thing breathing softly against my breast spoke to me and made my spirit soar. And for the first time, I knew that this was what my mother had meant when she said I must serve the spirits of our children and our children's children. Right then, I resolved that I would love and protect this child so that someday he could be a strong king.

The doctor said, "Majesty, if you please, we should inspect the baby." He held out his hands.

I gave my baby to him. Underneath the blanket, the baby jerked as he left my arms. He moaned and squeaked again. The doctor set the bundle on the mat and unwrapped my son from the blanket. The baby lay naked before us, tiny and red. The doctor rolled him onto his stomach. Suddenly Han-sook gasped and brought her hands to her mouth. A servant did, too. The doctor looked at the baby, and then he raised his eyes to me.

"What is it?" I breathed.

The doctor turned the baby to show me what they were looking at. On my son's lower back was a bulbous, purple sac. I looked at the doctor, who stared back at me. "It is the spine defect," he said.

"What does it mean?" I whispered.

The doctor rolled the baby on its back. The baby jerked with his torso and arms, but his legs didn't move. The doctor ran his fingernail hard along the bottom of the baby's foot. The baby didn't move his legs.

"No!" I cried. "No!"

Han-sook barked at the servants to leave, which they all quickly did. The doctor lifted the baby from the floor and wrapped a blanket around it. "What are you doing?" I demanded.

"Majesty," he said, "a child with this condition will not see five days. I must take him now."

I pushed myself up on my elbows. Spikes of pain stabbed at me from between my legs, but I pushed them aside. "No!" I said. "Give him to me."

The doctor held on to the baby. He shook his head. "Majesty, this is best."

"Give him to me or I will have your head!" I shouted. The doctor nodded and gave my son to me. I pressed him to my breast. The baby moaned and fell quiet again. "Help me to my bed," I demanded. As I clutched my son, Han-sook and the doctor lifted me onto my bed and put cushions around me for support. When they finally found a position where my pain was bearable, I said, "Leave me now."

The doctor and Han-sook left my bedchamber, and I was alone with my son. I ran my hand over his legs, and they didn't respond to my touch. I pinched his thigh hard, wanting desperately for him to feel the pain. Again, he didn't respond. I brought his mouth to my breast and teased his lips. He pouted, but did not open his mouth.

And as he slept, I cried. I tried to stifle my crying so I wouldn't disturb my baby, but my chest heaved and sobs escaped my throat. My son slept through it, innocent of his terrible fate, or perhaps at peace with it. It was the spine disease that destroys a newborn's nerves. First the legs, then the torso. Then, death. Five days, the doctor said. Five short days.

I held him tight as the seconds and minutes and hours rushed by.

They came for him in the morning of the fifth day. It was two guards from the Taewŏn-gun's staff, and a tearful Han-sook let them in. I had not left my bed and had not let go of my baby since he was born. No one had visited me, save Han-sook, who brought me tea that I drank, and rice that I refused. I had Han-sook keep the doors closed and forbade her to light the lamps. I was grateful that she never once asked me to give my baby to the doctor.

My son was still alive that morning. He had suckled every day, though each day was weaker than before. He no longer fussed or cried, almost as if he knew it was useless for him to protest his fate. Or perhaps he didn't have the energy for it.

The guards bowed at the door and came to the bed. They said they had orders from the Taewŏn-gun to take the baby. I protested and ordered them to leave. The guards said that the orders had the king's blessing. And so they took my baby from me.

At first I tried to resist them. I truly did. But I didn't have the strength to fight two strong men with orders from the Taewŏn-gun and the king. And inside, I knew I had to let them take my son. He was dying as the doctor had said he would. Though I would always love him, I would never again hold him close, feel his quick breathing against my body, suckle him at my breast.

I let them take my son. And when they did, I did not cry. Instead, I rolled to my side and embraced the fading warmth of him.

EIGHTEEN

I cannot say how many days or weeks I stayed in my bedchamber with the walls closed to the sunlight and the lamps unlit. Perhaps it was more than a month. I ate very little and refused to let anyone see me, save Han-sook. Every day, she brought tea and broth and encouraged me to eat. She changed my linens and bathed me by hand. On warm days, she opened the wall to the courtyard to let in fresh air. I never once went out. We didn't talk about what happened outside of my bedchamber, and we didn't talk about the baby. She constantly asked if she could do anything for me, and I always said no.

Inside my dark bedchamber, the spirit of my dead son haunted me. He was everywhere—as a baby lying next to me in bed, as a boy playing on the mat near my bed, as a man in the dark corners staring at me. I had trapped my son's spirit inside me because I had kept him with me those five days. So I ordered shamans to come and set my son's spirit free, so it could go to heaven. The shamans came and prayed, lit incense, and chanted as I lay in bed with my silks tight around me. After five days, my son still haunted me and I sent the shamans away.

Late one night I lay half-awake in my bed, numb with hopelessness. I believed that I would die in my bedchamber, and truly, I wanted to. Then a sound came from my study. At first I thought it was the

Taewŏn-gun's guards coming to take me away or perhaps to kill me. I almost hoped it was. The sound came again, and I listened more closely this time. It sounded like crying. I thought it was the spirit of my dead son. Weak and confused, I crawled out from under my blankets and put on a robe. I lit a candle and took it to the door of my study. I peeked inside but didn't see anything. As I turned to go back to bed, I heard the crying again. It sounded like the wailing of my mother those last days before she threw herself into the Han River. I lifted the candle to the room, and it cast long shadows against the walls. I thought I saw a ghost move next to the tapestry with the two-headed dragon. I took an unsteady step inside the study. "Ummah?" I whispered. "Mother?" The sound of my voice fell silent inside the room. I went closer to the tapestry. I lifted the candle to the dragon. Its eyes glowed in the candlelight with a piercing stare, as if it was trying to tell me something. Its claws reached for me, and its tongues seemed to move up and down. I had never seen it like that before, and it scared me. I took a step back, but the dragon continued to stare and its tongues still flicked. I couldn't tell if it was mocking me, pleading with me, or sending me a warning.

"What is it?" I shouted at it. "What do you want from me?"

I heard voices saying, "One Korea." I covered my ears to silence them, but they did not go away. I looked at the tapestry and I decided that I hated it. Why should I be the one to speak for the spirit of Korea? I never wanted to be queen. I never wanted the responsibility to bear a prince for the king and the country. Let the king's concubine be the queen and give the country a prince. I no longer wanted the heartache.

Still the dragon stared. The voices shrieked, "One Korea! One Korea!" I tried to shake them out. Then I lunged for the tapestry and clawed it off the wall. I crumpled it in my hands and threw it on the floor. I stomped on it with my bare feet and kicked it to the side. "Go!" I screamed. "Leave me alone!"

Leave me alone. I remembered the day my mother said the same thing to her orchids. I knew my mother was insane then, and as my own words echoed off the walls, I thought now that I might be. I stood over the tapestry breathing hard, trying to understand what I had just done. The voices went quiet.

"Majesty!" someone said from the other side of my study. "What is the matter?"

In the shadows, Han-sook stood in her nightclothes, wringing her hands.

"Burn it," I said, pointing to the tapestry. "I do not care what it says I must do. I never want to see it again."

"But, my lady," Han-sook pleaded, "you love that tapestry."

As I stood above the tapestry staring blankly at Han-sook, I was completely confused. At that moment, I wasn't sure why I was there, in my study with the tapestry crumpled at my feet. I thought I might be walking and talking in my sleep and all I needed to do was wake up from this nightmare and everything would be all right. But I knew it was not a dream.

I sighed and leaned heavily against the wall where the tapestry had been. Han-sook ran to my side. "You are not well, Majesty."

"I think you are right," I said, and I let my lady's maid lead me back to my bed.

As Han-sook arranged the blankets around me, I looked at her and said, "I must leave Gyeongbok Palace. This place haunts me. Tomorrow we will move to Deoksu Palace, where I will be safe. Tell Kyung-jik. I want to leave in the morning."

Han-sook nodded. "Yes, Majesty. I believe a change will be good for you. I will make the arrangements." When she had placed my blankets just so, she sat on the floor next to my bed and watched over me as I slipped into a restless sleep.

Deoksu Palace was nothing like Gyeongbok. It was not far away, nearer to the Han River, and much like Gyeongbok before it was rebuilt.

Years earlier, several palace buildings had burned down and now there were only a few structures left, none nearly as grand as the new ones in Gyeongbok. But I chose to come here primarily because the Taewŏn-gun never visited it. He preferred his new, extravagant quarters in Gyeongbok or spending quiet days in the Changdeok East Palace old gardens when he wanted to get away from Gyeongbok's comings and goings.

It was midday when my procession arrived at Deoksu. We had walked through Seoul, my royal palanquin flanked by eight guards, led by Kyung-jik. Nearly my entire staff followed in wagons and on foot, thirty people in all. Two carts carried my wardrobe, books, bat chest, and desk from my study. Three more carried supplies from Gyeongbok—food, clothes, and necessities for my staff. As we walked past, people on the streets bowed. I watched them through the curtains of my palanquin, and wondered if under their breaths they were cursing me for making such a sickly prince that he had to be killed.

My staff had warned Deoksu that I was coming, and they were ready for me when we arrived. Unlike the grand new gate at Gyeongbok, Deoksu's gate was old and small. The eunuchs had to lower my palanquin to fit underneath it. Inside, there was a rank of guards and the palace staff standing in a line. They bowed at the waist when I entered the courtyard. I stepped out of my palanquin, and Han-sook and Kyung-jik helped me into my new quarters. The queen's quarters consisted of only two rooms—a main anteroom and, behind it, a bedchamber. It was small and dark and smelled musty. Han-sook followed me in. She apologized for the palace's disgraceful state and promised that they would quickly make it appropriate for me. In my weakened condition, the trip had made me tired and I said I wanted to rest. Han-sook led me inside the bedchamber. It was less than half the size of my bedchamber in Gyeongbok. There were no paintings on the walls or fancy Chinese chairs and tables. It reminded me of my tiny room in the House of Gamgodang. The palace staff had put fresh silks on the bed and had opened the wall to the small courtyard to let in fresh air. Small and unadorned though it was, I felt safe there.

As Han-sook helped me into bed, I said, "Give me some time to sleep, but not long. I must get to work."

"You will have plenty of time to do your work, Majesty," Han-sook said gently. She smiled at me and left. As I lay on the bed, I could feel the place where my dead child rested against my chest for those five precious days. I tingled where his lips suckled my breast. I squeezed my eyes closed, and with effort, I pushed him away and collapsed into a deep sleep.

When I awoke, the sun outside the courtyard was at its early-morning angle. I had slept nearly an entire day. When I got out of bed, I felt better. I was hungry. I thought about scolding Han-sook for letting me sleep so long, but I realized she was doing what she thought was best for me.

"Han-sook!" I called.

My lady's maid came running into my bedchamber wringing her hands. "Majesty," she said, "are you all right?"

"You let me sleep too long," I said. "But I think it is good that you did." Han-sook lowered her head and smiled.

I went to the anteroom as Han-sook followed. There, they had set up my desk and bat chest. On the wall behind the desk hung the tapestry with the two-headed dragon. I remembered how the dragon had glared at me in the middle of the night, demanding that I listen to it. I remembered how I thought its tongues moved. I remembered the voices crying, "One Korea."

"Han-sook," I said, "I ordered you to burn that tapestry."

Han-sook said, "I'm sorry, Majesty. I did not hear your command. Shall I have it burned now?"

I looked at the dragon. I wasn't sure how I felt about it now. I didn't know if the thing was my tormentor or my guide. Perhaps it was both. I sensed that if I'd had the tapestry destroyed, it would have haunted me for the rest of my life.

I didn't answer Han-sook. I went to my desk and sat on the cushion. There in that small, musty room, with a full day's rest, the spirit of my dead son did not haunt me. But I was weak and my head wasn't clear. I needed to do something to get my mind straight. So I ordered Han-sook to get my books for me.

I spent the next several months in my study in Deoksu reading, trying to forget that I had failed to give my husband a son and my country a prince. But no matter how hard I tried, I could not forget my son. He was always with me, and after a while, I realized he always would be. I sat under the two-headed dragon trying not to let it drive me crazy like the spirits had done to my mother. Each time I looked at it, I wondered why it hadn't helped me bear a healthy prince. I went to bed each night afraid that the two-headed dragon would wake me and torment me as it had done before, but it never did.

During those months, I didn't ask what happened at Gyeongbok Palace. I assumed they did not miss me and, in fact, were glad that I had decided to live in self-imposed exile in Deoksu. One day news came that the king's concubine, Gwi-in, was pregnant and that if she had a son, the Taewŏn-gun would make him the crown prince and elevate Gwi-in, a daughter of the Yi clan, to princess consort. This news threw me back into depression. I didn't feel like reading anymore. I ate less and slept long hours. I lay in bed and pictured the statuesque Gwi-in with her belly growing large and her delivering a healthy son. I pictured Gojong, my husband, beaming with pride that he had finally produced a proper heir to the throne. I hated the pretty concubine and the healthy baby growing inside her.

One fall afternoon I put on a robe and went out to the courtyard. The courtyard was small and quaint with only a few pots and statues here and there. It reminded me of the courtyard at the House of Gamgodang. At one end, Han-sook had placed an orchid in the sunlight that was now in bloom. By chance, it was the same as my mother's favorite—cream-colored with a blue and pink center and a long yellow pistil. I went to it and smelled it. Its perfume filled my senses, and for a moment, it brought me home to my mother's garden. I pictured her before she got sick, gently pinching off the orchids' spent blossoms, singing softly to herself. My parents were older—nearly thirty years—when I was born. They had been married over thirteen years before I arrived. Thirteen years without a child. I had never thought about that before. But it must have been true that they, like me, had tried for years to have a baby. Perhaps my mother had lost a child, just as I had. Perhaps she had lost more than one.

As I smelled the flower and admired its soft white petals and bright-yellow pistil, I realized that I could not let the death of my son destroy me. Yes, I had lost a child, my son. He would always have a place in my heart, and it would take effort to leave him behind, but I couldn't stay in the dark forever. Perhaps it was what the two-headed dragon had tried to tell me that night in my bedchamber. I had a responsibility to my country. I was the queen and I must be the queen.

I called for Han-sook. She came into the courtyard and said, "Yes, Majesty?"

"Have the servants draw a bath and fetch my day-robe," I said. "Get me something to eat, too."

"Yes, my lady," Han-sook said, and she scurried off.

A few hours later, I had bathed and my maids had braided my hair and helped me into my day-robe. Servants had brought barley tea, rice and bulgogi, kimchi, and sweet dduk. I was surprised at how good it all tasted and ate everything they brought. Han-sook ordered the servants to fetch more, but I told her I'd had enough.

Over the next several days and weeks, I grew stronger. I ate and slept well. I tended to the orchids in my courtyard. I read books in the morning and took strolls in the afternoon. I thought about my years as queen. I thought about my decision to be a dragon queen. I thought of my dead son. I thought of the sons and daughters I would still have someday. I wanted them to have a strong mother. I remembered my lost uncle. I had promised my aunt I would find him, yet I still did not know where he was. And I thought of Korea. Its king was weak, and the Taewŏn-gun was interested only in staying in power—so much so that he was willing to align with the Japanese barbarians. My children—dead and unborn—needed me to be a dragon queen. And so did my husband and my country.

One fall morning when the wind promised change, I went to my study and called for Han-sook. "Fetch Kyung-jik and come back here," I commanded. "We have important matters to attend to."

"Yes, Majesty," she said, and hurried to find Kyung-jik.

A few minutes later, Kyung-jik and Han-sook stood before me as I sat at my desk. I had opened the wall to the central courtyard to let the cool fall air sweep away the staleness inside the room. It was a bright day, and the fresh air smelled sweet and clean. My sergeant of the guard looked handsome and strong in his uniform. My lady's maid, dressed in her hanbok, looked mature and composed. They had been loyal and true over the years, and I prayed that I could trust them now. With what I planned to do, if they proved to be disloyal, it would cost me my life.

"Sit," I said, "and listen to me well." They both sat on cushions in front of my desk. "I believe the palace wants to take my crown, but I will not let them. I have lived here in exile long enough. It is time for me to take my rightful place again on the throne."

"Yes, Majesty," they both said in unison.

I continued. "I want the palace to think I'll be content to stay here, so be careful what you say. There will be spies at every station."

"Yes, Majesty," they both said again.

"Kyung-jik, I want ten of your best men whom you can trust. Train them well and put them at the gate and around my quarters. They must be on guard every hour of the day. Then get word to your uncle, Minister Kim. Have him arrange a meeting with me and the leaders of the clans. It must be held in secret, somewhere away from here."

"Yes, Majesty," he said.

"Han-sook," I said, addressing my lady's maid directly, "send someone to the House of Gamgodang to bring my aunt; her lady's maid, Eun-ji; and my uncle's valet, Mr. Yang, here to live at Deoksu. I fear for their safety. Then arrange a meeting with the king. Away from here, at the royal tombs at Donggureung. Tell him he should come without Lady Min or the Taewŏn-gun. Tell him I want to talk to him about our dead son."

"Ycs, Majcsty," shc said.

I stood from my desk and looked out on the palace grounds. "Finally," I said, "as of this moment, no one is to mention my son to me. Ever. If they do, I will banish them to the streets. Is that understood?"

"Yes, Majesty," they said.

I turned to them. "It is important that you do your jobs well, and be on high alert. We are all in danger," I said. I gave them both a serious look. Then I said, "I plan to impeach the Taewŏn-gun and take over the government."

NINETEEN

It was a long journey from Deoksu Palace to the royal tombs at Donggureung, and even longer from Gyeongbok. I chose it in part for that reason, thinking that if Gojong agreed to meet me there, he would bring a small entourage and no one important from the palace. I also chose it because it was the final resting place of King Taejo, the first king of the Chosŏn Dynasty.

I wasn't sure my husband would accept my invitation. A long trip would take him away from the palace for an entire day, and he disliked leaving the comfort of his lavish quarters in Gyeongbok. I hadn't seen him since before our son was born, and I wasn't sure how he felt about me after I had failed to give him a healthy son. But though we were not close as husband and wife, we had shared something over the previous few years—a passion and a connection. I hoped that our shared frustrations would bring us together at Donggureung.

So when the king's courier delivered the message saying my husband would meet me, I was relieved. I truly wanted to talk to my husband about our son. And without the king, I would never be able to challenge the Taewŏn-gun. Then they would toss me aside and I would live in exile, not a dragon queen, not even a stone queen. I wouldn't be a queen at all.

On the day I was to meet the king, my eunuchs carried my palanquin nearly all morning on the journey to Donggureung. The tombs were deep in the hills east of Seoul. It was a lovely day, not hot or humid. Lazy white clouds drifted across the sky above grass-roofed country houses. In the distance, farmers harvested grains as their livestock grazed on the season's last greens.

I could tell my porters were tired when we got to the tombs. They jostled and tipped my palanquin more than they should have. I had them lower my palanquin at the simple wooden gate. The head porter lifted the curtain and I stepped out. All around, the forested hills were beginning to turn to their fall colors. Through the gate, a stone path led to a small, single-roof temple with red beams and a tile roof. Beyond the temple, a hill led to nine *neung* tombs for past kings and queens. Covered in closely trimmed grass, the tomb-mounds were ten feet high and surrounded by stone statues of guards and animals. Squat balustrades circled some of the tombs.

With Kyung-jik and two of his men behind me, I walked through the gate, past the temple and up the hill. I went to the tomb of Taejo. I had been here years earlier with Gojong, Lady Min, and the Taewŏn-gun, and I felt the ancient king's spirit then. Now, as I beheld the grand tomb of Chosŏn's first king, with its stone statues, columns, and totems, the spirit was strong in me again. I tried to hear what it was saying, but I could not.

I looked back down the hill and saw the king's entourage slowly making its way along the road to the tombs. His entourage was smaller than usual. Nevertheless, it was impressive. At the lead was a horseman carrying the king's pennant. Twelve skilled eunuchs carried his palanquin, and a dozen guards rode in dazzling raiment, many on stately Datong horses. A cart filled with provisions and pulled by two draft horses followed behind. I was relieved to see that the Taewŏn-gun's palanquin was not part of the procession.

The king's retinue stopped at the gate, and the porters skillfully lowered his palanquin to the ground. The king stepped out. He wore a loose white robe over his short frame and a squat black hat on his head. He looked around and spotted me. As he made his way up the hill followed by two guards, the rest of his entourage began unpacking the cart and setting up a small tent and picnic for us.

Beads of sweat had formed on his forehead when my husband reached me in front of King Taejo's tomb. He took out a kerchief and wiped away the sweat. I bowed lower than usual. "My king," I said, "it is good to see you."

As I stood in front of him, I couldn't tell if he felt the same about seeing me. He looked tired, more than he should have from a three-hour junket. He looked sad, too. His skin was pale, and there were deep circles around his eyes. His goatee was now full like a man's, but it was messy and untrimmed.

"Leave us," I said to the guards. Kyung-jik and his men left at once, but the king's guards stayed. He looked at his men and waved his hand. They turned and followed Kyung-jik down the hill.

"I was told you were sick," he said.

I nodded. "Yes, it is true. I was in despair about our son."

"Yes, well," Gojong said, and looked away. In his face, I saw that our son's death hurt him, too. I hadn't thought that it would. But of course, it made sense. The sickly child we had conceived reinforced the image that he was weak and unfit to rule the country.

I lowered my head. "I am sorry I did not make a proper son for you. It broke my heart that he was born that way. I was not a good wife."

Gojong continued to look away. "Gwi-in is due to give birth any day now. My father says if it is a son, it will be the *wonja*, the king's first son. Then my father will proclaim him to be the crown prince and Gwi-in princess consort. She will make a good princess consort." He turned and lifted his chin at me.

Anger swelled inside me. If I didn't act quickly, if I couldn't convince my husband to stay with me, the Taewŏn-gun would banish me from the palace or perhaps have me killed. And just like Gojong, I, too, wanted to prove that I was worthy of the crown they had placed on my head. If they banished me from the palace, I would never have that chance.

I pushed my anger aside and said, "Will you walk with me?"

Gojong nodded, and we began to stroll along King Taejo's tomb. "Thank you for coming here to meet me," I said. "I thought this was a fitting place for us to talk. Great kings and queens are buried here. I can feel their spirits. Can you?"

Gojong looked at the mounds and then at me. "These are just stones and hills," he said. "I don't know about spirits."

"They speak to me," I said, "although I do not understand what they are telling me. I wanted to come here to listen to them. I had hoped that you would hear them, too."

"Is that what those books teach you? How to speak to ghosts so they can tell you what to do?" The king shook his head. "Maybe I should read them, too."

We'd come to the end of the tomb and turned the corner. The warm midday sun was on our backs. The spirit of Taejo was whispering in my ear. Now, this close to the great king's tomb, its voice was clearer. "You are the spirit of One Korea," I thought I heard it say.

I held my eyes forward as we walked on. I had a determination that I'd never had before. It was as if King Taejo was lifting me up, urging me on. Finally I said, "You and I will make another son. I promise he will be healthy and strong."

"How could you know?" Gojong asked.

"I think it might be what the spirits are telling me. And when our son is born, *he* will be the crown prince. You will pronounce him so because *you* will be the king."

"What do you mean?" he said. "I'm already the king."

"Are you? If so, why does your father say who will be the crown prince? Why does he make the decisions for the country while you rot in your quarters with your pipe, wine, and women?"

The king sneered. "If Gwi-in gives me a son, everyone will know that I am the king."

"Will they?" I said. "Will Gwi-in help you so that you do not have to depend on your father? No. She is your father's tool to keep you in your place."

The king stopped walking. I had never before talked to him this way, and he was clearly flustered. "You should not say things like that to me," he said. "I am your husband and king."

I turned to him. "Then *be* my husband and king," I said. "Change your ways and stand tall. You must take control from your father. You have told me you wanted to do so. Do it now. Do it alongside me."

Gojong sighed and looked at his feet. In his white robe and short black hat, he looked small and weak, not like a king at all. "I don't think I can. It is not in me to challenge my father."

"It is in *me*," I said tapping my chest. "I can do it for both of us. If we do not take over, your father will drive me from the palace and will keep you in your quarters, nothing more than a puppet while he plots with the Japanese. Together, we can become the *true* king and queen and create a strong nation. They gave us our crowns. Now we must take them."

Gojong lifted his face to me. "I have tried to change my ways," he said, his eyes pleading with me to understand. "I did for a time when you were pregnant. I thought the prince should have a strong father. But when the baby died . . ." He looked at his feet again.

In his face was the pain of our lost son. I had the same pain during the months I spent in the darkness of my bedchamber at Gyeongbok. I had it still. I touched his arm. "We will make another son. But we can only do it if we are together. I will help you, but you must help me, too."

My husband shook his head. "I don't know if I can. I've never been able to challenge my father."

"You don't have to," I said. "We will have the clans do it. They will support us in an impeachment of the Taewŏn-gun. Your father's taxes are crushing them, and they fear the dangerous game he plays with Japan. With their support, we can take over the government. It will be a peaceful transition."

"What about the Japanese?" Gojong asked. "They will not stand by and let us take over."

I nodded. "I will deal with the Japanese," I said.

We had circled Taejo's tomb and now stood where we had started. I turned to the king. "Do not tell anyone about this, not even Lady Min. Your mother would support us in this to regain her stature in the palace. But I do not trust her adviser, Mister Euno. He doesn't work for her. He spies for your father, but he doesn't work for him, either. He is a Kokugaku scholar and believes that Japan should rule all of Asia. I suspect that he is an agent for the emperor of Japan."

"I never did like him," the king said.

"So will you join me?" I asked. "Will you help me take control of the government so you can be a proper king?"

"I do want to be a proper king," Gojong said simply.

"Then you must also give up your pipe and wine and lazy ways. You cannot be a proper king if you are ruled by them."

Gojong let out a snort. "I know what I have to do," he said. "Just be sure that you don't get us both killed."

I nodded and looked out over the forest surrounding Donggureung. "Yes, my king," I said. "I will be careful."

We walked back down the hill and through the gate where, under a white tent, our servants had spread a table of food and drink. When we got there, one of Gojong's servants bowed to the king and motioned that something was ready for him inside his palanquin. Gojong raised a hand and shook his head, and the servant bowed away.

And under the warm sun, we sat together and ate our lunch as husband and wife.

The Taewŏn-gun's impeachment depended on the clans' support. Although the yangban didn't trust me, they absolutely despised the regent because of his policies and taxes. The clans had had enough and wanted the Taewŏn-gun out. I prayed that they would support my plan to remove him from power. If I was wrong and they supported the regent, the palace would probably execute me for treason.

I met with them in secret, in a farmer's home late at night. Minister Kim had arranged the meeting. Kyung-jik helped me escape Deoksu Palace unseen through a back gate. I was dressed in a court lady's robe and Kyung-jik wore peasant's clothes as we navigated the narrow streets. The house was a short distance outside the city, not far from Mount Bukhansan. When I went inside the low, dark room, the clan leaders stood and bowed. There were five in all—heads of the Min, Ch'oe, Pak, Kim, and Chung clans. I had met each of them before in official meetings or at palace dinners and celebrations. However, this was the first time I had met them all together, and it was the first time I had met them without the Taewŏn-gun present.

We sat on cushions, the five in a row in front of me. As lamps cast our shadows against the farmhouse walls, they listened as I presented my plan. I had to choose my words carefully because I did not want to appear ambitious or disrespectful of my father-in-law. I said only that the king was going to assume control of the government and that we wanted the clans' support. I told them that the king, inexperienced as he was, would still have the Taewŏn-gun's advice, and that I would advise him, too.

Jae-kwon Pak nodded at me. He was tall and thin and had a long neck. He sat with his back to the fire and his face in darkness. "We cannot bear the taxes the government has imposed on us," he said in a reedy voice. "Will you advise the king to reduce them?"

"Yes, Jae-kwon, the taxes you pay are high," I said. "They have hurt members of my own clan as well. I will advise the king to lower them for all of us."

The head of the Kim clan, Yun-sik Kim, leaned forward, making his shadow grow large on the wall. He was elderly and had a long white goatee. His eyes were watery and gray from decades of reading Confucius. "What about your reforms, Majesty?" he asked. "You have a great interest in the outside world. We fear that you will bring strange ways to Korea."

I shook my head. "I understand your concern, Yun-sik. I believe we must keep pace with the rest of the world. But you are right. We cannot lose what we have, and I will be careful what I push for so that we stay true to who we are."

Chul-son Chung spoke up. He was a large man, and his robe stretched tight across his stomach. The fire was full on him, making his face look orange. "Will you appoint only members of the Min clan in official positions?" he asked in a gravelly voice. "Or will other clans share control of the government?"

"That is an excellent question, Chul-son," I said with a nod. "I believe that the rivalry between our clans must end. We must be one nation, not divided and at war, clan against clan. Therefore, I will appoint the most able men no matter what clan they are from. They must, however, be men we can trust."

Then Ik-hyun Ch'oe cleared his throat. One of Korea's most esteemed Confucian scholars and an important adviser to the palace, Master Ch'oe was the most powerful man in the room. He opposed the Taewŏn-gun's rule, often disagreeing openly with the regent on domestic policy. Ik-hyun was younger than the others, and his beard was not gray. He wore the blue robe of a wealthy man. He sat aside the fire, putting him half in shadows. "Will you push for independence or will you keep us a Chinese protectorate?" he asked with penetrating eyes. "I do not trust Empress Cixi, but I trust Emperor Meiji even less."

"You are wise, Master Ch'oe," I said. "I believe we should strive for independence, but we must be clever about it. We should not trust, either. Both must be contained by the other. Now, Japan is the aggressor. We have reports that they are modernizing their military. I will only align with China to keep Japan at bay."

Ik-hyun said, "What you are asking will put us all in danger. The Taewŏn-gun and his supporters will try to kill us. However, if you agree to stay neutral and keep the foreigners out, if you agree to lower our taxes, if you agree that all clans should share power, I will support your move to impeach the Taewŏn-gun." With this, all the leaders nodded and agreed to my plan. They said they would request a meeting with the Taewŏn-gun as soon as possible to ask him to step aside. When I stood to leave, they bowed. Pleased with myself, I joined Kyung-jik and we made our way through the night and snuck back inside Deoksu Palace.

While the clans arranged their meeting with the Taewŏn-gun, I continued to stay quiet in Deoksu Palace. I didn't attend important state meetings or set foot in Gyeongbok, even for the formal affairs that I typically hosted. When Kyung-jik reported that the palace passed a new law or issued a decree, I made no comment even if I disagreed with it. When Gwi-in gave birth to the wonja, the Taewŏn-gun named him Crown Prince Wan-hwa. He even threw a party for the new prince and elevated Gwi-in to princess consort. This was an awful slight to me, and it hurt my stomach. I vowed that someday, I would put Gwi-in—the full-figured beauty whom my husband had an eye for—in her place. But for the time, I stayed quiet. I didn't send messages to anyone in Gyeongbok, not even my husband. I read poetry and studied the old classics. I spent hours in my courtyard tending to my orchids. I wanted the Taewŏn-gun to think I had placed myself in exile at Deoksu for my failure to provide the country with a prince.

Finally, as fall yielded to winter, Kyung-jik reported that at a grand meeting at Gyeongbok Palace, Ik-hyun Ch'oe, along with the heads of the other clans, had demanded that the Taewŏn-gun step down. Since all the clans stood against him and the king declared he was ready to take his place at the head of the government, the regent could not object. He agreed that Gojong had come of age and was now the head of state and that he, the regent would be an adviser to his son. Of course, the Taewŏn-gun assumed that his son could not handle the difficult task of running the government. He knew that the king didn't know anything about politics, economics, or foreign affairs. The Taewŏn-gun had only agreed to step aside because the king would need his father to run the country exactly as he had before.

And so he did—until one month later, when I returned to Gyeongbok Palace and took my place on the throne next to my husband.

TWENTY

The first thing I did when Gojong and I took control of the government was to find my uncle. My aunt, Eun-ji, and Mr. Yang, had come to live with me in Deoksu Palace, and I brought them with me to Gyeongbok. It had been over a year since the Taewŏn-gun's guards arrested my uncle, and my aunt was sick with worry for him. With the king and me now in charge of the palace guard, I promoted Kyung-jik to the rank of captain and tasked him with finding out where they had sent Chul-jo. A few days later, Kyung-jik reported to me that my uncle was alive, held prisoner on Tsushima Island in the strait between Korea and Japan. I ordered his release and directed that a ship go to Tsushima to bring him back to Seoul at once. The minister of foreign affairs reminded me that Tsushima was part of Japan and that "the dwarf barbarians to the east might refuse to allow our ship to land there." I sent the ship anyway with Kyung-jik and twenty soldiers on board and a letter from me saying that if any Japanese official blocked my efforts to free a member of the Korean royal family, I would personally take up the matter with Emperor Meiji. The ship sailed and two weeks later, my uncle walked through Gwanghwamun Gate and into the waiting arms of his most grateful wife.

Days later, after my uncle had settled into his new quarters at Gyeongbok, I sent for him. It was midafternoon when a guard showed him into my study. I'd had my staff return my quarters to exactly the way it was before I left for Deoksu Palace. My desk was in its place, and the tapestry with the two-headed dragon hung on the wall behind it. When Chul-jo came in bowing low, I sat high on a cushion at my desk. He was thinner than the last time I had seen him, and gray streaked his close-cropped hair and goatee. I directed him to sit in front of me.

"Are you well?" I asked.

He didn't raise his eyes to me as he had done before when he had helped me with my education. "I am, Majesty," he said.

"How did they treat you in Tsushima?"

My uncle smiled a little. "They are Japanese, Majesty. They think Koreans are dogs."

"Hmmm," I said. "Well, now you are here."

"Thank you, Majesty, for freeing me. I am glad to be back."

"You have heard that King Gojong and I have taken over the government?"

"Yes, Majesty, I have."

"Gojong still seeks advice from his father and doesn't always listen to me. But I will prevail."

"It is important that you do," my uncle said. "I fear that the Japanese are far ahead of us in modernizing and will use it to their advantage."

I nodded. "You have said that before and you might be right. I agree with the Taewŏn-gun that we must stand alone from China, but my father-in-law gives too much to Japan. The yangban want things to stay the way they are so that they can keep their position at the top of society. The military is arrogant and believes they can defend our land from invaders with modern weapons. The scholars refuse to lift their eyes from their books. Most here in the palace want to pursue a policy of isolationism."

"What about the merchants and peasants?" my uncle asked. "The throne represents all Koreans, not just the yangban. What is their opinion?"

I paused at his question. "I don't know," I said finally. I shook my head, stood, and faced the tapestry. "Uncle, I asked you here because I have a mission for you. I want you to go to Tokyo to see firsthand what is happening there. Then I want you to sail to America—San Francisco and New York. See if the reports we have of their fantastic inventions and powerful armies are true. Then come back here and tell me what you learned. Your trip will take months, maybe as long as a year. But we must know what we are up against."

My uncle nodded. "That is a good idea, Majesty. I am honored to do this for you."

"I will have the palace arrange for your travel. You must go in secret so as not to alarm the Chinese and Japanese. You will carry my royal seal. You must leave as soon as everything is ready."

"Yes, Majesty," he said.

"While you do that, I will make a secret trip to China to meet with Empress Cixi. I want to talk to the empress about Japan."

"That is wise, Majesty. The Chinese must be handled carefully."

I sat at my desk again and looked at my uncle, who still hadn't lifted his eyes to me. I was glad to have him back. He was one of the few people in my life I could confide in. "Uncle," I said, "tell me about my mother. The spirits that haunted her when she . . . died."

My uncle didn't answer right away. He looked at his hands as if they held the words to explain my mother's condition. Finally he said, "As I told you before you became queen, your mother was a spiritual woman. When she was young, the spirits filled her with light and let her see things others could not. But later, they haunted her and turned her dark."

"What happened? What made her change?"

My uncle continued to look at his hands. "Your father and your mother tried for years to have children. She was pregnant many times but wasn't always able to carry the baby all the way to the end. She gave birth to a few but they did not live long. Each time, your mother turned darker. You were the first—and only—to survive, but by then the spirits of all the children she had lost had started to silence the spirits she'd heard before."

What I suspected was true. Like me, my mother had known the loss of a child. Knowing this put my childhood into perspective—why my parents were older, why they cherished me as they did, how the spirits of her dead children had driven my mother mad. I prayed that the same would not happen to me.

My uncle finally looked at me. "Why do you ask these questions about your mother?"

I sighed. "While you were away, I lost a child. It was a very dark time for me. Its spirit haunts me. Others do, too. They are trying to speak to me, but I do not understand them. I pray they do not drive me mad like they did to my mother."

He gave me a gentle smile and said, "Perhaps the spirits will make you strong."

I smiled back at him. "Have safe travels, Chul-jo," I said.

Since the clan leaders had made good on their promise to impeach the Taewŏn-gun, I stayed true to my promise to replace government officials with members of their clans. Lady Min, seeing my new status as a way for her to get back into the government, tried to influence my decisions. She still wanted the Mins to overthrow the House of Yi, and promoted Mins who were loyal to her clan. I, however, was growing tired of the infighting between the clans. They had been fighting for hundreds of years, and I believed the clan system was something that kept us from becoming a unified nation. So, in spite of her petitions, I appointed people who I thought were most suited for the position no matter their clan affiliation.

I also didn't trust Lady Min because she relied on the advice of Mister Euno. The Japanese man with his Western-style suit and top hat didn't show himself much around Gyeongbok. He stayed behind the scenes, whispering advice in Lady Min's ear and, I suspected, in the Taewŏn-gun's ear, too. I still saw him practicing his martial arts movements early in the morning behind his quarters. Though he was now middle-aged, his military arts moves were those of a much younger man. Occasionally I sought Mister Euno's advice on protocol when a dignitary visited, but mostly, I kept him at a distance.

I also kept my promise to lower taxes on the yangban. It was not that I believed the taxes on the wealthy were too high. I did so because I needed their support and I knew that lowering their taxes would place them in my favor. The Taewŏn-gun fought me on this, and admittedly, I objected only half-heartedly and readily accepted compromises. And I was careful not to press for changes that would be too contentious. I wanted Gojong to feel comfortable in his new role as the head of government, and I didn't want to give my father-in-law a reason to fight with me. Someday I would have to make bold moves, but for the time being, I wanted peace.

Even so, I knew that the Taewŏn-gun worked behind the scenes to steer the country in the direction he thought it should go. He often left Gyeongbok for days, saying he was resting at the East Palace or visiting relatives somewhere outside of Seoul. Once, one of my palace watchers reported that he saw Mister Euno go with the Taewŏn-gun when he left early in the morning. Then I knew that my father-in-law was secretly meeting with the Japanese.

During this time, my relationship with Gojong started to grow into something more than a man and a woman trying to give the country a prince. I could tell the king was making an effort to stop drinking and using opium. It was a struggle for him, and there were times I saw that he had fallen back into his habits. Still, he was trying, and for the first time since I'd become his lawful wife, I began to respect him. When he tried, he paid attention in our afternoon meetings, although his attention often faded well before we were done. And when it was the right time of month, he and I tried to make a son. After each time, I prayed that we had made a baby again, a son, a prince for our people. But month after month, my bleeding returned and when I told him about it, Gojong would turn me away.

Several months after the king and I had settled into our roles as heads of government, I set out for Peking with a dozen guards led by Kyung-jik, eunuch porters, and a secretary. Only a few trusted advisers knew about my voyage to meet with China's dowager empress so as not to alarm the Japanese. We boarded a boat that would take us down the Han River, across the Yellow Sea to the Chinese seaport of Tianjin. The boat was a three-masted junk with red winglike sails and a menacing-looking dragon for a masthead. The junk wasn't the largest ship in our navy, but it was one of the fastest, and captained by Korea's most skilled naval officer. They set up quarters for me in the forecastle. Inside there was a desk, a large bed, and a chair that faced a porthole. At first it amused me that they bolted everything down, but this was my first long voyage at sea, so I wondered and worried why they felt the bolts were necessary. They lashed my palanquin to the main deck. My porters and guards took up quarters on the second deck, and the secretary shared the mate's quarters.

We set sail on a fall morning with good winds. By midday, we had navigated the Han River and were on the open sea. I sat in my chair gazing out at Korea through my porthole. As the boat cut through the waves toward China, the shore grew smaller and smaller. When it completely disappeared, I panicked. My breathing was short and my heart raced. I ran to the foredeck's rail and frantically searched the horizon for my country. I only saw the rolling swells. I wanted to order the captain to turn the boat around and head back to Seoul. But weeks earlier, I had sent a message to Empress Cixi requesting an audience with her and she had accepted. I had no choice. I had to go on.

I went back to my quarters to try to calm my nerves, but I couldn't. I tried to understand why I was panicking. I had always enjoyed traveling throughout Korea, and I enjoyed the seashore. But I had never been this far out to sea, and I had never been to where I could not see my country. Something inside me was missing.

I went to the trunk I had brought along, which was filled with papers and books. Inside I found *Songs of Dragons Flying to Heaven*. I sat in my chair and read the poems and songs inside. Eventually my panic eased.

The weather was in our favor and we made good time. For most of the four-day sail, I stayed in my quarters so that the crew could do its job instead of always stopping to bow to me. There, I read *Songs of Dragons Flying to Heaven* from cover to cover, practiced my Chinese, and rehearsed what I would say and how I would conduct myself with Empress Cixi. Midday on the fourth day, the bowman called out that the hills of Tianjin were in sight, and soon we were in port. We moored the ship to a dock and headed for Peking. For two days, my porters carried me in my palanquin through countryside and villages that looked just like home. The Chinese were short and dark compared to my people, but they looked more prosperous. They didn't bow or even pause as my palanquin passed by. Instead, they went about their work, leading oxcarts filled with goods, tending to rice paddies, or building houses.

Finally we arrived in Peking. The city made me feel like we were in Seoul, only it was larger, more crowded, and some buildings were taller. But when we got to the Forbidden City in the center of Peking, I knew we were in a country far grander than Korea. I had seen paintings and sketches of the Chinese royal palace, but they did not do it justice at all. In Korea, the Taewŏn-gun had raised taxes and raided the treasury to build Gyeongbok into a grand palace, but it was nothing like this. The Forbidden City grounds were twice that of Gyeongbok, and there were twice as many buildings, too. A moat as wide as a river surrounded the entire palace. The central gate with its double pagoda roof and red stucco walls was much taller than Gwanghwamun Gate. The latticework was more intricate, and, where the roof tiles in Gyeongbok were gray-green, all the roofs here were gold. Seeing China's grand palace, I wondered if my country would ever be able to get out from under its influence.

The palace's sergeant of the guard and six of his men carrying gold armament met us at the gate. My guards and porters waited outside as the sergeant escorted me and my secretary through courtyards lined with marble statues and past massive halls decorated with gold emblems, lions, and dragons. We climbed white marble stairs to the Hall of Preserving Harmony—the empress's throne room. The Chinese sergeant told the secretary to wait outside the hall. Then he escorted me inside. The hall was not as large or ornate as the throne room in Gyeongbok, and it was much older. However, the small size and simple decorations somehow gave it more nobility than ours, as if it was unnecessary for the Chinese to flaunt their power. In the center of the room was a gilded throne on a small dais. A rosewood chair sat at the foot of the dais. The sergeant at arms invited me to sit. "Her Majesty will be here soon," he said with a bow.

I had expected a grand reception with Chinese dignitaries waiting to greet me, and afterward, an elaborate feast hosted by Empress Cixi. It was clear, however, that no such reception was forthcoming. I wondered if I had made a mistake coming here. Although we had corresponded, I had never met the Chinese empress before. She was older than me—nearly old enough to be my mother. She had been a minor concubine of Emperor Xianfeng, and when he died from a life of overindulgence, Cixi's son was his only male progeny and the young boy became emperor. Cixi took power by having the men Emperor Xianfeng had appointed to act as regents for his son beheaded. She was intelligent, shrewd, and ruthless, and ruled her country with an iron hand. The reports were that no one bested Empress Cixi.

She marched into the throne room alone, wearing a black robe decorated with dozens of the Chinese symbol for longevity in gold leaf. She was petite like me, but her countenance filled the room. Her hair was fashioned so that it surrounded her face like a picture frame. She held her chin level and her eyes forward. She walked with short but deliberate steps. She made no notice of me as she mounted the dais and took her seat on the throne.

I thought her royal secretary would announce me and that the empress would have secretaries and ministers with her. Instead it was just us two—China's notorious dowager empress and me. Somehow, being alone with her intimidated me more than if she had brought a dozen advisers.

She finally acknowledged me. "So you are the young queen I have heard so much about," she said. Her voice was that of a much larger woman.

"Yes," I said without adding the title "majesty" as I should have, given that I was her guest. "And you are the Chinese dowager empress."

She took a fan from inside her robe and opened it. She began to fan herself. "What brings you here, so far from home?" she said, looking down at me. "Surely, you wouldn't make such a trip if you did not have something important on your mind."

I had practiced how I would engage the Chinese regent to gain an advantage. I let some time pass and returned her stare. I sat back and relaxed my posture. I gave her a most diplomatic smile.

"What is it?" Cixi scolded as if I was a child. "Don't sit there and pose for me like a cat. Tell me what you want."

Cixi had caught me off guard and now *she* had the advantage. I took the smile off my face and corrected my posture. "I have come here to talk to you about Japan," I said, "and about relations between our two countries. I have come here for advice . . . Majesty."

"Ah, little Japan," Cixi said. "A handful of modest islands populated by dwarf barbarians. What do you want to know about them?"

"My father-in-law, the Taewŏn-gun, plots with them. He thinks they will protect us and help us be independent from China. I do not trust them. I believe they want to rule us."

"Of course they do!" Cixi said. "Study your maps. The Japanese believe your peninsula is a dagger pointed at their heart. They are ambitious. They want to rule Asia. Taking Korea is their first step. You have minerals, forests, and resources that Japan needs."

"I have seen the maps, Majesty, and I know why Japan wants us," I said, trying to recapture some standing with the empress. "I am here to seek your assurance that you will keep them away. If they take the peninsula, they will be at your doorstep."

The empress shrugged. "They are already at our doorstep. They fight us for control over islands in the East Sea. Their warships raid our merchant ships. I tell you, young queen, someday we will have to go to war with them for control of your country. And when we do, we will teach them a lesson."

I took a moment to absorb this. Then I said, "I have learned that Emperor Meiji modernizes his military."

"Meiji," she snorted, "I think he is younger than you." She glared at me and fanned herself faster. "Yes, Meiji. He and his reformists have embraced the West's ways. But I don't believe fancy new weapons from Europe and America will defeat us. We have our own modern weapons."

"So if they move against us, will you help?"

Cixi grinned at me and her eyes narrowed. "And I suspect you will ask them for their help against us. You are like a rabbit between two angry tigers. And the tiger that wins gets to eat the rabbit."

"But only if one tiger wins, Majesty," I said.

She threw her head back and laughed without covering her mouth. "Ha! You think you are clever. Well we will see about that. Of course, Japan and China are not the only tigers in the forest. There is Europe, the mongrel Americans, and the boorish Russia, too. Their eyes are also on you."

I nodded. "Yes, I know. For the time, I am concerned about Japan. Can I count on your help if they threaten us?"

Cixi turned her head to the side. "It is best for us if the Japanese pirates stay out of Korea."

"Thank you, Majesty," I said. "You are truly a great leader as I have been told. I am pleased that we are allies."

"Allies?" the empress said, raising her chin at me. "Is that what we are? For hundreds of years, your little peninsula has depended on us. Your coming here to see me tells me that you still do. But now, as Japan grows more powerful, you want reassurance. Okay, ally, you have it. Send regular updates to me. Let me know if the Japanese threaten."

"I will, Majesty."

She closed her fan and stood from her throne. She came down the dais to me. As she approached, I fought the urge to lower my eyes. She pressed her fan against my neck. "Take care to keep your head attached, young queen," she said. Then the great dowager empress of China walked out and left me standing alone in the throne room.

TWENTY-ONE

When I got back to Korea, my pact with Empress Cixi emboldened me in my clashes with the Taewŏn-gun. I started to disagree with him on most everything. I opposed a strong alliance with Japan, and I had to keep my promises to the clan leaders, which usually put me at odds with the regent. But I often took the position I did simply to oppose him.

This, however, pushed Gojong closer to his father. Now that he had produced a healthy heir to the throne with Gwi-in, the king had a newfound confidence bordering on arrogance. He paid attention all the way through the afternoon meetings and asked good questions. A king was slowly coming out. However, having wasted his youth in slothful decadence, he didn't have the knowledge or experience he needed to rule the country on his own. He still needed someone to lean on, and more and more, that someone was his father.

So I went to work on my husband. I appealed to his pride, telling him he was a great king. I complimented him on his decisions when he made them on his own. I pretended to accept his son with Gwi-in as being the true crown prince. I even gave the child small gifts and saw to it that Gwi-in was well cared for, though inside, I greatly resented having to do so. The king strutted around Gyeongbok like a rooster among hens. But I knew that his outward confidence covered a profound insecurity. He was the son of a strong father who had never shown him any respect. It's why he had retreated to wine and the pipe as a young man and why he had let his father run the country for so long. And though he didn't know it, it was why he needed me.

One night when Gojong and I were together in his bed, I said, "You are a great king, my husband. I am proud of all you have done. But you depend on your father too much. It makes you look weak. And a king who looks weak will not be the king for long."

He grinned at me. "You want me to side with you, don't you?"

"It is normal for a king to support his wife," I replied. "But your father was the regent while you were young. When you depend on him as you do now, it appears to everyone that he, not you, runs the country."

Gojong sat up on the bed with his legs folded underneath him. He turned serious. "I want to be a good king," he said. "But it is difficult. I am not always sure of myself. Sometimes, I get afraid."

It was the first time my husband had confided in me that way. I was heartened and encouraged that he did, but I knew that I could not turn him so easily after a lifetime of living under the harsh hand of his father.

I sat up and moved next to him. "If you are afraid, you can trust me," I said.

Gojong did not respond. After a few minutes, he sent me back to my quarters.

Over the next few weeks, the king started to disagree with his father more and more. It was difficult for Gojong, and he often backed down. One day in the afternoon meeting, we were discussing a proposal from America to establish stronger diplomatic relations with them. "I do not recommend this, Majesty," the Taewŏn-gun said in his high-pitched voice. "It is a dangerous precedent."

The ministers said nothing so the king said, "What is the queen's opinion on this matter?"

From my position behind the king, I said, "I believe strong diplomatic relations are an effective way to ease conflict."

The king said, "She makes a good point, Father."

The Taewŏn-gun scowled. "You concede to your wife too often. When will you learn to stand on your own?"

The room went as still as death. Gojong looked at his hands but his jaw was tight. After a few long seconds, he pushed himself off of his cushion and stormed out of the room.

That night when we were together, the king paced across his bedchamber and kicked at a cushion. "He thinks I'm a fool," he complained. "He has always thought I'm a fool."

"You are not," I said. "You are a great king, my husband."

"I do not want him in the meetings anymore," he declared.

I said, "It would be perfectly appropriate if you sent him to live in Changdeok Palace. He enjoys the gardens there."

"How do you think he will take it?" Gojong asked.

"Why does it matter?" I asked. "You are the king!" Gojong stared at me and nodded.

Early the next morning as the king stayed sheltered in his quarters, he sent guards to his father's residence to take the Taewŏn-gun and Lady Min to Changdeok palace. If there was an outcry from the regent or from those loyal to him, it never reached the king's ears.

And so finally Gojong and I ruled Korea without the Taewŏn-gun.

But with the Taewŏn-gun gone, I had a different problem. Now that my father-in-law was out of sight, I couldn't keep an eye on him. He was free to plot with Mister Euno and the Japanese on how to get rid of me and take over again. So I placed spies among the staff at Changdeok, but the Taewŏn-gun and Mister Euno were cautious and my spies learned nothing. I was certain that the Taewŏn-gun, having ruled the palace for so long, had spies in Gyeongbok. I had to be careful about what I said and did.

A year after I sent him on his mission, my uncle returned from Japan and America. I was almost as glad to see him as his wife was. He looked grizzled and exhausted from his time abroad. His hair and goatee were now mostly gray. I let him be with his wife for a day and then had him report to me in my study. I sat at my desk when he came in. He bowed.

"It is good to see you, Uncle," I said.

"It is good to be back, Majesty," he replied, standing at the door, holding a brown leather satchel. "I am told the Taewŏn-gun is no longer involved in the government and you and the king now have complete control.

I motioned for him to sit in front of my desk. "Control is an illusion," I said as my uncle sat on a cushion in front of me. "I only do my best, as you told me to do so many years ago." My uncle smiled.

"Uncle," I said, "you have made your trip to Japan and the United States. Tell me, what have you learned?"

My uncle frowned and hesitated. Finally he said, "I have learned that I was born in the dark. I went out into the light, and, Your Majesty, it is my displeasure to inform you that I have returned to the dark."

"Tell me about the light," I said.

He took out photographs and drawings from his satchel and placed them in front of me. He leaned back and paused as if he was searching for the words to describe all he saw. He said, "Majesty, the new world is like nothing you could imagine. What they call the Capitol Building in Washington, DC, is as white as snow and as tall as a mountain. In Chicago, there are buildings that reach twelve levels high with boxes on steel ropes that carry people to each level. In San Francisco, there are factories able to produce hundreds of items every day. They have inventions so elaborate that the mind cannot possibly comprehend how they work. And electricity, Majesty! Lamps and motors and all manner of inventions powered by electricity! They say that American cities and factories will run on it in less than ten years. They have telegraphs throughout the country, and someday they will have telephones, too." He pointed to the photographs and drawings he had placed in front of me. "I have brought you evidence of all these things."

I examined a tintype of the US Capitol Building with a group of men posing in front of it. The white-domed building was enormous and reminded me of how I felt when I first set foot inside Gyeongbok Palace. I looked at another photograph of a factory with a huge steam engine powering a wheel as tall as two men. The wheel turned a machine that spun dozens of spindles holding thread. I had read about many of these things, but seeing them in these photographs and hearing my uncle's descriptions made me realize that I had underestimated how far the rest of the world had gone.

"What about weapons?" I asked.

My uncle sighed. "I regret to tell you that the American and European weapons we have seen on our shores are just the beginning. They now have cannons that can fire heavy shells vast distances. They have rifles that a soldier can fire twenty times in a minute and kill a man a half mile away. They are building iron warships that our wooden ships could not possibly destroy."

"I see," I said, picking up a drawing of a man standing in front of a cannon much taller than he was. "And the Japanese? What did you learn about them?"

"Japan is not far behind, Majesty. They have opened trade to America and Europe to acquire these technologies. They are building at an alarming pace. I'm afraid that very soon Tokyo will be a city far greater than Seoul. There are pictures of Tokyo there, too."

"That is a most disturbing report, indeed," I said. "Based on what you saw, what do you recommend that we do?"

My uncle shook his head. "I fear for our country, Your Majesty. We must open our shores without hesitation, to modernize this still ancient kingdom."

I looked at him. It had been difficult for him to give me such a grave report, but I was grateful that he had the courage to do it. He was someone on whom I could depend, and with what I faced, I would need him. "Thank you, Uncle," I said.

He looked at me eye-to-eye. "Ja-young, I told you years ago that it will be very difficult to be the queen. Back then I could not imagine how difficult it would be. But I believe that you are the one chosen to lead us during these hard times."

He stood, bowed, said, "Your Majesty," and left my study.

I examined the photographs, drawings, and reports. Everything he said was true. It was clear that we were far behind the rest of the world. I set the papers down and closed my eyes. I imagined Korea with the inventions I saw in the photographs—factories run on electricity, telegraph lines crossing the peninsula. I pictured Seoul filled with tall buildings with lifts on steel ropes. I saw a powerful army with iron ships and cannons that could reach great distances. And I knew what we had to do. We had to negotiate trade deals to acquire the new technology. We had to accept foreigners on our shore with their eccentric clothing, mannerisms, and ideas. They would try to force their religions on us and change our way of life. But we needed to do it for the sake of our country, and we had to do it quickly. I had promised the clan leaders that I would not push for change. They were traditionalists—especially the powerful Ik-hyun Ch'oe—and they would fight any moves I might make to modernize. If I succeeded, we would quickly become a very different country. But at least we would still have a country.

The biggest challenge, however, was that we would have to raise taxes. The new technologies and weapons would certainly be expensive, and we had nothing valuable to trade. We had minerals, but no way to extract them in quantities needed for trade. We had labor, but not the trained workers the West would want to employ. We had very little capital, and the only way to get it was to raise taxes.

I shared the report with the king and told him about my plans. He agreed that we had to talk to the clan leaders about it.

Since I had met with Empress Cixi, I encouraged the king to conduct important meetings in the throne room instead of the meeting rooms of Sajeongjeon Hall. For these meetings, I dressed in ceremonial robes with painted hems instead of my usual day-robe. I acquired a fan made from ivory with a dragon design on each leaf. I had my maids put up my hair in a way that made me look taller and more majestic. I took care to control my posture as Mister Euno had taught me so many years earlier. And that is how I, along with the king, met the clan leaders.

The king sat high on the red throne with the gilded top, and I sat at his side when Kyung-jik led them past the massive red columns to the foot of the dais. Behind us hung the tapestry with the scene of trees and mountains, and the sun and moon in the sky. The leaders came in single file in their scholar's white robes and black hats. They stopped and gave us an almost pious bow. There was Yun-sik Kim of the Kim clan, Chul-son Chung of the Chungs, a representative of the Lee clan, and another from the Paks. And leading them all was Ik-hyun Ch'oe. They folded themselves onto cushions and looked straight ahead.

The king said, "Good men, I have called you here because we have something important to discuss with you. Since we have taken over the government, we have reduced your taxes and have not pursued reforms. We have appointed honest men from all clans to government positions. We have kept Westerners from our shores. We have kept our promises to you. However, I regret to say we may not be able to keep them any longer. The queen will explain."

I rose from the throne, careful not to stand in front of the king. The leaders kept their eyes forward, but underneath their black hats their eyes followed me. "Gentlemen," I said, "Our king is a great leader, and I am humbled to serve him. He has asked that I share a report I received that has shaken us. And now you must hear it, too."

I told them what I had learned from my uncle. I told them of the great cities of San Francisco, Chicago, and Washington, DC. I told them about the tall buildings and the new factories run by electricity. I told them about the modern weapons that could kill at great distances. I showed them the photographs and drawings my uncle had brought from his trip. "It's called the Industrial Revolution," I said. "I have read about it, and I believe that those who embrace it will conquer those who do not. And I'm sorry to say, Japan is one that embraces it. They are far ahead of us. They already have a modern military. We must change—and quickly—or we will never be our own nation."

I took my place next to the king again and let my words sink in.

Finally Chul-son Chung spoke. "Who has given you this report, Majesty?"

"My uncle, Chul-jo Min," I answered.

"Ah," he said with a simple nod, "your uncle. A Min."

"Yes, a Min," I said. "And a good and true man." Chul-son did not reply.

Yun-sik Kim leaned forward. "Certainly, Majesties, you do not mean to embrace the West. Let them have their modern ways. We are Koreans and must remain true to who we are."

The king looked sideways at me indicating that I should answer. "Yes, the king and I also want to stay true to who we are. But how can we if we are a conquered nation?" Yun-sik did not reply.

Jae-kwon Pak shook his head. "To build such a country would require raising taxes, which we cannot afford to do," he said. "I believe our best policy is to stay away from this Industrial Revolution and keep our money."

"We do not want to raise taxes, either," the king replied. "But what good is our money for if we don't have a country?" Jae-kwon did not reply.

Finally Ik-hyun Ch'oe cleared his throat. "I have heard on good authority that China and Japan are fighting each other. If we stay neutral, they will let us be."

"Master Ch'oe," I said before the king could reply, "I have met with Empress Cixi, and she has vowed to stand by us. But we must not depend on them. We must take action for ourselves. We cannot build a wall and hide inside our country. The wind will find a way in."

The scholar lifted his eyes to me. "We are a country with deep roots, Majesty. If we stand fast, no matter how hard the wind blows, it cannot penetrate our soul."

The leaders nodded at Ik-hyun's words.

"Our soul," I repeated as I returned his stare. As I looked down at the men in their white robes and black hats, I heard the spirits of Korea's past kings and queens shouting at me. "One Korea, One Korea" they said. These men, these scholarly men, did not hear their cries. And they refused to see what was clear before their eyes. I was furious with them. As the king nervously looked on, I marched past him down the dais steps and stood directly in front of the ministers. I pointed my fan at them. "You talk of staying true to who we are, but who are we, really? What kind of nation will we be in these modern times? You say that the rest of the world will let us be. Well, they will not let us be. They are circling over us like buzzards over a dead cow. Your way would allow the buzzards to tear us apart. I will not let them! The king and I have sworn to protect our country. The spirits of our ancestors and the spirits of our children and grandchildren demand that we take action. And we will."

I turned to Ik-hyun Ch'oe and addressed him directly. "You, Master Ch'oe, you should know better than to bury your head in your books and let our country perish. You are not blind to this. You *choose* to be blind. You, who have so much to offer, should help me."

Ik-hyun Ch'oe addressed the king directly. "Majesty, if our situation is as dire as the queen says, you should seek the Taewŏn-gun's help. He is more experienced in these matters."

And there it was. The clever Master Ch'oe was trying to play the Taewŏn-gun and me against each other for the mind of the king. With my father-in-law and me fighting, the clan leaders would have more leverage with the king and Master Ch'oe would become more powerful than he already was.

"Kyung-jik!" I called, still staring at Ik-hyun.

My guard came running. "Yes, Majesty," he said.

"Escort these men from the palace. The king does not need advice from men who cannot see."

As Kyung-jik led the clan leaders single file out of the throne room, I went back up the dais next to the king. His brow was furrowed and he looked at his hands. "I hope you know what you're doing," he said.

TWENTY-TWO

Over the next several years, the king and I did exactly what I told the clan leaders we would do. I convinced Gojong to raise taxes to build a modern army and acquire new technology. We established government bureaus to deal with foreign relations with the West, China, and Japan. We started a department to import Western goods. We created a bureau of the military to modernize our weapons and strategies, and even invited the Japanese, Chinese, and Americans to help train our army. We had the mint create and distribute new coins to stabilize our currency so we could trade with other nations more efficiently.

And it worked. Within only a few years, our economy started to grow. The chungin was opening successful businesses and trading with the West. Nations began to invest in Korea. New technologies like bicycles and photography started to creep in. Throughout the country, people were fascinated with all the new inventions from the West.

I was proud of what the king and I had done for our country. Korea was on its way to becoming an independent nation. We were on our way to being One Korea.

But there were problems, too. In the new order, the yangban were losing their status at the top of society. Their initial complaints grew into outright defiance, and they threatened to overthrow the palace.

The scholars feared that they were losing control of the country's soul because Christian missionaries crossed the peninsula, spreading their beliefs to Koreans eager to learn about the West. The foreigners introduced peculiar foods and clothing, dubious medicines, and strange ways of thinking. Some of my countrymen embraced the changes while others opposed them. Clans and classes still argued with each other, and their feuds were becoming deadly. I had expected that my reforms would cause problems, but I hadn't expected the problems to be this severe. It felt like my plans were falling apart. Nevertheless, I believed that I had us pointed in the right direction.

During these days, I became pregnant again. As my belly grew, I worried, and I prayed that this time I would deliver a healthy son for my husband and my country. I didn't have the morning sickness this time around, and I felt good throughout the pregnancy. I was careful to do exactly what the doctor instructed. I cut back my work schedule and let Han-sook pamper me as only she could. I ordered monks to pray for my baby. I had shamans make charms for my bedchamber and say chants to chase away evil spirits. Every day I drank ginseng tea, and at night Han-sook burned amber to help me and the baby inside me sleep.

My belly grew large, and then one day in early spring, I delivered a baby boy. When the doctor declared that he was healthy and strong, both Han-sook and I cried. When the doctor gave him to me, I held him close and was grateful to feel his little legs kick. He looked up at me and pursed his lips into a most dramatic pout. Then he pushed out a cry befitting a child twice his size. I put him to my breast and he sucked greedily. I immediately loved him as I had loved my first, sickly son. I named him Sun-jong—"rising dragon"—and I vowed that someday he would be king.

Naturally, Gojong was pleased that his lawful wife—and not just one of his consorts—had given him a son. So when my son grew into a toddler who ran around Gyeongbok as if the entire palace was his playground, I convinced Gojong to declare Sun-jong Korea's true crown prince and to remove the title the Taewŏn-gun had given to Gwi-in's son. And when he did, I stripped Gwi-in of her title as princess consort and banished her and her son to a small, cold village in the north.

One summer morning, I watched as my son played with his toy sailboat in the lake surrounding the Hyangwonjeong island pavilion. I held my young crown prince's slippers as he waded in the water. I delighted in watching Sun-jong play. He was full of life and curious about everything. His boat was a birthday gift from Emperor Alexander II of Russia. It was blue and had three sails and a toy cannon on the foredeck that Sun-jong pretended to shoot at pirates. "Boom! Boom!" Sun-jong said.

As my son played, Kyung-jik came marching toward me from the other side of the lake. His square jaw was set as he bowed. "Majesty," he said, "there has been a development with the Japanese. The king requests your presence in Sajeongjeon Hall immediately. He has assembled the ministers."

I waved to Sun-jong's nurse who was a few steps away. I gave her my son's slippers. "Let the boy play a little longer, then take him to his quarters to rest," I said.

"Yes, Majesty," she said, and assumed a position next to the prince.

As Kyung-jik and I crossed the central courtyard toward Sajeongjeon Hall, I asked, "What is happening with the Japanese?"

"They have gunboats at Ganghwa Island," he answered.

I wasn't surprised at this. I had believed that modernizing would help us stand up to other nations. But as I feared it might, it had exposed us, too. Once the foreigners started to do business with us, they coveted our country. They saw the potential in our land and in our untapped labor. But mostly, they looked at the maps as Empress

Cixi had said, and saw that our peninsula was strategically important to anyone who wanted to rule Asia.

And no country was more covetous of us than the Japanese. They were one hundred miles from our coast and far ahead in modernizing their nation. They had their eyes on us, and now they had gunboats at Ganghwa Island at the mouth of the Han River.

I hurried into the meeting room with the long, low table. Gojong sat on his high cushion and the ministers talked in hushed tones in their places around the table. They were all there, except Minister Kim, whose place was empty. Gojong's brow was furrowed and he bit his thumbnail. When I came in, he quickly motioned me to sit next to him. As I sat, the room went silent.

"My guard tells me the Japanese have gunboats at Ganghwa Island," I said. "What do they want?"

The foreign affairs minister held out some papers. "They demand that we sign this trade agreement, Majesty."

"Let me see it," I said, and the minister gave it to me. It was an unequal treaty like the ones that Westerners had forced on Asian nations for decades. It stipulated that Japan would be able to sell their goods to us without tariffs while we would pay stiff tariffs on everything we sold to them. It further stated that the Japanese had the right to be in our country whenever and wherever they pleased, and that while here, they were exempt from our laws. Our people, however, would not have the same rights in Japan. They also demanded payments from us for past wars' "injury." In essence, the treaty, if it could be called a treaty, was the first step in giving the Japanese control over our country.

I pushed the papers back to the minister. "What will they do if we do not agree?"

"They say that they will force it upon us, Majesty," the minister said.

Gojong looked at me. "We don't want war with the Japanese," he said. "I think we should sign it."

I paused for a moment as the ministers waited for my reply. I tightened my jaw and said, "If we sign this, what will they demand next? They will not stop until they have complete control and we are nothing more than a Japanese colony. No! We must tell them very clearly that we do not accept this one-sided treaty."

Gojong shook his head. "I don't know. My father has close relations with the Japanese. Perhaps we should ask him what to do." Several ministers nodded in agreement.

I looked around the table at them. I did not respect even one of them. They all had private goals that were not in line with mine. Some were probably working for the Taewŏn-gun. Some might be spies for Empress Cixi. Others might be spies for the Japanese. The only one I could trust was Minister Kim, and he wasn't here.

"Where is Minister Kim?" I demanded. All the ministers kept their eyes low and didn't answer.

"Call my guard!" I said to the court secretary. Soon, Kyung-jik was at the door. "Find Minister Kim at once and bring him here," I ordered.

After Kyung-jik left to fetch Minister Kim, I said, "The rest of you, leave me with the king." One by one, the ministers filed out of the room with bowed heads, leaving Gojong and me alone.

As we sat on our cushions, I thought about how I would convince my husband to take a stand against the Japanese. Over the years, he had come to depend on me as we ran the country from this room. He usually agreed with what I wanted to do, and the few times we disagreed, I let him have his way. He was the king, after all, and his was the final say.

I turned to him and said, "My husband, this is a most serious situation we are in. We must make the right decision or we could lose everything, including our crowns."

"My father knows the Japanese," Gojong said. "We should consult with him."

"Your father?" I pushed myself up off my cushion. "Your father favors the Japanese. He will tell you to accept this treaty, and in short order, you will have to abdicate your throne to them. You are the king! And you must protect your country from the Japanese thieves. It is your duty."

Gojong shook his head. "If we do not sign this treaty, they will declare war. And if they win, they will kill us both."

"Yes, they might," I replied. "But we are the king and queen. It is our duty to fight for our country. For the sake of our people, for the sake of our son, fight with me."

Gojong didn't answer right away. Under his furrowed brow, he tried to gather the courage to take my course of action. After a few minutes, he stood and went to the door. Before he left, he turned to me and said, "Tomorrow I will go to Changdeok Palace to see if my father can negotiate a better agreement for us."

After Gojong left, I stormed back to my quarters and sat at my desk under the two-headed dragon. I was furious with the ministers and with my husband. We had come so far, but now the Japanese were making their move. And we were vulnerable. We hadn't completed modernizing our military as the Japanese had done. The military's old guard complained about having foreigners train them and had threatened mutiny. I no longer had the clan leaders' support, especially the powerful Ik-hyun Ch'oe.

As I thought of all the problems I faced, my anger turned to despair. I stood and faced the two-headed dragon. I looked into its eyes. "Have I taken the right path?" I asked it. "Am I doing what I should do?" It had been a long time since the dragon had spoken to me, and I desperately needed it to speak to me now. It stared back and said nothing.

A while later, Kyung-jik came to my door. "Majesty," he said, "I have the most disturbing news about Minister Kim. He is dead, Majesty." He looked at his feet.

"Your uncle is dead?" I said. "I am sorry, Kyung-jik. How did he die? He has not been sick."

My guard's jaw stiffened. "His wife believes that he was poisoned. Their old cook left them two weeks ago for reasons they do not know. They had a new cook who disappeared late last night when the minister fell ill."

"I see," I said.

"That is not all, Majesty," Kyung-jik said. He raised his eyes to me. "The new cook was Japanese."

I sat at my desk, and for the first time since I had become queen, I was afraid. Though I had always been careful, I had never really feared for my life. But the Japanese were closing in. They had gunboats less than fifty miles away from Gyeongbok Palace, and it was clear that they were willing to use them. They probably wanted to kill the king and me to move us out of the way. But if we tried to save our heads by agreeing to their demands, they would strip us of our power and force us to be figureheads over a country that they controlled. It would be awful to have to sit obediently on the throne while the Japanese stripped away everything that was Korea. It would be better to fight, even if it would cost us our heads.

"Kyung-jik," I said, "double the guard around the palace, day and night. Make sure you trust the men you have on watch."

"Yes, Majesty," he replied.

"Then go at once to Changdeok Palace and arrest Mister Euno. Bring him to the throne room. Be careful with him. He is skilled in the martial arts. You will need several strong men to subdue him."

"What shall I say are the charges, Majesty?"

"Disloyalty to the throne," I said. "Go now. Be quick and be sharp. There is danger in every shadow."

My sergeant of the guard bowed and hurried out the door.

I called Han-sook and had her fetch my grandest ceremonial robe. Though it was a hot summer day, I had my maids put on an extra layer of petticoats to fill me out. As two maids fanned me to keep me cool, two more maids put my hair high and pinned it with my largest gold binyeo. When they started on my face, I said, "Make me look especially royal today." They applied heavy lines on my brows and extra powder to my skin. They painted my lips red. They helped me into my robe. The heavy robe was several layers of gold and red silk with the queen's pheasant pattern on the chima and a dragon on the chest. When they were finished, Han-sook held a mirror in front of me. In the reflection, I saw a dragon queen.

I took my ivory fan and tucked it inside a fold of my robe. And then I went to the throne room to wait for Kyung-jik to bring Mister Euno to me.

The sun had crossed halfway around the sky when the procession of guards and Mister Euno passed under the Gwanghwamun Gate and marched through the central courtyard toward the throne room. I sat on the throne as the procession entered with Kyung-jik in the lead. When they got close, I saw that my guard's lip was swollen and he tried to disguise a limp. Behind him, a foot shorter than Kyung-jik, Mister Euno walked in his Western coat and top hat. They had bound his hands behind his back and tied a rope around his neck that the largest guard held with two hands. They stopped at the foot of the dais.

"Kyung-jik," I said, "have one of your guards gather the ministers and bring them here. They need to learn what courage is."

"Shall I fetch the king, Majesty?" Kyung-jik asked. It was an appropriate question. As queen, I should not meet with the ministers without the king. But I knew the king would not approve of what I was about to do. So I answered, "No."

My sergeant of the guard waved one of his men to fetch the ministers. I looked down on Mister Euno who stared straight ahead. I fanned myself as we waited in silence for the ministers to arrive. I started to hear the spirits calling me. It was the first time in years that I had heard them. Their voices were far away, and I couldn't hear what they said. I prayed that they would approve of what I was about to do.

After a while, the ministers entered the throne room single file, flanked by the guard who had fetched them. "You are permitted to stand there," I said, pointing with my fan to the dais's left side. "Watch and learn what we must do if we are to keep our country." The ministers went to where I pointed and quietly stood with their eyes low.

I turned my attention to Mister Euno. "Kyung-jik," I said, "have the prisoner kneel. He made me the queen, now he should show respect for his creation."

Kyung-jik pushed the Japanese man to the floor, more roughly than necessary. Mister Euno kneeled on the stone floor and kept his eyes level.

"Mister Euno," I said, "you once told me that you are a Kokugaku scholar—one who believes in the Japanese way. I have since studied the Kokugaku. I have read all of the books and learned their teachings. They not only believe in the Japanese way, they also believe that Japan is destined to rule all of Asia."

I opened my fan and started fanning myself with it. "Tell me, Mister Euno, is that what you believe, too?"

Mister Euno didn't raise his eyes as he said, "Majesty, I am here to serve you and the king."

The spirits' voices were louder now. It was a cacophony of words and cries. I could not make out what they were saying, but I could hear that they were angry. I lifted my robe, went down the dais steps, and stood in front of Mister Euno. Kneeling on the stone floor, his top hat nearly reached my chin. I thumped the top of his hat with my fan. "You say you serve me and the king. But how can you serve us if you believe we should be ruled by Japan?"

"It is true, Majesty, I also serve Emperor Meiji, but only to help you on his behalf."

"Help us on his behalf," I parroted. "Why then, Mister Euno, does your Emperor Meiji have gunboats off of Ganghwa Island, not more than a two-hour sail from the palace gates? Why does he insist that we agree to a treaty that subverts us?"

Mister Euno lifted his eyes to me. "He brings the treaty so he does not have to go to war with you."

I returned his stare as I fanned myself again. The spirits cried out, and I could start to make out their words. "One Korea," they said. "One Korea!"

I said, "Yes, you are a true Kokugaku scholar, Mister Euno. Just like Emperor Meiji and his rebels."

I closed my fan and tucked it inside my robe. "Your emperor wants an answer about this treaty. Well, I will give him one."

I turned to the ministers who were watching me without moving. I said to them, "And now, ministers, you will see what a queen must do for her country."

The spirits in my head were shouting now. "One Korea! One Korea!" I held out my hand to Kyung-jik. "Give me your sword," I said. Kyung-jik hesitated only a moment, then took his sword from inside his uniform and gave it to me.

"Hold him fast," I said. Kyung-jik motioned to the large guard with the rope around Mister Euno's neck. The guard cinched the rope tight as Kyung-jik held Mister Euno's shoulders down.

I stood in front of the Japanese man with the sword in my hand. I had never held a sword before. In my hand, Kyung-jik's sword was heavy but balanced. The steel gleamed and I could see the edge was sharp. The weapon's life-taking power was intoxicating, and it made me feel like I was someone different, almost like a god. With the sword's tip, I pushed off Mister Euno's top hat exposing his topknot. Mister Euno didn't move as I grabbed his topknot with my free hand and held it tight. I placed the sword's sharp edge on his neck. The spirits were screaming now, "One Korea! One Korea!" I slowly raised the blade and held it high over the Japanese man. And then I heard a voice say, "Kill him!" I swung the blade toward his neck. At the last second, I lifted the sword and sliced off Mister Euno's topknot. And then the spirit voices went silent.

I took a step back with Mister Euno's topknot in one hand and the sword in the other. Without his topknot, Mister Euno's hair fell around his head in short black strings. He kept his eyes forward, but there was fear in his face. He breathed fast.

"A Kokugaku scholar wears a topknot to show his devotion to his beliefs," I said, pointing the sword at him. "Well, you no longer have a topknot. It is mine now and I will keep it as a reminder of the Japanese way."

I handed the sword back to Kyung-jik. With Mister Euno's topknot in my hand, I marched back up the dais steps. I turned and stood high above Mister Euno and the ministers. I thrust the topknot toward Mister Euno. "As for the answer to the treaty, I will use you to send it. My guard and his men will take you to Ganghwa Island at once. There, they will beat you until you are near death. Then they will give you to the captain of the Japanese gunboat. That is my answer to Emperor Meiji regarding this unequal treaty. And if you are ever tempted to come back, remember Kokugaku scholar, how today I showed you the *Korean* way." I nodded at Kyung-jik, and he and the guards led Mister Euno out of the throne room.

I turned to the ministers who stood motionless with their eyes wide. "And that, ministers, is what we must do to save our country from the Japanese," I said.

The minister of trade lifted frightened eyes to me. "They will kill you, Majesty."

I glared at him. "Pray that they do not, minister," I said. "Because if they do, they will kill our country, too."

King Gojong went to Changdeok Palace that night instead of the next morning as he had said he would. Before he left, he did not talk to me about what I had done with Mister Euno, but I knew how he felt. Though he, like most everyone, disliked the Japanese, he feared them and was angry with me for acting on my own and putting us in grave danger. I had made a move that forced Japan's hand. Everyone—the king, the Taewŏn-gun, the ministers, the clan leaders—would now have to choose if we would be an independent country or if we would let the Japanese take us over. I wasn't sure what the answer would be. Like a child, my husband had chosen the protection of his father. The ministers had always been afraid of the Taewŏn-gun, and now I had made them afraid of me. They would now have to choose sides. Some would choose the Taewŏn-gun. I prayed that a few would come to my side.

But by acting on my own with Mister Euno, I had committed an offense to the king. I had also made clear my hatred of the Japanese. It gave the Taewŏn-gun and the Japanese an opening, a reason to remove me from the throne. Perhaps what I had done would save Korea. Perhaps it was a mistake. Or maybe, the spirits had driven me mad as they had done to my mother.

TWENTY-THREE

Several days later, I walked with Sun-jong and Han-sook through the palace grounds. My son, dressed in his little white robe, skipped along the stone paths and climbed on the statues and parapets. It was a hot summer day with menacing clouds rising over Mount Bukhansan beyond the north palace walls. The palace was quiet, as it had been since my ordeal with Mister Euno. All around us, the guards stood watch with eagle eyes—two now where only one used to be. The palace staff attended to their duties with their heads low and talked in whispers as they passed by each other. Gyeongbok smoldered in the summer heat.

Outside the palace walls, the smoldering had burst into fire. The Taewŏn-gun had made his move, and I had to admit, it was brilliant. He and his operatives had convinced the public that my actions over the years had made Korea vulnerable to the Japanese. He incited the residents of Seoul to revolt against me and encouraged rioting in the streets. He brought the old-guard military to his side, promising them that he would return the military to the way it was before. As the Taewŏn-gun stayed safe in Changdeok Palace, the rioters captured two palace ministers and lynched them, dragging their corpses through the streets. And they were hunting for others. I worried for the people who had supported me over the years. I worried about my uncle and aunt, who had moved back to the House of Gamgodang.

The Taewŏn-gun had also turned the people against the Japanese, telling them that the dwarf barbarians wanted to take over Korea. With the Japanese under fire, I couldn't appeal to the Chinese for help. Empress Cixi was most likely amused by the reports she got—the Koreans revolting against her Japanese foes. If I asked her to intervene, she would refuse and let the fighting continue.

As for the Japanese, the Taewŏn-gun's maneuver had paralyzed them. With thousands of Koreans looking for Japanese to kill, they had to keep their gunboats at Ganghwa Island and suspend their demands for an unequal treaty until the rioting subsided.

And my father-in-law now had the king on his side. Gojong had come far, but he would always need someone strong like me or his father. This time, he had chosen his father. Certainly, it was safer for him at Changdeok under the Taewŏn-gun's protection than with me at Gyeongbok. The former regent controlled the rioters and the old-guard military. He had been a Japanese ally. But by fleeing to the protection of his father, the king had practically abdicated his throne to him.

I was terribly disappointed in my husband, and, truthfully, I was disappointed in myself, too. I wasn't able to bring my husband to my side. Since we had started to work together without the Taewŏn-gun, and especially since the birth of our son, we had grown closer. It still wasn't the love that I had seen in my parents when I was young, but it was more than we'd had before. The king wanted another son, and we'd spent many nights together in his bedchamber. I often stayed the entire night. Then in the morning, we would talk about Sun-jong, how he was growing so fast and what kind of king he would be someday. Gojong loved Sun-jong and, I think, he was grateful to me for giving him such a wonderful child. He was also grateful that I helped him rule the country without his father. I had helped him become a man. But was he a king?

My move with Mister Euno had forced the question on him, and he had answered that he did not have the heart for it.

When Sun-jong, Han-sook, and I came to the lake surrounding Hyangwonjeong island pavilion, my son took off his blue slippers and splashed his feet in the water. He peered in the lake for koi. My heart went out to him. He was innocent of everything happening around him. He didn't care about the Japanese or the soldiers or the rioters only a few miles away. He only cared about catching a fish.

As I watched Sun-jong play, I summoned the courage to do what I must do. I motioned my lady's maid next to me. "Han-sook," I said, "you have been a loyal lady's maid. But now I must ask you to do more. Take care of the prince. See that he is safe and that he knows his mother loves him. It is your most important duty now."

Han-sook nodded. "Yes, Majesty."

"Take him away today, and do not bring him out of hiding until you are sure it is safe." I turned to my lady's maid. "I am trusting you with my son's life," I said.

"I understand, Majesty," Han-sook said with a nod. "I will not let you down."

I knew she wouldn't. I had come to love her as I would have loved a sister. I often wished I could open up to her, share my desires and fears with her, talk to her as I imagined one would talk to a sister. But I was the queen and she was my servant, and neither she—nor anyone—would ever be a friend like that to me. It was the price I had to pay to wear the crown.

I turned to my son. "Sun-jong, come here."

Sun-jong kicked the water and didn't come. "Son!" I said. "Come and listen to what I have to say. It is important that you do."

"No!" he said. "I want to catch a fish."

I went to him and crouched to his level, soaking the hem of my robe. I took him by the shoulders. He looked down and pouted. "Listen to me," I said. "Today you will leave the palace with Han-sook. When you are away, you must do as she says."

"I don't want to go away," he said, splashing water at my robe with his foot.

I nodded. "I know, but you must. You must do this if you are going to be king someday."

My son grinned and said, "Then I can tell everyone what to do!" He pulled away from me and pointed to a tree. "You, squirrel, come down from that tree!" He pointed at the lake. "Fish, come here so I can catch you!"

I smiled. "Yes, like that, my son. But if you are to be king, you must go with Han-sook."

Sun-jong frowned and nodded. "Yes, Ummah," he said.

I stood and said to Han-sook, "Go now." As Han-sook took my child by the hand and led him away, my heart broke. I thought I might never see my little prince again. The Japanese, the rioters, and the Taewŏn-gun would be at the palace soon, and they were coming for me. I prayed that my son would escape, and they would not come for him, too.

As I strolled through the palace courtyard alone with my thoughts, the dark clouds over Mount Bukhansan slid over the palace threatening a summer storm. I was the only person of authority left in the palace. The ministers were running from the mobs that were trying to kill them. Over the past few days, the administrators had quietly left, too. Their staffs soon followed. Other than servants and guards, everyone had abandoned the palace.

Suddenly there was an explosion from deep inside the city. I turned to look. Far beyond the palace walls, a house had caught fire. The flames created an orange dome against the low clouds. Orange embers like glowing bees danced high above the fire. Far away, people shouted. As the flames subsided, the shouting grew louder. It sounded angry and mean. I saw the glow of torches. The rioters were slowly moving toward the palace.

I rushed to my quarters. I flung open the door to my study. It was dark inside, and all I could see were shadows. I looked at the wall behind my desk where the tapestry with the two-headed dragon hung. It was dark. I went to the wall for a closer look. The spirits were speaking again. With each step I took toward the tapestry, my heart beat faster and the spirits spoke louder. And then I saw that the tapestry was gone. The voices screamed, pleaded, and cried. They were the ghosts of the dead kings and queens of Korea. They were the voices of my mother and father and of my dead son. In the jumble of words, I couldn't make out what they were saying, but it wasn't "One Korea" as it had been before. I shook my head to make them stop. I put my hand over my ears. Eventually one word rose above the rest. It was the word, "run."

I ran out to my courtyard. The wind had come up, and it swirled inside the confines of the courtyard. On the horizon toward the center of Seoul, I saw the angry orange glow was now near. I heard footsteps behind me. I gasped and turned around. A shadow moved toward me. I took a step back. Then I saw the shadow was Kyung-jik dressed in the loose clothing of a sangmin commoner. He wore a dirty white peasant hat and a shirt closed at his chest. His pants were bound at his ankles.

"What are you doing here?" I demanded.

"Sheee," he said, placing two fingers on his lips. "Please forgive me, Majesty, for not following proper protocol, but we must leave at once." He held out dark-green clothes to me. "Take these. Put them on. Quickly!" I took the clothes from him and saw it was a sangmin woman's scarf and robe made from coarse wool. I pulled off my hanbok and put them on. The robe was too large for me, so I started to cinch it in at the waist. "No," Kyung-jik said. "Keep it loose. It will make you look larger."

I did as he said and he inspected me carefully. "Your hair," he said.

"Yes. I know what to do," I replied. I pulled out the binyeo and pins that held my hair in the queen's style and tossed them to the ground. I twisted my hair into a peasant's braid and pinned it. I put on the scarf and looked at Kyung-jik.

"One more thing," he said. He reached to the ground and scooped a finger of soil from between the flagstones. He stood and faced me. "Forgive me, Majesty, but your face . . . is too . . ."

"Do what you must," I said.

He rubbed the soil into his hands and pressed his fingers and palms against my face. I closed my eyes. It was the first time he'd ever touched me. His hands were strong but gentle. He moved them over my forehead, on my cheeks and chin. The soil was gritty against my skin, but he didn't hurt me. He took his hands away and I opened my eyes. He examined me again and said, "Follow me."

We moved quickly through the palace shadows to a gate on the west side, where two guards stood. When they saw us, the guards drew their swords and said, "Halt!"

Kyung-jik positioned himself between the guards and me. "Let us through," he said.

"Who are you?" one guard demanded.

Kyung-jik stepped forward and put his hand on the handle of his sword. "It is me, Kyung-jik, sergeant of the queen's guard."

The guards did not move, and I was afraid they didn't recognize us. Or maybe they were part of the rebellion. I stepped around Kyung-jik. I pulled off my scarf and stood tall before the guards. "I am your queen," I said, leveling eyes on them. "Now step aside and let us through."

The guards hesitated a moment and then one said, "Yes, Majesty." They stepped aside and bowed as Kyung-jik led me through the gate and out into the streets.

I put the scarf back over my head, and we started down the cobblestone street. The voices in my head were not as loud now, but I could still hear them begging me to run. I started at a fast pace but Kyung-jik said, "Slowly." He did not address me as "Majesty." "Bend forward," he said. "Like me." I saw that he slouched forward and, in his peasant clothing, no longer looked like my tall, handsome guard. I nodded and slouched forward, too. We maintained that posture as we walked to where the cobblestones changed to dirt streets.

"We have to make it to the river," Kyung-jik whispered. He pointed the direction for us to go. Here and there people ran in the streets toward the orange glow in the sky. They were all dressed in rags. Their hair was greasy and their faces smudged with dirt. Some had rags for shoes.

We turned toward the Han River. As we made our way past dark houses and markets closed for the night, we came closer to the rioters. Their shouting was louder now, and I could make out what they were saying. "Burn down the palace!" and "Kill the queen!" The glow from their torches lit the sky only a few streets away. Kyung-jik and I came to a fork in the street. "This way," he said, and we turned away from the rioters. I had to fight the urge to run.

A way along the road, there was another mob. They, too, were marching toward the palace, and they started to merge with the first mob, trapping Kyung-jik and me between them. I wanted to turn around, but Kyung-jik kept moving forward. Soon the rioters were all around us. "Kill the queen!" they shouted as they marched. "Burn down the palace!" They thrust their torches above their heads. They spit and cursed. Some gripped swords in their hands. Others had clubs.

One rioter bumped into me, knocking me to the ground. I looked at him. His clothes were nothing more than rags. His teeth were stained yellow. His face was gaunt and his eyes were full of rage. In his hand he held a short sword.

"Who are you?" the rioter asked, pointing his sword at me.

"She is my sister," Kyung-jik said, stepping between us.

"She is pretty," the rioter asked. "Are you yangban?"

"No," Kyung-jik answered. "We work for Master Pak near the river. She is a cook and I am Master Pak's stablemate. We are trying to get home."

"Hmmm," the rioter said. "You do not look like a stablemate and she doesn't look like a cook. If you truly are, you should join us. We are taking the palace and throwing out the queen!"

"Sir," Kyung-jik said, "I, too, wish the queen was not on the throne. But I cannot join your revolt. My sister and I must get home. Our master is waiting for us."

The rioter nodded. "You had better get home quickly with your pretty sister," he said. "There will be blood tonight." The rioter turned away and fell in step with the rest of the mob. "Burn down the palace!" he shouted, thrusting his sword into the air. "Kill the queen!"

We moved through the mob with our heads low. We walked more quickly than before, and soon the rioters were behind us. Kyung-jik put a hand in front of me. "Slow," he said. We slowed our pace, and before long the mob's shouts and the light from their torches grew dim.

"Where are we going?" I asked.

Kyung-jik kept his eyes forward. "There are horses waiting for us. They will take us to the countryside where we can hide."

"How long must I be there?"

"I do not know," he said.

"Why do I have to pretend to be a cook?" I asked.

Kyung-jik stopped and made sure no one was near. He took my arm and made me face him. He looked at me directly, which he had never done before. "Listen to me," he said. "The Taewŏn-gun and the Japanese are hunting you. If they find you, they will kill you. We must pretend to be commoners, and therefore you must act like one. I am sorry, Majesty," he said, "but that is the way it must be."

"So I am no longer the queen . . . ," I said.

"For now, Majesty," he said. "Also, I can no longer call you 'Majesty,' but I don't know what to call you."

I pointed for us to walk on. I let him go ahead of me, as a common woman should. "My mother's name was Soo-bo," I said. "That would be a good name for me." Kyung-jik nodded.

"Soo-bo," he said, and we made our way south to the Han River.

TWENTY-FOUR

Present day. Seoul, Korea

A loud banging outside jerks me out of the trance I'm in from Anna's story. I hear people shouting. Inside the room with its wooden columns and painted beams, people start to move. There's a sudden draft, making the fireplace fire flicker. Someone runs up to Anna, who still sits on the throne in her red and yellow hanbok. She leans in as they whisper something to her. She nods and the messenger runs toward the shouting. Anna turns to me. Her painted face and extravagant hairdo still intimidate me. "It appears that we have visitors," she says calmly.

"Visitors?" I ask.

"Your friends have found us," Anna says.

Well, it's about time the cavalry came to my rescue, but I'm not sure how I feel about it now. I'm relaxed here, and I have to admit that I'm engrossed in Anna's story. And I really don't want to face hours with the Seoul police, the CIA, and everyone at State who'll want answers about my little ordeal here. Guess I have no choice, though. They've come to get me.

The pounding outside stops. I hear people arguing. They're speaking English and the tone is distinctly military. Jesus, it's the marines.

These guys don't screw around. If they think I'm in here—and clearly, they do—they won't back down until they have me safe in the back of a Humvee speeding toward the nearest US base.

"You're screwed," I say to Anna. "Sorry. Guess the rest of your story will have to wait."

She smiles at me as if she knows something I don't. "We shall see, Mr. Simon," she says.

I shake my head. "Anna, don't fight these guys. They train for this sort of thing. It's what they live for. People could get hurt."

"A few people hurt is better than millions dead," she says. "Anyway, I assure you that everyone here—and outside—is more than willing to make that sacrifice."

"Outside?"

The voices at the door get louder. Words I can't quite make out are angry and threatening. Sounds like demands, ultimatums. This isn't good. The guards standing behind me aren't moving. I wonder what they'll do with me if all hell breaks loose. Best to stay put, try to stay calm. If the marines break in, hit the floor, don't move. The arguing stops. Guess the jarheads have decided to stop talking. I look at Anna. She hasn't taken her eyes off me. She wears an almost arrogant smile, and I wonder if this junior state department aide knows what's about to come raining down on her pretty little head. Probably not. I almost feel sorry for her.

I hear something from beyond where the arguing was. I crane my neck to listen. It's faint, like it's coming from blocks away. It's chanting. Hundreds of people, maybe thousands. I can't hear what they're saying, but it sounds like it's in Korean. It doesn't sound angry or agitated. Just chanting. Two words, over and over again. It's coming from all sides. It grows louder and louder.

Anna continues to stare at me with her smile. But now I see that it isn't as arrogant as I thought it was before. Her eyes say it. It's conviction.

Passionate, burning, desperate *conviction.* I can feel her flame. It's almost erotic.

I see Anna mouth words as she stares at me. I realize that she's chanting in unison with the crowd outside. I can't quite make out what she's saying. I watch Anna more closely and listen to the crowd. Then I hear it. *"Han hangug! Han hangug!"* I search my Korean for a translation. When it comes to me, I'm stunned. "One Korea!" the crowd chants. "One Korea!"

My God, they're her people. It sounds like thousands of them chanting the words that Anna's story is about. Good move, Anna. Check and mate. Who are you, anyway? You send the comb with the two-headed dragon to the president of the United States to get our attention; you kidnap me to listen to your story as you sit there on a throne dressed like a queen; you mobilize a huge crowd to keep the US Marine Corps Special Ops from rescuing me. You're not just some junior embassy aide. *So who the hell are you?*

I look behind Anna at the tapestry with the two-headed dragon. I remember the part in her story about Minister Kim saying that each time the tapestry appears, a great leader rises. Damn, is it possible? Anna? I close my eyes and shake my head. The fog in my brain reminds me that I haven't slept for nearly two days. All this drama must be getting to me, playing with my head. Queens and death threats and armies with nuclear warheads and angry mobs and the damn Japanese, Russians, and Chinese, and now I just want to talk to Jin-ee about passion.

I open my eyes. Anna is coming down the dais steps toward me. She stops and faces me. She puts her hands at her waist, left over right. She folds her legs underneath her so that her chima flows out all around her. She puts her hands on the floor in front of her and bends to place her head on them. She stays like that for several seconds. Then she sits up and looks at my feet. This close, she's even more striking than when she was on the throne. Sitting on the floor, she looks innocent, like a young girl dressed up in a queen's costume. It's as if the queen on the throne minutes earlier is gone, replaced by a young woman. She looks vulnerable, almost needy.

"The rest of my story is the most important part," she says. "It's about"—she looks at me—"the people."

"The people?"

"Isn't that why you are here, Mr. Simon?" she whispers. She sighs and looks down again. "When Queen Min was a young queen, she didn't know her people. She lived a privileged life inside the palace and only saw her subjects through the curtains of her palanquin. She didn't know them, Mr. Simon. She didn't know them, yet she was trying to build a nation for them. The spirit of One Korea is the spirit of *all* Koreans, not just the kings and queens. Not just the yangban or one clan. It is of all people. And she didn't know them."

Anna's eyes turn to me. "You don't know them, either, Mr. Simon. Yet you will help make decisions that will affect them far more than the people of the United States. And you don't know them. I beg you, please, listen to the rest of my story."

She straightens her back. "But I'll tell you what." She points toward the door with her chin. "Outside, they want to take you away. They want to take you back to where they can tell you what *they* think you should put in your report to the president. So if you want to leave rather than hear the rest of my story, I won't stop you. It's an important decision, Mr. Simon. Important for this country, but it is important for you, too, I think."

Two hours earlier, I would have bolted for the door. Now, I'm not so sure. I look at Anna and all I see is Jin-ee. Intelligent, tender, poignant . . . beautiful. Back then I was so in love with Jin-ee that I thought I'd break. But it wasn't just her. It was all the possibilities. For me, for her, for us . . . for the world.

Looking at Anna now, I realize that my slide into the problems with Jin-ee began here at the embassy when I was about Anna's age. Jin-ee wanted to take a few years off, live among the rice farmers and fishermen, learn to make silk and celadon pots. She wanted to go to North Korea to see what was happening there. "Let's do it," she pleaded.

I considered it. I really did. Jin-ee's enthusiasm was intoxicating. But I had just gotten a promotion with a healthy raise. More responsibility, money. More status. So I said no and stayed buried in my work at the embassy. Jin-ee never pressed me on it again—at least not that I'd heard.

Now, Anna's story has sparked the fire in me that I had before, the fire that I found out a few days ago Jin-ee never lost. I want to know more about this country and these people. I want to hear the rest of Anna's story.

I point at the door. "What should I say to hold off the jarheads?" I ask.

Anna looks pleased. "Tell them you need another hour."

"I doubt if they'll listen. They're marines, after all."

"Trust me. It's an impressive crowd outside. They don't want a situation."

I nod and one of the guys behind me leads me up a few stairs to a door. I stick my head through, and there outside in the daylight are a dozen Korean men standing in the tae kwon do ready stance facing a handful of US Marines who are pointing M16 rifles. The chanting from behind the marines is loud. "Han hangug! Han hangug!" When my eyes adjust to the light, I look for the marine in charge and spot a stiff-jawed lieutenant. From behind the Koreans, I shout to him that I'm fine and that I'm here by my own choice. In a voice that would intimidate a prizefighter, he orders me to come with him. In my gut, I feel the defiance I had twenty-five years earlier when Jin-ee and I faced the police on the Michigan campus and tried to stop them from tearing down the old student union. It's exhilarating to feel that passion again. "No, lieutenant," I say, wishing I could tell him to go to hell instead. "I'll take full responsibility. Please back off. I'll be out in an hour."

The lieutenant puffs out his chest. He again orders me to come with him as if I'm a recruit on the first day of boot camp. "Go to hell," I say, and slip back inside.

When I return to my chair in the big room, Anna has assumed her position on the throne. In her spectacular regalia, she looks like a terrible, powerful queen again. I sit and cross my legs.

"The people," I say to her.

She smiles back at me. "Yes, the people," she says. "The *true* spirit of One Korea."

TWENTY-FIVE

1882. South central Korea

Kyung-jik pulled his horse to a stop on a rise in the road a mile or so from a small village nestled in a shallow valley. My horse, used to following Kyung-jik's horse, stopped without me pulling on the reins. The horse's hooves were still wrapped in rags that silenced them when we were on the cobblestones of Seoul. It wasn't yet light, but through the early morning fog I could see we were in the low hills between the mountains and sea. Among the hills I could make out geometrically shaped rice paddies, and in the flats, green pastures with cattle and sheep. The village houses, maybe thirty in all, were scattered throughout the valley. They were small and low and had grass roofs.

Kyung-jik had chosen his most loyal guard to escort us. The man had met us with horses at the Han River and hadn't said a word all night as we rode through a soft rain along a quiet country road south of Seoul. From behind me, the guard rode up to Kyung-jik, and together they studied a house on the village edge. The house was not large, but it was half again as large as the others nearby. It was the only one with a tile roof. Next to the house was a long wooden building with a brick chimney at one end.

As Kyung-jik inspected the house, I was glad I had made him the commander of my guard. He was smart, skilled, and loyal. He was big and strong and dedicated to his craft. Once I saw him in a courtyard in the palace grounds practicing swordsmanship with other guards. He wore only a *mawashi* loincloth and the sweat on his smooth skin glistened in the hot afternoon sun. The muscles in his back, shoulders, and legs were well defined. He had his dark eyes focused on his opponent and his square jaw set. When they lunged at each other, Kyung-jik's moves were swift and true, and his opponent quickly submitted. When they saw me, the guards stopped practicing and bowed. I believed I blushed a little when, for just an instant, my eyes met Kyung-jik's.

My horse pawed at the ground as Kyung-jik and the other guard exchanged a few words. Kyung-jik dismounted. He came to me and held out a hand. "We are going to that house," he said, "but we must go on foot. If we take the horses, the neighbors will be suspicious."

I took his hand and slid off my horse. I was wet and cold and tired from riding all night. But I was safe, away from the mobs and assassins in Seoul.

"Who are we staying with?" I demanded. "What clan are they from?"

My guard did not answer as he should have. Instead, he handed the horses to the other guard and pointed to woods not far off the road. "Go there and stay until dark," he said to the guard. "Take off the saddles and the rags from their hooves and bury them. Then, make your way back to Seoul. If anyone asks you about the horses, say that you were hired to deliver them to a stable in Seoul. Go now, before the light comes."

The guard pulled on the reins, and the horses followed him single file back down the road. I stood alone with Kyung-jik. He nodded toward the house. "We are going there. The man who lives in that house is named Suk-won Min. He is a distant cousin of your uncle and he is a potter. His wife is Ki-soo. They know who you are, but no one else does. For those who don't know who you are, we will tell them this. You and I are brother and sister. We are guests of Suk-won because our home was burned by the rioters in Seoul."

Kyung-jik looked at me and raised a finger. "Remember, you are not safe, not even here. The villagers must not know who you are. As I have said, for the time, you are not the queen. Your name is Soo-bo. And as a common woman, you must not demand answers to your questions as you did just now. I cannot treat you like a queen, nor can Suk-won and Ki-soo. And you must not act like one, either. I am sorry."

I nodded. "Of course, you are right," I said. "I will play my part. But I'll need to get messages to my allies. I'll need to get a message to Empress Cixi, too."

"I have made arrangements for that," Kyung-jik said. "Give your messages to me. I will see that they are delivered."

As we started toward the house, the sun, softly filtered by the low, thin clouds, began to rise beyond the hills. The red sky slowly turned blue. After the rain, everything smelled clean and new. Some ways down the road, mud stuck to my feet and I slipped. Kyung-jik grabbed my arm to keep me upright. "Thank you," I said as he steadied me. It was the first time I had ever said "thank you" to him.

When we neared the house, I said, "If you please, kind brother, I would like to ask a question. How long will we be here?"

Kyung-jik smiled at my acting and nodded. "I do not know, Soo-bo," he answered.

The potter's house reminded me of my father's house. It was not large and proper like the House of Gamgodang with its many outbuildings and formal gardens. Rather, it had the look and feel of a workingman's home. A low wall surrounded the house, and a small, well-kept vegetable garden was along one side. The gray-green roof tiles were properly maintained—in line and straight. On the other side of the house was the wood building I had seen from the road. It was twice as long and twice as tall as the house. The sides were open and inside were two large brick mounds. The one in back had a chimney that rose above the building's roof. Off to one side was a huge stack of firewood.

As I stayed outside the wall, Kyung-jik went to the door and announced himself. The door opened and a tall, angular man exchanged a few words with Kyung-jik. The man looked at me and nodded. Kyung-jik came to me. "Come," he said. "That is Suk-won. They have been expecting us."

Kyung-jik led me to the house. When I stepped inside, Suk-won stood next to his wife, an attractive woman who was as short as her husband was tall. They looked silly standing there trying not to bow to me. Ki-soo held her hands at her waist in front of her, one hand squeezing the other so hard they were turning white. Suk-won pressed his arms along his side. Tall and lean as he was, he reminded me of a statue. They didn't look at me, but they didn't keep their eyes low, either. They looked to the side, trying to obey the orders to keep my cover, but at the same time trying to show the proper respect for their queen.

I immediately liked them. They had the look of honest, robust people who respected the throne. Their house was simple and clean, with only a few decorations in the room. Kindness and integrity showed in their faces and hard work creased their hands.

I went to Suk-won who still didn't look directly at me. "Master Min," I said to him. "My guard tells me that for my protection, I must not act as the queen. And therefore, for my protection, you must not treat me like one, either. Anyway, I think it will be difficult for us to live together if you and your wife are always so stiff and refuse to look at me."

He turned nervous eyes toward me. I almost laughed at him. "Well, that is a start," I said. "Now, I am tired from riding all night. Do you have a place for me to rest in this fine house?"

At this, Suk-won relaxed a little and nodded. "Yes," he said. "We have prepared a room. My wife will show you."

Ki-soo, still trying hard to strike the right pose, led me to a room off the back of the house with a sliding latticed door leading to a quaint courtyard. The room had an earthy smell, but the bed was soft and the ondol heating had warmed the room. I stripped off my wet clothes and crawled into the bed. I slept the entire morning.

When I awoke, I went out to the courtyard. The fog had moved off and the sun was high, making the courtyard bright. A Chinese stone bench sat under a small persimmon tree. All throughout the courtyard were superb celadon pots. I sat on the bench and took in the sun's warmth, thinking over what had brought me here. I had always been careful not to shame the Taewŏn-gun, and I even let him stay close to the king. We'd had many differences over the past several years, but I never thought he'd try to have me killed. I had underestimated him—his need to stay in power, his ego, his hatred of me. From now on, I would have to regard him as the mortal enemy he was. When I took the throne again—if I took it again—perhaps I should have him killed to show everyone that I was indeed a dragon queen.

And then there was Gojong. My husband had fled from my side at the first sign of danger. The king was weak, unable to stand on his own. I couldn't curse him for his weakness—that was the way he was. I had to blame myself for not being the strong one he turned to. I had thought my move with Mister Euno would show him that I was strong like his father. But perhaps it was a foolish thing I had done. It was an emotional, undisciplined outburst that had given the Taewŏn-gun and the Japanese an excuse to throw me off the throne.

A door opened from the main room, and an old man stepped into the courtyard. He was short and thin, and his long beard was pure white. His head was bald except for a strip of white hair over both ears and across the back of his neck. He wore loose, dark clothes. He tapped a cane on the ground in front of him.

"Earlier, I heard the voice of a stranger," he said, tilting his head. As he moved closer, I saw his eyes were pale and lifeless. "I was not told we would have visitors. Pray introduce yourself so we are strangers no more."

"My name is Soo-bo," I said, standing up from the bench. "Soo-bo Min." I realized I hadn't bowed to the elderly man, as a commoner should. But then again, he was blind.

"Soo-bo of the Min clan? Hmmm," he said in a most knowing way. "I knew a Soo-bo from the Min clan who lived near the Han River with her daughter. She would be older now and I hear in your voice that you are young."

"I'm sure we have never met," I said quickly. "May I know your name, sir?"

The old man moved closer. His white beard and bald head shimmered in the midday sun. His eyes, lifeless though they were, twinkled under pure-white eyebrows. "I am Woo-jin Min," he said. "I am Suk-won's uncle."

"I am honored to meet you, *samchonim*," I said, showing him respect by using the honorific for "uncle." But since he was blind, again I did not bow.

"What do we owe your visit to?" the old man asked. His voice matched his small size. It was thin and halting, but he delivered his words deliberately and with authority like a *mudang*—a shaman priest.

"My brother and I came here because our house was burned by the rioters," I answered. "I am not sure how long we will stay."

"Are you yangban?"

I wasn't sure how to answer this. Kyung-jik had only said to say that we were brother and sister. He did not say what class we were or what we did in Seoul. I decided I should use the story he'd told the rioter on the street—that I was a cook and he was a stablemate for a wealthy man in Seoul. "No, samchonim," I answered. "We are sangmin."

The old man nodded. "I ask because your manner of speech is that of a yangban. And I sensed that you did not bow to me, your elder, when we met just now." He grinned a blind-man's grin, and waved his hand. "No matter," he said. "I must get to work. Suk-won is waiting for me." He tapped his cane and headed for the large, two-story building.

"What work do you do, samchonim?" I asked before he left the courtyard.

He stopped and turned his head halfway back to me. "I am the one who forms the clay into pots," he said. And he disappeared around the back of the house.

I went through the house and out the front door. I stood in the path leading to the road and looked around. I had never seen a village or a workplace like this up close. Since I'd become queen, I'd lived inside the palace and had only seen villages, farms, and factories from inside my palanquin while traveling to a picnic or an official function. I felt vulnerable to be here like this, out in the open. But it was liberating, too. It was as if the palace and my troubles were on the other side of the world, though they were only a half-day's journey away.

I heard thwacking behind me and turned to look. In the enclosure between the house and wooden building, Kyung-jik and Suk-won were working on a mound of clay in the hot midday sun. My guard had his shirt off and pounded the clay with a large wooden mallet. After a few strikes, Kyung-jik leaned on the mallet while Suk-won—with his long, sinewy arms—used a wide paddle to turn the clay Kyung-jik had just pounded. After three or four turns, Kyung-jik resumed his pounding. Though they could have only been working together a short time, they moved in unison like a fine Chinese clock. Thwack, thwack, thwack, turn. Thwack, thwack, thwack, turn. Sweat poured down Kyung-jik's chest and back, and his face showed that he enjoyed the hard work. Suk-won seemed pleased, too, though his job was much easier. I guessed that he was happy to have such a strong man as Kyung-jik helping him.

Ki-soo came outside and stood alongside me. She was about my height, though she looked to be much stronger than me. Together we watched the men work. She still seemed nervous to be with me. "Why do they beat the clay?" I asked, trying to make her comfortable.

"To mix it and get rid of the air bubbles," she answered.

I said, "I suppose the more they mix it, the better the pots will be."

"Yes, you are right, Majesty, um, Soo-bo," she said. "Although I think my husband mixes it more than is necessary."

"He has to get rid of the air or the pot will explode when it is fired. Am I correct?"

"You know about making pottery," Ki-soo said, relaxing some.

I smiled at her. "I read a lot. Where does the clay come from?"

Ki-soo pointed across the field with her chin. "It comes from swamps near the sea at Ansan," she said. "It is the perfect clay for white celadon, but unlike other clay, it is full of impurities, which we must remove. It is backbreaking work, so Suk-won is the only one who uses that clay. The pounding and kneading is the last step."

"Who do you sell your pots to?" I asked.

Ki-soo said, "Suk-won and his uncle are known to make the finest white celadon in Korea. We sell to yangban and have even sold pieces to the palace. Our business has suffered since the new taxes, though. People don't have money for pots anymore. We barely earn enough to get by."

She suddenly remembered who she was talking to. Her eyes went wide and she stiffened. "Please forgive me," she said quickly.

I grinned at her. "I, too, think the king and queen should be hung for their contemptible taxes!" I said, jerking my chin up. "Then you could sell more pots!"

Ki-soo hesitated for a moment. Then her face slid into a grin. "Well, they do not have to be hung," she said, shaking her head. "They should just lower the taxes and concern themselves more with the people."

We stood for a minute smiling at each other, and I could tell my initial opinion of her and her husband was correct. They were honest, honorable people. I was lucky that they had agreed to hide me while half of Korea wanted my head. They were taking a big risk, and I vowed that someday I would reward them for it.

I looked back at the men. "Kyung-jik says we don't know how long we will be here," I said. "I will get bored with nothing to do. How can I help?"

"Oh," Ki-soo stammered. "We have no need for your help."

I turned back to her. "Kyung-jik says your neighbors will be watching. I cannot act like a queen with nothing to do at a pottery factory. I should work so they don't become suspicious. What can I do?"

Ki-soo took a second to think. "I know," she said. "Since we've had to let some of our help go, Suk-won's uncle sits at the wheel alone most of the day. He gets bored with no one to talk to, and he does like to talk. It makes me sad to see him alone. Perhaps, once in a while, you can sit with him as he works. Would that be too much to ask?"

"I like to talk, too," I answered. "I would be happy to sit with him."

"I must warn you about Woo-jin," Ki-soo said. "We did not tell him who you were. He has many friends, and he is not always careful about what he says." She shook her head. "He often says the most unusual things that no one understands. It's as if, though he is blind, he sees what others do not."

"I see," I said, remembering my uncle said the same thing about my mother and me. "Perhaps I can learn something from him." I went to the big building to sit and talk with the blind man who saw what others did not.

TWENTY-SIX

I found Woo-jin inside a shed next to the big wooden building. The shed was made from planks and had a crude door hanging on leather hinges. Here and there, streaks of dusted sunlight angled through cracks in the walls. Tables with carving tools sat against one wall, while huge pots with lids on them leaned against one another. In the shed's center were dozens of pots in various stages of completion. Some were plain. Others had been etched with intricate patterns of plants and cranes and dragons. They were all dried clay, not yet glazed or fired.

Bathed in a cut of sunlight, Woo-jin sat on a stool at a stone wheel that was two feet off the ground. He pumped his legs up and down to drive the mechanism that made the wheel turn with a low grinding sound. On one side of him was a mound of gray clay; on the other, a bowl of water. Over his half-bald head, he had tied a red scarf that made him look like he was a master of the military arts. He leaned over the wheel with his eyes closed and his head turned to the side. His long fingers and hands, slick with mud, caressed a ball of clay. He pressed his thumbs inside the ball hollowing it. As the clay turned, he pinched, squeezed, and pulled at it. Little by little, the clay rose into the shape of a pot. He dipped his hands into the water and began where he had left off, all the while pumping his legs to keep the wheel turning steadily.

It was hot inside the shed, and beads of sweat formed and ran down Woo-jin's head as he worked. His red scarf caught the sweat before it could drop into the clay.

I stood for a long time watching him. The wheel's smooth movement and the clay's gradual ascent in Woo-jin's hands were hypnotic. It was as if the blind man was bringing a dead lump of clay to life, like a phoenix rising. He was on the pot's stem now, pinching the narrow opening ever so carefully. At the top, he gently turned the clay out to form the lip.

When he was done, he stopped pumping his legs and the heavy wheel ground to a stop. The pot stood tall and proud in the center of it. The curves, the size, the shape of it were in perfect proportion. It was a majestic thing, worthy of a place in any king's palace. Woo-jin slowly ran his hands from the pot's base to the top, caressing it as if he loved the thing he had just made. Then suddenly he lunged at it and pounded the pot back into a lump of clay.

I couldn't believe what I just saw. He had made what looked like a perfect pot. I shook my head and stepped inside the shed. "Why did you destroy it, samchonim?" I asked. "It was perfect!"

The old man turned to me. "Ah," he said, showing no surprise at me being there, "it may have looked perfect to you, but it was not to me. My family has been making pots for hundreds of years. We have a reputation to uphold. If we let every pot go, our reputation will suffer."

I pulled up a stool and sat next to him. "What was wrong with it?"

Woo-jin thought about my question for several seconds. His white eyebrows twitched. Then he said, "I cannot say so that you will understand. It wasn't the shape, or the dimensions, or the thickness of the walls. All pots are unique in those respects. No, it was what I felt inside. The pot's spirit was not what it should have been."

"The pot's spirit?"

He reached for the lump of clay on the wheel and found it with his hands. He dribbled water on it and started to form it into a ball again.

"There are spirits in all things," he said as he worked the clay. "The mountains have a spirit. The trees, the sea, this wheel, the clay. If you are lucky and listen carefully, they speak to you. Then you will know who they really are."

"Yes," I said, "I hear spirits sometimes. I don't always know what they are saying."

"Perhaps," Woo-jin said, raising a muddy finger, "you are not listening completely."

I thought of when I had heard spirits. Most times, they had scared me. I had fought them and tried to make them go away. But there were times I had heard them clearly. I'd heard them in my sick infant; in Sunjong, my young prince; at the tomb of Taejo; in an orchid in full bloom; in the two-headed dragon in my tapestry. I had heard them say, "One Korea." I heard this and more, but I hadn't always understood them. Perhaps the old potter was right—I hadn't been listening completely.

"I want to learn how to hear the spirits in the pots," I said, "and the spirits in other things, too. Can you teach me?"

"Hmmm," Woo-jin said. "Are you willing to listen completely, no matter what they say to you?"

"Yes," I answered.

He nodded and began pumping his legs again to turn the wheel.

Over the next several weeks, Kyung-jik and I settled into a routine. Kyung-jik slept in a corner of the big building in a bed he made out of straw and a blanket. He would always rise before the sun to start working the clay. It was a grueling process. Men delivered raw clay on oxcarts and dumped it in the yard next to the big building. Suk-won and Kyung-jik would spend hours picking through the new clay by hand to remove sticks, pebbles, and blades of swamp grass. Then they would press the clay through a series of goat-hair screens, each one finer than the previous one to remove the impurities. When they finished screening, they put the clay into large troughs and washed it three or four times. Then they beat it and kneaded it for hours before Suk-won said it was ready. It was incredibly hard work that Kyung-jik relished. At the end of each day, so much gray clay covered him he looked like a ghost. Sometimes I laughed at him, but never so he could see me.

I slept in the small room off the courtyard, and every day I arose with the sun. Since I was not the queen here, I helped with the cooking and household chores. Ki-soo was embarrassed that I did. She told me they used to have a housemaid and two workers to help Suk-won prepare the clay. I told her I didn't mind helping. It gave me something to do, I said, and reminded me of when I was a girl and helped my mother. Ki-soo seemed to accept this, although I could tell she was still embarrassed. In the afternoon, I sat with Woo-jin as he made pots.

We'd been at the potter's house for several weeks when the Ch'usŏk celebration began. Ki-soo and several women from the village had spent days in the potter's house preparing for the three-day harvest festival. From the back of the house, they dug up tall narrow *tok* pots that they had buried the past spring. Inside the tall pots were various types of kimchi: spicy fermented napa cabbage, daikon, and cucumbers. In the kitchen, women from the village made *japchae* noodles, pork spine stew, *jeon* pancakes with fish, green onion and spinach salad, pork bulgogi. They pounded cooked rice and sugar into paste for dduk, enough for dozens of the half-moon cakes. They crushed persimmon berries and roasted barley for bori cha. They brought out the soju.

Of course, the food was much simpler than the fancy delicacies the palace cooks prepared for feasts at Gyeongbok. They didn't have quail eggs in soy sauce, or squid garnished with sturgeon roe, or salmon from the North Pacific, or beef from Manchuria. But the feast here had a hearty, unassuming feel like I remembered from when I was a girl. It was straightforward and honest and I realized that unlike the palace feasts, this one was wholly—and in many ways more—Korean.

Since I had to pretend to be somebody other than the queen, I helped with the preparations. I didn't mind. I had always helped with the Ch'usŏk feast when I was young, and I still remembered how to do most things. In fact, I enjoyed it. It was a welcome change from the pressures of running the country and fighting the Taewŏn-gun. Mostly I helped with the dduk because that was the main fare at the festival and it was something I'd always done when I was a girl. Ki-soo had told the village women the same story about me—that Kyung-jik and I were siblings whose house was burned down by the rioters because we were Min. All of the women accepted the story and treated me kindly. All, that is, except Chae-won.

Chae-won was a Yi. Before I met her, I learned from Ki-soo that she was from a yangban family in Jeonju. Her parents, unable to find a yangban man willing to marry their unattractive, ill-tempered daughter, made her marry a farmer here in the village. According to Ki-soo, she hadn't been happy since the day she arrived. "Be careful what you say to her," Ki-soo warned. "Chae-won has two faces and she has a loose tongue."

I first met Chae-won when we worked on the dduk together with Ki-soo and two other women named Mee-su and Coh-ri. We were at the kitchen table in Ki-soo's house. We were filling the rice cakes, some with bean paste, others with roasted sesame, and some with honey. Chae-won sat across from me. She was older than me, and wide in the body with a thick neck and small eyes. She always scowled. Even her smile was a twisted grimace. She eyed me suspiciously as if she thought I was about to steal something from her.

As we worked, Chae-won pounded and poked at the rice cakes as though she was angry with them. "I only like the cakes made with honey," she grunted. "I don't know why we make the ones with bean and sesame."

"The children feel the same as you," Ki-soo said. "They bite into a cake and if it isn't honey, they put it back. I like them all, however." The other women nodded in agreement.

"I do the same as the children," Chae-won said as she jabbed at the rice with her stumpy hands. "If it is not honey, I put it back."

"Those with bites in them don't get eaten," said Mee-su. "Then we must feed them to the pigs."

"I do not care," Chae-won sniffed. The others looked sideways at each other and shook their heads.

The women talked about many things as we worked. I had to be careful not to show who I was, especially with Chae-won watching my every move. So I just listened. They talked about the upcoming harvest, how fast their children were growing, how the behavior of birds and the color of the leaves foretold a mild winter. And they talked about what was happening in Seoul.

"I think the rioting is dreadful and unnecessary," Mee-su said, pinching rice flour into a half-moon cake. "People were killed for nothing."

"They are angry," replied Coh-ri, spooning the sugary rice from a bowl. "The government takes too much from them in taxes and spends it on their palaces and fancy lifestyle. They do not care about the commoners."

"I agree with the rioters," Chae-won said, not doing anything. "I think they should chop the king's and queen's heads off." She cocked her head at me. "What do you think, Soo-bo?"

I spooned bean paste into some rice flour. "I'm more concerned about the Taewŏn-gun," I answered. "He gives the country to the Japanese to stay in power."

Chae-won eyed me. "That is the same thing the queen worries about," she said.

Coh-ri spoke up. "I worry more about China. They've dominated us for hundreds of years. I think Japan should put them in their place."

Mee-su shook her head. "Japanese, Chinese . . . it doesn't matter. We are Koreans. We should just be Koreans."

To that, all the women nodded, save Chae-won who fingered honey out of a bowl and ate it.

The first day of Ch'usŏk began with paying respects to ancestors. In the morning, each family laid out food on the table in their house so that the spirits of their ancestors had something to eat during the three-day celebration. Suk-won and Ki-soo laid out a modest spread—what they could afford during these hard times. They burned incense to invite the spirits in, and they lit candles so the spirits could find the meal that was prepared for them. And when it was ready, Suk-won, Ki-soo, and Woo-jin, dressed in their finest hanboks, faced the table and bowed all the way down until their heads were on the floor. They stayed like that for a while, showing respect to those who had come before. Then they stood and invited Kyung-jik and me to do the same. Kyung-jik went first in a short, embarrassed bow. He didn't stay bowed for long, and then it was my turn.

Ki-soo had given me one of her hanboks for the celebration. At first, she offered her best one, but I refused, explaining that it would give away who I was. So she gave me her secondary hanbok, a yellow and blue one which was the right length, but too big around the chest and waist. We cinched it in and it fit perfectly.

Dressed in Ki-soo's hanbok, I stepped in front of the table with its simple food, candles, and incense, and something came over me. This was not a public display at the palace that I had to put on for all to see. For the first time since I was young, this was something simple, genuine, and sincere. Here I could feel the spirits and my own spirit, too. I tried to listen carefully as Woo-jin had said I should. I bowed as Mister Euno had taught me. I faced the table with my head low. I cupped my right hand over my left. I bent at the knee and lowered myself to the ground so that my hanbok spread out around me. I placed my hands on the floor, still right over left. I slowly bent at the waist and brought my forehead to my hands. There I stayed. And though I had my eyes closed, I saw the ghosts of my parents. They were there with me just as they were when I was a girl. I prayed to them, to my father to help me think, to my mother to help me feel. The ghosts of my own children—the one dead and the one living—were there, too. And the ghosts of the kings and queens all the way back to King Taejo and the spirits of my descendants all the way forward to the end of time.

I cannot say how long I stayed bowed like that. It could have been a short time, or it could have been very long. When I finished, I stood and faced the others. Kyung-jik looked anxious, as if he wanted to get the Ch'usŏk celebrations done with so he could get back to the hard work of preparing clay. Suk-won and Ki-soo lowered their eyes as if they didn't want to intrude on my private thoughts. Woo-jin tilted his head high like a blind man does, and smiled.

Suk-won and Ki-soo's house was the largest in the village, so that is where the public festivities took place. There were games, dancing, and music outside on the fine, fall day. Kyung-jik took keen interest in the games, especially those that were physical in nature. He was the best at *jegichagi*, keeping the bean-filled sack in the air with his feet longer than anyone else. When it came time for *juldarigi*, Suk-won and the men from the west vigorously recruited him for their side of the tug-of-war contest, telling him that if their team out-pulled the east, the harvest would be particularly good that year. The east team went for him, too, saying that if *they* won, the coming winter would be short and mild. The west team countered, telling Kyung-jik that the east had won several years in a row and that the winters had been just as long and harsh as always. Eventually Kyung-jik agreed to go with the west team, and Suk-won led them in a cheer.

Before the contest began, the village offered sacrifices of food and charms to the earth goddess, Teojuchin. Then the contestants of each side, dressed in white robes, danced and circled around the other, raising their heavy braided ropes over their heads to make them look like serpents. As they danced, they chanted and hurled insults at the other team. After some time, they looped the two ropes together and the contest began. The west team put Kyung-jik at the front of their rope and Suk-won just behind him. Across from him was Chae-won's farmer husband, Hyeong-ju, big and strong from a lifetime of hard work. When they took hold of the rope, the men set their jaws and focused on the other side. Then, as the women and children waved flags and banged on cymbals and drums, the men began to pull. At the start, Hyeong-ju gave a mighty tug, causing many men on the west team to tumble forward. Kyung-jik dug in and held steady. When Hyeong-ju made another strong pull, Kyung-jik pulled back, giving his teammates time to regain their feet. Then Kyung-jik leaned into the rope and the entire west team leaned with him. Soon, the east team members were falling forward. Hyeong-ju tried to stem the west team's advance, but Kyung-jik kept pulling. The muscles on his arms and back bulged out. Before the east could gather their feet, Kyung-jik shouted, "Pull!" and the west team gave it all they had. Hyeong-ju took a step forward and several more of his teammates stumbled. Then Hyeong-ju stumbled, too, and the contest was over. The west team let out a cheer, and their women and children waved flags and banged their cymbals and drums. Kyung-jik set down his rope and faced Hyeong-ju and they bowed to each other. The west team lifted Kyung-jik on their shoulders and paraded him around as if he was a king. My guard seemed a little embarrassed by the ordeal, but I could tell he was pleased, too. As he bounced on the shoulders of Suk-won and his teammates, something stirred inside me. Naturally, I was proud of him, but it was something more, too.

After the midday meal, the men and children went to the field in front of Suk-won's house to fly kites. The children wrote their names on their kites so that evil spirits would blow away with the wind and not haunt their sleep. They tossed the kites into the air, and the children bounced and shouted with joy as the kites rose high. The kites were much simpler than the ones they flew at the palace, but against the mild blue sky, I thought they were beautiful. They were all colors—blue, red, yellow, and green. Most were plain, but one was shaped like a tiger, and another like a dragon. They had colorful ribbons off the sides and long tails that twisted and curled like a serpent's tail in the breeze. The kites soared and my spirit soared with them. I felt the spirits of the children who had written their names on the kites. And my spirit held hands with the spirits of their parents on the ground, watching their joyful children. For the first time in my life, I felt the spirit of my people, the true spirit of my country. I was their queen, but I'd never gotten to know them. Here in the afternoon sun sitting among these simple people, I became one of them. And as the kites flew so high that I thought the sun would swallow them, I vowed to always remember who they were. They were my people. They were Korea.

When the children grew tired of flying their kites, we gathered in the clearing aside Suk-won's house for music, dancing, and storytelling. I sat alone, happy to take it all in without having to be careful not to expose who I really was. I still wore Ki-soo's hanbok and had my hair pinned back in a braid. The young girls danced the *buchaechum* in their hanboks and bright-red fans. Accompanying them, a man plucked a seven-string *geum* guitar, another played a *sogeum* flute, and a third pounded a *janggu* drum. The music and the dancing were not very good—certainly not what I was used to. But the soulful way they played and danced somehow seemed to be more Korean than what was performed at the palace.

"What do you think of the dancing?" a voice said from behind me. I snapped out of my trance and turned around. There in front of me was Chae-won. She wore a green hanbok that stretched tight across her stomach. She fanned herself with a Chinese fan. I forgot to give her a small bow as I should have since she was my elder. "The girls are beautiful," I answered. "I especially like their red fans."

"They are not so good," Chae-won said. "When I lived in Jeonju, the dancing and music was much better. The food was better, too. The Yi clan is much more skilled at celebrations, as they are in most everything." She looked down her nose at me. "I would think the entertainment in Seoul is better, too. Is it not?"

"That depends on what better is, Chae-won," I answered. "This here, I think, is perfect."

"Perfect? This?" Chae-won sniffed. "When I first saw you, I thought you were a person of taste. You held yourself that way. But now I am not so sure. Your parents must be uneducated sangmin. Why aren't you with them for the Ch'usŏk festival?"

"My parents died when I was young. And they were educated well enough," I said with some force.

"Well, apparently their education did not pass on to you," she said, fanning herself.

My blood boiled, and I almost lashed out at her as I would have if I didn't have to pretend not to be queen. Instead, I glared at her and said nothing.

"Hmmm," Chae-won said with a nod. "I see you struggle to hold your tongue. Perhaps, you are hiding something."

Chae-won's mouth twisted into her scowling smile. Then she walked away.

TWENTY-SEVEN

"She knows," I said to Kyung-jik. "Chae-won knows who I am and she is a Yi!"

My guard and I were in the courtyard behind Suk-won's house. It was the end of a long day. Kyung-jik had changed out of his muddy clothes and washed. He had pulled his hair into a short tail. It was still wet from washing and was black and shiny like a raven's feathers. The night had the dusty smell of late summer. In the corners of the courtyard, the first leaves to fall rustled in the gentle breeze. The air was dry and the stars twinkled brightly above.

Kyung-jik looked down. "I will keep an eye on her. You have to stay in hiding for a while longer."

"I hope we don't have to move," I said. "I want to stay here."

"I know," he said. "I would like to stay, too. It is peaceful."

"Yes," I nodded, "it is."

We were quiet for a while. Kyung-jik looked at the ground as if he was trying to find something he lost among the cobblestones. I studied him. I thought how peaceful it would be if he and I were husband and wife, living here, him working for Suk-won and me raising chickens and growing vegetables in a garden. I thought about lying next to him at night, massaging his aching shoulders after a hard day's work pounding the clay. I thought of making love to him. But I knew it could never be.

I pushed these thoughts aside and asked, "What do you hear from Seoul?" Since we had arrived at the potter's house, I had given Kyung-jik messages to deliver to my allies and to Empress Cixi in China. When they answered, he would deliver their messages to me, here in the courtyard. I didn't know who he used to deliver my messages and I did not care. That they got through was my only concern.

Kyung-jik said, "The Taewŏn-gun is back in the palace. He told everyone that you were dead and staged a spectacular funeral for you. I heard they dressed a dead woman in your robes and marched it through Seoul for all to see. But the people are not fooled. Most believe you are still alive.

"He did that?" I asked, shaking my head. "Well, the people are right. I am still alive." I grinned at Kyung-jik. "What about the Japanese?" I asked.

They have troops throughout Korea, north and south. They are angry about the riots that killed many of their soldiers. The Taewŏn-gun has ordered our military to stand down. He undoes all of your reforms."

"What do the people think?

"Everyone wants the Japanese to leave, although I think many are glad the Taewŏn-gun ends your reforms.

"What about China?" I asked.

Kyung-jik nodded. "We sent your message to Empress Cixi. She has promised to send troops. If she does, I believe the Japanese will back away. And then you can retake the throne."

"Have you heard from the king?"

"He does nothing," Kyung-jik said, his chin tightening. "He says nothing."

"Have you any news about my son?" I asked.

"No. I am sorry."

I sighed. "Well, let us pray that Cixi is true to her word and sends troops. I worry about our country with the Japanese."

"Yes," Kyung-jik said. "I think it would be best if we returned to the palace soon." As the leaves danced in the corner and stars twinkled above, he lifted his eyes to me. There, deep inside, was passion and longing. He looked at me as if I was the only woman in his world and that he would do anything for me. He loved me, it was plain to see. At that moment, I wished I could fall into his embrace, kiss him, make love to him. It would be the first time I had ever known true love and I wanted it so. But I could not. I was the queen and I would be until my last day. And a queen must make sacrifices for her position. She could never make love to her guard.

It took some effort for me to look away, but I did and said, "Yes, I want to get back to the palace soon. Keep me informed of what Cixi does." I looked at him. "I am tired and it is time for bed. Good night, my loyal guard."

He smiled sadly and said, "Good night, my queen."

The next day, I helped Woo-jin with pot making as I did most days. He never started work until the afternoon. The old man preferred to sleep late and have his morning tea and rice cakes when the rest of us had our midday meal. Suk-won didn't mind. The turning was a small part of pot making, yet it was the most difficult to do well. Apparently, Woo-jin did it very well indeed.

On any given day, the old man might produce five pots. On a good day, it was seven; on a bad day, only three. More than half the time, he would carefully form the clay into what looked like an excellent pot only to smash it back into a ball. "Bad spirit," he would say, and he would start over.

I say that I helped, but I didn't do much. Occasionally I fetched more clay, went to the well to fill his bowl with water, or brought him tea and rice cakes when he was hungry. Mostly I talked with him.

We talked a lot about pot making. He said that being blind was an advantage for him. Instead of using his eyes to form the pot, he depended on his hands. "Hands tell you much more than your eyes can," he said. He said that in his hands, the clay would tell him what it wanted to be. Sometimes it wanted to be tall and narrow. Other times it wanted to be short and round. But only when the clay was a pot did it reveal its spirit. Then he would read the pot's spirit and if it wasn't what it should be, he had to destroy it before the clay hardened, trapping the spirit inside.

He said that people often showed him pots made by someone else and asked his opinion of it. He would feel the pot to detect its flaws. "I can tell if it's a Chinese pot or Japanese pot," he said one day as he took a break. "They both make excellent pots. Still, Korean pots are the best. Especially mine." He grinned.

"Can you feel the spirits in Japanese and Chinese pots?" I asked.

"Of course!" Woo-jin said. "As I have said, all things have spirits."

"What do the spirits in their pots tell you?"

The old man sat at the wheel and thought for a minute. He said, "The Chinese spirits are old and proud. They are like an ancient Buddhist scholar who is content just to be. It is good, I suppose, to be content. I do not think it is good to be too proud, however."

"And the Japanese pots?"

"Hmmm." Woo-jin nodded. "Yes, the Japanese. The spirits in their pots are proud, too, but they are not at all content. I feel fire in them, especially the newer ones."

"Can you teach me how to feel the spirits in the pots, samchonim?"

The old man lifted his head. "Get a pot I made yesterday. The taller one with the narrow neck. Be careful with it. It is special."

I went to where Suk-won placed the pots to dry. The ones made recently were darker than those that had completely dried. Among the five darkest ones sat a tall one with a narrow neck. I carefully picked it up and brought it to the wheel.

Woo-jin felt it and said, "Yes, this is the one. Put it in the center of the wheel." I did as he instructed. "Now, sit here." He moved off his stool and sat on the ground with his legs crossed underneath him. I sat at the wheel. "Before you reach for the pot, close your eyes," he said. "Can you feel it in front of you?"

"I think so," I said.

"Now reach for it. Find it with your hands." With my eyes closed, I reached out with both hands and touched the pot. It was cool and the drying clay was grainy. The curves of it matched the curves in my fingers and hands.

Woo-jin said, "Keep your eyes closed and run your hands from the bottom to the top. Tell me what you feel."

I moved my hands to where the pot touched the wheel. "I feel the base of it," I said. "It is heavy and strong."

"Yes, yes," Woo-jin said. "Keep going."

I ran my hands up. "From the base, it grows out and becomes delicate and fine in the middle."

"Go on."

"Now it turns inward and I feel the strength in it again, like shoulders on a man." I moved up to the neck. "And here, it is delicate again, but the lip makes the narrow part strong."

"Good," Woo-jin said. "Now do it again, but this time feel inside it. That is where its spirit is, in the center. Try to feel it breathing."

I slowly ran my hands along the pot again. I tried to feel the spirit, but all I felt was clay. "I . . . I don't feel the spirit," I said, opening my eyes.

"That is because you think this is just a pot, but as I have said, it is more. You must believe in its spirit. You must call for it and connect with it using your own spirit."

I took my hands from the pot. "Can you feel my spirit, samchonim?" I asked.

"I can," Woo-jin answered.

"What does it tell you?"

"You have a strong spirit but it is confused."

"How can I make my spirit so it is not confused?" I asked.

Woo-jin didn't reply right away. He sat aside the wheel with his dead, white eyes pointing up as if he looked for the answer to my question somewhere in the air. After a while he said, "Put the pot back with the others." I did and he pulled himself to the wheel. He reached for fresh clay and placed it on the wheel. He pumped his legs once to make the wheel turn. He positioned the clay in the center of it and began pressing it into a ball.

Then he said, "All spirits are connected—the tree to the mountain, the wheel to the clay. You to me, and each of us to everyone and everything. The dead and the living and all to come. It is all one mind. You will discover your own spirit through all things and all people. Many find it in nature. The mountains, the rivers, the animals. I, myself, feel it most in a strong storm," he said with a crooked smile. "You must open yourself to all spirits. Listen to them with untainted ears. When they speak to you and when you try to understand them, you will know your own."

"Yes, I have felt the spirits more since I have come here," I said. "But sometimes I hear spirits that scare me."

"You must not be afraid," Woo-jin said. "The spirits are trying to make a connection between all things to preserve the one mind. You are lucky to hear them. You are their vessel, the link between heaven and earth. You only differ from the one mind as a drop of water differs from the ocean. You are the same in kind and value. You with the strong spirit must be an expression of the one mind."

"One mind," I said as the blind man prepared the clay for turning. "Tell me, samchonim, can the one mind be for a country, for a people?"

He grinned. "The one mind is for all things. But yes, it can be for a country and one people, too."

"For Korea?"

He nodded. "Yes, for Korea. One mind. One Korea," he said, and he began pumping his legs to turn the wheel.

One day, Woo-jin did not go to the wheel. He sat in the courtyard clutching a blanket around him looking content with the job he had done turning pots the weeks before. I asked Suk-won why his uncle wasn't working that day. He said it was because it was time to fire the pots.

By then there was a large assortment of Woo-jin's work in the shed's drying area. Most were plain, but into a few, Suk-won had carved intricate designs. Some designs had plants and birds; others had mountain scenes and lakes. The day before, they had dipped each pot into a white glaze and then set them all out to dry.

I asked Suk-won if I could help with the firing. "Are you sure?" he asked. He, like Ki-soo, was still uncomfortable having me do anything that a queen wouldn't do. I always had to tell them that I enjoyed helping. And I must admit, I felt responsible to them because my taxes had caused them to lose their help.

"Yes, of course," I answered. "I want to."

"You can help Ki-soo place the pots inside the kiln."

And so I went to the big building and crawled inside the kiln to help Ki-soo stack the pots for firing. It was fortunate that we were both small. The kiln was short and narrow and I had to squat to fit inside. From outside, Suk-won handed a pot to me. In turn, I handed it to Ki-soo who carefully placed each pot on the tile shelves inside the kiln. She placed the smaller pots farther down and the larger pots on the top shelves. "The heat is greater up high," she explained. "The larger pots need more heat." While we did this, Kyung-jik brought in firewood from outside. He placed it next to the brick oven, and soon, the stack was taller than he was.

When we had placed the pots in the kiln, Suk-won sealed the opening with bricks. Then he and Kyung-jik stacked wood into the oven. Ki-soo went into the house and returned a short while later carrying a tray with tea, two cups, and a candle. Tapping his cane in front of him, Woo-jin followed her from the house to the kiln. Ki-soo placed the tray at the oven's mouth and lit the candle. She poured tea into the cups. Woo-jin and Suk-won kneeled and bowed to the kiln with their heads on the ground. When they finished bowing, Suk-won took one cup of tea and put the other one into his uncle's hand. They both took a sip and then poured the remaining tea in their cups onto the kiln. "Tea for the fire spirit," Suk-won said. He and his uncle bowed again.

Then Suk-won took the candle and lit the fire. The flames quickly filled the oven, and its red heat poured into the kiln. He took a step back. "It will be four days until we know," he said, gazing into the flames. "One day for the firing and three days for the pots to cool."

"Four days until you know what?" I asked.

"Until we know how many good pots we have made. In some firings, only one in ten are acceptable. In a good firing, it is one in five. I hope this will be a good one."

"What do we do now?" I asked.

"My uncle and I will keep the fire going for one day. It must stay at the right temperature or the pots will not turn out well. We know the fire is the right temperature by the sound it makes." He looked at me. "There is nothing more you can do."

Ki-soo took the tray with the tea and candle and went back to the house. Kyung-jik left to fetch more wood. Woo-jin sat on the ground with an ear to the oven, and Suk-won stood and watched the fire.

I decided to take a walk along the river to see if I could hear the one mind.

When I set out, the wind blew gently from the east and I could smell the seasons changing in it. I had put on an outer robe and walked along the path to the stream where, when spring's water ran high, they would load narrow boats with pots packed in straw for the trip to the market in Pyeongtaek. I looked at the sky, hoping to hear the one mind. A flock of white-cheeked starlings practiced their flying before their migration south. They swooped close to the ground and then circled high. Hundreds of birds flew as one, and I remembered that Woo-jin said that everything is connected, just as each bird is joined to the flock.

I looked at the forest. The trees were turning yellow, orange, and red. Here and there, a leaf snapped off in the breeze only to swoop and circle like the starlings before it found its place on the ground. I thought of how when the leaf returned to the earth, the trees tapped its remains for food. Leaf and tree separated and connected again.

I reached the stream. It was at its late summer's flow, gently gurgling over gravel runs, into pools, and out of the pools into runs again. I thought of how the water flowed to the sea and how a storm took it up and tossed it high against the mountains where it returned to the stream. Everything was connected.

I walked along the stream, among the spirits of nature. I listened for the one mind. I listened for my own spirit, too. Since I had come to the village, I had heard the spirits of my parents and of my children, and I had touched the spirits of the children who flew kites. Now I felt the spirits of the birds, the trees, and the spirit of the stream. I still could not hear the one mind, but the spirits no longer frightened me.

I came to a shallow pool in the stream and sat on the bank. Underneath me, the grass was dry and the earth was cool. The starlings flew overhead and the leaves on the trees quaked, snapped off, and then drifted in the air. And there, among the reeds across the stream, was a red-crowned crane. The tall bird with a white body and little red cap stood still as a statue staring at the water in front of him. After some time, he turned his head ever so slightly as if he saw something in the water. Without causing even the slightest ripple, he carefully took a step forward. I smiled to myself, remembering how a lifetime earlier, I had watched the cranes on the Han River with my mother. Her ghost was there with me now, watching, hoping the crane would spear a fish so we could cheer and clap as we did then.

I sat still and watched the crane for a long time. After a while, the starlings, the trees, the stream, the crane, and the ghost of my mother sitting next to me all came together around me and inside me. I let them flow through me, and I knew it was the one mind. I wanted to grab it, make it mine, but I knew if I did, it would fly away. Instead I sat, listening, feeling, trying to connect with it as Woo-jin said I should. But before I could, something moved in the grass on the other side of the stream. I looked there but saw nothing. I went back to watching the crane. My mother no longer watched it with me. She was looking at the grass beyond it. Now, however, it wasn't my mother when I was young. It was the ghost of her in those last days before she died.

I looked back at the grass beyond the pool. Again something moved. And then through the blades came the face of a tiger.

At first I thought it was coming for me, but its eyes were focused on the red-crowned crane. The tiger was through the grass now, inching closer to the crane. It was a magnificent animal—streaks of orange and black, sleek and powerful, unblinking yellow eyes. As it moved forward, the crane continued to stare at the water, unaware of the big cat behind him. I wanted to shout to make the crane fly away before the tiger could strike. I opened my mouth but nothing came out. I tried to stand and wave my arms, but the ground held me firm. My mother was panicked now, just as she was in her garden that day. She screamed at the tiger.

But she wasn't screaming at it to spare the crane. She screamed at it to let me, her daughter, live.

The tiger took another careful step, and then it struck. I gasped and brought my hand to my mouth as the tiger leaped onto the crane before it could fly away. The crane let out a frightful cry. Water splashed all around as the bird flapped its wings and frantically kicked its legs. But the tiger had it, and with one shake of its head, it broke the crane's neck and the bird hung limp in the cat's mouth. The tiger stood with its paws in the water and casually looked from side to side as if it was terribly pleased with what it had just done. First it looked at the bank from where it had come. Then it looked upstream, and then across it. And then it looked directly at me.

I locked eyes with the tiger and I couldn't move. It was as if its yellow eyes hypnotized me. It looked at me with the crane in its mouth and its chest moving in and out with every breath. Its tail slowly swung from side to side. It dropped the crane on the riverbank and stared at me with its mouth half-open. Its lips curled into a snarl, and a low rumble came from deep inside. Its tongue was pink and its fangs were ivory.

This close to the tiger, I became someone different, someone I hadn't known before. I was connected to the birds in the flock, the stream, and the ocean, the tree and the fallen leaves. I was connected again to the children flying kites, the dancing girls, and to the musicians and their music. And I was connected to the tiger. I was able to push myself off the ground and face the tiger. "Go away," I shouted across the stream. The big cat continued to stare at me with its mouth open, but it no longer snarled. "I am the spirit of the people and you are the spirit of the animals," I said. "We are one and you must not hurt me. Go now. Take your kill to your cubs and leave me be. Someday, we will meet again."

The tiger took two more breaths and closed its mouth. It turned from me and looked downstream. It flicked its tail and turned back to the crane. It took the dead bird in its mouth, slowly climbed up the bank, and disappeared in the tall grass.

I quickly walked back up the stream and to the path leading to the village. I reached a rise in the hill, and when I saw the village, I stopped. There, in front of Suk-won's house, were ten palace soldiers on horseback. I looked behind me. The tiger had not followed me. The white-cheeked starlings were gone, too. I looked back at the village. The soldiers had spotted me and were driving their horses toward me.

TWENTY-EIGHT

The soldiers were on me before I could run. Their horses snorted and stomped as they pulled up in front of me. One soldier dismounted. On the chest of his black tunic was the flying five-toed dragon, the emblem of King Gojong.

He approached and bowed. "Begging your pardon, Majesty," he said, "you must come with us."

"What do you want with me?" I demanded. Though I tried to sound like the queen, my heart pounded in my chest.

"The king wishes to see you."

"I will not go back to the palace as a common prisoner," I said. "If the palace wants to kill me, you will have to do it here."

"Majesty," the guard said. "The king is waiting for you at the potter's house."

"The king is here?"

The guard offered the reins to me. "If you please, Majesty, take my horse."

"No," I said, "I will walk."

I walked up the path toward the house while the guards followed behind. As I neared, the soldiers there bowed as they did when I was at the palace. Off to the side, they had bound Kyung-jik at the hands and two guards, both with blood on their faces, held him firm. My guard looked at me, worried. At the big building's far end, black smoke poured out of the kiln chimney high into the air. Suk-won stood at the door watching me.

"The king is inside, Majesty," the guard on foot said.

I strode past the bowing guards to the door of the house. I pushed it open. Ki-soo was inside looking terrified. When she saw me, she pointed to the lattice door leading to the courtyard. "The king is out there," she said.

I went through the house and stood in the doorway to the courtyard. There, alone, was King Gojong, sitting on the bench sipping tea. He wore a black cap and a gray riding robe closed with the king's medallion.

When he saw me, he set his tea down, took off his cap, and stood. This took me by surprise. The king never stood for anyone, not even me. "Come, my wife," he said, "have tea with me."

"Have you come to take me back to the palace so your father can kill me?" I asked without leaving the door.

He looked hurt at my question and shook his head. "My father does not know I am here. I left the palace in secret well before the sun rose. I rode on horseback all morning to see you. As you know, I do not like riding horseback. It hurts my legs. I much prefer my palanquin. But I want to talk to you."

"If the Taewŏn-gun knows where I am, he will send his assassins to kill me."

"He doesn't know. I found you through Lady Min. It seems my mother favors you. Or perhaps she favors the Mins over the House of Yi." He waved his hand. "It doesn't matter. It is all so foolish. Anyway, in secret, I asked her to find you. I thought because she is a Min, she would know where you were. And she did."

"Lady Min . . . ?" I said.

"Yes." He pointed at the bench. "Come. Sit. I want to talk to you." I went to him and we sat together.

"Will you have some tea?" he asked. "I will pour it for you."

"You, the king, will pour my tea?"

He answered by taking the pot and filling my cup. I noticed lines on his face that I hadn't seen before. He looked older, more mature. He looked tired, too.

I took a sip of tea. "How is our son?" I asked. "Is the prince safe?"

"Yes," the king replied. "I had him brought to the palace. My father wishes him no harm."

"I'm thankful for that," I said. "I have worried about him." I let relief at the news of my son sink in for a few seconds. Then I said, "So, my husband, you say you want to talk to me. What about?"

Gojong leaned his elbows on his knees and stared at the courtyard stones. "The Chinese army is at the Yalu River," he said. "They are coming to drive the Japanese out."

"Yes, I know," I said. "Empress Cixi promised me she would protect us from Japan."

Gojong said, "My father plays a risky game. He used the dwarf Japanese to take power, and now he wants them to leave. But he is afraid of the Chinese. He thinks they will have his head."

"His head might be the price he pays for collaborating with the Japanese," I said.

Still leaning forward, the king shook his head. "I don't know what to do. You have always been better at things like this. That is why I came here . . . to ask what we should do."

"You want *my* advice?" I took another sip of tea and held the cup in my hand. "You ran to your father when I defied the Japanese. You did not come to my rescue when he turned the people against me. They wanted to kill me, and you did nothing."

He looked at me with sad eyes. "I'm sorry I left you," he said. "I was afraid. But if you come back, I will never leave you again, even if they try to kill us. Please, my wife, believe me."

I glared at my husband. But in his face, I saw how desperate he was, how much he needed me. In my mind, he was still the spoiled boy king who depended on his father. Yet he had risked his life and defied his father by coming here to talk to me. He wanted to stand up to his father once and for all, and he was asking me to help him.

My heart went soft. At that moment, I believed that someday I could love him. He wasn't tall, handsome, and brave like Kyung-jik, but he was my husband. We had made a prince together. For a while, we'd been able to work together. Perhaps we could work together again.

I slipped my hand into his and he squeezed it. It was the first time we'd ever touched like that. There was love in it. He pulled me to him in an embrace, and our hearts beat together. For the first time since that fateful day when they married us, King Gojong was my true husband.

After a few moments, he pulled away. "When the Chinese come, return to the palace and we will rule our country together. But I must ask for this. Please, do not have my father killed. Send him to China where he will not drive us apart. Lady Min begs for his life, too."

I sat up straight. "Your father will always want to run the country. He will plot with the Japanese, even from China. Mark my word, if we let him go, he will return someday."

The king tried to look brave. "If he tries to return, I will fight him alongside you."

I relaxed a little. I said, "I promise that if the Taewŏn-gun is killed, it will not be on my order. I cannot say what the Chinese will do, although I will get word to Empress Cixi that it is my wish to let him live. As for what to do regarding the current situation, do this. Give the Japanese what they want to make them leave. Give them an apology for the soldiers killed. Offer reparations if that's what they want.

Anything, as long as their troops leave without a war. When they are gone, you and I will take back the palace. Then we will set our country in the right direction again."

King Gojong nodded. We sat for a few minutes more, and then he pointed to the house. "I must go. I am going on to Pusan," he said. "If I go there, I will lead our enemies far away from you. When they catch up to me, I will tell them I was afraid of the Chinese and wanted to get as far away from the north as possible. People in this house should say that my stop here was to rest and water the horses."

I raised an eyebrow. "That is clever. Is it your idea?"

Gojong grinned. "It is."

"Well," I said, "it seems you have good instincts for politics after all."

We rose from the bench and the king faced me. "I am glad I came here," he said. "I am eager to see you again at the palace when the time comes."

We embraced again. Then together we went through the house and out the front door. He mounted his horse, and, though he rode it awkwardly, I was filled with pride for my husband as he and his guards rode down the road, on to Pusan.

The Chinese army crossed the Yalu River that day and occupied Seoul in less than three days. The Japanese, outnumbered and not willing to go to war with a much larger country, offered no resistance and pulled back to the south. As I had predicted, the Japanese agreed to a complete withdrawal only if they received a formal apology and financial reparations for the soldiers the mobs had killed. King Gojong agreed to their demands as I had told him to, and Japan and China signed a treaty. The treaty stipulated that both countries would remove their armies from the peninsula and notify each other before intervening in Korea again. As I had requested, the Chinese did not kill the Taewŏn-gun. Instead, they took him to Peking where he would stay under house arrest. Finally there was peace in my country, and I could go back to Gyeongbok Palace and take my seat on the throne.

But first we had to take the pots out of the kiln. As Suk-won had said, it took three days for the pots to cool after their day in the fire. Even then, when Suk-won unsealed the opening, it was warm inside. When Ki-soo climbed in to retrieve the first pots, she had to use lamb-skin gloves to handle them. I offered to help. "Thank you, Majesty," Suk-won said, addressing me as queen now that there was no need to hide my identity. "That is not work for a queen." Of course, I could have insisted and they would have had to let me do it. But I knew it would have embarrassed them to have their queen inside the hot, ashy kiln so I didn't press it.

Kyung-jik and I stood by as each pot came out. Woo-jin sat on the floor with his face turned to the roof and an ear toward the kiln as if he could hear how the pots turned out. When Ki-soo handed a pot to him, Suk-won did a quick check of it. Then he set it on the ground alongside the kiln. When they had all the pots out and Ki-soo, sweaty and covered with ash, climbed out from the kiln, Suk-won said, "We will have to do a more thorough examination, but at first check, I would say it was an excellent firing. One in three looks to be acceptable."

Woo-jin clapped his hands. "How did the one turn out?" he asked.

Suk-won picked up a pot. It was the tall one with the narrow neck that Woo-jin had me feel when I said I wanted to know the pots' spirits. Suk-won turned it over and around and I saw that they had carved a design into it. "It looks perfect, Uncle," Suk-won said.

"Let me have it," Woo-jin said with his hands out.

Suk-won gave his uncle the pot and the blind man ran his hands over it as if it was a most precious thing. Then he cradled it like a baby. He threw his head back and smiled broadly. "Yes," he said. "As I had hoped, it is worthy of a queen."

He reached out a hand, and Suk-won helped him stand. Woo-jin held the pot out to me and bowed. "Majesty," he said, "we made this one for you. Please accept it as our gift."

I took the pot from the old man. In my hands, it was light and warm like a newborn baby. And it was exquisite. The celadon glaze had the radiance of jade and the clarity of spring water. I studied the carving. There, in hundreds of tiny strokes, they had carved a two-headed dragon with five toes. It was the same dragon as was on my tapestry. I ran my hands over the pot and in the center of it. I felt its spirit. It was the spirit of One Korea.

Suk-won said, "Woo-jin suggested the figure of the two-headed dragon. I thought it should be a crane for longevity or the queen's medallion. But my uncle was quite adamant that it be this design. I hope you like it, Majesty."

With the pot in my hands, I looked at Woo-jin. "Samchonim, you had your nephew carve this design before the king came. A dragon with five toes? You knew who I was all along, but you never indicated that you did."

Woo-jin grinned as a blind man does. "Your position never came up when we talked," he said simply.

Kyung-jik said, "Majesty, Woo-jin is the one who conveyed messages for you. He has many connections."

I looked at Ki-soo, who had tried to wipe the sweat and ash from her face but only left it a smear. "You told me Woo-jin didn't know who I was," I said.

Ki-soo nodded. "I apologize, Majesty. I see now that it is I who did not know about him."

I faced Woo-jin. "A two-headed dragon, samchonim?" I asked.

"I thought it would be a design to remind you of our talks," he replied. I wanted to ask him more about what he knew of the two-headed dragon, but I decided this wasn't the time or place.

"Suk-won," I said, "you and your uncle are fine potters indeed. Good people like you make me proud of our country. Thank you for this gift. I will take it to the palace and put it where I will see it every day to remind me of your kindness."

He bowed to me. "We are honored, Majesty."

Two days later, Kyung-jik informed me that it was safe to go back to the palace and that my entourage was on its way to take me there the next day.

"Shall I have them bring your palanquin, Majesty?" my guard asked.

"No," I replied. "I will ride on horseback where I can see my people."

"As you wish, Majesty," Kyung-jik said.

"Tell me," I said, "how did you know Woo-jin? How did you know that you could trust him with our messages and that he would have a way to deliver them?"

"It was my uncle, Minister Kim," Kyung-jik answered. "Years ago, he told me about the blind potter in this village and said that if you ever needed help, I should go to him. When the riots started, I contacted him and he said I should bring you here."

"It makes me sad that Minister Kim is dead," I said. "You and he saved my life. When I return to the throne, I will make you a general."

"Thank you, Majesty. It is my honor to serve you, no matter what my title is." He bowed low.

"I want to go early tomorrow," I said. "I want to see my son and I have much to do."

"Yes, Majesty. I will make the arrangements."

Kyung-jik bowed again and went off to carry out my orders. As he walked away, I thought of what could have been if they hadn't chosen me to be queen, if somehow Kyung-jik and I could have met—me an orphan girl, he a young palace guard. We could have had a good life—him practicing his swordsmanship and me soothing his sore muscles at night. It certainly would have been simpler than being queen. But that wasn't what had been chosen for me. I had to be the queen, and he had to be a general in my army.

I went to the big building to find Woo-jin. I wanted to ask him what he knew about the two-headed dragon. I wanted to know if he knew anything about my tapestry and the words, "One Korea." And I wanted to thank him for teaching me about spirits.

I pushed open the door, but he was not at the wheel. I went back outside and found Suk-won packing the fired pots in straw for storage until spring. There was a pile of broken pots next to him. He picked up a pot and examined it carefully. He brought it close to his face and ran a finger over it. Then he threw the pot on the pile of broken pots where it shattered into pieces.

"What was wrong with it?" I asked.

"Majesty," he said with a nod. "I did not see you."

"Why did you destroy that pot?"

"It was flawed," he said. "There was a small impurity in the glazing. Most people wouldn't notice it, but I could not let it go in good conscience."

"Of course," I said with a smile. "I am looking for your uncle. He's not at the potter's wheel. Do you know where he is?"

"I don't know, Majesty. We won't be making pots until I prepare the new clay, so he might be in the village. He has friends there."

"Well, I should not go there to find him. My appearance would cause a stir now that everyone knows who I am. I will go for a walk instead."

Suk-won looked at the sky. "It is a good day for it," he said and returned to his pots.

I hadn't told anyone about the tiger I had seen at the stream days earlier. With Gojong coming from the palace, it had left my mind.

Now, I thought it best to keep my encounter with the tiger to myself. And it seemed like it had been a dream, although I knew it wasn't. I didn't want to press my luck with the big cat, so I went into the woods instead of down to the stream.

Suk-won was right; it was a good day for a stroll. It was more like summer than fall, warm and still. The sun was high, and only a few clouds moved slowly across the sky. I followed a path into the woods. The leaves still clinging to the aspen trees fluttered softly. A woodpecker flitted from tree to tree. It was cool and pleasant, and soon, I was far into the woods. I remembered the tiger and thought I might be too far from the house. But before I turned to go back, I saw a thin line of smoke rising just off the path ahead of me. I took a few steps more and looked closely. There was Woo-jin, sitting in a clearing alone, smoking a bamboo pipe. Sunlight shined on the blind man as if Cheonjiwang, creator of heaven and earth, put the sun in the sky to cast its light on just him. Woo-jin sat on the ground with his legs crossed underneath him. He wore a white robe and a small black cap on his half-bald head. He rolled his head back and forth as if he was in a trance.

I thought I should let him be, but before I could leave, Woo-jin called out, "Come, Majesty. Sit with me so we can talk once more before you leave."

I went to him. "How did you know someone was there, samchonim?" I asked. "And how did you know it was me?"

"I felt your spirit, of course," he replied. "Anyway, I knew you would come. I called you."

I sat on the ground in front of him. He took a puff on his pipe and blew a curl of white smoke into the sunlight. The smell of tobacco hung in the air. "The older I get, the more I like my tobacco," he said. "I like my soju, too." He grinned.

"You should not be here alone, samchonim," I said. "I saw a tiger the other day."

"The one at the stream?"

"Yes, it was by the stream."

"I know that tiger," Woo-jin said. "We talk sometimes. What did he say to you?"

"He said nothing," I answered. "He just growled at me."

"Begging your pardon, Majesty, but he always says something. What did his spirit say?"

I nodded. "I told him we are all part of one spirit and he agreed."

The blind man smiled his smile. "Yes, that is what we talk about, too."

We were quiet for a moment. Then I said, "I want to ask you about the pot, samchonim. The one you gave me. How did you know about the two-headed dragon?"

"Ah, the two-headed dragon. What do you know about it?"

I told him what Minister Kim had said about the two-headed dragon on my tapestry, how it was made by order of King Taejo, how the tapestry appeared to a leader in times of crisis, and how it had come with the message, "One Korea." I told him how Minister Kim had said that I was the one it had come for.

"Yes," Woo-jin said, "that is all correct. Minister Kim got that information from me."

"From you, samchonim?" I said.

"Majesty, my people and I are the ones who sent the tapestry to you."

"I see," I said. "Tell me more."

Woo-jin tapped the bowl of his pipe against his hand to clear the ash and put it in the pocket of his robe. He raised his face to the sky. "The two-headed dragon," he said. "One head looks east and one head looks west. One protects us from Japan and the other from China. That is why King Taejo had it made. He wanted Korea to be independent and free. However, we face challenges not just from China and Japan. Our greatest challenge has always been coming together as one nation."

"One nation, samchonim?"

"Yes!" he said, turning his face in my direction. "You see, the dragon's heads not only face east and west, they look in opposite directions. That is because King Taejo wanted our nation to be for all Korean people. Not just for the people of the south, but for the people of the north as well. And not just for the yangban, but for the commoners—the chungin, sangmin, and even the nobi. It also looks forward and back. Back to the Three Kingdoms and forward to the generations to come. The dragon has two heads but only one body. It begs us all to be one people, one nation, one Korea. When Minister Kim said you were the one the dragon came for, Majesty, he meant that you are the spirit of One Korea."

"Why me, samchonim?

"Because the spirit is in you," he answered, simply.

"Yes, I feel it," I said. "Are there others who know about the two-headed dragon?"

"We are a secret society, but yes, there are many. Your lady's maid, Han-sook, is one."

"Han-sook?" I exclaimed. I shook my head. It was almost too much to take in. "I never imagined it."

"As I said, Majesty, it is a secret society."

I was quiet for a while as Woo-jin's information sank in. Then I asked, "How can I do it, samchonim? How can I be the spirit of One Korea?"

"Listen to the people, Majesty. Speak for everyone."

"Yes, the people," I said. "But what about the tiger?"

"Do not fear the tiger. He can only kill your body. But he knows he cannot take your spirit, which is what he wants most. That is why he growls."

I sat for a while longer and said nothing. Then I said, "I will do my best, samchonim. I will do my best to speak for the people. I will be the dragon queen."

He smiled a little. He took out his pipe and pushed tobacco into the bowl. He struck a sulfur match and lit it. The smoke curled up and caught the sunlight. I stood and walked down the path back to the house.

TWENTY-NINE

It was still dark outside when I awoke the next morning. It was much earlier than when I usually got up, and the house was quiet. I wrapped a robe around myself and went to the courtyard. I sat on the bench and watched the sky beyond the hills turn from black to red and then orange. A new day was coming, and I felt more ready for it than any other day I could remember. I sat for a while enjoying the sunrise. Then, as the light came up in the courtyard, I kicked over a pot so that it clattered on the stones. Seconds later, Ki-soo was at the door wrapping a robe around herself. "Majesty," she said, "you are awake so early!" I grinned at her.

The previous night, they had brought my dark-blue traveling robe. Ki-soo helped me put it on and closed it with a gold queen's medallion. She put my hair up in the queen's style and pinned it with an ivory binyeo. She applied powder to my face and red paste to my lips as Han-sook did when I went outside the palace. When we were done, she studied me. "You look like a queen again, Majesty," she said with a pleased look.

"Thank you, Ki-soo," I replied. "Thank you for everything."

Ki-soo bowed low and said simply, "Your Majesty."

The sun was still below the horizon when I stepped out of the house. Though I had told Kyung-jik I didn't want it, they had brought my palanquin along with eight eunuch porters. They were waiting for me at the front of the house along with ten guards—four on horseback and six on foot. They all bowed to me when they saw me.

"Kyung-jik," I said, "I told you I did not want my palanquin."

"Many apologies, Majesty," Kyung-jik said. "They did not get my message in time. But it is a fortunate mistake. The guards tell me there are still those in Seoul who wish to kill you. It would be safest if you returned to the palace inside your palanquin."

"I do not care," I said. "I will ride instead. Use the palanquin to carry my pot with the two-headed dragon. When we go, put guards around me, but only a few. And do not announce me to the people on the streets as we ride. I don't want my return to be a spectacle."

"As you wish, Majesty," Kyung-jik said.

"However," I said, "have a guard carry the queen's banner."

I was anxious to see my son, and, to my surprise, I was anxious to see my husband, too. I told Kyung-jik that we should set out right away. He mounted his horse and led four guards and me on horseback. Kyung-jik insisted on carrying my banner as he rode tall in the saddle. The road was dry and the day was pleasant, so we made good time. After a short distance, the palanquin, porters, and guards on foot fell out of sight behind us. I, like the king, was not a good rider, and I was sore and tired when we arrived at the outskirts of the city. Even so, I rode with my back straight and my eyes on my people. When the people of Seoul saw the procession, they paused from what they were doing and lowered their heads. I could see several of them steal a look at me. They looked surprised to see me outside my palanquin. A few seemed angry. I tried to reach out to their spirits, to hear my people. Their spirits were confused, as if they didn't know which way to turn. "They need a leader," I said to myself. "They need a dragon queen."

We went on into the heart of Seoul to where more people were on the street. Kyung-jik looked from side to side, carefully watching as we rode. Where the crowd was thickest, a mother pulled her young daughter aside and made her bow. The girl was the same age as I was when I saw Lady Min with my mother. She wore rags and, in spite of the cold, she had no shoes. I watched her as we went by. Before we could pass, she looked up, and for an instant our eyes met.

"Halt!" I said. The procession stopped and Kyung-jik rode up to me.

"What is it, Majesty?" he asked.

"Help me down," I said. He dismounted and helped me down from my horse.

With Kyung-jik at my side, I approached the girl. She had her head down, and when she saw I was coming to her, she began to shake. Her mother pulled her close to her side.

"Do not be afraid," I said. "I am not a snake. I will not bite you."

The girl continued to shake and now the mother did, too. "How old are you, young one?" I asked.

"She is six years, Majesty," the mother said unsteadily.

"What is her name?"

"Her name is Soo-hee, Majesty."

"I have a son who is about your age," I said. "I am going to see him now. His name is Sun-jong. He likes to fly kites during festivals. Do you like to fly kites, too?"

In a voice I could barely hear, the girl said, "I have never had a kite."

"Well, you shall have one. I will see to it."

"Thank you, Majesty," the mother said. The girl still shook.

I sighed. I took the queen's medallion from my robe. I crouched and held the gold medallion out to the girl. She lifted her head and looked at it with frightened eyes.

"I want you to have this, Soo-hee," I said. "It is the queen's medallion. Having it means that you are special." The girl did not reach for it, so I took her hand and pressed the medallion into it.

"Mother," I said, standing straight again, "use the medallion to buy shoes and clothes for your daughter and for you, too. Show it to the merchant and have him send the charge to the palace. Let your daughter keep the medallion if she wants."

"Thank you, Majesty," the mother said.

The girl looked at the medallion in her hand. She no longer shook.

I stepped back and looked at the crowd that was watching my interaction with the girl. Everyone bowed to me again. "My people hear this," I shouted at them all. "Spread the word. Your queen returns. I return for the people. Not for the yangban, not for the rich merchant or the scholars or for the royal family or for the Mins. I am here this time for everyone. For one people, one nation. For One Korea." Several in the crowd lifted their heads and looked at me surprised. "Spread the word," I said again.

I went back to my horse, and Kyung-jik helped me mount it. "See that the girl gets a grand kite before the new-year's celebration," I said to my guard. "It should be a dragon kite."

"Yes, Majesty," he said.

We arrived at Gyeongbok late in the day. The first thing I did after we dismounted and walked inside the palace was look for my son. As I walked across the courtyard, I asked Kyung-jik, "Where is Sun-jong?"

"The prince is with your lady's maid, Majesty. He waits for you in your private courtyard."

I quickened my steps as I went to my quarters. I went through the entry and out to the courtyard. There, sitting on the cobblestones with Han-sook was Sun-jong, playing with toy soldiers carved from ebony. When he saw me, he shouted, "Ummah!" and ran to me. He threw his arms around my waist and hugged me.

"My son," I said, returning his hug, "I am pleased to see you. How have you been?"

"Han-sook and I had adventures!" he said, pushing away. "We hid in the forest and then went to some people's house. Then we came here and I was with *Appa*. Where did you go?"

"I was in the country learning how to make pots."

"You can make pots? I want you to teach me."

"It is very difficult to make pots," I said. "But if you want, someday I will show you how it is done."

"Good," he said.

"I want to hear about your adventures," I said. "But first I must talk to Han-sook. Will you tell me later?"

"Yes, Ummah," he said, and went back to his toy soldiers.

I looked at Han-sook. She had a gentle smile on her face and lowered her head in a bow. "Majesty," she said, "it is good that you are back."

"You have done your duty well," I said to her. "I shall not forget."

"Majesty, as I have said before, I live to serve you."

"And I am fortunate for that," I replied. "Come to my study with me. I have some things to tell you."

Han-sook ordered a maid to watch over Sun-jong and together we went to my study. There, behind my desk, was the tapestry with the two-headed dragon. I was pleased to see it. As I looked into the dragon's eyes, I vowed to not be afraid of it when it spoke to me and to listen to it more carefully. I sat behind my desk. It was good to be back, although it was different. Now I felt my responsibility to my people stronger than I ever had before. I had not known them until now. I vowed I would never forget them.

"Han-sook," I said. "I wish to see my uncle. Arrange an audience for him."

Han-sook lowered her eyes. "Majesty," she said softly, "I am sorry to tell you that your uncle was killed."

With this news, sadness replaced the joy of seeing my son and being back in the palace. In my mind, I pictured my uncle with his handsome face and onyx-black eyes. I couldn't believe that I would never see him again or have the advantage of his advice. I felt guilty for putting him in a position close to me. I thought of my poor aunt and how much she loved her husband. I vowed that I would help her. After a minute I asked, "Who killed him?"

"The official statement is that he was killed by the rioters, Majesty."

Then my sadness turned to anger. "The rioters incited by the Taewŏn-gun," I said.

"It could have been the Japanese," Han-sook said quickly. "Or one of the clans that hates the Mins."

No, it was the Taewŏn-gun and I knew it. I wanted to break my promise to spare my father-in-law's life. I knew that if I sent a message to Empress Cixi, she would gladly comply and chop off his head.

"What about my aunt, my uncle's butler, Mr. Yang, and the head housekeeper, Eun-ji?"

"They are still at the House of Gamgodang."

"Tell the palace secretary to give them good positions here at the palace," I said. "I want them paid well. As for my uncle . . . ," I stopped for a moment and remembered my gentle uncle with his soft eyes. I had grown to love him like a father. But I was the queen and, no matter how much I ached for revenge, I had to think of my country first. And so I sighed and said, "I will issue an order that there will be no retaliation for his murder. It is time we stopped fighting each other."

"Yes, Majesty," Han-sook said.

"One last thing, Han-sook. It's the two-headed dragon. I know about the secret fellowship, and I know that you are a member." My lady's maid lowered her head. "I think it is good that you are. It appears that I am part of it, too."

"I am glad you are, Majesty."

"So this is what I want you to do," I said. "I want you to arrange for artisans to make talismans for those in the fellowship. Let them choose what they want to have to remind them of their commitment to the fellowship. For me, I want to have something that I will use every day. It should not be a weapon or armament. It should not be something only a queen would have.

"How about a comb, Majesty?" Han-sook said.

"Yes," I replied, "a comb. But though a comb is a common thing, it should be fit for a queen so that all who see it know that the queen supported the society of the two-headed dragon."

"Yes, Majesty. A queen's comb."

"You must do it in secret because if the Chinese or Japanese discover us, they will be angry and try to end our movement. Go, do this at once."

"That is a good idea, Majesty," Han-sook said. She bowed out of my study, and I began planning the future of my country.

In the first day after I returned, I issued a decree that there would be no retribution for crimes committed during the uprisings and had it delivered to all corners of the country. I hoped that it would quell the hostilities between the clans and classes. In spite of my decree, there was still fighting throughout the country—clan against clan, traditionalists against progressives, pro-Japanese against pro-Chinese, poor against rich. I had to do something to get my people focused on something bigger than their centuries-old feuds.

So in the weeks and months that followed, I set about building a nation for my people. I could tell Gojong was nervous about my actions, but he was true to his promise and supported me. Even with the king behind me, the ministers protested, reminding me that my earlier efforts to modernize the country had led to the uprisings. And because my reforms cost money, there were complaints among the yangban and merchants about their high taxes. I remembered the poor people I had seen on the street. I remembered how Ki-soo had said the high taxes had hurt their business. I wanted to lower the taxes; I truly did.

But I had come to believe, like the Taewŏn-gun, that it was time to end China's authority over our country and stand as an independent and free nation. I believed it was only a matter of time before Emperor Meiji would have a fully modern army and China and Japan would go to war for control of my country. If we were ever going to stand on our own, we had to modernize and we had to do it quickly. For that to happen, we had to stop fighting among ourselves. We had to stop pretending that we would be fine with our heads in the sand, content to be the Hermit Kingdom. We had to invest in modernizing our country, which meant we had to keep the taxes high. It was a painful decision, but I was convinced that it was the right thing to do.

In the years that followed, I pushed through my reforms. We laid telegraph lines and built roads and bridges. We built sewer and water systems and started an electric grid. We imported farm implements, seeds, and livestock, and built dams for irrigation. Merchants opened new business and traded with foreign countries. We opened public schools, and soon, literacy in Korea increased dramatically. Several newspapers started publication.

We began to modernize our military, too. We imported weapons from Japan and America. We brought in instructors from America to train our troops in modern warfare. We created a military school and an officer's training program.

But the most important change I made was for equal rights for my people. I oversaw the end to slavery. The yangban objected to this and fought it. So I removed their legal privileges, stripping them of their power and effectively ending the caste system.

And I granted equal rights to women. I ended restrictions on when women could leave their homes, where they could go, and who they could see. I endorsed Asia's first all-girl academy in Seoul. It was the first time in history that a Korean girl, commoner or aristocrat, had the right to an education.

In less than a decade I had Korea on its way to becoming a modern, Westernized country that, in a few years, could stand on its own against Japan, Russia, the United States, and even China. Koreans, north and south, rich and poor, were beginning to come together to form a country. I hoped and prayed that for the first time in our history, we would finally be one nation, independent and free. We had made great progress, but we needed a few more years.

Just a few more years.

One summer day nearly three decades after I'd become queen, Kyungjik delivered a report to the afternoon meeting and it was not good news. "The Japanese have sent troops to confront the Chinese troops in our north," he said, standing at the head of the table dressed in his new blue and red officer's uniform. "They are marching toward Seoul. I think Peking will declare war."

Though my reforms had begun to build a nation, the changes had caused strife, too. Two months earlier, a group of traditionalists had taken up arms to protest the foreigners who had come to Korea to help enact our reforms. I asked Empress Cixi to help us put down the uprising. She had sent more troops than necessary, and they easily chased the rebels back into their homes. But Chinese troops in Korea were the perfect excuse for Japan to challenge their long-time adversary to the west. Tensions and distrust between the two countries had only grown over the years, and Emperor Meiji apparently believed that his new modern military could finally defeat the Chinese. So even though the Chinese agreed to pull out after they had put down the uprising, Japan sent thousands of troops to the peninsula. Now Japanese soldiers were in the south and marching toward Seoul.

It was a precarious situation, and I needed advice from my ministers who sat at the table across from Gojong and me. Another seat was empty, and now there were three ministers absent. After Kyung-jik bowed and left the room, I asked, "Where is Minister Pak?"

The palace secretary stepped forward and said, "Majesty, he did not report today."

"Why?" I demanded.

"I have received no word, Majesty," the secretary replied.

"I see," I said.

I looked at King Gojong sitting just ahead of me. My husband sat straight in his chair with his eyes forward. Though he tried not to show it, he looked worried.

I addressed the ministers. "Advisers," I said, "what are your thoughts on this matter?"

Not a one spoke up. They sat mute like stone statues in white robes with their legs folded underneath them, not daring to make eye contact with me. I was convinced that, like Minister Pak, most of them were planning to leave now that the Japanese had sent their troops. They looked like rabbits poised to run from a fox.

"Don't you understand?" I pleaded. "The future of our country is at stake. We have come so far but we are in danger of losing everything."

Minister Chung cleared his throat. "Majesty, if there is war between Japan and China, the Chinese will win. Then we can go back to the way it was before."

"The way it was before . . . a protectorate of China," I said. I shook my head. "And if Japan wins, we will become its colony and we will lose everything we have worked for. Well, I will have something more. I will have a unified nation independent from all others. One people, one nation. One Korea. Isn't this what you want? Isn't that what our people want? Is there not one among you who will support our cause?"

Still they said nothing and the room was silent for some time. Gojong continued to look worried. I wanted to be angry with the ministers, but I couldn't blame them. They were not the ones who were ultimately responsible. I was the one who had pushed for all of the changes. They had put the crown on *my* head, not theirs.

"Go now," I said finally. "Tell your people that their queen will fight for their country."

The ministers stood as one and quickly left the room. The king sat a while longer. Then, without saying a word, he left, too.

THIRTY

Late fall 1894

The society of the two-headed dragon made my comb from tortoiseshell and gave it a solid gold rim. The inlay of the two-headed dragon with five toes on each foot was made from the finest ivory and looked almost real. Every morning I combed my hair with it when I arose, and every night before I went to bed. When I was done combing my hair, I always asked the dragon if I had been a good queen. He never once answered me.

I didn't need his answer. I knew I had failed. I hadn't been able to build my nation quickly enough for it to stand on its own. As Empress Cixi had said years earlier, Korea was in the middle of a fight between two tigers. If China won the war, they would reassert their dominance over East Asia and we would continue to be their protectorate, unable to rise from their shadow. It would be as Minister Chung had said, "the way it was before." If Japan won, Korea would be their first conquest on the way to building an empire in East Asia. If they controlled our country, there would be no telling what they would do to us.

While war raged on the peninsula, I was a prisoner inside the palace. The king and I were unable to leave or even send messages to anyone. The Japanese occupied Seoul and had soldiers just outside the palace. They were pushing the Chinese back across the Yalu River and were winning important battles on land and at sea. There were no afternoon meetings anymore, the ministers long ago having run off to hide from the Japanese. I spent my days alone at my desk. On the tapestry behind me, the two-headed dragon mocked me.

Kyung-jik was a prisoner, too, and he raged like an angry bull. He forced his men to practice hand-to-hand combat with him for hours every day until he—or more often, they—could no longer stand. King Gojong spent his days in his library, trying to learn what he should have learned decades earlier. My son was now a man and had married a lovely girl from the Min clan, arranged, of course, by me. The prince had grown to be much like his father—soft in stature and character. I loved him just the same. He was a good husband and had a good heart. I prayed that someday he would have a country to rule.

I went out to my courtyard. Weeks earlier, the hot and humid days of summer had given way to the crisp days and cool nights of fall. I pulled my robe tight around me and sat on the Chinese bench. On a table next to me, Han-sook had set out the year's last orchids. She knew I liked the cream-colored ones with a blue and pink center and a long yellow pistil—the kind my mother had grown. Their perfume was light this time of year, but I could smell them just the same. Their colors were fading and I knew that in only a few days, the blossoms would die and fall.

I heard a screech above me and looked up. There high in the sky was a flock of red-crowned cranes heading to their wintering grounds in southern China. I remembered when I had seen them while sitting in my uncle's bamboo grove the day they told me I would be queen. It was spring then, and the cranes were flying north to their breeding grounds in the lowlands of Manchuria. I remembered how I had felt that day, that something important was about to happen to me. The same feeling was heavy on me now. I tried to send my spirits to the cranes so that I could fly away with them.

Han-sook came into the courtyard. "Majesty," she said, "is there anything you need?"

I didn't answer right away. She was in her later years now, only a few years from being an old woman. All the same, she carried herself with grace and humility.

"Come," I said. "Sit with me." I had never offered to have my lady's maid sit with me as if we were equals. She did not hesitate and sat on the Chinese bench next to me.

She didn't keep her eyes low as we both looked out over the courtyard. "I have heard the war will be over soon," Han-sook said without addressing me formally. "They say that the Japanese will win."

"I have heard the same," I replied. We were quiet for some time. Then I said, "I want you to remove the tapestry with the two-headed dragon from my study. Give it back to our people."

"That is a good idea," Han-sook said. "I will have it done right away."

"One more thing," I said. "There is no telling what will happen once the Japanese take the palace. They will most likely bring the Taewŏn-gun back from China, though he is an old man and will be nothing more than a figurehead. I want you to leave. They will not stop you. Go to where you will be safe. Go soon."

My lady's maid looked out over the courtyard and shook her head. "Oh, my queen, I will never leave your side," she said. "As much as it hurts me to disobey your command, I must this one time. I would rather die than leave you."

She turned and smiled at me.

We sat for some time, looking out at the courtyard, smelling the orchids' sweet blossoms. Finally she said, "I have had one of your servants fetch a book from the king's library. It is *Songs of Dragons Flying to Heaven*. I know you like those poems. I thought you would enjoy reading them today."

"Yes," I said. "I would like that."

She stood and said, "It has been my life's greatest honor to serve you, Your Majesty."

I said, "Thank you, Han-sook." She bowed low and left the courtyard.

I went into my study, and there on my desk was *Songs of Dragons Flying to Heaven*. I took the book from my desk and sat on the floor in the middle of my study. I saw someone had marked a page with a silk ribbon—likely it was Han-sook. I opened the book to the page and read the poem there.

The flying dragons of Chosŏn
Everything they did was blessed by heaven
Their spirits harmonize with the ancient ones.

I closed the book and set it aside. I searched for the meaning in the poem. I wondered if heaven had blessed me and if I had harmonized with the ancient ones. I wondered if I had been one of the flying dragons of Chosŏn. Though now the ancient ones' spirits were everywhere around me, I doubted if I had become a dragon. Since the war between the Japanese and Chinese had started, the spirits scared me again and haunted me at night. I was glad Han-sook was taking away the tapestry with the two-headed dragon. I thought about throwing my comb with the two-headed dragon into the palace pond. I wondered if I was going crazy like my mother.

That night, though he had not called me, I went to King Gojong's quarters. I found him alone in his library reading a book. He sat on the floor with a candle for light. His mustache and goatee were long now and starting to gray. His face was pale, and he looked older than his years. When he saw me, he motioned for me to sit with him. As I lowered myself on a cushion, he closed his book.

"I see, husband, you are reading John Stuart Mill's *Principles of Political Economy*," I said.

"I do not understand it," the king said, shaking his head. "Production and distribution and capital and how governments make decisions. It all seems so silly."

I nodded. "I thought so, too, when I first read it. But there is merit to it. It explains things."

"Yes, you were always smart with books," he said, pushing the book aside. "It didn't help us, though. Did it?"

"No," I said, "it did not."

"What do you suggest we do now? How do we save our country? How do we save ourselves?"

"I fear it is too late to save our country," I answered. "Japan will win the war. They will take Korea for themselves. I pray for our people."

Gojong nodded. "Yes, it seems that way."

"As for us," I said, "you should go to the Japanese without me. Though he is in the eighth decade of life, they will bring back your father from China. He won't harm you. The Japanese will put you on the throne only as a figurehead. But you will still be alive."

"What about our son?"

"They will not harm him or his wife, either. His fate will be the same as yours."

"And what about you?"

I didn't answer him. I took his hand and looked at him. His eyes were moist. My heart broke. He was my king who, thirty years earlier, I had promised to serve. And my service to him had led to this. "I am sorry, my king," I said.

"Why do you say you are sorry, wife?" Gojong asked. "Do you think you are a failure?"

I looked into our hands and nodded.

The king shook his head, "No one is a failure who has done their best."

At that moment, I truly loved the man sitting next to me who was my husband and king. In spite of his weak character, in spite of having a dominating father who had used him all of his life, he had become a man and a king. I squeezed his hand, and he pulled me in close. We kissed a most tender kiss. And for the first time in my life, I knew a man's love. We embraced for some time, and then pulled away. There were tears running down my husband's face.

He smiled sadly. "My queen," he said.

A tear ran down my face, too. "My king," I replied.

THIRTY-ONE

Present day. Seoul, Korea

"Did she fail?" Anna asks me as she sits straight-backed on the throne and glares down at me. "Tell me, Mr. Simon, what do you think? Did she fail as queen?"

It's a good question and I don't have an answer, so I say nothing. Outside the room, it's been quiet since I told the marines to back off. Thank God for that, but I doubt they'll stay cool much longer. Those guys get twitchy when they're not in control.

Anna gives a signal and two women come to her. They start working on her hair. One pulls out the binyeo as another takes off her wig. Anna's hair falls down to her shoulders. Two men go to the tapestry with the two-headed dragon and take it off the wall. They roll it up and carry it away.

"Do you remember what happened to Korea after the Sino-Japanese War?" Anna asks.

I sort of do. Probably not in the detail that I should. "Tell me."

Anna emits a sigh as if I'm a student who hasn't done his homework. "The Japanese won, of course," she says. "Empress Cixi spent the money the Chinese had raised for modernizing their military on rebuilding the summer palace to celebrate her sixtieth birthday. I've seen her palace. Lakes, gardens, and pavilions built among hills. You should visit it someday, Mr. Simon. It's spectacular. But it cost China the war and its dominance in East Asia. They could no longer protect Korea, so Japan took over. Their troops never left the peninsula."

The women have brushed Anna's hair and pinned it back in the business style she wore when I first saw her. Now they go to work on her face, removing the powder and red lipstick.

I want to show Anna that I know something about Korean history, so I speak up. "After that war, the Japanese went to war with Russia. Nicholas II wanted to colonize East Asia, just like the Japanese. The Japanese won that war, too. Decisively. It was the first military victory of an Asian power over a European one."

"Yes," Anna says, "it was significant for Japan. What's also important is the treaty the two countries signed to end the war."

"The Treaty of Portsmouth," I say, feeling smug that I remembered it.

"Correct. You recall that President Theodore Roosevelt negotiated it."

"Of course," I say. "He won the Nobel Peace Prize for it."

"That's true. But what most people don't know is that at the same time, he negotiated a secret agreement with Japan. The agreement stated that if Japan didn't interfere with America in the Philippines, they could do anything they wanted in Korea."

"I didn't know about that," I admitted, my smugness fading away.

Anna continues, "As a result, Japan turned this country into a slave state. They annexed the peninsula in 1910 and for thirty-five years did their best to wipe out everything Korean. It wasn't until the US defeated Japan in World War II that they were forced to leave. And you know what happened then."

The women finish removing Anna's makeup. Two more come with a sheet and lift it to Anna's neck. Behind the sheet, I see that they are helping her take off her queen's attire. One carries off the robe that

Anna wore. Another provides a shoulder for her to lean on as she slips on her skirt.

"Yeah," I say. "A divided country with the communists in the North and the capitalists in the South. The Korean War. A standoff ever since. And now the mess we have today."

"The mess we have today," Anna repeats. "The mess you need to report on to the secretary of state and the president." She finishes dressing and the women drop the sheet. Without her regalia and makeup, she's no longer a terrible, beautiful queen. She's back to being just a junior embassy aide. In my job, I outrank her by quite a bit, but here, now, I don't feel like I do.

I look around and see that we're alone. The fire in the fireplace has died to glowing embers, and there are only a few candles still burning. The room smells musty again.

Anna comes down the dais and sits on the step in front of me. I see that she is holding the comb with the two-headed dragon. "Mr. Simon," she says, "may I call you Nate?"

"Sure."

"Nate, have you seen the State Department documents from WikiLeaks regarding our policy on East Asia?"

"I don't pay attention to documents from WikiLeaks," I reply. "I get the real thing."

"You get what they want you to get," she replies with a look. "What they want you to believe is that we have this altruistic foreign policy to promote a democratic world order. It's supposed to be ruled by international laws and connected by free markets."

"And what's the problem with that?" I ask. "Free markets have made the South Koreans extremely successful."

"Financially they are. But are they happy? South Koreans are far down the list of the happiest people in the world. And we don't care about international laws. The WikiLeaks documents prove it. We prop up lawless regimes. We support anyone as long as it's in our financial interest to do so.

"And we don't believe in fair markets, either," Anna continues with fire in her eyes. "We only care about market dominance. Profits from supposedly fair markets flow to Wall Street without the cost of a physical occupation of the countries we dominate. And market dominance trumps any commitment we have to human rights or state sovereignty."

I think about what she says. She has a point. It's the same point of view I had twenty-five years earlier. I feel the righteous indignation that I did then. "State sovereignty," I say. "Like an independent and free Korea."

"Yes." Anna nods. "An independent, free, and *united* Korea. One Korea."

I shrug. "So what do I put in my report to the president?"

Anna shakes her head. "I don't know. I really don't. But I think the answer is in how you answer my question. Did she fail, Nate? Did Queen Min fail as queen?"

I take a second to think. Then I say, "It's in her spirit, isn't it? The spirit of Korea."

"Yes, the spirit of One Korea," Anna says. "Her spirit, the spirit of these people, the spirit of this nation."

We're quiet for a while. Then she opens her hand. There is the comb with the two-headed dragon. It looks different to me now, almost like a sacred thing. "I have to keep this," she says. "It's my duty to preserve it and support what it stands for."

I look at the tiny ivory dragon. It seems to stare at me, pleading with me to understand what it's saying. I lift my eyes and take a hard look at Anna. "Who are you?" I ask.

She stares at the comb in her hand. "Years ago, my Korean grandmother gave me this comb and told me that I am a direct descendant of Queen Min," she says. "It explained the spirits I'd struggled with since I was young. It was the queen's spirit inside me. So I'm at State to work for America. But I am a child of Korea, too. I love both of my countries, the one that gave me life and the one that gave me a family. I want to help them both."

I nod and then motion toward the door. "What do I tell them about you?"

She grins. "If you tell them about my involvement here, I'll go underground. If you don't, I stay in my job at State. Either way, I'll be fine."

She slips the comb in her pocket and stands. She extends a hand and I shake it. "Good luck, Anna Carlson," I say.

"Good bye, Nate Simon," she replies. Then she turns and disappears into the room's blackness.

It's another fifteen-hour flight back to DC. Second one in four days. The plane hasn't even taken off and I'm exhausted. It was a grind when the marines, CIA, police, and God knows who else grilled me all night about my little affair. "They were Koreans. They wanted to give me *their* take on what we should do with their country." I told them the truth. Well, mostly. I didn't tell them about Anna.

Then there was the meeting with the CIA about the comb. I said the Koreans took the comb from me. Turns out, those guys had it all wrong anyway. Thought the dragon and the words "One Korea" were a message from the North that they're willing to go to war for control of the entire peninsula. I didn't tell them I knew what it really meant.

The airplane points down the runway, and they hit the throttle. The engines roar to life, and we rumble into the air. Soon we're flying high over Seoul. I look down at the Miracle on the Han River. Hundreds of apartment buildings, thousands of cars and trucks and buses, and millions of people. I feel their spirit. They are Korea, a divided people yearning to be at peace, yearning to be one nation. One Korea, just like Anna said.

Anna. Damn, that woman has guts. I'd shown up at the embassy the next morning and there she was wearing a smart black suit and her hair up like nothing ever happened. She nodded a greeting at me and didn't say another word for the rest of my time there. When I snuck a look at her in our meetings, I couldn't believe what she'd done. She has what I used to have, what Jin-ee still has. Conviction, courage, passion. I did the right thing by not giving her up.

The jet hums softly and the cabin is quiet. We turn east and head out over the Sea of Japan. The sky in front of the airplane is dark. Fifteen hours. By chance, Derek the flight attendant is on this flight, too. I grab him and ask for some coffee. As he goes off to get it, I take my briefcase from under the seat. I open it and take out the report I've started. The damn report. Only a handful of people get to give reports to the secretary of state and president. Still not exactly sure how I'll color it. I certainly don't know what my final recommendations will be. But the more I work on it, the more Queen Min's spirit pushes its way into it. I think about Anna's question: *Did she fail?* I think maybe the queen didn't fail and something about that needs to go into my report. I vow to read more about Korea's last queen when I get back. I'll also read the WikiLeaks documents that Anna talked about. Have to do it on the q.t.; the big brass doesn't like it when guys like me know too much.

I chuckle to myself. What a rebel I am, secretly reading leaked government documents. I feel like when I was in college with Jin-ee, all upset about this or that. Oh, yeah, Jin-ee. She'll want to read the WikiLeaks reports, too. We'll do it together, at the kitchen table. We'll read the especially shocking passages aloud to each other. "Our country is better than this," we'll declare. Then we'll find a protest group or something to express our rage. We'll take the kids with us, show them what's important in life. Hell, State will probably fire me for it. Then we can show the kids how to really change the world. I'm excited just thinking about it.

I can't wait to tell Jin-ee.

OCTOBER 8, 1895

They had planned it for when the moon was new and the night was deep. Twenty men crouched in the shadows outside a rear gate of Gyeongbok Palace. They were dressed in black with scarves covering their heads and faces. Only their eyes were uncovered. They moved silently as one. They approached two guards at the gate. One guard slouched against the wall, asleep. Days earlier, the other had sold his loyalty to them for fifty yang.

As they approached, the men in black drew swords and pistols from underneath their garments. One went to the sleeping guard and slit his throat before he could make a sound. The other guard looked uneasily at his partner gushing blood at his feet. One of the twenty—short with intense eyes—gave him a pouch containing fifty yang. The guard looked first at the pouch, then at the man in black. "Open the gate," the man demanded. The guard unlocked the gate and cracked it open just wide enough for one man.

One by one, the twenty slipped through the gate. They were at the edge of a courtyard surrounded by many buildings and lined with persimmon trees.

"Who's there?" shouted someone from the other side of the courtyard. "Guards, report!"

The short man in black gathered his men. "The fox is three buildings in," he whispered. "Half of you to the right, half to the left. Go now, for the glory of Japan!"

A bell rang out, and palace guards spilled into the courtyard with swords and pistols drawn. They looked around. They spotted the intruders and attacked.

The bell's toll woke her from her sleep as she lay in her bed. When she heard the shouts and swords clash, she sat up and wrapped the covers around her as if they would somehow protect her. Outside, there was a pistol shot, then another. Men shouted out.

They have finally come. All of her efforts to prevent this day had been in vain. Could she have prevented it if she'd had more time, if she'd had more skills? Had she failed?

The shouting drew near. A woman's scream was cut short. "That's not her," a voice said in Japanese.

"Over here!" another one shouted.

Her lady's maid rushed into her bedchamber. "Majesty, you must run!" the lady's maid cried.

"It is too late for me," she said. "Save yourself."

"I will not! I will tell them that I am the one they want."

The lady's maid ran to the chest next to the queen's bed, and took the queen's medallion. She stood at the door.

The head of the palace guard came running from his quarters. He clutched his sword. Two of his men were with him. "General," one said, "they are going for the queen!" When they got to the queen's quarters, there were men dressed in black at the door. The three guards threw themselves on the men. A shot rang out, and one guard collapsed to the ground. With a sweep of his sword, the other guard killed a man in black. Two intruders jumped on the guard and quickly sent him to the ground. His blood ran onto the cobblestones.

The general lunged with his sword and killed two intruders before they could face him. Another shot the general in the chest. Blood oozed into his white shirt and ran down his torso. At first the shot stunned the general, but then he set his square jaw and charged. He plunged his sword into the shooter, killing him. Others jumped on the general and delivered stabs and blows that would have killed any other man. Covered in blood, the general swung his sword wildly, and the men in black fell back.

"Step away," a voice said from behind. The men in black stepped aside and there in front of the general, was the short man holding a pistol. Breathing hard and spilling blood on the ground, the general looked into the man's eyes. He had seen them before.

"You are brave, Kyung-jik," the short man said. "But you cannot save her." The man raised his pistol and shot the general between the eyes. The general dropped his sword to the ground with a clang and fell dead onto the cobblestones.

They were just outside. She pushed the bedcovers off and folded her legs underneath her. She rested her hands on her knees and opened her palms toward the ceiling. She leveled her chin and closed her eyes. Her black hair fell down her back. She forced herself to breathe slowly.

She was overwhelmed with sadness as a thousand years of history swept over her. She could not bend its long arc. She had not made a difference. A tear ran down her cheek as she said a prayer for her people.

The door swung open and men clutching swords rushed in. Her lady's maid stood in front of them. "I am the one you have come for!"

she screamed. "See? I wear the queen's medallion." She thrust out her hand to show them the medallion.

The short one came forward. He reached up and slowly took off his scarf exposing his face. His hair and long mustache were completely gray now, but his eyes were focused and sharp. On top of his head, he wore a topknot. The lady's maid's eyes went wide. "Mister Euno!" she gasped. The short one motioned to another. "Kill her," he said. The other intruder thrust his sword into the lady's maid's throat. She uttered no sound as she collapsed to the floor.

The assassins stood in the room with their swords drawn, staring at the woman dressed in white and kneeling on the bed before them. She sat the way he had taught her a lifetime earlier. Her eyes were closed. Her lips moved in a silent prayer. Tears ran down her cheeks.

Mister Euno went to her. He took a moment to admire her beauty. He saw that she held her shoulders down and back, and her head level and straight. Her arms gracefully curled down to rest on top of her legs. "Perfect," he whispered. And then he plunged his sword into her heart.

The room is suddenly bright, the air is suddenly warm. She hears no more shouting or gunfire. She is weightless and rises above her bed, floating like the red-crowned cranes above the Han River. She wears the robe with one hundred fifty-six pairs of pheasants in the chima and thirty gold dragons in the hem. She wears the ebony wig from her wedding day. In her hand is the comb with the two-headed dragon. Her face is dusted and her lips are painted red. Tucked in her arm is *Songs of Dragons Flying to Heaven*.

There are many people in the room. She sees her mother and father as they were when she was young. She sees her uncle and aunt. All four smile at her and nod their approval. She sees her lady's maid, Han-sook, and her guard, Kyung-jik. They bow to her respectfully. She sees Woo-jin, the blind potter, at his wheel turning a pot out of clay. She sees her sons, the one that died and the one that lived. They are happy, mischievous boys splashing in the pond, trying to catch koi fish. She sees her husband. He is dressed in his finest king's regalia and sits high and proud on his throne. He looks at her lovingly.

She floats outside her bedchamber high above the palace. She sees the gray granite mountains and the white foam seashores. She sees the terraced rice paddies, the villages in valleys, and the cities in the flats. She sees the Han River from its source high in the Taebaek Mountains to where it spills into the Yellow Sea. She sees children flying kites, the elderly and the newly married. She sees the yangban, sangmin, chungin, and former slaves. She sees soldiers and merchants, scholars, Buddhist monks, potters, farmers, women in the paddies harvesting rice, miners in the north, fishermen in the south. She sees young women in schools. They all reach for her as she flies and they chant, "One Korea! One Korea!"

She looks back to the Three Kingdoms of Baekje, Silla, and Goguryeo, and to Tan'gun, the father of Korea. She nods to the great Emperor Taejo of Chosŏn. All the kings and queens who came before her are there. They, too, are chanting, "One Korea! One Korea!"

She looks forward to her children's children and all of Korea's future children. She sees great cities with millions of electric lights and swift carriages made from iron, and buildings as tall as mountains, and giant steel birds carrying people inside. She sees armies of nations with terrible weapons facing each other at a line that divides her country. She sees that her people are afraid. Some are bent under the tyranny of foreign nations. Some are bent under the tyranny of one man. They cry to her, "Why are we not free? Why are we not one?"

She embraces them all, back to the Three Kingdoms and forward through the generations to come. She is the link. She is the one mind.

She is the breath. She is where north meets south, east comes to west, and heaven joins the earth. She is the axis mundi. She is the mountains and the sea and the great cities. She is the Han River. She is both the tiger and the crane. She is the then, she is the now, and she is what will be. She is one, and she is all.

And as she soars high above her country in her queen's regalia, she cries out, "Hear me! I am the Dragon Queen! I am the spirit of One Korea!"

AUTHOR'S NOTE

THE "ONE KOREA" DREAM

In a windowless hotel meeting room in northern South Korea, twenty South Korean families sit quietly waiting to meet their loved ones from the North. The men wear dark suits and have fresh haircuts. The women wear unpretentious dresses that the authorities told them to wear. The children at their sides are on their very best behavior. The families have with them small, inexpensive gifts that the armed soldiers who watch their every move have carefully inspected.

These people are here because the allied victory over Japan in World War II separated thousands of families just like theirs. When Japan surrendered after a brutal thirty-five-year occupation of Korea, what to do about the peninsula was little more than an afterthought. It was left to two young American officers, who proposed that the Russians occupy the peninsula above the 38th parallel and the Americans occupy the land to the south. The Russians agreed and, as the Americans were mopping up in Japan, the Russian Army marched into Korea and stopped at the 38th parallel. Weeks later, the Americans hastily sent troops to the south and Korea has been divided ever since.

Immediately after World War II, negotiations between the US and Russia failed to unify the peninsula under one government, neither side willing to compromise their political ideology. The result was the Korean War fought between Russia/China/North Korea and America/UN forces/South Korea that killed 1 million combatants and 2.5 million Korean civilians. It ended in a stalemate with the exact same division at the 38th parallel. Then Korea became a front line in the Cold War between the US, the Soviet Union, and China. And while the Cold War supposedly ended with the fall of the Soviet Union in 1991, the world is still fighting over Korea. In fact, a sign at US Camp Bonifas one mile from the 38th parallel proclaims that the Korean Demilitarized Zone is "The Most Dangerous Place on Earth."

In a 2014 survey by Seoul National University, 70 percent of South Koreans said they were in favor of reunification. (Because North Korea is a closed nation, their opinions are impossible to determine.) However, they are concerned about the enormous financial burden it would place on their country. The 2014 World Factbook estimates that GDP per capita in South Korea is twenty times higher than in North Korea. By comparison, West Germany's per capita GDP was only three times higher than East Germany's and reunification there has cost Germany an estimated two trillion euros and counting. Experts agree that the only way Korean reunification can succeed is through the cooperation and financial assistance of the US, Russia, China, and Japan—countries that haven't agreed on much of anything since World War II. Korean reunification remains the world's greatest political conundrum.

Even so, Queen Min's dream of an independent and free "One Korea" is a goal of both North and South Korea. In June 2000, the two governments adopted a five-point joint reunification declaration.

1. The South and the North have agreed to resolve the question of reunification independently and through the joint efforts of the Korean people, who are the masters of the country.
2. For the achievement of reunification, we have agreed that there is a common element in the South's concept of a confederation and the North's formula for a loose form of federation. The South and the North agree to promote reunification in that direction.
3. The South and the North have agreed to promptly resolve humanitarian issues such as exchange visits by separated family members and relatives on the occasion of the August 15 National Liberation Day and the question of unswerving Communists serving prison sentences in the South.
4. The South and the North have agreed to consolidate mutual trust by promoting balanced development of the national economy through economic cooperation and by stimulating cooperation and exchanges in civic, cultural, sports, health, environmental, and all other fields.
5. The South and the North have agreed to hold a dialogue between relevant authorities in the near future to implement the above agreements expeditiously.

This agreement led to a brief period of cooperation between the two countries. However, the military provocations of the North and the conflicting superpowers' goals for the region ended this era before any real progress was made. Today, tensions between the North and South—and between the superpowers with respect to the two Koreas—are higher than ever.

And so the people in the hotel room sit and wait to meet their loved ones. Although they can barely afford the fees and bribes for these meetings, they feel lucky to be here. When their loved ones finally come through that door, they will only have a precious few hours to be together. As they wait, they pray that the dangerous conflicts between the North and South, and the machinations of their superpower allies, don't end these meetings. And like Queen Min, they dream that someday the two Koreas—and their families—will be permanently reunited in One Korea.

William Andrews

ACKNOWLEDGMENTS

A book like this is never a solo effort. I owe a debt of gratitude to my friends and family who have supported me over the years. A special shout-out to the good people at Lake Union Publishing who have helped make this book all it could be. And, of course, an extra special thank-you to my researcher, first editor, sounding board, encourager, and love of my life, my wife, Nancy.

SELECTED BIBLIOGRAPHY

This is a work of fiction. As such, I took some liberties with history for dramatic purposes. Nevertheless, I did my best to portray Queen Min as I saw her and stay as true as possible to the history and culture of Korea in the late 1800s.

If you want to learn more about Korea's extraordinary last queen and about the fascinating and often tragic history of the Land of the Morning Calm, below is a bibliography of books I found useful.

On Korean History

Breen, Michael. *The Koreans: Who They Are, What They Want, Where Their Future Lies*. New York: Thomas Dunne Books, 2004.

Cumings, Bruce. *Korea's Place in the Sun: A Modern History*. New York: W. W. Norton & Company, 2005.

Eckert, Carter J., Ki-baik Lee, Young Ick Lew, Michael Robinson, and Edward W. Wagner. *Korea Old and New—A History*. Cambridge: Korea Institute, Harvard University, 1990.

Oberdorfer, Don. *The Two Koreas: A Contemporary History*. New York: Basic Books, 2001.

Pratt, Keith. *Everlasting Flower: A History of Korea*. London: Reaktion Books, 2006.

Seth, Michael J. *A Concise History of Korea: From Antiquity to the Present*. Lanham, MD: Rowman & Littlefield, 2006.

Two Fictional Accounts of Queen Min

Buck, Pearl S. *The Living Reed*. New York: Moyer Bell, 2004. Fourth printing.

Oh, Bonnie Bongwan Cho. *Murder in the Palace*. CreateSpace Independent Publishing Platform, 2016.

AUTHOR Q & A

Q: What inspired you to write this book?

A: There is a reference to Queen Min in my first book about Korea, *Daughters of the Dragon: A Comfort Woman's Story*, so I had to learn about her. When I did, I saw what a fascinating person she was and decided to write her story. She is widely considered the greatest monarch in Korean history since King Taejo, founder of the Chosŏn Dynasty. The Koreans worship her.

Q: What did you like about her story?

A: Her strength and intelligence. She is a hero among Koreans in the same way that Abraham Lincoln or Theodore Roosevelt is to Americans. She gave her life to make Korea independent and free.

Q: There's a lot of history in this book. Is it accurate?

A: First, please know that I'm a storyteller, not a history expert. Still, I tried to make this book as historically accurate as possible. I did a ton of research and got help from several history experts. But I did take some liberties with history for the sake of storytelling.

Q: Just like *Daughters of the Dragon*, you seem to vilify the Japanese. Is this fair?

A: It's different in *The Dragon Queen. Daughters of the Dragon* exposes the Imperial Japanese Army that raped hundreds of thousands of Asian women during World War II, an unforgivable atrocity that the Japanese have never really apologized for. In *The Dragon Queen*, the Japanese behave exactly like the rest of the modernized world, trying to colonize other, less modern nations.

Q: Do you think Queen Min's vision of One Korea will ever be realized and North and South Korea will reunify?

A: See the Author's Note. I don't think it will happen without a lot of pain and suffering. I hope and pray for the people of both countries.

One last thing. I'd like to ask readers to please go to their online retailer and write a review of this book. Or, send me an e-mail at bill@williamandrewsbooks.com. It's the only way I can get feedback from my readers.

ABOUT THE AUTHOR

Photograph © 2013 Greg Thoen

For more than thirty years, William Andrews was a copywriter and a marketing/brand executive with several Fortune 500 companies. For fifteen years, he ran his own advertising agency. At night and on weekends (and sometimes during the workday!), Bill wrote fiction. His first novel, *The Essential Truth,* won first place in the 2008 Mayhaven Contest for fiction.

The Dragon Queen is Bill's fourth novel and is the second book in his trilogy about Korea, which includes *Daughters of the Dragon: A Comfort Woman's Story* and a planned third book, *The Society of the Two-Headed Dragon.*

Today, Bill is retired and focused on his writing. He lives in Minneapolis with his wife, who's been an inner-city schoolteacher for thirty-two years.